NIGHTSHADE
ACADEMY

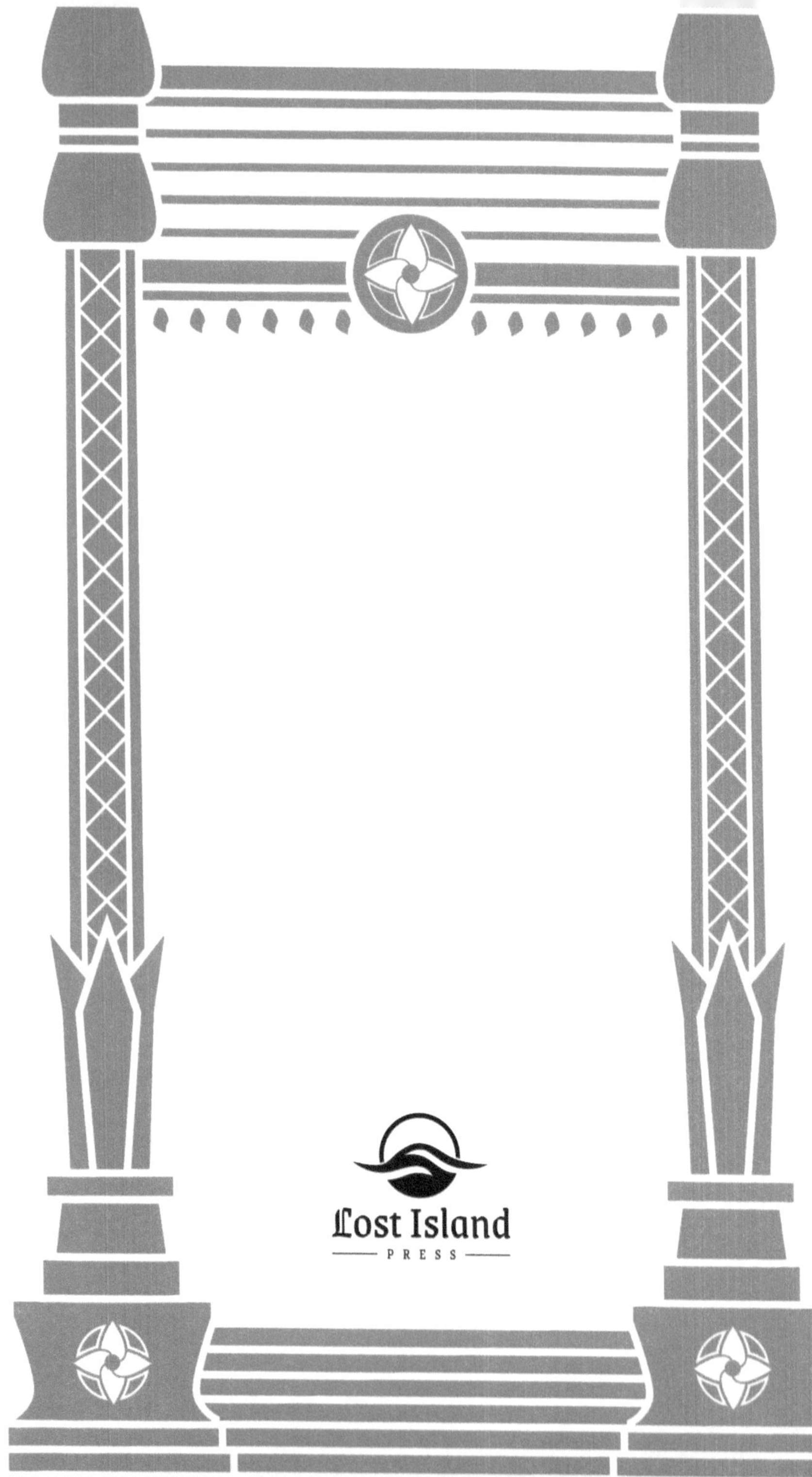
Lost Island
PRESS

NIGHTSHADE ACADEMY

BELLADONNA, BOOK 1

MEL TORREFRANCA

Nightshade Academy
Copyright © 2023 Mel Torrefranca

Library of Congress Control Number: 2023920548

ISBN 978-1-962876-00-1 (paperback)
ISBN 979-8-9850102-6-8 (ebook)

Cover design by MAD Book Covers
Select interior illustrations by Gonzalo Mansilla

Lost Island Press LLC
Oro Valley, AZ
lostislandpress.com

GUARDIAN DIVISIONS

RESEARCH   DEFENSE   MEDICAL

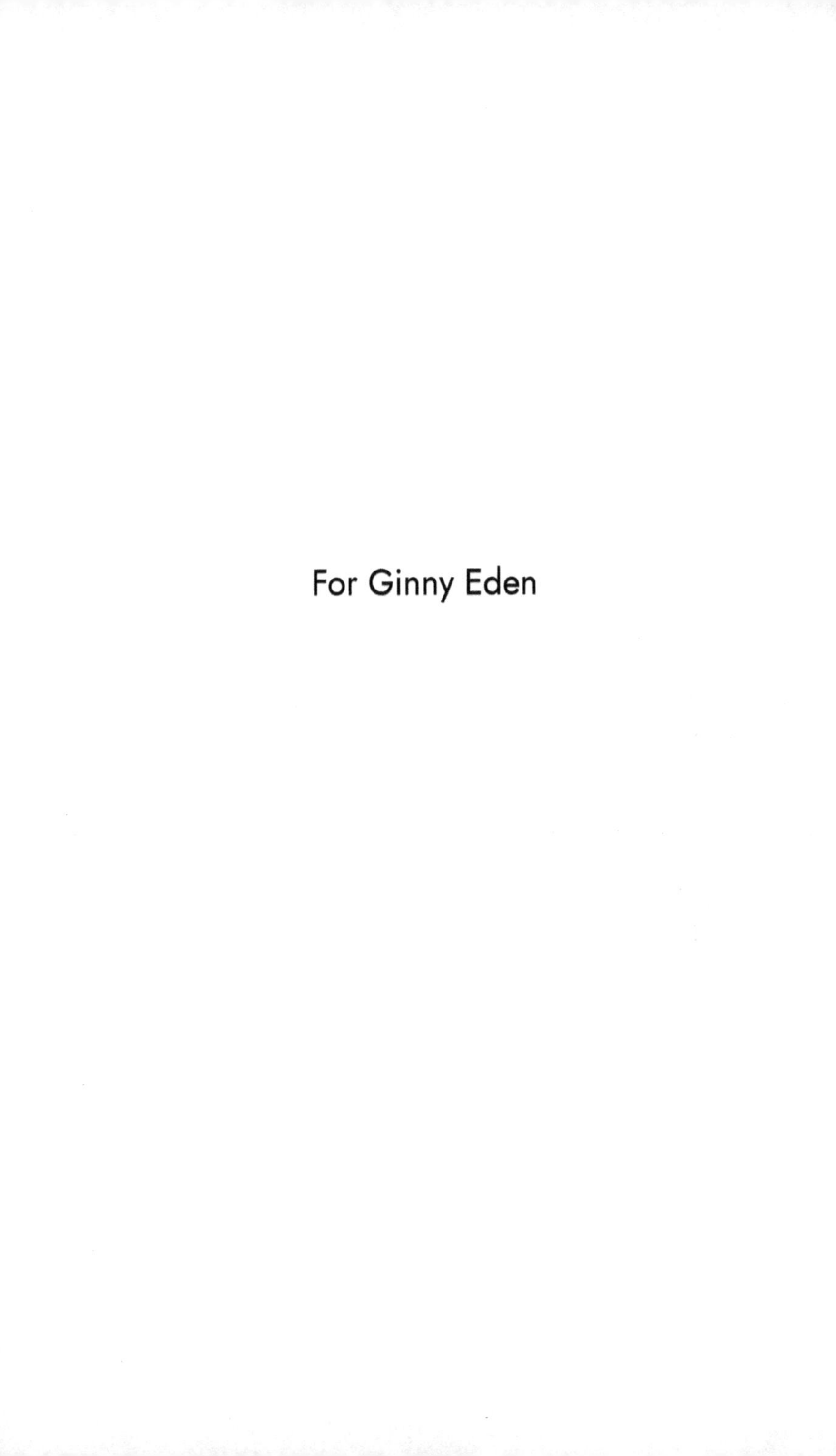

For Ginny Eden

HIDE AND SEEK

Two years and four months ago…

Yahshi Konya was an easy target. His scarlet coat restricted his movement, crinkled with every step, and stood out against the evergreens. The farther he ran, the louder the tracer's cackling echoed through the woods.

"You're wearing red!" he yelled, tackling Yahshi onto the dirt. "Like a bullseye!" The tracer laughed in his face before darting off to hunt his final target.

Stupid coat.

Yahshi dragged himself to their imaginary Detainment Facility, a designated area marked with an outline of logs—courtesy of Quax Avarium. He stepped over the boundary to join his fellow thirteen-year-old detainees.

"Welcome back, Yahshi. I'm surprised he didn't trace you faster with a coat like that."

"You look like a tomato with arms and legs."

That's it. Yahshi flung his coat to the ground.

"You'll get sick," Quax warned.

"It's either get sick or get caught," he said, clutching his arms with a shiver.

"Silly move, Yahshi." Alora Valentine marched toward him, her short hair jumping on her shoulders. "Now your teeth will chatter, and I'll hear you."

"I bet if I borrowed your mittens, you'd trace me even faster." Yahshi eyed the bright fabric around her hands, the cause of her equally pathetic performance.

"They're *light green*," she said, convinced her mittens camouflaged into the woods.

"They're yellow." He leaned in with a smirk. "Truly, banana yellow."

Her smile faded as the other detainees burst into laughter. Everyone knew she was color blind, a fact about herself that she hadn't fully accepted.

"Quax..." Alora said. "Are my mittens really yellow?"

"Ugh! Can we start the round already? Lunch break doesn't last forever." Quax pointed at the previous tracer, who was already back with his final target.

"Fine," Alora said, leaving the Facility to assume her new role. The criminals got into position as she pressed her forehead against a tree. "One, two, three..."

They shot off, scattering about the woods. Yahshi was searching for a clump of thick bushes to hide between when a whisper interrupted him.

"Psst! I've got the perfect spot."

He trailed behind Quax, brows high. *What'd he do this time?*

They weaved around tree trunks and stepped over mossy logs, traveling so deep into the woods that Yahshi feared they wouldn't hear the bell ring.

"How far are you taking me?" he asked.

"Oh, stop whining. We're already here." Quax crouched by a low pile of logs. "Well? Have a look for yourself."

It wasn't until Yahshi leaned over and squinted that he noticed the strings binding the logs together. He opened the makeshift door, revealing a secret ditch large enough to hold two people.

Yahshi's jaw dropped. "You're kidding. No wonder you stayed late after school yesterday."

"No, no. I was studying. At first. Then I realized I really wasn't in the mood to read, *but* I was very much in the mood to build the best hiding spot in the history of Sitra, which is probably a nonexistent standard, but I digress." He climbed into the hole and hugged his knees. "Now hurry up and get in! She's stopped counting."

Yahshi was a full head shorter than him, so he didn't have to hunch over, even after they dragged the door shut. Light streamed through the cracks between logs, illuminating Quax's proud grin.

"If only you put this much effort into your scores," Yahshi muttered, earning an elbow jab from Quax.

"Shut it."

He chuckled, leaning his head against the dirt wall—but the vibrations of footsteps chased his humor away. *Something's off. Those strides are too long to be Alora's.*

"Do you hear that?" Yahshi whispered.

"Shh!"

They held still as the clunky footsteps approached, causing pebbles to trickle down the walls. Yahshi waited for the disruption to pass, but it halted right above them.

A bronze eye peered through a gap in the door.

"I know you're in there," taunted the intruder, sending a chill down Yahshi's spine.

The voice gave him away. Sixteen-year-old Chima Fernis made a hobby of tormenting students, identifying one target and destroying their dignity before cherry-picking his next victim. And his current cherry was none other than Quax's older sister, the girl who never snapped back, no matter how many bruises he left or insults he dished.

Yahshi understood exactly why Chima was here. If he couldn't destroy Cal Avarium directly, perhaps targeting her little brother would change the game.

The door shifted, and Yahshi gritted his teeth. *I have to do something.*

As light flooded the hideout, he sprang at Chima, knocking him down with pure momentum.

"Quax!" Yahshi yelled. "Run!"

Chima stared up at him with a smile, making no effort to get up.

"Run!" he yelled again, pinning Chima beneath him. He heard Quax jump out of the hideout, but the laughter of two boys cut his fleeing short.

"Let go of me!" Quax shouted, his boots shuffling against the ground.

Chima's not alone.

Yahshi threw a fist at the bully, but Chima snatched his wrist before it could land.

"Better not be after my eyes," he sang, wrenching Yahshi's wrist until his skin burned.

Before he could retaliate, someone grabbed him from behind.

"Leave us alone!" Yahshi elbowed the boy and broke free, but Chima was already back on his feet to capture him.

He struggled as they threw him against a tree, binding his arms behind it with scratchy rope.

"Keep the little one out of my way," Chima ordered, slapping the dirt off his pants. He crept toward Quax, who another boy was pinning down.

Yahshi settled to catch his breath.

"You can mess with me," Quax said, "but leave Yahshi out of this!"

"Oh, relax," Chima said. "We won't hurt him if you cooperate."

As strong as Quax looked, he was a dramatic boy, the kind to complain for ten minutes about a paper cut, and he wouldn't stand a chance against them. Yahshi pushed his fingers into the knot, hoping to undo it without the boys noticing.

"Ah, Quax Avarium. It is so nice to finally meet you." Chima towered over his prey. "Although, I'm sure your sister's told you enough about me already."

"She—she doesn't care about you," Quax spouted.

"Yeah? You guys hearing this?" Chima paused, cueing his friends' laughter.

Yahshi applied more pressure to the knot, wincing as the rope scraped a layer of skin.

"Alright, she doesn't give a damn about me." Chima leaned over. "But what if I spit in your face, huh?"

Quax shut his eyes when he spat.

More laughter.

"Huh?" Chima wiped his lips on his sleeve. "Would she give a damn about that?"

Quax tried to launch himself into a seated position, encouraging Chima's friend to drill him down harder. The twigs beneath him dug into his wrists, and he cried out in pain.

Yahshi threw himself forward, trying to leverage his weight and snap the rope.

"Let him go!"

Chima faced him with a jolt of his head, and Yahshi froze.

"Shut it, *convert*." His piercing gaze lingered for only a moment before he grabbed a pocket knife from his coat, refacing Quax. "Cal thinks that if she ignores me, she wins."

Yahshi's heart raced as he resumed tugging, but the rope refused to give way.

"She wants me to believe there's nothing I can do to make her fear me." Chima slammed his shoe into Quax's stomach, leaving him choking for air. "But there is *one* thing, isn't there?" He squatted and pressed the rusty blade to his neck.

No, he wouldn't. He wouldn't dare.

"Please, don't hurt me," Quax said, the color draining from his face.

"Alora!" Yahshi yelled, spotting two yellow dots in the distance. "Help!"

Chima's friend held a hand over Yahshi's mouth, muting him. His pleading eyes tracked Alora as she sprinted away, hopefully to alert their instructors. The school staff never interfered with social matters outside the classroom, but they would need to step in today because Chima had taken his bullying too far. Murder was *illegal*, a violation of Imperial Law.

Illegal. That's when it dawned on him. To kill was to buy a one-way ticket to the Detainment Facility—the real one. Surely Chima knew that. There was no way he'd destroy his life just to make Cal snap.

Yahshi's eyes widened. *He's bluffing.*

"P-Please." Tears rolled down Quax's cheeks. "Please don't hurt me."

"Okay," Chima said, nodding. "Alright, deal. But in exchange, why don't you tell me one good reason why you deserve to live, huh?"

Quax cried harder. "Please!"

"If you wanna live so bad, tell me *one reason* why I shouldn't bury you in the grave you dug up for yourself." He nudged him with his boot. "Go on. You have ten seconds."

"Chima!" Yahshi shouted.

"Ten, nine..."

"Don't do this!" he continued.

"...eight, seven..."

"The guardians *will* find out!"

"...six, five..."

"They'll lock you away. You know that!"

"...four, three..."

Chima trailed off, his countdown swallowed by the hammering rhythm of approaching footsteps. His friends jumped and backed away like they'd seen a ghost.

As a figure shot toward them, Yahshi's stomach folded into itself.

Chima was raising his chin to face the interrupter when a stocky log struck his skull. He collapsed, the knife slipping from his grip.

Cal Avarium dropped to her knees, log in hand. "You can't win," she spat.

The air flew out of Yahshi's lungs. He watched, petrified, as Chima's fingers searched the dirt for his pocket knife. Cal waited until he grabbed it before swinging her log down a second time.

The forest screamed with Chima's friends—branches swaying, leaves rustling. Yahshi could hear every squawking bird, every distant footstep, every panting breath. The air tasted like iron and salt and—

Blood. It rolled down Chima's face, pooling into his ear.

Cal roared through gritted teeth as she reeled her log back.

"Stop!" Yahshi snapped to his senses, yanking at the ropes again. "Don't—"

He gasped as warm blood splattered across his face.

"Cal," he whispered, *"please."*

Chima's friends grabbed her log. She resisted, grunting as she clung to it, but they managed to yank it free.

Her black hair thrashed in the wind as she curled over and sobbed.

He was only bluffing. Yahshi's head trembled and ached. *It was only a game to him.*

While the boys backed away, her brother sat up next to her, blood mixing into his tears. Cal had never been the warmest older sister, and Quax had sometimes expressed concern over whether she cared for him at all. But at that moment, he stared at the girl who saved his life with unconditional admiration.

Yahshi looked away from the siblings, gagging at the sight of Chima's brain.

"Cal," he choked out, "what have you done?"

In embracing your duty as a guardian in the Force, you shed the trivial pursuits and heavy burdens of your prior life, reborn through devotion and discipline as an embodiment of the Empire's unyielding glory.

THE GUARDIAN HANDBOOK

PART 1

CORRUPTION

CHAPTER 1

RABBIT HOLE

I vow to serve the Empire with absolute devotion.

♫ SPANISH SAHARA · FOALS ♫

Cal Avarium was not human. Even in her recent portrait, featured in the latest issue of *Capital Weekly*, she looked exactly like she had two years ago. From her porcelain, ageless skin to her silky, midnight hair, Cal was nothing but a lifeless statue of perfection.

Seeing her name gave Yahshi goosebumps. Cal had been the only student from Sitra selected for Belladonna Guardian Academy in decades, so the community relished her success. They'd pasted her *Capital Weekly* article by the door to Sitra Market, ensuring her inked face greeted every resident entering the busiest building in town.

The Belladonna Prodigy, Yahshi read. *Commander Cal Avarium of Sitra, 18, breaks record as the youngest unit leader in guardian history.*

The four-petaled flower emblem branded into her forehead marked her as a member of the Force. She was wearing their iconic uniform—a dress shirt and tie, armored vest, and black overcoat with golden lining. Her hair was slicked back into a low bun, not a single strand out of place.

1

And yet, despite her powerful presence, she still looked like a child.

Lightning struck. He glanced over his shoulder, ensuring the road was clear, before peeling the article from the wall and tucking it into his book bag.

The market door creaked open.

"Hey," Alora said. "Just saw your father in there."

Yahshi snapped his bag shut. "What are you doing here so early?"

"Better question..." she said, drawing out the phrase. "What are you hiding in your bag?"

"Homework."

"*Homework*, on Selection Day Eve?"

"I mean, I have a lot of missing assignments, so..."

Alora ran her fingers along the wall, humming in curiosity. Her hand paused right where the article used to be.

"Silly move, Yahshi. I saw the news about Cal on my way in. The paper's gone, but the glue residue isn't. See? Right here."

"Sorry." He wiped his palms on his pants. "I'll put it back."

"No need."

"You won't tell anyone about this, right?"

"It never happened." She faced him and leaned against the wall, arms crossed. "I just hope you remember how awful Chima was. He hurt a lot of people."

"But he never killed anyone."

"He probably would have. Eventually, considering the path he was on." She looked away. "Maybe if I tried to fight instead of running for help, he'd still be around right now—bullying people, hurting them, *killing* them."

Yahshi raised his head as the clouds darkened, and a few sprinkles met his cheek.

"Yeah," he said, "it's much easier to believe that, isn't it?"

Her eyes jolted back to his, and he strangled his bag strap. *Good going, Yahshi.* He knew better than to question the Force's narrative publicly. Chima was evil. Cal was a hero. That's what the guardians ruled after she spent four months behind bars. That's why they pardoned her and gave her a spot in the Academy program. *That's the Force's story, so that's the only truth.*

Alora's gaze softened. Droplets dotted her black hair like stars, and for some reason, Yahshi decided he could trust her to keep this discussion between them.

"Remember when we were in primary school," she said, "and we'd compete for the highest scores?"

He tucked his hands into his pockets, concealing a grin. "That was a long time ago."

She chuckled. "I miss it. Everything was simple back then. Things just worked without a thought, you know?"

"I do," Yahshi said, recalling his life before the incident. He missed studying after school until the sun vanished, fueled by the challenge. Students would return his smiles in the hallways, and instructors would praise him and Alora for their scores. But with a few swings of a log, it all slipped between his fingers.

Alora opened a yellow umbrella when the sprinkle turned to rain. She owned a lot of yellow things. *I wonder if her favorite color's actually green.*

"Maybe it's odd to say this, considering we've hardly talked since... *the incident*," she said. "But I still feel like I know you. And the people who say you lost your way are the same people who never really had the best scores back then. Sometimes I wonder if that means something."

The rain dampened his shirt. "Why are you telling me this?"

"Because I think you're smart, Yahshi. You always have been. And it scares me."

When he realized what she was hinting at, it scared him too. He would never wish to drag Alora down his rabbit hole—not when she still had everything in her grasp.

"Sorry. I've gotta go. You know, help with the bread."

"Sure. Okay." Alora smiled under her yellow shield, protected from the rain. He envied her.

"I'll see you in class," Yahshi said, and opened the door.

He trudged into the bustling market, instantly weighed down by the roaring discussion about tomorrow afternoon's selection ceremony. Two years had passed since Cal entered the program, and six months had passed since her graduation. It was time for the guardians to announce the next cycle of fifteen- and sixteen-year-old trainees.

He kept his head low as he rushed for his father's bread stand, ignoring stares from residents theorizing whether or not he'd be selected. Despite his visible discomfort, their eyes tracked him like he was a lab project.

"Yahshi, my man! Take in the spotlight!"

"Yahshi, Yahshi, Yahshi! We're famous this week. Famous!"

Two classmates appeared on either side of him, matching his pace. He made a point not to look at them.

"Rumor has it you failed every selection exam. A failure that grand deserves a medal!"

"Maybe it's time to go home, *convert*."

"You could join the Underground. Jar up some eyeballs."

Yahshi's jaw tightened, and his classmates scattered before his father could spot them. How ironic that they had no problem shaming him for being born in Eastern Territory but wouldn't dare offend adults. The word *convert* had become a cheap insult among teenagers—many of whom couldn't even remember the Eastern raids.

"Morning, Father." Yahshi joined Martu behind the stand. "Nearly sold out already?"

"Everyone's in a good mood today. Optimism does wonders for business." Martu's smile widened as a customer set two coins on the table. "My, you're just in time. Bread's going fast." He slipped the money into a velvet pouch. "Yahshi, get a wheat loaf ready."

The woman grinned. "You remembered."

He leaned forward and winked. "I wouldn't dare forget a smile like yours."

Yahshi cringed as the woman burst into laughter. He could feel her eyes drift to him as he began to wrap her loaf in brown paper.

"I remember when you were just a little one," she said. "You're of selection age now, aren't you?"

"Yeah, I am," he replied, forging his enthusiasm.

"I bet you did wonderfully on the exams. You were always a clever one."

Yahshi secured the paper with a string. "I did alright."

"Humble as always, I see."

No, not humble. He handed her the wrapped loaf. *Just a liar.*

The woman smiled at Martu before leaving, and Yahshi flinched as a girl stepped into her place. He nearly thought it was Cal pointing to a loaf of sourdough. She had the same silky hair and narrow face, but her skin was slightly darker, and when he stared into her sea-foam eyes, they seemed real—not like Cal's, which he'd always described to himself as marbles.

Yahshi peeked at the girl as he wrapped her loaf. *She looks a bit older than me, but I don't recognize her from Sitra Secondary.* He could have identified her hometown by the color of her shirt, but she wasn't dressed in a uniform. *Why would she skip school on Selection Day Eve?*

Yahshi smiled, offering her the bread, and she snatched it before bolting away.

"Hey!" He stepped forward, but Martu stopped him by the shoulder. "Father, let me—"

"No."

He pulled his shoulder free, scanning the crowd for the thief—but she had vanished.

"As the Eastern saying goes," Martu continued, "have faith in kindness, and it will always repay you."

"So that's it? We let everything slide?" He faced his father. "People do horrible things, and we gloss it over like it never happened?"

Before Martu could reply, applause erupted in the room, and customers dispersed to make way for fifteen-year-old Quax Avarium. He was wearing a sage green shirt and khaki pants identical to Yahshi's, but his school uniform had been tailored flatteringly using money from Cal's family pension. A designer bag from Vakoi City hung from his shoulder—and his face, as usual, was beaming.

The applause died off as he approached Martu's stand, but the stares and chatter lingered.

"Morning, Martu," Quax said.

"What a pleasure to see you!" Martu ruffled his hair. "My, how you've grown."

"I know, I know." Quax cringed through a smile as he flattened his hair back into place. "It's been ages since I last came to the market. I've been so busy studying for the selection exams, but now that I'm through with them, I can't stop thinking about your bread. I'll take one of my favorites—*if* you still make it."

"Of course I do." Martu started to wrap a cheesy bread. "You've earned yourself a big day tomorrow."

"Yeah, tell me about it." He forced a grin. "Thought I'd walk to school early with Yahshi today, for old time's sake."

Yahshi shook his head. "I need to help with—"

"Don't be ridiculous," Martu cut in. "It's a special occasion. I can manage alone for one day."

"Thanks." Quax set four coins on the table and took the bread. "Keep the change."

"Why thank you, Quax." Martu glanced at Yahshi as though he were saying, *I told you so. Kindness always finds a way to repay us.*

The two boys walked down the road toward Sitra Secondary, only a few minutes from the market. To their right stood the woods where the incident occurred.

"What are you looking at?"

"Sorry." Yahshi pried his eyes off the trees. "I thought I heard something."

Quax frowned before blinking his confusion away. "Well, I've been meaning to talk to you. Tried to find you at school yesterday after we got our scores back, but you disappeared during lunch. And I wasn't able to stop by your house last night either. We had my tutor over for supper."

"Sorry about that." It was an empty apology, and they both knew it.

Quax bit into his cheesy bread, his stare pressing for an explanation. Yahshi broke eye contact to signal that he wouldn't be giving one.

The silence between them deepened with every step. *I can't remember the last time we walked to school together like this.* Ever since Cal's selection, Quax had been obsessing over scores, fitness, and social status to increase his chance of getting selected.

Everything's changed.

Memories of pre-incident evenings at the Avarium household flickered through his mind. He recalled how Cal would take her plate to eat and read in the other room, leaving Quax picking at his food. Yahshi would suggest they go outside after supper to cheer him up, which always worked.

Quax would demonstrate his latest contraptions like tripwire-activated diversions or cleverly concealed ditches. Then they would lie on the grass, and he'd tell him about his grand dream of designing buildings with the most elaborate secret passageways and security mechanisms. Yahshi would listen in fascination, because a grand dream was something he never had.

Yet here Quax was, throwing that precious dream away.

When they arrived at Sitra Secondary, the other early students were watching a guardian unit secure a *Happy Selection Day* banner to the outdoor stage. Their strapped primary tools demanded fear, but their smiles drew people in. *If Cal's a guardian, what does that say about them?*

While Quax smiled at the unit from afar, Yahshi scowled at the fence dividing the school courtyard from the woods. The community infrastructure bonus from Cal's time in the program had funded its construction not long after the incident.

"Alright, look," Quax said, his smile fading. "I know you've been avoiding me."

"Avoiding you?" Yahshi asked. "Why would I do that?"

"Because you don't want me to get selected."

"No. I mean, not *no* like I don't want you to get selected. Of course I want you to get selected."

"Really? Because I've been preparing for tomorrow for nearly two years, and you've hardly been there." Quax crossed his arms. "I really wish I could leave on good terms with you, because after tomorrow, who knows when I'll see you again? It could be months, and if I graduate, it could be years before—"

"Have you ever considered the possibility that you won't get selected? And honestly, would that be so bad? What if the guardians aren't who you think they are?"

"I knew it. You're still thinking about Chima."

"No." Yahshi stepped back. "No, of course not."

"You don't trust the guardians, so you're trying to stop me from becoming one."

"I'm sorry. I shouldn't have—"

"No, Yahshi. You don't get to do that anymore. You don't get to sneak around and make ridiculous claims and take it back with an I'm sorry or an I didn't mean to. So for once, just once, tell me the truth—did you sabotage my selection exam?"

"What?"

Quax handed Yahshi a score sheet from his bag. "Have a look for yourself. High nineties in every category except for our most recent exam. Do you really think I'd get a sixty-three on a multiple choice test about the Atherus War?"

"I didn't do this."

"It's not that you don't want me to succeed. You're just... so brainwashed that you think you know what's best for me. This is your weird, twisted way of trying to save me."

"That's ridiculous." Yahshi's grip on the page tightened. "I didn't sabotage your exam. How would I possibly pull that off, anyway?"

"I don't know! You're the one who broke into the Fernis household last year."

"I didn't *break in*." Yahshi scanned the courtyard, paranoid the other students had heard despite the distance. "The door was unlocked."

He had slipped inside, hoping to find something that would paint Chima as a murderer and put his doubts to rest—but the house was empty.

"And I know that was wrong, okay? I was being obsessive, but I'm past that now. I swear."

"Yeah? You swear?" Quax asked. "Open your bag then. Let me see what you're keeping in there, because I doubt it's the hundreds of homework assignments you didn't turn in this term."

He shielded his bag without thinking, and Quax scoffed.

Great going again, *Yahshi. Keep defending yourself, and he'll assume you're lying anyway.*

With a sigh, he returned the score sheet and opened his book bag. Inside were over a dozen *Capital Weekly* articles about Cal—two years of collecting and analyzing.

Quax snatched the papers and began to flip through them.

"You're right. I haven't moved on completely," Yahshi admitted. "But you have to believe me when I say I had nothing to do with your low score. Whatever happened, I wasn't involved."

His eyes widened. "This isn't healthy."

"Quax..."

"You were at the top of our class once. Remember that? Now your grades are in the pits. You're throwing away your future, and for what? To read too deep into something my sister did to protect me? Something she did to *save* me, because she *loves* me?"

She didn't save you because she loves you, Yahshi wanted to say. *She saved you because she hated her circumstances. She saved you because students bullied her for being quiet and eating lunches alone. She saved you because she was tired of being the victim.*

"I'd like to leave Sitra knowing you'll stop this." He fished for Yahshi's gaze, but he wouldn't look at him.

"I'll stop. Let's just—let's talk about something else." Yahshi reached for the articles. "Here, let me—"

"You're *not* getting these back."

"Hey!" He stepped toward him, but Quax maintained his distance. "Really, I-I need those!"

"That's exactly the problem." Quax stopped, his expression hardening as he tore the stack in half. The ripping noise sliced through the air.

Yahshi gritted his teeth and lunged, sending a fist flying. Torn pages fluttered around him like confetti as Quax yelled out, cupping a hand over his eye. It took a few seconds for Yahshi to realize what he'd done.

"Quax! I-I'm sorry!" He hobbled as though he'd taken the hit himself. "I didn't... mean to."

"Typical," Quax said.

Yahshi unraveled his fist, his knuckles tingling from a punch he'd thrown out of impulse. He thought of Cal in the woods, swinging that log down over and over.

What have I done?

As muttering students closed in on the scene, he fumbled to gather the pieces before they could read his annotations.

"Are you okay?" Alora asked.

Yahshi looked up as he grabbed the final piece.

"Yeah," Quax replied. "Thanks."

Shoving the articles into his bag, Yahshi jumped to his feet. The students parted, allowing a convenient exit as he ran for the road. *How dare they allow me to flee?*

He'd nearly reached the end of the courtyard when a calloused hand snatched his wrist.

"Yahshi Konya," a stranger called, stopping him.

He looked back at a middle-aged man with a trimmed beard, a bandaged forehead, and eyes that burned to stare into. He was wearing the uniform of a Sitra Secondary instructor, but Yahshi didn't recognize him.

"You did well," the man said, and with a grin, released Yahshi's wrist.

CHAPTER 2

SELECTION CEREMONY

I vow to partake in Imperial ceremonies when called upon.

♬ BABYLON - BARNS COURTNEY ♬

Yahshi and his father lived on the outskirts of town, where grassy fields and evergreens stretched between houses. This was the first place Martu had moved to after the Atherus War, and it was the only place Yahshi had ever called home.

Leaving his sandals on the porch, he made a beeline for the kitchen, where he chucked his tattered articles into the trash. *There has to be a way to fix this.*

He brought a stack of dusty homework assignments to the oak dining table—a gift from the Avariums. Quax's parents had helped Martu settle into Sitra after he converted twelve years prior, assisting him with housing, furnishing, and securing a market stand. *But in return for their kindness, I hurt their son.*

For hours he sat there, searching for a manageable assignment, but the concepts flew over his head. The sun was setting when Martu returned, empty bread baskets in hand.

"Are you... doing homework?"

Yahshi slammed his pencil down. "I'm trying to."

"What happened?"

"I... punched Quax."

"What?"

"He got a hold of my articles about Cal, and he ripped them, and I... punched him." He shook his head, turning to meet his father's widened gaze.

"You promised to keep those articles at home."

"I shouldn't have had them in the first place."

Martu's grip on the baskets tightened. He set them on the countertop as he eyed the ripped pages in the trash. It was silent for a while before he clasped his hands together.

"Why don't we get some practice in?" His tone was oddly cheerful.

"Right now?" Yahshi asked.

"Why not? We can talk about this. Move around a little. It might help you sort your thoughts."

He glanced at his homework assignments. *I guess I could use a break.*

On their way out, they stopped on the porch so Martu could light the brass lantern that hung by the door. Its wiry exterior strained the candlelight into flickering shapes.

"I still don't get why you light this lantern every evening," Yahshi said.

"It's an Eastern tradition." Martu smiled, his eyes glowing. "Your mother adored these kinds. Her father was a lantern-maker."

"Really?"

He nodded. "She helped your grandfather make this one."

"You never told me." Yahshi studied the lantern, its light warming his face. "I assumed you didn't bring anything to Sitra when we converted."

"Well, I didn't bring much. Just this lantern." Martu paused. "And you, of course."

"I see." Yahshi cracked a grin. "I come second to high-quality craftsmanship."

"I'm glad you know your place," Martu said, and they laughed.

As Yahshi led the way, he hopped from stone to stone—a childhood habit he couldn't shake, even on the worst days. His final jump landed him barefoot in the backyard, surrounded by shrubs and flowery weeds. The unkempt grass tickled his ankles as he left it behind, stepping onto a slab.

"Show me your stance," Martu said, his voice merging with the chirping of crickets and birds.

Yahshi raised his hands.

"Shoulders?"

"Right." He loosened them with a sigh. "Bad habit."

"Stop and Go?"

"Sure."

Martu joined him on the platform and mirrored his stance. "Now tell me—why *shouldn't* you keep the articles? Go."

Yahshi sprang forward with a jab, which his father leaned back to dodge.

"Stop," Martu said, and they held their positions.

"Those papers are ruining my life," Yahshi answered.

"How exactly are they ruining your life? Go."

Yahshi tried a combination this time. Martu dodged his first two punches and blocked the last.

"Stop," Martu said.

"I've fallen to the bottom of my class." Yahshi's posture softened, letting his guard down. "And I didn't wanna tell you this, but if I don't show progress this term, I'll be held back a year."

"Would that really be the end of the world?"

"What?" Yahshi frowned at his father, expecting him to dismiss the question as a joke, but his blank expression proved he was serious.

I'm failing. You're supposed to be angry. A surge of blood rushed to his head. *Why* aren't *you* angry? He threw a few distraction punches before pivoting into a kick.

Martu caught his leg, stealing control of his balance. With a few steps away, he sent Yahshi pummeling backward.

He winced as the hard platform pressed into his shoulder blades.

"I didn't say *go*," Martu said, peering down at him. "If you stop now, you'll never find answers. How are you okay with that? Go."

Yahshi attempted to spring to his feet, but Martu crouched, shoving his chest down. He held a pocket knife to his neck.

"Stop."

The blade sent a chill down his spine as he recalled what little he knew of Quax's older sister. As cold-natured as Cal was, he couldn't deny her talent. She would study far more than he ever had, and when she wasn't studying she'd be reading, solving puzzles, or going on extended runs—all while distancing herself from bullies and empathetic classmates trying to befriend her.

"Maybe Cal deserves to be in the Force," he said. "Maybe she's doing good for the Empire. And if not, there's nothing I could do anyway."

Martu stashed the knife and offered Yahshi a hand. "You're right," he said, helping him up. "You can't change anything now, but who's to say about the future? Your intuition is sharp, and it shouldn't be ignored. You never know when you'll be able to create real change."

Did you hear nothing, Father? I'm failing school. Why are you encouraging me?

Yahshi lowered his gaze, watching a trail of ants march across the platform in a single-file line, neat and orderly. For two years, he'd thought Martu was the one person who understood him, his one supporter—but he'd been leading him astray.

"I can assure you that many others are asking the same questions, but they're terrified," Martu continued, his voice strained. "It takes someone brave, like you, to pursue answers on their behalf." He lifted Yahshi's chin, forcing him to meet his gaze.

He could have sworn he saw a hint of moisture in his father's eyes.

"Does that make sense?" Martu asked.

"Yeah, I guess," Yahshi replied, but it didn't make sense at all.

I'll leave those articles in the trash, he decided. *I'll apologize to Quax tomorrow. I'll get my life back.*

Martu's brows furrowed as a raindrop splattered against his head. He looked up at the clouds, his lips spreading into a smile, and Yahshi looked up next.

Rain began to fall, trickling down their cheeks like tears.

"The sky weeps with us," they said in unison.

Martu had always described the island as bipolar. One moment the clouds would be bright, and the next they'd be raining a storm. One moment there would be peace, and the next there'd be war. The only consistency was the gray clouds. Rain or shine, East or West—those same clouds hovered over them.

"It may not feel like it now, Yahshi, but you're exactly where you need to be."

The following afternoon, nearly four thousand town residents gathered in the Sitra Secondary courtyard. Whether they knew Quax personally or not, they believed the Belladonna Prodigy's little brother could do nothing but win.

Yahshi wished he could skip the ceremony, but as a fifteen-year-old, his attendance was mandatory. He stood near the stage with over three hundred selection-eligible students from Sitra, all of whom were staring at Quax.

Did I really do that?

Quax's right eye was swollen half-shut, framed with blotchy clumps of violet.

"Wow, he looks awful."

"I heard Yahshi punched him."

"And he went for the eye! What a convert."

"At least Quax'll make a bold entrance at the Academy."

"Silly move, Yahshi." Alora appeared next to him. "You injured our star student."

"I know," he said firmly. "I messed up."

She looked back at the Avariums. "You're lucky his parents aren't throwing a fit. They're being all smiley with your father right now, like they're not angry at all."

"If the whole town wasn't staring them down, I doubt they'd be this forgiving."

"The staring is their fault for dressing up so fancy. They're fully confident he'll get selected, and they're not even hiding it."

Quax's father was wearing a sleek suit, and his mother was wearing a glittery dress that trapped every pair of eyes for a moment too long. They nodded at Martu with wide grins, likely assuring him that yesterday's scuffle in the courtyard wasn't a concern.

Meanwhile, Quax bit his lip and started to fidget with two quartz marbles Yahshi had gifted him for his eighth birthday. *He kept them, all this time?*

Yahshi dropped his head, eyes wide. "I can't imagine the pressure he's under right now."

"If he doesn't get selected," Alora said, "the island will—quite literally—sink."

Yahshi managed a weak chuckle. "So, did I miss anything at school yesterday?"

"Hmm, let's see… drama about Quax's eye, a lecture on Academy history, and tips for the ceremony. That's about it."

"What kind of tips? We just stand here, don't we?"

"They recommended we pack small sentimental items in case we get selected by surprise."

"Did you pack anything?"

"M-Me?" Alora said. "Why would you ask that?"

"Better question…" Yahshi said, drawing out the phrase. "What are you hiding in your bag?"

"Now you're being ridiculous."

"Your scores are almost as high as Quax's. It's not crazy to think you'd get selected too, and surely you know that, because you did pack your bag." He pointed to it, and she stepped away.

"Girls hardly get selected. The guardians have physical standards too."

He shrugged. "You were always a killer at tag."

As Alora laughed, Yahshi's smile faded, remembering his plan. "I should apologize."

She saluted him as he turned away. "Good luck."

The other fifteen- and sixteen-year-olds stepped aside as he passed, and by the time he reached Quax, a bubble had formed around them.

Quax's eyes were glued to the stage, but surely he knew Yahshi was there because he'd slipped the marbles into his bag.

"Quax," Yahshi said, holding his arms behind him. "I'm sorry. And I'm not just saying that. I mean it. I've been a horrible friend. You've been under so much pressure with everyone rooting for your selection, and I never stopped to notice. I was too worried about the possibility that you might leave someday. It wasn't just about the incident or my *stupid* investigation. Growing up, I assumed we'd stay in each other's lives forever, but as a guardian, you would—"

"Disappear," Quax finished.

"Yeah, like Cal."

He faced Yahshi. "Look, there's something you should know... I don't—"

"Welcome to the biannual selection ceremony!" a guardian shouted from the stage, prompting cheers. He had a four-petaled flower branded into his forehead, and his overcoat flowed past his white pants, nearly skimming his boots. Strapped to his back were two sheathed swords.

"What is it?" Yahshi asked.

"Not now," Quax muttered.

"My name is Commander Roz," the guardian said, and the cheering fell to the ground, dead. They all recognized his name—Commander Roz was one of three Academy guardians, a primary decision-maker in the selection process. His hosting of Sitra's selection ceremony, instead of any other town's, had to be a good sign. But while others crossed their fingers and met eyes in excitement, Yahshi squinted at the guardian. *His voice sounds familiar.*

"I am honored to announce the twenty Western students we've selected to train at Belladonna Guardian Academy this cycle." Commander Roz referenced a golden paper. "Limbo Brackle of Vakoi City, Ceylon Brackle of Vakoi City..."

Mumbling.

"Siblings?" Quax tilted his head. "That's a first."

"...Keiyo Pickett of Miranda, Vell Patura of Miranda..."

Yahshi gulped. He wasn't sure which pinched his nerves more—the thought of Quax getting selected, or Quax *not* getting selected. He counted names in his head as Commander Roz continued.

"...Dice Bayin of Frontal..."

Sixteen.

"...Pinto Dempsey of Frontal..."

Seventeen.

"...Sunna Rickabee of Nominner..."

Eighteen.

A brief pause. Somewhere out there, entire towns were cheering as their selectees' names were called. The town of Sitra waited for their chance to cheer too.

Commander Roz lowered the page and shouted, "Quax Avarium of Sitra!"

Yahshi gasped as the crowd exploded, screaming and applauding. He hadn't realized he'd been holding his breath.

"Congratulations, Quax," Commander Roz said. "Please say your brief goodbyes before joining me on stage."

Quax turned to Yahshi with a weak grin. "I'll miss you."

Yahshi wasn't sure how to feel about his selection, but he did know that he'd miss him too. He slung an arm around his shoulder. "Goodbye, Quax."

Alora shoved her way through the crowd, joining their bubble. "You better last a while. We could use better desks in the science room." She offered a hand, and Quax chuckled, shaking it.

"You've got a deal," he said, and with a boldening smile, left them behind.

He said goodbye to his mother first, who kissed him on the head—then to his father, who whispered something into his ear that he nodded to with watery eyes. And lastly, when Martu ruffled his hair, he didn't flatten it back into place.

All of Sitra watched as he walked toward the stage. They were happy for him and what his selection would bring to the community because Sitra had, once again, produced a star. But he was a shooting star whose fate was to flash by before vanishing, leaving behind only a lingering sense of awe. They were simultaneously lucky to have witnessed him and unlucky to have lost him.

Yahshi focused on their shared memories—their family suppers, walks to school, and games during lunch breaks. He focused on when the star was overhead rather than the moment it shot away.

"I can't believe he's actually leaving," Alora said.

Yahshi glanced at her with a smirk. "At least that puts you at the top of our class."

"By default. How shameful."

Quax joined the guardian on stage and bowed in gratitude. Only then did Yahshi recognize Commander Roz as the instructor who had stopped him by the wrist to praise him.

"That's strange," Yahshi muttered.

"What?" Alora asked.

"And finally," Commander Roz said, "Yahshi Konya of Sitra!"

CHAPTER 3

BLOOD BOUND

I vow to complete forty consecutive and obedient
years of service.

♫ ALL EYES ON ME · VINES ♫

Me, selected? Yahshi blinked. *That's impossible.*

Adults and younger children cheered, but his selection-aged peers mumbled in protest. They went to school with Yahshi, where he'd developed a reputation as the star student-turned-lowlife, the witness corrupted by trauma, the boy who never left the woods that day. He was anything *but* selection material.

"Yahshi," Alora said, removing an item from her book bag, "I want you to have these."

"Your yellow mittens?" he asked.

"They're light green," she corrected. "Just take them, to remember."

He didn't know what Alora meant by *remember*—all he knew was that she was trying to say goodbye.

"I'm not actually selected," he said, stepping away from her.

"Take them!" Alora shoved the mittens into his hands.

"Yahshi!" Martu yelled, emerging from the crowd.

He stuffed the mittens into his bag, and Martu embraced him.

"Father," he whispered, "there's been a mistake."

Martu pulled away, gripping his shoulders. "Then you go up there, and you tell him that." He lowered his voice. "Remember that you *always* have a choice."

Yahshi struggled to make eye contact with him.

"Do you promise to stay in Sitra?" Martu asked.

His eyes hopped from face to face as though he might find answers in the students around him. "I'm so confused right now, and—"

"Promise me." Martu's grip on his shoulders tightened, and Yahshi finally looked into his eyes.

"I promise."

Yahshi and Quax sat across from Commander Roz in the Sitra Secondary office. Above the only window was a portrait of Cal, and on the desk were two golden pages with a dagger between them.

"This meeting will take no more than ten minutes," Commander Roz said. "I'm going to explain why the two of you were selected and go over what we would expect of you as Academy trainees. At the end of this meeting, you will choose whether to sign the contract or pass on the opportunity. If you choose to sign it, you will leave for Belladonna Guardian Academy immediately.

"Let's start with Quax Avarium. I received amazing recommendation reports from your instructors on the social dynamics between you and your schoolmates."

"Commander," Yahshi said. "I-I shouldn't be here. There's been a mistake."

The guardian locked eyes with him. "Hold your tongue. You're exactly where you need to be." He returned his attention to Quax. "Like I was saying, with scores like yours, raving instructor reports, and a letter of recommendation from your combat tutor, selecting you was an obvious choice.

"Now, normally an obvious choice is an obvious choice, but considering your connection to Cal, I wanted to ensure the words of praise were more than a runoff of your sister's reputation. And I must admit, I was a little curious about you too, and six months of flipping through exam scores and instructor reports in my flat gets... dull. I decided to conduct a hands-on experiment to test how you'd respond to a situation of injustice, so I co-ordinated a grade change with Sitra Secondary for your last exam of Selection Season. I observed your response from a distance the next morning with a single question that would determine your selection—would you let the injustice slide in fear of conflict, or would you embody the nature of a guardian and stand up for what's right?"

Yahshi bit his lip. He and Quax hadn't fought over a misunderstanding —they'd fought over a test.

"Surely enough, you worked with the information you had to draw your own conclusion and confronted Yahshi. You proved how much you care about your selection, but most of all, you proved how much you care about doing the right thing."

Yahshi caught a glimpse of Quax through the corner of his eye. He desperately wished he could read him, but his face held no expression. Did he feel Commander Roz had played him, or was he proud of himself for passing the test?

"And next, Yahshi Konya," Commander Roz said. "Eastern convert and son of Sitra Market vendor Martu Konya. I heard from Cal that you have a history of combat experience under your father's guidance."

"We train for recreation," Yahshi said. "It's just a hobby."

"Every skill of mastery begins as a hobby," Commander Roz countered. "I also dug into your school reports from Sitra Primary. You were at the top of the class every year without fail. And yet, over the past two years of secondary school, your scores have steadily declined."

"School's been getting harder," Yahshi muttered.

"If that were the case, we'd see the same pattern with other students, but we don't. Your pitiful scores are not the case of school getting harder, but your life getting busier. You've started to help your father manage his stand at Sitra Market. Is that correct?"

Yahshi nodded.

"I assume your recreational training and vendor responsibilities take up a significant portion of your day. Your father's demands for your involvement in his life have limited your study time."

He said nothing. It was true that Martu had expected more help from him since the incident.

Commander Roz leaned in, resting his elbows on the table. "And all of that doesn't account for your investigation."

Yahshi froze. "What investigation, Commander?"

"I know you've been questioning the Force. Your instructors say you've been poking your nose into Chima's social circle and reading articles during lectures."

"Oh." He should have known his instructors would notice. "Well, I've moved on from that."

"Rest easy. You're not in trouble. When the other Academy guardians and I heard about your skepticism, we were more intrigued than anything else. Your investigation has contributed to your academic decline, but it's also demonstrated your all-consuming devotion and intensity of focus. You were willing to punch Quax, a childhood friend, to protect your articles. You're intelligent, and you care immensely about what you value. Those are exactly the qualities we look for in a potential guardian. What the Academy program will do is help you direct that energy into a productive outlet rather than a destructive one."

Yahshi had never thought of what his life would look like as part of the Force—or part of anything, for that matter. With pitiful scores in secondary school, his career options after graduation were limited to the lowest tier. He had fallen into a ditch, but the guardians were kind enough to throw him a rope instead of burying him.

"Yahshi, we're offering you a chance to build a new reputation and make a difference for the better. Your peers and instructors may not consider you selection material, and perhaps your father may have doubts, but I fully believe in you. There is no mistake here. We look for performance, but we also look for potential."

Commander Roz paused, and Yahshi used the space to soak in his words.

He wished he could hear them a billion times, looping like a never-ending melody.

"Before accepting this deal, it's imperative that you understand the full ramifications of joining the program. Allow me to summarize the contract's five points." Commander Roz pushed the golden pages closer to them, and Yahshi squinted at the clusters of tiny text.

"Number one: As trainees, you will have no contact with anyone from your old life for the duration of your time in the program. There will be no visits and no exchanges of letters or gifts. You will engage socially with guardians and trainees, unless otherwise organized by the Force.

"Number two: On the first day of every month you're in the program, your immediate family will receive a two-thousand-coin pension, and your hometown will receive five times that as a bonus in their monthly infrastructure fund. The first payments will be delivered today, assuming you sign the contract.

"Number three: We run a competitive program that requires your complete dedication for success. You will not get many days off, and you will not have the privilege to travel freely. You will need to follow a strict schedule that demands growth under pressure.

"Number four: If you are filtered from the program, but the Empire requires additional guardians in the Force, your partial training experience may subject you to a mandatory service call, regardless of your graduation status.

"And lastly, but most importantly, number five: You must understand that only five of twenty trainees will graduate from the program eighteen months from today. These five trainees will be finalized after nine months and required to serve forty years after graduation. However, prior to the tenth month, you are welcome to filter yourself from the program before any life-altering commitments are made. In fact, we encourage it. If you cannot handle the separation from friends and family, are mentally or physically unable to maintain the Academy schedule, or experience doubts about your career path, you are not fit for guardianship, and you should leave before it's too late. Bear in mind that your family pension and your community's infrastructure bonus will cease upon returning home.

"If you accept your selection, take this dagger." He slid the tool between them, and a dull beam of light reflected off its blade. "You must sign the contract in blood to reflect the weight of your decision."

Quax didn't miss a beat before grabbing the dagger and slitting his thumb. With a wince, he brought his finger to the contract, and the wound left a surprisingly large stain. Yahshi was sure his blood must have seeped through the page.

Commander Roz bandaged Quax's thumb and cleaned the blade with a handkerchief. He placed the dagger on the table again, but Yahshi didn't reach for it.

I should go, shouldn't I? Staying behind would deprive Sitra of the bonus infrastructure funding, and the town would blame him for it. *I can leave any time before the tenth month, anyway. I should stay for a few days before giving up my spot, that way they'll receive at least one month's bonus.*

But if he joined and ended up liking it, would graduating as a guardian be so bad? He would live in Vakoi City among the most influential figures in the Empire, and the people of Sitra would respect him again.

As a result, however, he would hardly see his father anymore. Would Martu despise him for breaking his promise, leaving him in Sitra, all by himself? *How am I supposed to choose between my father and a bright future?*

"Could I have some time to decide?" Yahshi asked. "I'd like to speak to my father about this."

"I'm afraid this decision is yours to make alone," Commander Roz said. "And you must decide now."

I could be a guardian? Yahshi stared at the dagger for what felt like a lifetime. *Is that something I want?*

He flinched as Commander Roz stood.

"I believe you've made your decision." The guardian collected the signed contract and headed for the door. "Quax, follow me."

As their footsteps echoed through the office, Yahshi's chest tightened, and he could hear his pulse in his ears. This was the opportunity of a lifetime. If he were to leave the dagger on the table, at best, nothing would change. At worst, he would ruin his life more than he already had. He would forever wonder what could have been if he had simply signed the contract.

Yahshi narrowed his eyes, swiping the dagger.

I'm sorry, Father.

He gritted his teeth and applied too much pressure to the blade against his thumb. A yelp left his lips as blood spilled across the page in more than one spot, blurring the text.

I've made my choice.

Their footsteps halted as Yahshi pressed his thumb to the contract. Despite his urge to wince, he pushed even harder. For the first time, he had a plan of action, a direction, a wild dream. He chose to believe in a life outside of his rabbit hole.

CHAPTER 4

ORIENTATION

I vow to report suspicious activity within or outside the Force.

♫ SWIM TO THEM - RYAN LOUDER ♫

They left Sitra in a vault, a mode of transportation exclusive to the Force. While Roz guided the horses from the exterior driver's seat, Yahshi and Quax sat across from each other in the wheeled aluminum passenger box.

I never imagined the inside would look like this. Yahshi studied the barred windows near the roof that hardly filtered light, his stomach churning as the box swayed.

"Before the ceremony began," he muttered, "what were you gonna tell me?"

They hit a rugged patch of road and gripped their benches, anchoring themselves.

"Forget it," Quax replied.

Yahshi couldn't be sure he'd heard him correctly over the clomping of horse hooves.

"What?"

"Forget it!"

He gulped, fishing for Quax's gaze. "This is all... pretty crazy, right?"

"I'm not in the mood, Yahshi."

"Well I wasn't planning for things to turn out like this either, but is it really so bad?"

Quax finally made eye contact. "My entire future's on the line."

Now it was Yahshi looking away, his vision tilting as he lost his sense of up and down. "So you think that's all I do?" He tightened his grip on the bench, and the pressure stung his injured thumb. "Mess things up for you?"

"You gave me a black eye."

"And I apologized. You know I'd never do something like that again."

"I *never* know with you. That's the problem." Quax rubbed his temple, sighing. "Our goodbye was perfect, exactly what it should have been, but now everything's twisted... and *weird*."

"Why?"

"Because *you're* here."

They traveled the remainder of the hour-long trip in silence. Yahshi's dizziness and the lack of scenery gave him no choice but to burrow into his mind. He listened to the dirt crumbling beneath the wheels, mentally replaying their meeting with Commander Roz. He nearly convinced himself he'd imagined it when the vault came to a jagged stop.

The door swung open, and light filled the passenger box.

"Come on out," Commander Roz said.

Yahshi's jump from the platform left him stumbling down a forested road.

Commander Roz caught him by the shoulder. "Vaultsickness. Gets the best of us."

Quax jumped next, landing with a solid thud.

"Orientation will begin in the common room shortly." Commander Roz gestured to the roadside. "Welcome to the Academy."

An icehouse and a horse stable hid in the shadows of nearby trees, beyond which was a grassy field surrounding the main building. Streaks of gold shined through gaps in the clouds, illuminating the Academy in a natural spotlight. Its gable displayed the golden four-petaled flower emblem, and its dark shingles swirled into pointed peaks.

Yahshi and Quax crossed the field, entering a courtyard with benches and an elevated statue of Emperor Vakoi. A muscular frame filled his royal gown, and his hair flowed symmetrically over his shoulders.

After scaling the steps, they halted at the door.

"What happened yesterday stays between us," Quax said.

"Of course."

He opened the door, and Yahshi's jaw dropped as he followed him inside.

The common room walls arched into a curved ceiling decorated with portraits of the Vakoi Empire lineage. Natural light gleamed through crystal-clear windows, which reflected the flickering flames of torches on the walls. And at the heart of the room, a few boys occupied a posh lounging area, their feet propped up like they'd lived here forever.

Two of the boys were identical, apart from one having a bird silhouette tattoo on his neck. Their classy uniforms and carefully crafted hairstyles confirmed them as the Brackle siblings from Vakoi City Secondary. With an upbringing among royalty and the most influential figures in the Empire, Yahshi wondered how long they'd last. Students from the capital were too entitled and delicate for the program. *Or so I've heard.*

The boy sitting across from the twins was dominating the conversation, his expression animated as he gestured with every word. He had a mole on his left cheek, wavy hair that fell to his chest, and a black shirt identifying him as a student from Miranda Secondary—the school with the best selection track record in the West.

"There's no way!" shouted the boy in the black shirt. He rushed from the sofas, smiling so widely that his dimples looked like stab wounds. "I was sure I must have misheard. *Two* selected from Sad Sitra this season?"

"Sad Sitra?" Quax asked. "Is that really what we're known as?"

"Before your big sister turned out to be a prodigy, at least." The boy smiled at Quax without offering Yahshi a glance. "I'm Keiyo Pickett"—he tugged his black shirt—"of Miranda, if you couldn't tell."

"Quax Avarium."

Keiyo chuckled. "Yeah, I know." He waved a finger at Quax's face. "What's with the eye? Looks painful."

"Eh. I've had worse."

"Ooh, alright, *tough guy*. Come have a seat!" Keiyo led Quax toward the twins, and Yahshi stayed behind because the invitation clearly didn't extend to him.

"How many from Miranda this season?" Quax said as they walked away.

"Just two," Keiyo replied, as if *two* weren't enough. "Me and that girl over there." He pointed to a trainee who was leaning against the wall with her arms crossed.

Yahshi frowned. *It's that girl from the market.*

"Let me tell you—her selection was a wild surprise," Keiyo continued, his voice hardly audible over the distance. "Horrible attendance."

Yahshi took a deep breath and marched toward the girl in the black shirt. *What would the guardians see in a thief?*

She was watching a pair of rowdy boys engage in a pushup competition when he planted himself next to her.

"So, why'd you do it?" Yahshi asked, testing whether she remembered him.

"Because I had to." She shrugged. "And I like sourdough."

"Sitra's far from Miranda. At least an hour on foot."

"It's easier to steal from strangers."

"But why would the guardians—"

"They're not looking for star students. They're looking for well-intended criminals." She finally faced him, her brows furrowed with a slight pout.

"I'm Yahshi."

"Vell."

"How old are you?"

"Fifteen."

"Me too." He studied her face. "You look older."

"And you look younger."

The front door opened, drawing their attention to the latest pair of arrivals. The shorter one had a chiseled jawline and a red bandana around his forehead, while the taller one had soft cheeks cradled by his curly hair. A leather patch covering his right eye spread murmurs across the room.

"Poor depth perception," Vell noted.

Yahshi glanced at the floor before meeting her eyes. "Is that a problem?"

"It won't hurt him much out there, but at the Academy, he's disadvantaged."

"Maybe he has formal training to compensate."

"That's true. I know Keiyo worked with a private combat tutor."

"Quax did too."

"And you?"

"My selection wasn't planned."

She paused. "Mine wasn't either."

Once all twenty trainees had arrived, a bug-eyed guardian burst into the common room. She had a bow and a quiver of arrows slung across her back.

"Quiet up!" yelled the guardian, her voice stabbing their ears. "Keep the noise down. What is this, primary school?"

The room silenced. Yahshi and Vell made eye contact before joining the others gathered by the lounging area. Keiyo and the Brackle twins were sitting up straight now, their feet on the ground.

"My name is Professor Embre, and I'll be your Research instructor during your time here." She paced back and forth, her dark locks whipping around her with every pivot. "I worked at the Investigation Office for four years before joining the Academy staff. You're my third cycle of trainees, and it's an honor to welcome you here today."

It doesn't sound like an honor.

Professor Embre halted, crossing her arms. "For those of you counting your fingers—I'm twenty-eight. And by the way, there's a thing called *mental math.*"

"Feisty," said the boy with the bird tattoo. His brother elbowed him in the side.

"Let's get you settled. Follow me to the second floor. *Quietly.*" She led them to a spiral staircase, and the trainees slowed to observe the railings' carvings.

"I said *quietly*, not slowly. You'll have plenty of time to stare at wood this evening. Right now, we need to get you sorted into your living quarters, after which you'll have ten minutes to change into your uniforms. When the bell rings, head straight to the fourth floor for a Defense demonstration with Commander Roz. Leave your book bags and any other belongings behind. Understood?"

"Yes, ma'am," the trainees chanted.

"It's *Professor*," she snapped. "You see the Research Division badges on my shoulders, do you not?"

They filed into the second-floor lobby, which featured novels by renowned Vakoi City authors, classic board games, and tins of throwing darts with feathered tips. Ten numbered doors led to their quarters, dozens of cork targets on the walls between them. *We'll be living together from now on, almost like a family.*

"When I call your name, please enter your assigned quarter." Professor Embre retrieved a golden paper from her overcoat. "We have one girl this cycle, so Vell Patura—Room 1 is all yours."

Vell flinched as every trainee in the lobby faced her. She fled into her quarter and slammed the door.

Professor Embre scowled at Room 1 before referencing her paper again. "Quax Avarium, Keiyo Pickett, and Sunna Rickabee—the three of you will share Room 2."

Three boys stepped forward, and Yahshi identified a new face—Sunna had the palest skin among them, with freckles that covered his neck and arms like a splattering of cornstarch over dough. He picked at his thumb bandage as he followed Quax and Keiyo into the room.

"The other quarters will have two trainees each. Limbo Brackle and Rugan Whitter—you'll take Room 3."

One of the boys who stepped forward was the brother with the bird tattoo. Yahshi made a mental note to associate the symbol with the name *Limbo.*

"Yahshi Konya and Pinto Dempsey—you'll take Room 4."

Yahshi stepped forward in unison with the tall boy from Frontal Secondary. He wasn't sure why Pinto made his shoulders go stiff. Perhaps it was the eye patch, or perhaps it was—

No, it's the eye patch.

He followed Pinto into Room 4, which was larger than his house back home. It came with a private restroom, a sliding glass door to the balcony, and lavish furniture that put the common room to shame. They each had their own bed, dresser, desk, and nightstand.

"Wow, this room is incredible," Pinto said, spinning around with his chin high. "And there's designs on the ceiling. Who even looks up there?"

Yahshi approached the bed to his right, where a trainee uniform and a pajama set rested on the blankets. He held the pants against his legs, testing their length.

"And these golden silk pajamas, have you felt them?" Pinto rubbed the material as though he were petting a cat. "Fabric made from worm saliva doesn't deserve to feel this great."

"These pants look like the perfect size," Yahshi concluded.

"They must have taken measurements from our school health evaluations."

"Isn't that risky?" Yahshi plopped the pants onto his bed. "You'd think they'd tailor our uniforms *after* we signed the contract."

Pinto laughed. "As if anyone *wouldn't* sign it."

Remembering Professor Embre's instructions, they began to change into their uniforms. Their dark pants were thick yet breathable, and their vests had flower emblems embroidered at the heart with golden buttons of the same symbol.

Pinto smiled at the mirror, securing his silky blue tie. "It's Yahshi, right?"

"That's me."

"Let me show you something." He pulled a bamboo journal out of his bag. "Handmade, can you believe it? The paper's refillable too."

"Uh..." Yahshi forced a smile. "Cool."

"Did you bring anything with you?"

He hesitated but opened his bag. "All I have are some late school assignments for Sitra Secondary—which I guess I don't need anymore—and these... light-green mittens."

"They're yellow."

Yahshi chuckled. "Right?" He crossed the room and set the mittens on his nightstand.

"It's a rather hot time of year for mittens, don't you think?" Pinto asked.

Yahshi paused, frowning at the fabric. "Yeah, I suppose you're right." Only now did he wonder why Alora had brought them to the ceremony.

Oh no. The ceremony. How is Father taking the news?

Pinto sighed. "Okay, what's with the face?"

"What face?"

"The one you're making right now. You look sick." He gasped. "*Are* you sick?"

Yahshi shook his head, eyes on his thumb. "I'm just worried I let my father down today."

"Why would you think that?" Pinto asked, a touch of humor in his tone. "You're doing everyone in Sitra a favor, especially him. Just think of the pension, and the honor!"

"My father doesn't care much for money or honor. I'm his only family, and he has no idea when he'll see me again. He must be heartbroken."

"Oh," Pinto said, his voice deepening. "I had to leave someone really important to me too. We could both hardly bear it." He clutched his journal, the color draining from his face. "But training here is the opportunity of a lifetime, and it'd be a shame to let bitter feelings get in the way of that. They'll come to understand our choice with time."

"I hope you're right," Yahshi said.

"Me too."

The training room had no windows—only torches. It was monochrome with the exception of a circular, emerald-green area in the middle of the floor, about ten steps in diameter. Guardian tools and training equipment were scattered about the walls like decoration.

Yahshi and Pinto stood near the door, watching Quax juggle his marbles from across the room.

"I don't know how you do it," Keiyo said.

"Whoa..." Sunna's eyes followed the marbles in a circular pattern. "Mesmerizing."

Pinto rolled his eye. "The brother can juggle marbles. What a prodigy."

"It's not easy to juggle small objects," Yahshi said, recalling how long Quax had spent practicing.

"Impressive or not, Professor Embre made it clear that we're supposed to leave all personal belongings—"

The metal door slid open, and Vell rushed inside. She was the only trainee without a navy-blue tie, which made a few boys chuckle.

"I feel like something's"—Limbo smirked, tightening his tie—"*off.*"

Yahshi's cheeks warmed as though the embarrassment were his own, but Vell seemed unfazed. One by one, she stared back at the boys watching her until they broke eye contact first. Quax turned around when she looked at him, stashing the marbles in his pocket.

"She has an edge," Pinto said. "I heard that's good in the program. The nice ones don't last."

"Are *you* nice?" Yahshi asked.

He shrugged. "Maybe."

The door slid open, and a guardian sailed into the room. "I'm Commander Roz, your Defense Division instructor..." He stopped when he noticed Vell. "Do you not like your tie?"

"I don't think *it* likes me," Vell said.

"Well, I'm sure it'll warm up to you tomorrow," Commander Roz said. "I'll see to it."

He nodded before eyeing the other trainees. "As you all know, the Academy only permits five graduates every two years. But who can tell me what determines those graduates?"

Quax's hand shot into the air. He likely squeezed information out of his combat tutor, a former trainee who had almost graduated during a previous cycle.

"Yes, Quax?"

"Filtrations. Tests of essential guardian skills."

"That's correct. Trainees who pass the tests will keep their spot at the Academy, while those who fail will be filtered from the program and sent home. After nine months, only five trainees will remain, their graduation ensured. Those five will move on to shadow real guardian units and undergo personalized training.

"Consider the program's first half an opportunity to prove that you deserve a spot in the Force. Don't get too comfortable, because with comfort comes laziness. Any questions?"

Yahshi had several, but he didn't know where to begin.

"Yes, Pinto?" Commander Roz called.

"I have two questions. First, how often will these tests occur?"

A few boys made eye contact, mocking Pinto's serious nature.

"Sometimes they'll be random," Commander Roz answered. "Sometimes you'll be told in advance."

"Got it. And second, what will the tests consist of?"

"I'm glad you asked." Commander Roz gestured to the circular green zone. "Quax Avarium and Yahshi Konya, please enter the sparring range."

Yahshi glanced at Pinto as he left him behind, joining Quax in the green zone.

"Allow me to explain the rules of your first filtration." Commander Roz pulled a stopwatch out of his overcoat. "There are two ways to win a match. You can make your opponent tap out through force—or alternatively, you can push your opponent outside of the green zone. If you're unresponsive, it's an automatic loss. If the match lasts longer than ten minutes, it's a draw."

Yahshi gulped, mirroring Quax's fighting stance.

The guardian's stopwatch clicked.

"You may begin."

CHAPTER 5

FINISH YOUR SUPPER

I vow to uphold Imperial Law and Protocol without exception.

♬ NO REASON - BONOBO, NICK MURPHY ♬

Two years prior, Quax couldn't fight if his life depended on it—but today, he threw one punch after another, one kick after another, relentlessly.

Impressive. Yahshi smiled as he leaned back, ducked, blocked. *His hard work paid off.*

But then he remembered that losing this match would get him filtered.

I can't keep this up forever. He sidestepped around a punch, and for a moment, Quax's arm was extended, his face vulnerable. *I need to strike back.*

As Yahshi closed in for a hit, he got a painfully close look at Quax's eye. He thought of what he'd done in the courtyard and how he'd told Quax that he'd never do something like that again. Yet here he was, throwing another punch.

How did we get here? We used to be best friends.

Yahshi diverted his arm, intentionally missing Quax's cheek by a hair's width. He didn't resist when Quax swung him into an arm lock and forced him down. He didn't fight back, even with his cheek pressed against the floor, his arm aching.

But pain was pain, and he could only bear so much.

Yahshi gritted his teeth and tapped his palm against the floor, forfeiting the match. He couldn't tell which hurt more—the soreness in his elbow or the thought of explaining to everyone in Sitra why he hadn't lasted more than an hour in the program.

His arms trembled as he pushed himself up. As he rejoined the others, the trainees watched him with faces that said, *He's the first to go.*

"There will be three phases to this filtration, spaced three days apart." Commander Roz attached a four-petaled flower pin to Quax's collar. "You'll have one sparring opportunity for every phase. If you fail to earn your pin after three phases, you'll be filtered from the program."

Yahshi froze when Commander Roz faced him.

"The first phase will take place two weeks from today, so you have plenty of time to prepare."

I'm not getting sent home?

"With that being said, we still have a bit of extra time before the opening ceremony. Why don't we squeeze in one more sparring match against Quax? Any volunteers?"

Silence.

"Consider this phase zero, a bonus opportunity to join him in bypassing the filtration completely."

More silence.

"Just step forward." Commander Roz gestured to the green zone. "There's nothing to lose."

Limbo sent Yahshi a smirk. "Just our dignity," he whispered.

Yahshi lowered his head, and Pinto jumped in, saying, "He made a good effort."

"He couldn't land a hit," Limbo countered.

A surge of mumbling interrupted them as Vell weaved through the group. She faced Quax in the green zone, her stance too narrow, her shoulders too high.

The guardian's stopwatch clicked. "You may begin."

Quax lunged at Vell, who backstepped out of reach. She narrowed her eyes, glancing at his boots, then his face. When he tried to close the gap, she swerved around him, shoving her shoulder into his.

She's fast. I'll give her that.

But she wasn't strong. The shoulder bump hadn't disrupted Quax enough to clear an opportunity for her to strike. All it took was a few more steps and a shove for him to launch her out of the green zone.

Yahshi closed his eyes, refusing to watch. The choir of wincing confirmed that she'd struck the floor.

When he opened his eyes, Quax was offering Vell a hand. "Are you okay?"

She slipped her fingers into her pocket before accepting his help with a smile. Quax dropped her hand like it was a hot coal as soon as she was back on her feet.

She volunteered for this match. Yahshi squinted at Vell as she untangled a few strands of hair. *Why would she smile after losing?*

Vell craned her head to meet his gaze. He could feel her eyes piercing through him long after he looked away, tormenting him until the school bell cut through the air.

"Please head to the common room for Embre's opening ceremony," Commander Roz said.

Yahshi lingered as the others filed out, and with a deep breath, approached Commander Roz.

"Is something wrong?" asked the guardian.

"Commander," Yahshi said, "I'm a bit confused about why you paired Quax and me for this demonstration."

His silence pressured Yahshi to continue.

"It almost feels like you're trying to... pit us against each other." He bit his lip, bracing himself for Commander Roz to retaliate against his rude accusation.

But instead, he smiled. "Yahshi, you trust me, don't you? Everything we do at the Academy, we do for a good reason." Commander Roz didn't pause long enough to invite a reply. "Now if I were you, I'd hurry. Embre doesn't ignore tardiness."

Yahshi's jaw tightened. "Right."

The trainees sat in the common room's lounging area as Professor Embre, in excruciating detail, outlined the Academy schedule, rules to follow, and tips for success in the program.

"...You may skip classes if you wish, but that won't do you any favors. Unless you're sick or injured, I recommend you show up, and do so punctually. As for your time off the clock, rooms of instruction are open at all hours for studying and training independently. The only areas off-limits are the guardian quarters." She gestured to the door and stood. "That covers everything. Enjoy your supper."

The trainees headed for the dining hall as Professor Embre headed for the front door.

Yahshi glanced back. *Where is she going?*

The dining hall included round, four-seater tables and chandeliers with infinite candles. One wall was made entirely of glass, showcasing the field and surrounding woods. Gold and pink hues of sunset flowed between trees.

"Whoa, take a look at that glass," Pinto said. "It's incredible."

"What a gorgeous view," Yahshi said.

Pinto laughed. "I meant the window. It's massive!" He grabbed a tray from the serving table and shot for an open seat.

Yahshi grabbed a tray next, his mouth watering at the steak, vegetables, and package of crackers. But the cold steel against his thumb cut made him shiver as he turned to the tables. His eyes hopped from face to face.

Quax was sitting with his roommates, and Yahshi figured he should give him space.

He approached Pinto's table instead. "Can I join you?"

"You don't have to ask," Pinto replied, unfolding his table napkin. "It's... *odd* if you ask."

Yahshi pursed his lips and sat across from him.

Pinto gasped. "Are you seeing this?" He dangled the fabric in Yahshi's face. "My napkin has thin golden lines embroidered into it. They're so small you can hardly see them, but they're there."

He studied the fabric with a faked hum of interest. *How could he be so fascinated by a napkin?*

"I-I can't believe this all for us." Pinto spread the cloth over his lap. "With treatment this special, we might as well be royalty."

Yahshi grabbed his utensils, steam from the steak warming his face. *I can't remember the last time I had beef.* Even the best lunches at Sitra Secondary were vegetarian, under-seasoned, and always served cold.

His first bite dissolved in his mouth, the spices both foreign and comforting. It took all his strength not to stuff the food into his face with his bare hands.

"Hey," Yahshi said after a few minutes of enjoying the meal in silence, "where do you think Professor Embre was going?"

"What?"

"After the opening ceremony. She was leaving the building."

Pinto shrugged and prepared his next bite. "I don't know, Yahshi. She's a guardian. They're busy all the time."

"But she's an *Academy* guardian."

"What's that got to do with anything?" Pinto's grip on his fork tightened. "She's still a guardian in the Research Division. Maybe they need her in the Investigation Office sometimes."

"Sorry." Yahshi stared at his plate, stabbing a bite of steak. "I wasn't trying to annoy you."

"I'm not annoyed. It's just a... weird question, that's all."

As Yahshi chewed, his eyes drifted to Vell. She was sitting alone, cutting her steak into bite-sized pieces with jagged knife pulls. He figured being the only girl in the program must have felt isolating.

"Vell!"

They both flinched. Vell, surprised someone had called her name—and Yahshi, surprised that the *someone* had been him. She met his gaze.

"Do you... wanna join us?" Yahshi asked.

Pinto leaned toward him. "You know her?"

"Not really," he muttered back.

Vell studied the other tables as though gauging her options before walking over and sitting between them. A small object struck the floor as she scooted her chair in, and her eyes widened. She snatched the fallen marble and slipped it into her pocket.

Pinto cleared his throat. "That was…"

"Yes." Vell avoided eye contact as she resumed cutting her steak.

Yahshi mentally replayed the match. *Did she really steal a marble from Quax's pocket without him noticing? Without any of us noticing?*

"How?" Pinto asked. "It doesn't make sense."

Vell took a bite, offering no explanation.

"Why?" Yahshi asked, more curious about her motive.

"I just wanted to see if I could."

Pinto tugged her collar. "So you can't tie a tie, but you can pull off a discreet maneuver like that in the middle of a sparring match?"

She swatted his arm away. "They're completely different skills."

He blinked. "That's fair."

"Vell," Yahshi said, "I think you should return it. We all didn't bring much from home. It might be important to him."

"No, she can't do that," Pinto argued. "If she puts her cards on the table too early, she won't have any leverage."

"Huh," Vell said. "You're smarter than you look."

Pinto raised his chin. "What do I look like then?"

"Intimidating." She paused. "Childish."

"That's a bit contradictory, don't you think?"

"I've met intimidating children."

The door busted open, and a third guardian, likely in his fifties, rolled a metal cart into the dining hall. He had a pointy gray beard, bushy brows, and badges on his shoulders that marked him as a member of the Medical Division. Strapped across his chest was a bandolier of throwing blades.

"Doctor Blimmery, Guardian Blimmery, Blim Blim—whatever you'd like to call me is just fine!"

He bobbed his head back and forth, dancing to a silent tune as he delivered glasses of red juice from his cart. When he reached Yahshi's group, he set one by Vell and winked at her, making Pinto raise a brow. He served the boys their glasses next.

"Wow," Pinto said as Doctor Blimmery left their table. "This morning everything was normal, and now we've got fancy rooms, fancy clothes, fancy food—even fancy juice. It's more incredible than I imagined."

Vell chewed slowly, glancing at Pinto before stabbing her fork into a slice of meat.

"Surely you're pleased to be here," Pinto said in a questioning tone.

"I'm pleased for the pension," Vell said.

"The pension?" Yahshi asked.

"That's why we're all here."

"No, not all of us. We're still in a horrible state of conflict with the East." Pinto stared at the chandelier above them, his eye glimmering. "Some of us feel responsible for serving Emperor Vakoi and protecting our people."

"That's admirable," Vell said.

"You know, I really can't tell if you're being sarcastic or not." He sipped his juice and cringed. "Ugh. Retract *fancy juice* from my previous statement."

Yahshi took a sip next, his face contorting as he resisted the urge to spit it right out.

Pinto chuckled. "Did you not hear me warn you?"

Vell tried hers and broke out into a fit of coughs. "Tastes like poison." She slammed her glass down.

Pinto and Yahshi laughed, and she smiled at them for the first time.

"I'm Pinto Dempsey of Frontal, by the way. Yahshi's roommate."

"Vell. From Miranda."

"She steals bread," Yahshi added.

Vell coughed again.

"Steals bread? What does he mean by that?" Pinto looked back and forth between them. "Oh, come on. Don't just ignore me. Did you two know each other before getting selected?"

As Vell tuned out Pinto's follow-up questions, Yahshi noticed the bandana boy sitting with the Brackle twins.

"Hey, Pinto…" Yahshi said. "He's from your town too, isn't he?"

Pinto fell silent for an abnormally long time.

"Dice Bayin," he finally said. "I'd stay away from him if I were you."

Yahshi and Vell stared, awaiting his reasoning.

"He's from the East," Pinto explained. "He and his parents moved to Frontal when he was just a toddler, and I bet they're false converts, faking their loyalty to Emperor Vakoi to funnel information back East."

"Like spies?" Vell asked. "Why would you think that?"

"It's not like it hasn't happened before. Remember a few years ago when the Research Division traced over a dozen false converts living among us? Who's to say there aren't more?"

"But what makes you think Dice is one of them?" Yahshi asked.

Pinto shook his head, his upper lip curling in disgust. "In primary school, he wouldn't let me join him and his friends for a game of hide-and-seek. He said his parents didn't allow him to... *play with pirates.*"

Vell's lips twitched as she concealed a grin.

"The only kind of parents who could raise a kid to mock my eye are the ones who supported the Eastern raids. I wouldn't be surprised if they're affiliated with the Underground."

Yahshi grabbed his fork as a distraction, but he'd already lost his appetite. Due to one rude comment years ago, Pinto was making a wild accusation against Dice and his family. *Of course he hates converts. I should have known.*

His frown loosened at the sight of Commander Roz through the window, who was leading a white horse into the woods.

Pinto bit into a cracker, and his brows jumped. "Wow, it's buttery," he said, his voice muffled as he chewed. "I've never had a cracker that actually tastes buttery."

"They *are* pretty good," Vell said.

Yahshi spotted Doctor Blimmery chatting with the boys at Quax's table. He jumped to his feet.

"Where are you going?" Pinto asked.

"Restroom. I'll be right back."

Yahshi returned to the common room and planted himself at the door to the guardian quarters. His fingers barely grazed the doorknob, willing him not to enter, but he forced his grip to tighten with a twist.

The door creaked open, revealing a torch-lit stairway descending to the basement floor.

I need to decide if I'm staying here or not. He made his way down, shutting the door behind him. *I won't leave Father behind any longer unless I know I can trust the guardians.*

He reached the end of the stairway, finding himself in a dark room decorated with framed portraits of previous Academy instructors. He opened one of three identical doors, which led to a quarter twice the size of his own—and far more disorderly. There were open books on the floor, coats slung over chairs, and chipped teacups on the tables. But the imperfect humanity of the place somehow made it the most comfortable room in the Academy thus far.

Yahshi ran his fingers along a bookshelf, reading titles as he walked. *Guide to Natural Antidepressants, The Art of Silence, Cultural Significance of Belladonna...*

He gathered a stack of pages from a desk and flipped through them, stopping at a familiar title.

The Belladonna Prodigy.

The text matched the article he'd taken from Sitra Market, but this page was written in messier handwriting with scribbled-out words and phrases rewritten.

> Commander Cal Avarium of Sitra, 18, breaks record as the youngest unit leader in guardian history. After only six months in the Force, Emperor Vakoi promoted her to unit leader, acknowledging her effectiveness in tracing Eastern individuals affiliated with the Underground.

He skimmed the remainder of the article, which recounted Cal's achievements prior to her promotion. As expected, there was no mention of the incident when she broke Imperial Law. There was no mention of how she wasn't in Sitra when her name was called last Selection Day. There was no mention of the four months she spent in the Detainment Facility, locked up as a juvenile criminal.

They offered her a spot in the program even though she murdered Chima. Yahshi set the article down. *And then there's me, who spent two years trying to prove that Cal wasn't the heroic older sister the Force made her out to be. If anything, I should be a suspect of treason, but here I am.*

He thought of Vell, whom Keiyo revealed to have horrible attendance at Miranda Secondary, a school with more than enough eligible candidates. He thought of the six months of exams during Selection Season, all of which he'd failed and some of which Vell might have missed.

Do our selection exam scores mean nothing? What really *determines whether the Force wants us or not?*

"Doctor Blimmery?" someone called.

Yahshi spun around, and Professor Embre gasped. "For the glory of Vakoi, *what* are you doing here?"

"I'm sorry, Professor."

"Answer my question!"

"Uh…" He gulped, struggling to look her in the eye. "Commander Roz made me spar with Quax. It just… felt strange."

Professor Embre crept into the quarter, and Yahshi wished he could run from her without consequences.

"Yahshi, I vouched for your selection long before Commander Roz did. Your devotion and intensity of focus are exactly what the Research Division needs right now. The Underground is always one step ahead of us, and if we could have more clever people like you on the case, maybe we could change that.

"But this rabbit hole of yours is corrupting your potential to help our people, and it's destroying your emotional state. We're giving you an opportunity here to create a new life for yourself—a life where your actions benefit people, not hurt them. Wouldn't you like to move on, and feel better, and do good?"

He thought of Quax's black eye. "Of course I would."

"Then you need to understand that trust is a two-way street. If you don't trust us, we can't trust you. And if we can't trust you, we can't let you stay here. We can't help you." She lowered her chin, making her eyes look even larger. "Is that logic reasonable?"

Yahshi nearly replied, but she cut him off.

"Roz and Blimmery will hear of this. If you violate our trust again, we'll consider you a lost cause."

He nodded repeatedly, hoping the enthusiasm would calm her. "I understand."

"Good." The word sounded vicious—opposite its meaning. "Now go upstairs, and finish your supper."

CHAPTER 6

THE UNDERGROUND

I vow to defend Imperial Doctrine with my life.

♫ INDIGO - PIKOE ♫

The morning bell tolled, stirring Yahshi from slumber.

This doesn't look like home.

The ceiling that greeted him every morning was made of wooden panels, but this one had a seamless cream surface with four-petaled flower designs. He pushed himself into a seated position and spotted another bed across the room, perfectly made without a wrinkle in the blankets.

Right. I'm at the Academy now.

The stone floor chilled the soles of his feet, and he pulled his knees up in confusion. His morning routine was so ingrained in him that even the simplest of changes threw him off-guard.

Yahshi forced his feet to meet the floor, leaving his bed unmade as he dressed into his uniform.

I've been far too reckless. He brushed his teeth with toothpaste sweeter than sugar cane, and a comb steered his disheveled hair into place. *If I keep lying and sneaking around, the guardians will filter me before I decide whether or not to stay, myself.*

He washed his face like any other morning, but the water here wasn't cold. It was lukewarm and strangely unrefreshing.

Yahshi left his quarter to find Vell and Keiyo sitting on a sofa. Keiyo had his hair tied back into a low bun today, a few strands framing his face.

"Okay, so for the last step," he explained, "you bring it up through the big loop and then push it down through the small loop. Then you just wiggle around the top part until it's tight enough." He demonstrated with his own tie.

"Keiyo," Vell said.

"What?"

"You're explaining this horribly."

"Well, how am I supposed to explain it? Tying a tie is one of those things that you just have to *do*, you know?" He reached for her tie, and Vell watched him finish the last step for her.

Yahshi realized he'd been staring and shut the door, catching their eyes.

"Morning, Yahshi," Vell said.

"Morning," Yahshi replied, surprised she remembered his name.

Keiyo snapped his fingers, bringing Vell's attention back to him. "Do you need me to show you again?"

"I can remember." She smiled as she tightened her tie. "Thanks."

Yahshi was about to leave for the dining hall when the door to Room 2 swung open.

"That's the strangest thing," Sunna said. "I can help you look for it if you want."

"No, no. Don't bother." Quax crossed his arms. "It's just weird. I've never lost my marbles before."

"He's been on about this all night," Keiyo muttered to Vell before piping up. "Hey Quax! Maybe someone stole it—just to hear you say you *lost your marbles.*"

"Very funny," Quax said in a monotone, his gaze drifting from Keiyo to the girl next to him. "Vell, you did it."

Yahshi's eyes widened.

"Did what?" Her face didn't read as guilty or oblivious.

Quax pointed to her tie, and Yahshi cracked a grin.

"Keiyo helped me," Vell said.

"I saved her, is what I did," Keiyo corrected. "Did you guys see Commander Roz yesterday? He looked personally offended when he saw her without a tie."

"There's probably some kind of unresolved trauma there," Sunna said, which made Keiyo laugh.

"Also, Vell," Quax added, ignoring his roommates. "I wanna apologize for the sparring match yesterday. I should have let you win. I already earned my pin, so it's not like I had anything to lose, but I didn't think it through beforehand."

Vell shrugged. "Don't worry about it."

Yahshi chuckled, and Quax jolted his head, squinting at him. "What?"

He forced his smile away. "It's nothing."

"No, what's so amusing, Yahshi? Are you laughing at my eye?"

"Of course not. I feel awful about your eye."

"You should have Doctor Blimmery take a look," Sunna chimed in. "It's a bit more swollen than yesterday. Are you in pain?"

"I'm feeling *just fine*, Sunna. Thank you," Quax said. "I'm just waiting for Yahshi to explain what he finds so funny."

"I said, it's nothing," Yahshi insisted.

"Did you take my marble?"

His face ran hot. "Again, with the accusations?"

"Let's not jump to conclusions now," Sunna said.

"How would he even do that, Quax?" Keiyo asked, leaning back with a grin.

Quax marched up to Yahshi and stared him down. "Did you do it or not?"

Yahshi glared back at him. "I'll answer your question if you tell me how you got that black eye."

Quax's face turned red.

"I didn't take your marble," Yahshi said. "It was—"

Vell's departing footsteps cut him off. He stared at Quax a moment longer before following her.

"Vell," he called, "wait!"

He caught up halfway down the staircase, but she wouldn't look at him.

"Is something wrong?"

"I can handle myself," Vell muttered.

"Sorry," he said through a sigh. "It's just ironic how condescending he was when you're the one who stole his marble."

"He can think what he likes."

"But you're letting him underestimate you for no reason."

She met his gaze, her eyes cold. "This may be a shock to you, but we're not all here to show off."

The boldness of her words stopped Yahshi in his tracks. He watched her long hair sway as she continued down the staircase without him.

Yahshi grabbed a tray and scanned the dining hall for someone to sit with. He wasn't keen on sharing breakfast with Pinto after hearing his thoughts on Dice, but avoiding him would make evenings in their quarter awkward, so he joined his table again.

"Where were you this morning?" Yahshi asked.

"Professor Embre said something about a library on the third floor." Pinto leaned into a yawn. "I woke up early to do some research." His eyelids were drooping, his complexion dull.

"You look... a bit tired today."

"I'll feel better later. I'm not a morning person, that's all."

"Then why did you wake up before the bell?"

"Because I'm a motivated person. It's truly a cursed combination." Pinto finished his omelet, leaving the bed of rice beneath it untouched. "And to make matters worse, the coffee in that dispenser is so weak it might as well be green tea. If the guardians have a problem with coffee-dependent trainees, they could just say so. They don't have to play cruel mind games with me."

Pinto raised his ceramic mug to take a sip—only to discover there was no coffee left. "Sorry, I'm being ridiculous, aren't I?" He slammed the mug down. "To be honest, I couldn't sleep a wink last night. I kept replaying

Vell's match in my head, and I couldn't figure out how she managed to get that marble out of his pocket so discreetly. I thought I'd read a book on pickpocketing to ease my curiosity, but apparently it's not something you can find written tutorials for."

"Why does it bother you so much?" Yahshi took a bite of eggs and rice.

"I don't know. Sometimes I come across things I don't understand, and I feel this... *itch* to figure out what I'm missing. And the puzzle is all I can focus on." Pinto looked away with a chuckle. "That probably doesn't make any sense, but—"

"No, it does," Yahshi said. "I know exactly what you mean."

The lecture hall included ten desks, each with two chairs facing a blackboard. Above it hung a portrait of Emperor Vakoi, and beneath it stood Professor Embre, her eyes attacking every trainee who walked through the door.

"Yahshi."

He halted with a flinch.

"You're in the last row, far left."

"Yes, Professor."

Yahshi took his seat next to Quax's freckled roommate.

"Looks like we're stuck together." Sunna grinned. "It's Yahshi, right? From the lobby?"

He cringed at the memory. "Yeah, that's me."

"You gave him that black eye, didn't you?"

His jaw dropped. "I—well—"

"I figured." Sunna lowered his voice. "But it's alright. I won't tell."

As the bell rang, Yahshi smiled back at him.

"Good morning," Professor Embre said, projecting her voice more than she needed to. "I'm glad to see everyone's here on time. Please stand for the pledge of allegiance."

Their chairs scraped the floor as they stood, locking their eyes on the Emperor's portrait. "I pledge my allegiance to the Vakoi Empire," they chanted.

Professor Embre nodded, and they retook their seats.

"There's a stereotype in the Force that professors are stiff and pessimistic, which is accurate, and rightfully so. Those qualities are necessary for the Empire's safety. To prepare for the worst-case scenarios, we must first imagine them and live with the unfortunate knowledge that they *are* possible.

"Today we'll discuss our potential worst-case scenarios involving the Underground, a rebel group we've been dealing with since well before the Atherus War. After securing Eastern Territory, Emperor Vakoi ordered the Research Division to shut the Underground down, and twelve years later, we're still working on it. We catch more and more of their members—but never the last one. Why would they be so persistent if they weren't planning something unimaginable?"

As she paced behind her desk, the remnant specks of white chalk on the blackboard resembled stars. Yahshi stifled a chuckle at the image of Professor Embre floating in the night sky.

A few boys stared, killing his humor.

"Yahshi, you seem to be having fun back there, and I have reasons to believe you're extremely talented at imagining worst-case scenarios." Professor Embre halted in silence, allowing trainees to contemplate what she meant. "Why don't you brainstorm a potential problem we might face with the Underground?"

Yahshi folded his hands in his lap. "I-I mean, they're still—"

"Stand!"

He stood. "They're still loyal to—"

"Speak up!"

Limbo chuckled.

Yahshi took a deep breath before answering, "The Underground rebels are still loyal to Emperor Atherus, despite his death during the War, so maybe they're planning to strike back in his name."

"And what might that entail?" Professor Embre asked.

"What they did last time, during the Eastern raids."

"And what did the Underground *do* during those raids?" She asked the question as though the answer wasn't obvious to everyone.

"What?"

"What did they do, Yahshi?"

"Well, I mean…"

"He's spineless," Limbo muttered.

"Professor," Pinto said, "do we really need to—"

"Quiet, everyone!" Professor Embre yelled. "Yahshi?"

"I-I don't know."

"But you do."

"I don't!"

"Answer the question."

"Just answer the question, Yahshi," Sunna muttered.

"Okay!" he said. "During the War, a group of Easterners traveled West to raid our towns. They didn't kill anyone, but they always left a mark."

Professor Embre crossed her arms. "What kind of mark?"

"I don't—"

She was shouting again. "What kind of mark, Yahshi?"

"Eyes!" he shouted back. "They'd break into homes and gouge out people's eyes!"

Professor Embre smiled. "You may be seated."

Yahshi sat with a scoff.

"It's like she's out to get you," Sunna whispered.

"She definitely is," he whispered back.

"The War may be over, but we can't let our guards down," Professor Embre said. "We are never in a state of peace as long as the Underground exists. No one should have to face an Eastern raid again, and we must prepare for the worst-case scenario where—"

"I don't think it's just a worst-case scenario, Professor." Pinto stood of his own will. "What else would the false converts be channeling information to the East for? The Underground is plotting something horrible. If they took my eye last time, what's next?"

Quax turned in his seat to face Pinto. "The false converts? That was wrapped up years ago."

"And what other schemes could be operating without our knowledge?" Pinto countered. "For all we know, most of them went undetected. Now's not the time to risk letting converts like Dice into the Academy."

Professor Embre leaned against the blackboard, smiling as murmurs filled the lecture hall, eyes shooting to Dice and his yellow bandana.

Dice ignored their attention, glancing over his shoulder to meet Yahshi's gaze.

Does he know I'm a convert? Yahshi broke eye contact. *No, I've never spoken to him before. And it's not like Easterners look any different.*

"Seriously?" Quax said, shaking his head. "Just because you're a raid victim doesn't mean you can be an asshole to converts."

"You certainly wouldn't last in the Research Division," Pinto said. "You're far too trusting."

"Oh really? *I'm* too trusting?" Quax laughed. "Perhaps you should consider how you're currently rooming with your worst enemy."

Eyes drifted to the back of the lecture hall, where Yahshi sat beside Sunna, dumbfounded.

Professor Embre finally intervened, continuing her lecture by outlining the roles of guardians in the Research Division. Yahshi waited for Pinto to look back at him, but he never did.

"Hey," Sunna whispered, smiling lightly. "If it makes you feel any better, my best friend back home is a convert too."

"Stand wherever you'd like!" Doctor Blimmery shouted. "Two per table—that's the only rule."

Located on the highest floor of the Academy, the lab was more of a rooftop conservatory than a learning space. Doctor Blimmery's desk rested under a thick tree rooted in the floor, and the glass dome forming the walls and ceiling allowed light to nurture the potted plants inside.

"Wow, Quax. That eye is looking *impressive* today. You better put some ice on that thing." Doctor Blimmery headed for the door. "Let me grab some from the infirmary."

"Thanks, Doctor," Quax said.

Yahshi claimed a standing table, soon joined by Dice.

"Hey, Yahshi. I'm sorry about this morning. Pinto's never been easy to get along with."

He offered Dice a grin before diverting his focus to the tree, not in the mood for a conversation.

Dice tightened the bandana around his head. "Do you know what part of the East your father's from?"

"He doesn't really talk about it." A moment passed before Yahshi faced him. "Wait, why my father?"

"Huh?"

"Why my *father*, specifically?"

The door opened, and Dice turned to watch Doctor Blimmery return, clearly dodging the question.

"I've secured the ice!" the guardian yelled. "Can you catch it?"

Quax raised his palms. "I can try."

Laughing, Doctor Blimmery chucked the bag of ice across the lab.

"Oh, it's coming fast!" Sunna exclaimed.

Quax caught the bag, the ice clinking in his grasp.

"Nice one," Sunna said.

Keiyo leaned against his table, smirking at Quax. "I'm surprised you saw it coming with an eye like that."

Doctor Blimmery walked to his desk and clasped his hands together. "Alright, let's get to business! Who can tell me what the Medical Division does? Any hands? How about you, with the patch?"

Pinto flinched at his nickname, and a few boys laughed. He sent glares their way, shutting them up before answering.

"The Medical Division's role is to preserve life. They manage the largest Hospital on the island, located in the heart of Vakoi City," Pinto said, his words accelerating. "It's also where major medical discoveries and advancements are made. If it weren't for the Force's doctors, dozens of royal family members would have died young, including several of our late Emperors..."

Students grew restless as Pinto blabbered relentlessly. Vell leaned forward with her chin in her palm, and Dice started to tap his fingers against the table in an irritating pattern.

Limbo rubbed his bird tattoo with a scowl. "I hate this kid already."

"Keep your voice down," his brother scolded.

Yahshi leaned toward his table partner. "Why'd you ask about my father?"

"Forget it," Dice said, refusing to look at him.

Pinto paused for a breath before continuing. "Medical is also responsible for—"

"Alright, I'll cut you off there," Doctor Blimmery said with a chuckle.

"Thank the stars," Limbo muttered, which made Pinto scoff.

"I may look ridiculously young," Doctor Blimmery said, "but believe it or not, I worked in the Vakoi City Hospital for over thirty years before transferring to teach here at the Academy. The Medical Division is the most important guardian division there is."

"All three divisions are equally important," Pinto interrupted. "They work together to—"

"I was joking. Lighten up, kid." Doctor Blimmery flashed Pinto a disturbed look before smiling at the others. "Medical runs the Hospital in Vakoi City, but they also assist with tool production and development. Take this dagger, for example." He pulled the tool out of his overcoat. "You'll notice a familiar emblem on the bottom of its handle. Any guardian tools marked with this four-petaled flower are laced with serum sourced from a rare plant grown in the lab. Can anyone tell me what plant I'm speaking of?"

Pinto raised his hand again, and Doctor Blimmery sighed. "Yes, you again."

"You mean *poison*, Doctor," Pinto said.

"That's incorrect terminology in Medical. *Poison* implies detrimental intent. We refer to it as *serum*, or by the plant's name... which is?"

Pinto emphasized his raised hand.

"Anyone *besides* Pinto?"

Quax and a few other boys raised their hands next, and Doctor Blimmery dragged his dagger through the air as though he were writing calligraphy. The blade swerved from one boy to the next before landing on Vell, who hadn't volunteered to answer.

"How about you?" he asked. "What plant is the serum sourced from?"

"Belladonna," Vell said. "The plant has beautiful flowers, but every part is deadly—roots, leaves, petals, berries... With enough extracted poison on a blade, even a small cut is fatal."

"*Serum*," Doctor Blimmery corrected, less harshly than he had for Pinto.

"Serum," Vell echoed.

He tucked his dagger away. "And what would happen if you were to touch the plant without gloves?"

Vell trailed a finger along her palm. "I assume it wouldn't be fatal, but it might irritate the skin. Cause a rash, maybe."

"Perfectly stated," Doctor Blimmery said. "Belladonna is a powerful and discreet tool for defense, but it's also dangerous in the wrong hands. That's why only guardians can access it, hence our Academy's name."

He brought a pot to his desk. "This right here is a belladonna plant. It doesn't look all too special, right? Just an ordinary bush with violet flowers and a few ink-colored berries. If you were to see this plant in the wild, you might consider it harmless. You might even be enticed to eat one of its cute little berries. But this plant is a major two-faced liar. Eating about a dozen berries could kill a grown man, and our concentrated serum does the job much more effectively."

He plucked a berry and held it up for everyone to see.

I thought he said it caused rashes. Yahshi frowned. *Why isn't he wearing gloves?*

"Before I go over the different parts of the plant, does anyone have any questions?" Doctor Blimmery dropped the berry into the pot. "Yes, Yahshi?"

"Why didn't you—"

No, I can't ask that. Confronting the guardians with too many questions will give off the impression that I still don't trust them.

"Didn't *what*?" Doctor Blimmery prodded.

"Never mind," Yahshi said. "I figured it out."

"Are you sure?"

He nodded.

"Well, alright then."

As Doctor Blimmery introduced the different parts of the plant, gripping them with his gloveless fingers, Yahshi's gaze drifted to Vell. She was focused intently, as though she was genuinely eager to learn—as though she'd joined the program for more than the family pension.

"I swear," Keiyo told his roommates, "no one cared about me, but the second I start training for my selection, I'm an instant lady magnet. It's like the stars are aligned against me..." He trailed off when he noticed Yahshi standing by their table, tray in hand.

"Hey, Quax?" Yahshi said. "I just wanted to say thank you."

Quax tilted his head. "What for?"

Yahshi couldn't tell if he was asking the question genuinely or not.

"Look," Quax replied to his silence, "I spoke up because your roommate is a judgmental prick, and that's all there is to it."

Yahshi gripped his tray harder. "But you—"

"I don't have the energy for this, okay? Unlike you, I'm here to graduate."

Keiyo's smile morphed into a cringe. "Ouch."

"Quax..." Sunna said.

He broke eye contact with Yahshi, jamming his spoon into a bowl of beans. "Just stay away from me until you get filtered."

Yahshi turned his back to Quax but struggled to walk away.

"That was too far," Sunna muttered.

Dice gestured for Yahshi to join him and the Brackle twins, but he ignored the invitation and stormed to an empty table. His beet juice nearly spilled over when he slammed his tray down. The Academy was supposed to be his chance for a better future, but all he'd done was make enemies.

"Can I join you?"

A shadow cast over him, and Yahshi raised his chin with widened eyes.

"You don't have to ask," he choked out.

Pinto's lips twitched upward as he took a seat.

They ate lunch together in silence, occasionally making eye contact but never speaking. A friendship between them went against all logic—and yet, for a reason Yahshi couldn't identify, Pinto had chosen to share a table with him, and Yahshi had chosen to be okay with it.

CHAPTER 7

COLOR BLIND

I vow to maintain optimal health to maximize my use.

♫ THE UNKNOWN - SAINT CHAOS ♫

"Welcome to your first day in Defense training," Commander Roz said, passing out rolled strips of fabric. "In preparation for your upcoming filtration, the next two weeks will be dedicated to hand-to-hand combat. Classes will consist of group technique practice, followed by individual sessions until the bell rings."

Yahshi guided the wraps between his fingers and around his palms like a spider spinning a web. He had just finished his second hand when a tap on his shoulder turned him to Vell.

"Do you mind?" she asked, a mess of fabric dangling from her wrist.

Yahshi chuckled. "How did you get them all tangled like that?"

"Will you help me or not?" She held her hands toward him, diverting her gaze.

Yahshi suppressed his humor and started untangling her fabric. "You know, I find it hard to believe you don't have experience with this. Considering your... *history.*"

"A good thief never has to fight," Vell said, watching him work. "And they certainly don't need formal training."

Yahshi secured the fabric around her wrist. "There. First one's done."

"Thanks." She clenched and unraveled a fist.

"Careful, Vell," Limbo's voice intruded. "I heard Yahshi has a thing for eyes."

He ignored Limbo, shooting Quax a glare from across the training room. If he hadn't exposed him for being a convert, Yahshi could have left the eye-gouging jokes in Sitra.

The other Brackle twin grabbed Limbo's arm, guiding him away. "Ignore my brother."

As the pair disappeared, Vell yanked her hand out of Yahshi's grip. "I'll do the other myself."

And she did do it herself—perfectly—her eyes narrowed as she recalled each twist and turn.

"I'm surprised you remembered all that," Yahshi said. "I only showed you once."

"Should once not be enough?" she asked.

A sudden silence drew their attention to Commander Roz, who was waiting until all eyes were on him before providing further instructions.

"Today, we'll start with basic punches. This may be a bore to some of you, but enjoy the bore while it lasts because the program does not move at a slow pace." He demonstrated the steps as he explained them. "First off, position yourself into a fighting stance. The first punch from here is a jab, a straight punch with your leading hand. Are you following?"

"Yes, Commander," they chanted.

"Let me see them."

As they punched, Commander Roz turned from trainee to trainee, correcting their forms. They repeated this process with crosses, hooks, and uppercuts before drilling with the punching bags. Through repetition, the movements became second nature.

Eventually, the door slid open, revealing the other two Academy guardians. Doctor Blimmery elbowed Professor Embre in the side a few times until she smiled, likely to get him off her case.

"Now it's time to move on to individual training," Commander Roz said. "While you wait for your turn, you can either rest or train solo. We have all kinds of equipment at your disposal—weights, punching bags, retaliation boards... Pick your poison."

"Pick your *serum*, one could say," Doctor Blimmery added. Vell and Sunna laughed with him.

"Oh, come on," Pinto muttered under his breath.

"Pinto Dempsey, Limbo Brackle, and Keiyo Pickett—you're up first," Commander Roz announced.

Professor Embre marched toward a corner. "Limbo, let's go."

He rolled his eyes, following her. "Splendid."

"Be nice," his brother warned.

"Keiyo Pickett, we'll take the sparring range," Commander Roz said, leading him there.

Yahshi noticed that Keiyo was sweat-free despite the punching drills.

Pinto was already approaching Doctor Blimmery when the guardian said, "That means you're with me, kid."

"I know," Pinto spat.

Doctor Blimmery smiled at Vell as he passed her. "Hi, Vell."

She smiled back, and Pinto stared questioningly as he passed her next.

While waiting for their turns, trainees scattered to exercise equipment, but Yahshi and a few others lingered to watch the first individual training sessions.

He studied Pinto first, who was struggling to hit Doctor Blimmery's striking pads. At every attempt to land a punch, the guardian would pull the pads away and laugh at his reddening face.

"You can't get me with that attitude!" Doctor Blimmery taunted.

"I must admit," said Limbo's brother. "Pinto's skills have exceeded my expectations."

"He has perfect form," Yahshi agreed.

"He is pretty slow, though."

"Maybe he's self-taught. Practiced alone."

"That's what I've been thinking," the brother said, and they smiled at each other. "I'm Ceylon from Vakoi City, by the way." He held his hand out, and Yahshi raised his brows at the unusually formal gesture.

"Yahshi." He nearly shook Ceylon's hand, but a grunting noise distracted them. They turned to see Professor Embre stepping out of Limbo's rampaging path. He growled in response.

"Do you really think whining will help you win?" she yelled.

"Ah, and that's my brother," Ceylon said with a chuckle. "Limbo. He's a bit of a wildcard."

"What's the story behind that tattoo?"

"Identity crisis. Said he felt caged in—wanted to make a statement that he was more than my double. So, you know... birds. Freedom."

"That's surprisingly poetic," Yahshi said.

"He *is* a poet, actually."

"Really?"

"Don't repeat that. He would actually kill me." Ceylon's smile faded. "The freedom tattoo's ironic now, though. I don't think he wants to be a guardian. Trying to get selected has always been *my* thing. He's into the arts, like pretty much everyone at our school. It's what the City's known for—music, dancing, painting..."

"Then why'd he sign the contract?" Yahshi asked.

He shrugged. "Because I'm here, I suppose."

"That's time!" Commander Roz shouted. "Yahshi, you're with me."

He turned to Ceylon. "It was nice to meet you."

"Likewise."

On his way to the sparring range, he passed Keiyo, who finally had beads of sweat dripping down his face.

Yahshi took a deep breath as he faced Commander Roz, bracing himself for a tiring session, but the guardian didn't raise the striking pads. Instead, he stepped toward him, his presence bolder than ever. He was taller, his shoulders broader, his eyes darker.

"Embre told me about your little stunt yesterday," Commander Roz said.

"I'm sorry. I wasn't thinking."

"I don't hold it against you, Yahshi. She doesn't cut trainees any slack, but I knew your selection would result in some... inconveniences."

"I'm not trying to be inconvenient."

"All I ask is that you stay on track from now on."

"Of course," Yahshi said.

"I'm proud of you for choosing the Academy—for choosing to give yourself a chance." Commander Roz smiled. "Now, let's get to it. Hands up."

Martu had always insisted on training barefoot per Eastern tradition, so Yahshi wasn't used to fighting with boots on—their heaviness slowed him down. He punched and punched, losing himself in the rhythm as Commander Roz raised one pad after another, demanding a constant stream of energy. When the stream stopped, Yahshi leaned over and glued his eyes to the green zone, breathing heavily, the world spinning around him.

"Sunna, you're up next!" Commander Roz called.

Yahshi's vision darkened around the edges when he staggered off the sparring range. His head flooded with heat, and his knees gave out, making him stumble.

"Whoa!" someone said.

A hand gripped his shoulder to balance him. He focused on steadying his breath, and his vision cleared just enough to see a freckled face staring back.

"You okay?" Sunna asked.

"Yeah, I-I'm fine." Yahshi freed his shoulder, embarrassed at the knowledge that a few people must have witnessed his dizziness. "Thanks."

"You should sit down."

"I will." He wiped the sweat from his forehead. "Have fun."

Sunna chuckled. "Well, after seeing you, I don't think I'll have much fun. But thank you anyway."

The dizziness left when Yahshi reached the wall, but his exhaustion stayed. He sat on the floor and leaned back, his breath settling as he watched the other trainees exercise with unmatched determination.

Even at the Academy, nothing has changed.

He had come here for a better future, a life outside his rabbit hole, yet he had fallen back in without realizing it. He thought he'd reached the light at the end of the tunnel when he'd only reached the tunnel's entrance.

They all want this. His gaze swept across the room. *Surely I do too.*

So despite the fatigue and the churning of lunch in his stomach, Yahshi dragged himself to a punching bag.

After Defense class, the trainees stood in the field, smoldering in the afternoon heat. The clouds hung heavily in the sky, threatening to rain, but something seemed to hold them back.

"Field class involves practicing guardian skills in a less sterile environment," Professor Embre said. "Some days, we may see who can find the best natural remedies in the surrounding woods to cure a fake wound. Other days, we may practice stealth skills, such as walking quietly or listening for threats. Today, we'll be starting with the basics of"—she paused, building anticipation for a big reveal—"horseback riding."

No reaction from the trainees.

Professor Embre frowned in what looked like disappointment before leading them to the stable. "Those of you who progress further into the program will learn how to drive a horse-led vault, a crucial skill for every guardian, especially those in the Defense Division."

She demonstrated the steps to prepare a horse to ride, which included more equipment than Yahshi would have thought. The trainees practiced leading the horses, mounting them, and slowly riding them to the courtyard and back.

Yahshi had never ridden a horse before, and his arms tensed whenever it was his turn to grip the reins. What if the horse could not be trusted as a replacement for his feet? What if the horse would lead him in the wrong direction despite the reins in his hands, stealing all control? What if, in his effort to work with the horse, he would lean too much and pummel headfirst onto the grass?

But he reminded himself that if he didn't learn to trust the horse, he would continue to inch across the courtyard at a snail's pace, never to reach anywhere.

That seemed to help a little.

Yahshi showered, changed into a fresh uniform, and collapsed onto his bed. His body was so heavy he seemed to sink through the blankets, entering a warm and comforting abyss.

"You'll—"

He shot into a seated position. Pinto was standing in the restroom doorway, already showered and dressed after what felt like seconds.

"You scared me!" Yahshi exclaimed. He flopped backward onto the blankets.

"You'll go bald," Pinto finished.

"What?"

"Sleeping with your hair wet. It'll make you go bald when you're older."

He heard Pinto swipe a textbook from his desk and hop onto his bed.

"I didn't think you'd be superstitious," Yahshi muttered.

"All superstitions are rooted in truth. That's why they pass the test of time."

Yahshi lay there for a while, but he couldn't fall into a restful trance, so he sat up again. Pinto had a heap of pillows stacked behind him as he read a textbook.

I wonder what it's like to read with one eye. Yahshi watched him turn a page. *Is his range of vision cut in half, or does it not work like that? Does he need to move his eye more to see the words? Does he own more than one patch, maybe some in different colors? Does he need to wash them frequently?*

"What are you reading?" he asked instead.

"*History of Belladonna.*" Pinto flipped another page. "I found it in the library after lunch."

In the corner of his eye, Yahshi saw Alora's yellow mittens on his night-stand. Goosebumps sprang across his arms as he reached over and took them into his hands, processing how close they'd been to Chima's murder. After the incident, he burned the uniform and shoes he had worn in the woods that day. These mittens were the equivalent of a souvenir for tragedy, and for some reason, Alora had insisted that he bring them along.

"Speaking of lunch..." Yahshi inspected the inside of the mittens, searching for a note or something meaningful, but there was nothing. "You sat with me earlier. Why?"

Pinto shut his textbook. He stared at the cover while Yahshi stared at the mittens, and as though they were thinking in sync, they raised their chins and made eye contact in unison.

"After everything I said about Dice, you still joined me for breakfast," Pinto explained. "I figured that if you were willing to accept me despite my rudeness, maybe I could accept you despite your history."

Yahshi nodded. "I understand it, honestly. If my family were raided, I'd feel the same way."

"No, there's no excuse. I know that." Pinto closed his eye with a sigh. "The thing is... I'll never know which Easterners raided my family. It's much easier to blame all of them for it, as wrong as that may be." He paused. "I'm sorry for what I said."

"I'm sorry too, about the raid," Yahshi replied. "Do you... remember it?"

"Oh, I remember everything, although the faces are blurry." Pinto opened his eye like he'd awakened from a nightmare. "How about you? Do you remember moving West?"

"Not at all. I can't remember anything from the Atherus War."

"Nothing? Not even a vague memory?"

"I can't remember life in the East at all."

"You were three or four when you moved, right? You ought to remember *something* from back then."

"All I've known is... Sitra."

"I see." Pinto stared at his lap with a shake of his head. "And here I was judging you for being born in a place you don't remember. People aren't usually as forgiving as you. I have a habit of turning friends into enemies."

"Me too." Yahshi's gaze returned to the mittens in his hands.

Maybe I'm color blind like Alora, in a way. I may see things differently, but that doesn't make my vision true. He strangled the fabric. *Sometimes you should trust what the people around you are seeing, or you'll go your whole life thinking yellow mittens are actually green.*

"Those mittens," Pinto said. "Why did you bring them?"

"I didn't mean to. They remind me of something I haven't been able to forget, even all the way out here."

"Well, what is it?"

"Something evil." Yahshi opened his nightstand drawer and tossed the mittens inside. "But it's time to move on."

He finally decided that he wasn't here to please Sitra with a single month of bonus funding. This was an opportunity for him, not an obligation to his community.

He slammed the drawer shut.

I'm here to stay.

CHAPTER 8

SELECTION MATERIAL

I vow to wear my sanctioned uniform or formal wear,
even in repose.

♫ I'LL KEEP COMING - LOW ROAR ♫

"Why do you look so tired?" Pinto asked. "Your eye bags are getting darker every day."

"Every day..." Yahshi trudged down the dimly lit hallway, struggling to keep pace with his roommate. With such a monotonous, breakless schedule, he'd lost his grip on the concept of time. "How many days has it been, even?"

"It's day fourteen," Pinto said.

"There's no way we're two weeks in."

"We are. I've been counting."

Yahshi grabbed his pinless collar. "That means our first matches are tomorrow, aren't they?"

"That's right. And perhaps you'd remember the filtration if you slept enough. You realize how irresponsible it is to stay up past the night bell, right? With a schedule like ours, we need rest for our bodies to—"

"Just so you know," Yahshi cut in, "it's *your snoring* that's been keeping me up."

"My *what*?"

"Your snoring."

"I do not snore, Yahshi."

"How would *you* know?"

Pinto shook his head with a chuckle. "You're unbearable, you know that?"

Yahshi smiled. It was moments like these that made the program enjoyable. But soon enough they were always back in the lecture hall, the lab, or the training room—and he couldn't play the role of an ordinary fifteen-year-old anymore.

"Morning," he said, taking his seat.

"Good morning," Sunna chirped.

"You look happy."

"I may have spent the entire night perfecting my personal essay." He plopped a stack of pages onto his desk.

"Wow." Yahshi squinted at the tightly packed words. "That is... a lot of writing."

"Eleven pages. And I had to shorten it too. Where to begin with a prompt like that, right?"

After spending three days of recreation time agonizing over every sentence, Yahshi had completed the assignment with pride—but Sunna's effortless paper of greater length made him hesitate to pull it out.

The bell rang, prompting the pledge of allegiance. Professor Embre crossed her arms as they retook their seats. "I hope you remembered that your first assignment is due this morning."

The rapid crinkling of pages filled the room until every trainee had a stack in hand. Yahshi shrunk at the observation that his appeared to be the shortest.

"The prompt for this personal essay was for you to write about why you want to become a guardian," Professor Embre reminded them. "Now, before you turn your paper in, I want you to think about whether the reasons stated on your paper justify the grueling efforts this program de-mands."

Yahshi read his first sentence. *I want to become a guardian so I can protect the Vakoi Empire and the values that it stands for.* And then he decided, *It's way too vague.*

"By now you're familiar with the daily schedule and the workload required. You're two weeks in, and there are seventy-six weeks left to go. So, can you handle this? Because if you don't believe you're selection material, why the hell should we?" Professor Embre pointed to the door. "If you have even the slightest hesitation, I encourage you to leave now. Your family and hometown have already received one payment, and that's something to be proud of."

She paused to call on Yahshi's raised hand. "I thought we could filter ourselves any time before completing nine months in the program," he recalled.

"That's correct," Professor Embre said, "but today I'm opening the door *for you*, just to make that decision easier. We acknowledge the many external pressures to stay in the program, but you aren't trapped here. It's not shameful to leave."

Yahshi stared at the open door. Walking through it would ensure a lifetime of mediocrity. Returning to Sitra meant returning to the life he had come here to escape—selling bread in the market and falling behind in school with no career path or spectacular dreams.

He yawned. *I wonder why that doesn't sound so bad.*

A boy in the second row burst to his feet, drawing eyes from all directions. Yahshi couldn't see his face from the back of the room, but he did see his shaky grip on his folded essay.

"Professor!" the boy called in a quaking voice. "I'd like to leave."

His words sparked an uproar.

"Now?" said Pinto. "Really?"

Limbo rolled his eyes. "Wonderful timing."

"Guys," Keiyo said, leaning back with a grin, "calm down. He can ditch if he wants."

"Easy for you to say," Pinto muttered. "Some of us aren't built like—"

Professor Embre stomped her boot, silencing the room. She left her desk and held the door open for Rugan. "A guardian is waiting in the common room to escort you home."

Yahshi found it interesting that they'd already made preparations.

As Rugan stepped into the aisle, Limbo stood in protest. "Don't you dare leave."

Pinto stood next. "Wait a few days, at least."

Rugan held his head low as he rushed into the hallway, taking his folded essay with him. Professor Embre continued to hold the door open long after his footsteps faded.

Yahshi couldn't recall much about Rugan—not his hometown, favorite class, or roommate—but he did remember how he'd sit alone in the dining hall, fall asleep during lectures, and avoid eye contact with anyone who looked his way. He had been slipping, and now he was gone.

"Anyone else?" Professor Embre asked.

Yahshi thought of Alora's yellow mittens in his drawer. He thought of Chima in the woods. He thought of serving in the Force someday, dressed in the same uniform as Cal, working for the same cause.

A chill ran down his spine.

"What an idiot," Limbo muttered.

"Hey, we all saw it coming," Keiyo said.

"But not *this* soon," Limbo replied.

Yahshi's grip on his essay tightened. *What am I thinking? I'd be a coward to leave this early into the program, right?*

He sighed as Professor Embre closed the door. Life was easier without excessive questioning.

After collecting their essays, Professor Embre grabbed a piece of chalk, gripping it like a dagger. "Today we'll be reviewing the events that led to the War. Obviously the raids made us take down the Atherus Empire, but what led them to raid us in the first place?"

She wrote *Causes of the Atherus War* on the chalkboard, and Yahshi took notes until his hand cramped up. He couldn't risk forgetting even the smallest of details. With Rugan gone and nineteen trainees remaining, it finally sank in that most wouldn't make the final five. Getting selected was only a warm-up for the battle ahead.

Yahshi sipped his beet juice and puckered his lips. "Okay," he said, "what's wrong?"

"Nothing," Pinto said.

Not wanting to pry, Yahshi left it at that, but he couldn't stop wondering why Pinto had been so dull throughout lunch. Normally it was a challenge to get him to *stop* talking, not the other way around.

After field class, Yahshi ate supper alone and returned to his quarter right as Pinto hurled a textbook at the wall. It slammed onto the floor, and Pinto stood there, seething, struggling to catch his breath.

"*Really*, Pinto," Yahshi said, "what's wrong?"

"Oh, *everything's* wrong." Pinto plopped onto his bed and ran his fingers through his curls. "Rugan just took off and left this morning."

Yahshi frowned. "He was miserable in the program. He didn't belong here."

"Exactly. He was dead weight, the weakest link. If he had slugged himself through another day, one lucky trainee would have an easy match tomorrow. But now we all have to fight our hearts out. Except for Quax."

"It's not Rugan's responsibility to give us an easy match. You're taking this a bit too seriously."

"Well if you were in my shoes, you'd understand."

He crossed his arms. "What's that supposed to mean?"

"This is more than a game to me, Yahshi. I'm not here to just... give this a *good go*." Pinto looked up at him, his eye watering. "Being a guardian is all I've dreamed of. It's the only fulfilling career path I can imagine for myself, and I don't have a backup plan. Without a spot in the Force, what would I do then?"

Yahshi saw something in Pinto that he couldn't find in himself, and that *thing* left him speechless.

Pinto sighed. "Sorry, I'm being ridiculous, aren't I? Acting bitter isn't gonna fix anything."

"No, it's okay," Yahshi said. "You're not the only one who's been frustrated."

"But it's the frustrated trainees like Rugan who get filtered first. I need to pull myself together."

"You're fine."

"No, I'm not. I'm slipping."

"You're *not* slipping," Yahshi stated, arguing more for himself than his roommate. Part of him had wanted to leave with Rugan. *And I'm not slipping. I can handle this.*

Pinto left the conversation at that, grabbing his bamboo journal. His pencil rolled across the page in a smooth, endless flow.

"You've been writing in that book every day," Yahshi said.

"I've decided to document my time at the Academy."

"But you have a perfect memory."

Pinto's pencil paused over the page. "It's not for me." He shook his head before resuming.

Yahshi fought the urge to ask who it was for. "I'm heading to the library to study. Wanna join?"

"I think I'll sleep early."

"Are you sure?"

"I'm sure."

"Okay..." Yahshi said, cracking the door open. "Well, goodnight then."

He left Room 4, entering the lobby in unison with Sunna.

"Hey, Yahshi," Sunna said, struggling to close the door behind him. He had a stack of folded uniforms balanced in his arms. "You caught me. I'm moving out."

"Moving out? Like, you're leaving?"

"No, not like that. There's only eighteen guys left, so I'm reassigned to Room 3 with Limbo. You know, Rugan's old roommate."

"Oh!" Yahshi smiled. "Of course."

"What are you up to?"

"I was planning to catch up on some Medical reading."

"Darts?"

"What?"

"Do you wanna throw darts?" Sunna gestured to a target with his eyes.

"Umm...sure." Yahshi opened the door to Room 3 for him.

"What the hell, Sunna?" Limbo shouted as he entered.

"I'm moving in," Sunna announced.

"Oh, you have *got* to be kidding me!"

Yahshi chuckled at the thought of the two polar opposite boys rooming together. *I wonder if the Academy guardians put together odd pairs for their entertainment.* His humor died at the thought. *Is that why they paired Pinto and me together? An Eastern convert, rooming with a victim of the Eastern raids—surely that was intentional.*

Sunna returned and plucked a dart from a tin can. Yahshi watched him square himself across from a target and make his throw.

The dart struck one of the inner rims.

"Your turn," Sunna said.

Yahshi threw a dart next, and it landed one rim closer to the red bullseye.

"Nice one!" Sunna grabbed another dart. "So, how are you liking the Academy so far?"

"I'm not sure if *like* is the right word," Yahshi said.

"How are you *loving* the Academy so far?"

Yahshi laughed as Sunna threw his second dart.

"Ooh," he said, "bullseye."

"Does that mean you automatically win?" Yahshi asked.

"I think so."

"I guess we're tied now."

"Looks like it."

"This might be a close match."

"Let's hope we're not paired up in the"—Sunna's smile faded—"filtration too." He broke eye contact with Yahshi and began to toss a dart from hand to hand.

"How are you feeling about the first phase?" Yahshi asked. "Are you ready?"

"I'm not sure if *ready* is the right word."

"Are you *excited*?"

He chuckled. "No, not really."

A few moments of silence passed before Sunna stopped fidgeting with the dart. "Hey," he said, slipping it back into a tin, "you know what's odd?"

"What?" Yahshi said.

"I think Quax and Keiyo *love* the program. Everything about it. The training, the studying, the competition—it's got them hooked."

"How about you?"

"I enjoy some parts—scattered pieces here and there." Sunna met his gaze. "Do you think that's... wrong?"

"Why would it be?"

"Because Rugan didn't love the program, and now he's gone."

The next day, every trainee except Quax gathered by the sparring range. Yahshi noticed Dice standing next to him and recalled the day they'd been exposed as converts.

"Hey, Dice?" Yahshi muttered.

"What?"

"I'm sorry if I was rude to you."

"It's fine," Dice said. "We shouldn't enjoy our time here anyway."

Yahshi fished for his gaze, but Dice's eyes were locked on Commander Roz. The guardian stood frozen in the green zone as though he were a bell-activated puppet.

"Why not?" Yahshi asked.

And like that, the bell rang, and Commander Roz cleared his throat.

"This filtration will consist of three phases, spaced three days apart. If you fail to win a match after three tries, you'll be filtered from the program." He readied his stopwatch. "Today, nine matches are scheduled, starting with Yahshi Konya and Keiyo Pickett."

Keiyo walked onto the green zone first, tying his hair into a sloppy bun.

Here we go. Yahshi took a deep breath before joining him, knowing this would be a difficult match. He'd seen Keiyo transform into a different person during Defense lessons, skilled in both technique and strength. The click of Commander Roz's stopwatch would surely transform the deep-dimpled jokester into a ruthless weapon with a brain.

But instead, the click of his stopwatch morphed Keiyo into the image of Chima Fernis, bloody and bashed.

Yahshi dropped his arms with a gasp, looking around to find himself in the woods by Sitra Secondary. The chirping of birds and the rustling of leaves sounded precisely as they had during the incident.

Chima's bloody figure inched toward him, and Yahshi looked down to find a stocky log in his hands.

"Hit him, Yahshi."

Cal's voice appeared as though she were standing next to him, muttering into his ear—but no matter where he looked, she was nowhere to be found.

"What are you waiting for?" Cal added.

Yahshi's breath caught in his throat as he locked eyes with Chima.

But he's already bleeding, he mentally replied.

"He needs to know that he can't win."

Yahshi closed his eyes, refusing to watch the blood drip down Chima's face. *You went too far.*

"I did what I had to do, and so should you. To stay in the program, you need to win."

Maybe I don't wanna win.

"Either you win"—Cal's voice grew bolder—"or you end up like *him*."

A punch to Yahshi's face left him reeling. When he raised his stinging chin, Keiyo was ahead of him, *not* bloody and *not* bashed.

With each attack came a swift dodge from Yahshi. He waited for a chance to reverse the momentum, but Keiyo drilled relentlessly. It was only a matter of time before the ducks and dodges wore him down, leaving him no choice but to block Keiyo's attacks. Each impact sent jolts of pain through his arms, but his opponent didn't flinch once.

I can't last much longer.

Keiyo sidestepped one of Yahshi's weakening blocks, kicking him in the gut. The impact threw him off-balance, and he crashed onto the sparring range. Keiyo pinned him down before he could react.

Yahshi's eyes widened as a fist came toward him, striking his cheek like a rock. Spectators winced as he struggled to breathe. *I wish I landed in the black zone.*

His body begged him to tap out, but he didn't listen. As he attempted to free himself, Keiyo struck him again.

"Keiyo, stop," Sunna said, but a third hit made Yahshi's face burn anyway.

I can't win. It's over.

Another hit.

"That's enough!" Commander Roz yelled.

The pressure lifted. Yahshi lay on the floor, gasping for air as Keiyo peered down at him.

"Well, if nothing else," Keiyo said with a grin, "you're stubborn."

The matches continued without Yahshi, who iced his face alone in the infirmary. It was a plain room across from the lab containing a sink, an ice chest, and a wall of wooden cabinets stocked with medical supplies.

He was sitting on a bed, shivering in silence, when Professor Embre entered. The heels of her boots clicked sharply against the marble floor.

"I finished your paper." She dragged a chair in front of him and took a seat. "To be frank, it's repetitive and generic. I expected more from you."

His grip on the bag of ice tightened, increasing the pressure against his face and making him flinch. "I'm sorry, Professor."

"Don't apologize. Fix it." She tossed the papers at his lap. "You have three days. I want you to write me a new paper with the same prompt. And if it's not up to my standards, we're sending you home."

"You mean, I'll get filtered?"

"Being a guardian is not something you fall into out of circumstance. Even an ounce of hesitation will destroy you in our field of work. You need to want this, fully and truly. There is no space for regret. So you need to really dig, Yahshi. You need to dig, and you need to find a reason why you *bleed* to stay here."

She leaned forward, casting a shadow over him. "So rewrite this, and if it's not rewritten well, we'll know that you were never selection material in the first place. Because unlike what Roz may have told you, sometimes we do make mistakes."

CHAPTER 9

WEEDS IN A FLOWER BED

I vow to ingest serum daily to maintain the required tolerance.

♫ SOME KIND OF BERRY · MOUNTAINS OF THE MOON ♫

Yahshi's sixteenth day at the Academy greeted him with an aching back, a throbbing face, and a cramping leg. He'd spent the night wincing with every turn and shoving pillows against his ears in a failed effort to block out Pinto's snoring.

Before catching an ounce of shuteye, morning light began to seep through the balcony's glass door.

I need a break.

After getting dressed, he sat on a bench in the courtyard to watch the clouds brighten. It was still that hot and humid time of year when the air would dampen his clothes, even in the breeze.

A white rabbit hopped onto the courtyard, and Yahshi stood, resuming his long-paused game.

Let's see how close I can get.

Commander Roz had taught a step-softening stealth lesson a few days prior, so this was a perfect chance to test his new skill in a real-life setting.

Plus, he could use the distraction.

Heel to toe, Yahshi reminded himself as he crept forward. *Heel to toe.*

The rabbit was at the base of Emperor Vakoi's statue, nibbling at a weed between two bricks. He neared close enough to see its movements, like its nose twitching as it sniffed the weed, and its physical details, like thin streaks of brown against its predominantly white fur.

My younger self would be so proud. He chuckled at the memories of chasing rabbits across the Sitra Primary courtyard, managing to scare them away from a distance every time.

Oops. He halted as the rabbit's ears twitched toward the clouds. *You didn't hear me laugh, did you?*

The rabbit craned its head to stare at him.

Your eyes...

It took off, soaring across the field.

They look like belladonna berries.

The bell rang, calling him to breakfast. He waited until he lost sight of the rabbit before heading to the dining hall.

Meals at the Academy had become Yahshi's favorite parts of the day. At first he thought it was because the food was hot and the tables weren't grimy like they were at Sitra Secondary—but with time, he realized that he simply liked sharing meals with someone who appreciated his presence for a change. He didn't realize how tiring it'd become to watch students fight for Quax's attention until he no longer had to.

Your sister's amazing, they'd say. *I remember her being so quiet. She was always reading books. Does she still read books? What kind of books does she read? Do you read books too? Oh, you do? What else are you doing to increase your chance of getting selected? Oh, it's a secret? We're not going to steal your spot in the program! Just tell us, Quax! Tell us your secrets!*

Yahshi grabbed a tray of steak and eggs with a side of tomatoes—the dish his roommate had predicted the night prior. Pinto claimed to have deciphered the circulation of Academy meals by memory after unintentionally noticing patterns. Yahshi liked to believe he was lying—that somewhere in their quarter, he'd find a notebook with a log of every meal and corresponding calculations.

As he headed for Pinto's table, his gaze habitually drifted to Quax's eye. He'd been observing the healing process over time, watching the damage he'd caused gradually reverse. Not even the faintest hint of purple remained.

It's over, isn't it?

Quax and Sunna were laughing together—but Keiyo's gaze drifted to Yahshi, assessing the results of yesterday's match. Yahshi turned his head, not wanting to give him the satisfaction of seeing the bruises on his face. *I suppose I can't hate him for staring without being a hypocrite.*

"Morning," Yahshi muttered. He bit his lip to keep from whimpering as he scooted his chair in.

"Where have you been?" Pinto asked him, but his eye was on Vell, who was sitting alone as usual. "You never wake up before me."

"I had a hard time sleeping last night," Yahshi said.

Pinto finally faced Yahshi, and the fork fell out of his hand, clattering against his plate and drawing stares. "Your face! For the glory of Vakoi, it looks *way* worse up close!"

Yahshi leaned forward, hoping the others wouldn't get a clear sight.

"It was all red and swollen yesterday, but this is... *wow*." Pinto shook his head, lips parted in disbelief. "No wonder you couldn't sleep."

"Okay!" Yahshi held his head low, looking up at Pinto. "You can stop now."

Pinto's eye widened at the realization that he'd gone too far. He picked up his fork, and Yahshi followed suit. The eggs, steak, and tomatoes were perfectly seasoned, just like they always were.

Yahshi only took a few bites before setting his fork down with a sigh, knowing this wonderful meal marked the start of another not-so-wonderful day of training.

"I'm really tired, Pinto."

"No, you're not," Pinto said. "Don't fall for the trap."

"What trap?"

He cast a glance around the room before leaning in. "A few upperclassmen at Frontal Secondary were selected in the last cycle but didn't graduate. One lasted five months in the program, making the final ten. He calls the Academy guardians *gardeners*—says they water us with everything all at once and pluck the ones who don't grow right, like they're weeds in a flower bed. The first month is designed to overload us, but if we make it through, the program should calm down a bit."

"Are you calling me a weed?" Yahshi asked.

"I'm telling you not to be."

"Is it a choice?"

"I sure hope so." Pinto shrugged before staring at Vell again, and Yahshi found himself staring too. Her reserved nature gave him the impression that she preferred being alone—but lately, her self-isolation had sparked rumors of her downfall.

"Do you think Vell is... slipping?" Yahshi asked.

"If she was, why would she push herself so hard in Defense class?" Pinto countered. "She intends to make the final five. I know it."

"Then what are you so curious about?"

"Doctor *Blim Blim* called her his favorite yesterday."

"That was obvious already."

Vell squinted at her food, likely noticing their attention. Yahshi and Pinto faced each other again.

"I know, but that got me thinking," Pinto said in a hushed tone. "Usually the guardians select girls who demonstrate a fighting nature. You know, more aggressive. Like Commander Cal."

Yahshi accidentally inhaled a bite of eggs and coughed. He set his fork down with watery eyes, and Pinto frowned. "Did you know her well?"

"Uh... no. Not really." Yahshi shook his head. "*Hardly.*"

"Oh. Well, based on Doctor Blimmery's favoritism, I'd assume he's the guardian who vouched for Vell's selection. He must have recognized her obscure medical knowledge during Selection Season."

"But the selection exams were mainly focused on Imperial history, arithmetic, anatomy..."

"Exactly." Pinto pointed at him with a grin. "How many questions do you recall about botany?"

"None," Yahshi admitted. "But maybe the school—"

"—curriculum is different in Miranda? Sure, I considered that too, but Miranda Secondary has the highest selection rate among schools in the West.

Their curriculum is designed for success in the standardized selection exams, which don't contain questions about botany and certainly not about belladonna. Why would instructors waste time teaching a topic that won't help their students get selected? And if they did teach botany, for some impractical reason, why doesn't Keiyo share the same knowledge?"

"So you're wondering how Vell learned about belladonna?" Yahshi asked.

"*And* how Doctor Blimmery discovered her knowledge. He must know something about Vell that her exam scores couldn't indicate. The fact that Dice sat with her during supper yesterday makes me even more suspicious."

Yahshi observed the table where Dice, Limbo, and Ceylon were eating. While the Brackle twins chatted, Dice read a novel, occasionally looking up to contribute with a smile. The four-petaled flower pin attached to his collar stood out more than his neon bandana.

"She was paired against him, right?" Yahshi said. "He probably sat with her because he felt guilty for winning."

"I doubt that," Pinto muttered.

"You sure do hold a grudge."

"It's not just because he's a convert, Yahshi."

The door flung open, and Doctor Blimmery wheeled a metal cart into the dining hall. "Young men! Young men, listen up! And you too, young lady." He winked at Vell, and she smiled back. "I'm happy to announce that you workaholics have the day off."

"About damn time!" Limbo shouted.

Keiyo blew the guardian a kiss. "Thanks, Blim."

Yahshi smiled. "Perfect. I'll have time to write."

"Write what?" Pinto asked.

"*Study*, I mean."

Doctor Blimmery's cart creaked as he wheeled it from table to table, stopping periodically to serve glasses of red juice to the trainees.

Pinto narrowed his eye. "We're never served beet juice for breakfast."

"Well, it's our day off," Yahshi said, secretly pleased that something had finally thrown him off. "Maybe we have a different meal schedule."

"No," Pinto said. "Something's wrong."

When Doctor Blimmery reached them, he gave Yahshi a pat on the shoulder.

"You poor little guy! You better ice that face later."

"I will, Doctor."

The guardian flicked Pinto's collar. "Where's your pin, Pin?"

"That's not my name."

"I think it suits you." Doctor Blimmery set two glasses of juice on their table before wheeling his cart away.

Yahshi chuckled. "It's not a bad nickname."

"Nicknames are pointless," Pinto said.

"But a *pin* is sharp."

He groaned.

"Before I let you kids run wild, we have a quick Medical demonstration to get through." Doctor Blimmery grabbed a white briefcase from his cart's bottom shelf.

Pinto's face brightened. "I knew there was more to it."

"The belladonna plant is rooted in Western culture. It represents elegance, efficiency, and power—qualities every guardian should aim to embody. That being said, belladonna is a feisty little thing. We must take the necessary precautions to use it safely.

"Only guardians can legally grow, harvest, and use belladonna, but what might happen if it were to fall into the wrong hands—like the Underground's —or if a Defense guardian were to lose hold of a laced tool during an expedition into Eastern Territory? Yes, Keiyo?"

"The serum could be used against us."

"Correct," Doctor Blimmery said, "which is why it's important for guardians to build a tolerance to their own serum."

"Typical. He never calls on me." Pinto lowered his arm with a huff, and Yahshi frowned, urging him to let it go.

"Here's a fun secret," Doctor Blimmery continued. "We serve beet juice every lunch period for its health benefits, but also because its strong taste easily cloaks belladonna."

Limbo's jaw dropped. "We've been *drinking* it?"

He laughed. "Oh, stop with the looks. We haven't introduced the serum yet, but starting today, we'll be lacing your juice with increasing doses to condition your body to fight its toxins. Yes, Ceylon?"

"Are we required to drink it?"

"You're not *required* to do anything at the Academy, but if you'd like to succeed in the program, I'd recommend finishing your glass. Eventually, your tolerance will be tested.

"Now, I should warn you—the first dose can be... intense. We'll need to take this process slowly, so your lunch juice won't always contain serum. I recommend testing yourself daily on whether you can detect belladonna in your juice or not. Some guardians occasionally serve the Royal Family as taste-testers, so tolerance and *detection* are considered vital skills."

Pinto waved his arm in the air. "I have a question too, Doctor."

"Yes, *you*."

"What if the Underground also builds a tolerance to the poison?"

"*Serum.*"

Pinto rolled his eye.

"That's not something to worry about," Doctor Blimmery answered. "They would need access to belladonna, which mainly grows in the City Hospital's lab. It's rare to find it naturally, but even if they did, tolerance training is dangerous without professional guidance, and it's a skill easy to lose without maintenance. Staying immune requires frequent exposure for life. Those are the same reasons why Royal Family members don't risk undergoing this training themselves."

Yahshi's eyes widened as three Medical guardians entered the dining hall, identical briefcases in hand. Seeing new faces made him realize he hadn't seen *anyone* from the outside world in over two weeks. He'd nearly believed the Academy was all there was.

I wonder what it's like for them to return after graduation. He watched the Medical guardians wave at the trainees, grinning widely. *Is the dining hall nostalgic?*

"Oh, here they are!" Doctor Blimmery exclaimed. "I've invited a Medical unit from the City Hospital to join us."

"This can't be good," Pinto mumbled.

Yahshi considered the possibility of an Academy guardian requesting Cal's assistance in the program someday. He shivered at the thought of walking into the common room to find her standing there, waiting for him, the candlelight shining in her marbly eyes.

"So what now?" Keiyo yelled. "We drink this stuff?"

"Or you can filter yourself from the program if you prefer."

"Alright, I got the message, Blim." Keiyo raised his glass but hesitated to sip.

Quax took the lead instead, drinking the laced beverage as though he believed it was water.

I wonder if his combat tutor told him about tolerance training in advance.

"I don't taste the difference," Quax said, smacking his lips together.

"You will with time," Doctor Blimmery assured him.

Yahshi grabbed his glass. "Of all drinks to mix belladonna into, it just *had* to be this one." He swirled the red fluid around in a whirlwind.

"Well if we can handle beet juice, we can handle anything," Pinto said. "You first?"

"Sure." He watched Pinto's concerned gaze through the glass as he gulped the juice down.

"Ugh." Yahshi nearly gagged. "That's awful."

"Awful *worse?*"

"Awful *same.*" He puckered his lips. "I don't taste the difference either."

As Pinto took a modest sip, Yahshi stared at the obnoxious amount of liquid remaining in his glass. He normally left this beet juice untouched, but he knew finishing the full doses would be as crucial as showing up to Research classes, so he raised his glass again and chugged.

The slimy, bitter taste lingered on his tongue even after he set his empty glass down. He was one of the first trainees to finish.

"Are you okay?" Pinto asked.

Yahshi lowered his head to find that he'd set the glass on his scrambled eggs. He tried to move it onto the tablecloth, but it slipped from his grip and tumbled away.

"Yahshi!" Pinto shouted.

The sound of shattering glass echoed through the dining hall. Yahshi struggled to reply, a knot forming in his throat as he grasped for words that weren't there. From a distance, he heard Keiyo shouting.

"Hey, Sunna! Snap out of it!"

"What's wrong?" Quax asked.

The faces and tables and chairs blurred together in every direction Yahshi looked. He squinted, his vision focusing to see Sunna's arm go limp, red juice splattering over his uniform. A pool of laced juice resembling blood formed around his boots as he collapsed face-forward onto his half-eaten steak.

"Doctor!" Quax yelled. "Help!"

Yahshi's head whipped around as he observed the other trainees, his vision fading in and out. He saw the Brackle twins hunched over, gripping their heads. He saw Dice with a hand on his chest. He saw Keiyo shouting at Sunna, his words drowned in the chaos.

"Blim!" one of the Medical guardians called. "We've got two out!"

"They can't take the antiserum!" another guardian yelled.

"Get them transferred," Doctor Blimmery ordered with an unusual firmness to his tone. "Now!"

Yahshi urned to Pinto, whose face reddened before falling out of sight.

"Pinto!" Yahshi gripped the side of the table to hoist himself up, but his vision faded after a few steps. "Help!" he called into the darkness.

Someone bumped into his shoulder, shooting past him. His vision cleared enough for him to recognize Vell by the black hair that waved behind her like a cape. She kneeled at Pinto's side and tugged his limp arms.

Yahshi nearly called for help again when Vell looked up at him, her eyes narrowed.

"Quiet."

He trusted the confidence in her voice and glued his mouth shut.

"Wake up." Vell shook Pinto by his shoulders, but he remained unresponsive. She scanned the room to ensure no one was looking before jabbing a fist into his stomach.

Pinto's eye opened as he gasped for air. "What the hell?"

"You'll get filtered if you pass out," Vell muttered before raising her chin to the ceiling. "Doctor Blim!"

Unlike Yahshi, Vell was heard instantly by Doctor Blimmery, who rushed over. She stood and backed away to give him room.

Pinto grimaced, clutching his stomach as Doctor Blimmery hoisted him up into a seated position.

"Will he be okay?" Yahshi asked. His vision had steadied, but he could feel his grip on the table loosening against his will, and he feared he might fall over next.

"We have neutralizer in the City Hospital, but that's a last resort. He'll be fine right here as long as he takes the antiserum." Doctor Blimmery opened his briefcase to reveal vials of yellow fluid secured in foam slots. He popped the cork stopper off one and brought it to Pinto's lips. "Hey smart-mouth, you gotta drink this for me, alright?"

Clusters of trainees stumbled to the scene, watching in half-dread, half-curiosity as he poured the liquid into Pinto's mouth.

A few seconds later, he vomited across the glimmering floor.

Doctor Blimmery made an announcement in the lobby a couple of hours after breakfast. Only nine dizzied trainees received the bittersweet news first-hand, as many of them, including Pinto, were bedridden in their quarters.

"What took place this morning was more than a Medical introduction to belladonna tolerance. It was also a filtration," Doctor Blimmery explained. "Two trainees lost consciousness and couldn't take the antiserum. The Medical unit transferred them to the City Hospital for emergency neutralization, and upon recovery, they'll be sent home with their spot in the program revoked."

"What the hell?" Limbo jumped from a sofa. "It's not like they could control their reactions."

"I know," Doctor Blimmery said.

"That's not fair!"

The raw anguish in his voice made Doctor Blimmery raise a brow. "No, it isn't," he replied, "but that's how it works. Some kids aren't compatible with the program, whether it's their fault or not."

Yahshi's eyes drifted to Vell. She pressed the tip of a dart against her finger, testing its sharpness.

With only a few hours left before lunch, Yahshi crawled into bed. His belly burned, his forehead wouldn't stop sweating, and the soreness from yesterday's sparring match intensified. He desperately sought rest, but Pinto's tossing, turning, and groaning left him too concerned to sleep.

When Doctor Blimmery delivered a bowl of porridge, Pinto gagged with every bite, and Yahshi decided to watch his roommate suffer no longer.

He trekked to the library on the third floor, collapsed onto the nearest chair, and drifted to sleep.

It felt like only a few minutes had passed before the bell summoned him to the dining hall.

Two boys were filtered, he recalled, scanning the tables for empty seats. He'd been too disoriented during the filtration to notice who the Medical guardians had carried away.

His gaze landed on Quax and Keiyo. Sunna's usual spot at their table was empty.

Hopefully he's just resting, like Pinto.

Yahshi astonished himself with how much he'd grown to care about someone he sat next to during Research class and had once thrown darts with in the lobby. The new understanding that they could lose anyone—at any time—made even the most mundane moments with his fellow trainees memorable.

As he headed toward his usual table, intending to eat alone, Vell caught his attention. He slowed to a stop and thought about their encounter in Sitra Market, their first supper together at the Academy, and her bizarre choice to keep Pinto from getting filtered.

With a deep breath, he diverted from his path and approached her.

Vell raised her chin, locking eyes with him.

"Can I join you?" he asked.

She blinked a few times before nodding with the slightest hint of a smile.

CHAPTER 10

BE STUPIDER

I vow to support my fellow guardians, for we are one.

♫ FLEETING LIGHT - AMARANTE ♫

"Thank you for earlier," Yahshi said.

"It's nothing." Vell bit into her bread roll. "Pinto's your friend. I owed it to you."

"What do you mean?"

She took another bite, diverting her gaze.

As he waited for a response, he grabbed his fork, but the sight of chicken breast and salad made his stomach churn. *It must be the belladonna.*

Vell continued to eat, her appetite unaffected, and it became clear that she didn't intend to answer his question.

"Uh..." He cleared his throat. "How are you feeling?"

"Headache."

"A headache? That's all?" Yahshi looked around to see utensils shaking, food falling off them. He saw rubbing of eyes, sharp inhales of breath, scratching of skin.

"That's all," Vell confirmed, recapturing his attention. "You?" She brought a fork to her mouth with a steady hand.

"Well, I'm feeling okay after a nap," Yahshi said. "Pinto has it much worse. I suppose some of us are luckier than others."

"It's not completely luck. Reactions are based on various factors."

"Like what?"

"Height, weight, genetics, fitness, how much food is in the stomach..." Vell trailed off as she tossed the last bite of bread into her mouth.

"Food? In the stomach?"

"The more you eat beforehand, the slower the serum absorbs, and the milder your symptoms."

"Huh." Yahshi tilted his head. "So I assume you finished your breakfast before drinking?"

"I stuffed myself."

He chuckled. "You know a lot about this sort of thing."

Vell's brows knitted together. She finished her plate with a few rushed bites and stood from the table.

"Wait," he said. "What are you planning to do with your day off?"

"I'll be outside. I still can't make a horse trot."

"Well, could I come with you?"

"You already thanked me. What more is there to say?"

Yahshi shrugged. "There's always more to say, isn't there?"

As they rode their horses at a walking pace, a sense of dread loomed over him. He couldn't tell whether it manifested his concern for Pinto, his suspicions about Vell's reaction to the dose, or his stress over the personal essay he was so obviously procrastinating to rewrite.

"Is something wrong?" Vell said.

"Let's race to the courtyard," he blurted.

"What?" she asked, a twinge of humor in her tone.

He glanced at her with a smile. "You heard me."

"Aren't you dizzy?"

"I'm not *that* dizzy."

"I couldn't possibly win."

"Well, you could try," Yahshi said, urging his horse into a trot. The air washed over his face, taking his anxieties about the program with it. For the first time in days, he saw the Academy beauty his stress had clouded—the elegant architecture, the neatly trimmed grass, the expansive courtyard.

Vell's horse trotted up behind him, letting out a neigh. "I think I'm getting the hang of this!" she shouted. He had never heard her shout before.

"Go faster then!" Yahshi locked his eyes on Emperor Vakoi's statue and brought his horse into a gallop, racing toward it. Vell trailed close behind, threatening to overtake him.

As they neared the courtyard, the sense of dread returned, sucking the air out of his lungs. His gaze drifted to the surrounding woods to spot a familiar face staring back at him from the shadows.

Yahshi gasped and yanked the reins, bringing the horse to a jagged stop.

"Don't you have a paper to write?" Cal asked. It sounded like she was directly in front of him, not across the field—and when he realized this, her figure flashed forward and appeared at his horse's side.

Her stony eyes pierced through him, but he feared looking away more than maintaining eye contact.

"I'm taking a break," Yahshi muttered.

"Winners don't play two games at once." Cal's expressionless face distorted into Yahshi's for a split second before reverting. She was grinning now. "Winners are focused."

"You're not real," he said in a quivering voice. "Leave me alone!" He couldn't tell if he was speaking aloud or in his mind, but he didn't care. *I want her gone.*

But Cal remained.

"What's wrong?" Vell asked, pulling her horse up next to his. She stopped where Cal had stood, replacing her.

Yahshi scanned the area for Cal before sighing in relief. "Sorry. I thought I heard something."

Vell studied him with a slight nod. "You're intoxicated," she said, turning her horse around before either of them had reached the courtyard. "No more racing."

He was quick to agree. "Yeah, okay."

Yahshi followed her toward the stable, his heartbeat settling and his breath evening out. But occasionally, his gaze would drift to the trees, prepared for Cal to reemerge and haunt him again.

"Yahshi?" Vell asked, breaking the silence.

He pulled up next to her. "Yeah?"

"Why are you here?"

"At the Academy?" His shoulders tightened at the thought of his essay. "Well, it's hard to—"

"No. Here, with me." She paused. "Are you still mad?"

"Mad? Why would I be mad?"

"Because of the bread."

He concealed a grin. "You're still thinking about that?"

"I assumed you were still mad."

"You thought I was mad about the bread?"

"Now we're talking in circles."

"I'm just trying to clarify."

The air fell silent, and this time, it was Yahshi who chose not to answer her question. *She stole from me. I* should *be mad, shouldn't I?*

"If I knew I'd have to face you every day at the Academy"—Vell's knuckles turned white as she gripped the reins tighter—"I wouldn't have done it."

"Is that why you helped Pinto? Because you felt guilty?"

She hesitated. "On our first day here, I lied to you."

"About liking sourdough?"

"Well, it is my favorite, but that's not why I stole. It was for my mother. She's going through a hard time, and my family hasn't been doing well financially."

What kind of situation would put her family under such heavy financial stress? Miranda had the highest selection rate, which meant they had massive bonuses to boost their infrastructure. It wasn't as luxurious as Vakoi City, but it was as close as modest towns could get.

"I'm sorry to hear that," Yahshi muttered, knowing he shouldn't pry. "But I really don't mind, Vell. About the bread."

It was silent for a moment.

"What's your mother like?" he added.

Her eyes snapped to his. "Why do you ask?"

"I'm just... curious."

Her gaze softened as she looked away. "Despite her situation, she does everything she can to make us laugh. I don't know what I'd do without her." A smile tugged at the corners of her lips before she turned to Yahshi. "Do you miss your mother too?"

"I guess," he said, and his bland tone made her frown. "She fell sick during the Atherus War. I don't even remember her."

"She was... sick?"

"Not horribly, but it did get worse. My father thinks she could have recovered with medical help early on, but the War wasn't the best time to get sick. Hospitals were packed."

As a result of the Eastern raids, the West struck back, resulting in violent outbreaks on both sides of the island that continued for months until the Force burned the Atherus Palace down, ending the War. By the time Emperor Vakoi announced that he'd allow a single migration of Easterners to pledge allegiance to him and live better lives on Western land, Yahshi's mother had already passed.

"That's horrible," Vell said, her voice shaky.

He forced a smile. "It's okay."

"No," she said, "it's not."

He dropped his smile, looking over to meet her gaze.

"Sorry." Her tone was still harsh. "I'm just... it's sad to hear that."

Emotion. He saw it then. Something about his story had struck a chord with Vell, a girl who hardly expressed herself at all. And if the story had made her feel something, perhaps it could do the same for the Academy guardians.

"That's it!" Yahshi exclaimed, galloping toward the stable.

"Yahshi?" Vell called.

He secured his horse and sprinted to the library. His mother's story seemed to flow from his pencil as though the words were coming from an unknown source.

I miss this feeling. He smiled at the memory of his younger self solving complex math problems with pride. *I miss the academic challenge.* It was so much easier than the challenge of questioning the Force's morality. A paper like this was so effortless, so manageable.

He tightened his grip on the pencil as he crafted his concluding paragraph.

Her pointless death moves me to earn a spot in the Force and prolong our era of peace on the island. No one should ever experience what she went through.

As he read his essay, he couldn't shake the feeling that he had written a piece of fiction, not a paper based on reality. But he was tired of his questioning getting in the way of his success. So he read his essay again, and again, and again, and at some point the lines blurred together and everything became real.

Despite getting a meager three hours of sleep, Yahshi woke with a sense of clarity. *The program constantly outsmarts and surprises me. It's about time I make the first move.*

As he changed into his uniform, he spotted Pinto awake in bed, restlessly adjusting the strap of his eye patch. He always slept with it on, and Yahshi wondered what his face looked like underneath it—but of course, he would never ask.

"Pinto?"

His roommate groaned. "What?"

"Do you want me to bring up your breakfast tray?"

He still didn't open his eye. "No thanks."

"Are you sure?"

Pinto rolled onto his side, pulling the blankets over his head as he coughed. "Just let me sleep," he croaked. "Please."

When Yahshi arrived at the dining hall, Vell was just getting seated. He grabbed a tray and joined her.

"You weren't at supper yesterday," she pointed out.

"Listen," Yahshi said, accidentally slamming his tray down. "I've been thinking about the program. Just the way it's structured, and the filtrations, and... I realized we should help each other."

"We're competing," Vell said.

"For *five spots*, not one," he argued. "This doesn't have to be a game where everyone fights alone. We have our second phase tomorrow. I'll help you practice later, during recreation time."

"In *your* current state?"

"I'm bruised, not paralyzed."

Vell eyed the evidence of Keiyo's hits, which were already beginning to fade. "What's in it for you?" She took a bite of eggs.

"Yesterday's filtration came out of nowhere, and you were the only one prepared. A lot of guys here can fight and memorize facts from a textbook, but your medical knowledge is something only you have. It's a huge advantage in the program." Yahshi grabbed his pinless collar, lowering his voice. "My sparring matches have been far from impressive, but—"

"I know you can fight. Just tell me your plan."

"I'll help you get your pin." He leaned toward her. "Then, after the sparring filtration, you'll share your medical knowledge with me."

Vell studied the other trainees in the dining hall, many of whom had combat experience like Yahshi. They both knew this was a better deal for him than for her. But Vell had isolated herself from the other boys, and Yahshi was the only one offering help.

She met his gaze with a nod. "I'm in."

During recreation time that evening, Yahshi and Vell faced each other in the green zone.

"Tell me," she said, raising her hands. "What's my biggest problem?"

"You're too smart," he answered.

Vell scoffed with a grin. "I'm talking about combat."

"I am too." Yahshi mirrored her stance.

"What do you mean, I'm too smart?"

"I noticed on our first day here when you volunteered to spar against Quax." He circled her like a shark, and she pivoted in pace, her stiff posture and calculated gaze proving his point.

"You try to analyze your opponent—predict their next move—and it makes you freeze up. Once you're in your head, you've already lost."

She narrowed her eyes. "How do I fix it?"

"Be stupider." He smirked. "There's actually a game that helps with this."

"A game?" She asked the question as though he were joking.

"What?"

"I don't play games."

"Trust me, it'll help. My father and I came up with all kinds of training games. We had Stop and Go for practicing counters and Slow Motion for technique. This one's called Quiet Mind."

Yahshi nodded for Vell to make the first move—a hesitant jab.

He leaned back, dodging it. "What are you thinking?"

"That I can't fight," she replied.

"Well, stop it."

Vell threw a faster punch but failed to extend her arm properly. He grabbed and pushed her wrist until her hand met her collarbone.

"What are you thinking?" Yahshi asked again.

"That the last time I punched in a sparring match, Dice put me in an arm lock."

He released her wrist. "Forget about that."

This time, Yahshi threw a jab at Vell.

She stepped out of view, and when he pivoted to face her, a boot struck his stomach. "What are you thinking?" he asked, staggering a few steps away.

"That whatever I did kind of worked."

He shot forward, closing the gap.

Vell ducked under a punch, countering with a strike to his side as she dashed away.

A force hit the back of his knee, breaking his balance, and the impact of his back hitting the floor knocked the air out of him.

Vell's head popped into his field of vision as she leaned forward, brows raised.

"What are you thinking?" Yahshi choked out.

A smile spread across her face, which morphed into a laugh.

"Nothing," she answered, offering a hand.

CHAPTER 11

HER VOICE

I vow to obey orders from the Emperor and my superiors.

♫ EYES ON FIRE - BLUE FOUNDATION ♫

"Something's wrong," Vell said, watching Yahshi bite into a slice of toast.

He set his bread down and pressed the bruises on his face. They still hurt, but not horribly. Three days had passed since his match against Keiyo, and he thought the healing process was moving along fine.

"I didn't mean the bruises," she clarified. "You haven't been sleeping."

Yahshi swallowed, the dry bread scraping his throat on the way down.

"Is it *that* obvious?" he asked.

"It's the eye bags. And the oily hair."

"But I showered this morning." He ran his fingers through his hair, rejecting her claim about the oiliness, but the eye bags were likely true. *I can't keep up.*

"Second phase today," Vell said.

"Thanks for the reminder," he muttered, pushing his empty plate aside. *Any meal could be my last in the program.*

"Will Pinto be there?"

Yahshi shook his head. "He can walk around fine, but I doubt he could fight."

"At least he has a final shot in three days."

"Let's hope they don't serve our next dose before then."

Vell stared at him before taking a sip of watered-down coffee. "Might as well be tea," she said, and Yahshi grinned.

As they headed up the staircase after breakfast, Quax and Keiyo jogged past them. Yahshi caught a glimpse of the golden pins on their collars—symbols of victory that could have been his.

He crossed his arms, and Vell shivered. It was cold despite the hot weather, but perhaps the chill was only in their minds.

Yahshi trailed behind Vell in the lecture hall, slipping his rewritten paper onto Professor Embre's desk. He looked over his shoulder at the guardian as he walked down the aisle, expecting a glance of acknowledgment that never came.

For the second morning in a row, Yahshi sat next to an empty seat. He'd overheard Quax and Keiyo badgering Limbo, Sunna's new roommate, for updates on his condition. It was relieving to know that Sunna hadn't been filtered. *But I hope he's feeling okay.*

The bell rang.

"I see more empty seats than I'd like to," Professor Embre said after the pledge of allegiance.

Yahshi counted seven empty seats when there should have been three. Seventeen trainees remained in the program, but four had been too sickly to attend classes after the first dose. *I wonder how many of them will make it through the week.*

"If your roommate is still recovering, I ask that you pass today's news onto him," Professor Embre added.

News? Yahshi's eyes jolted back to her. *That can't be good.*

The air fell still, and he folded his hands in his lap, hoping for anything but another filtration.

"You have a history exam the day after tomorrow," she announced. "The trainee with the lowest score will be filtered from the program."

The lecture hall erupted with whispers and sighs.

"Quax?" Professor Embre called.

He lowered his arm. "What topics will the exam cover?"

"I will say only this—study smart, not hard." She paused as though she'd revealed the meaning of life before gesturing to Yahshi's raised hand. "Go ahead."

"That's the day before our final sparring opportunity with Commander Roz."

"All the more reason to earn your pin this afternoon." She smiled. "Agreed?"

The room seemed to tilt when he realized the guardians had purposefully overlapped filtrations. *They've turned overwhelming us into a game.*

Professor Embre called on another trainee, but Yahshi couldn't make out a single word that left his mouth. The noises around him muddled into a blur.

"You said it yourself..."

At the sound of Cal's voice, the lecture hall morphed into the woods by Sitra Secondary. Yahshi was no longer sitting at his desk but standing, dressed in a sage-green shirt and khaki pants.

"You need to win today," Cal finished.

Yahshi spun in place but couldn't find her. *Leave me alone!*

He jumped when Chima appeared in front of him, blood dripping down his face. His head was dented from a hit Yahshi knew he hadn't thrown, but the bloody log in his grip claimed otherwise. *Where did this come from?*

"Do it," Cal said, her tone sharpening. "What are you waiting for?"

He stepped forward, raising the log over his head. His arms trembled as he fought against an invisible power forcing him to swing.

"Cal," Yahshi yelled, "stop!"

He burst from his chair in the lecture hall, gasping. All eyes were on him as he pinched his pinless collar, his heart pounding so fast he feared it might explode.

Keiyo shot Quax a grin. "Why's he talkin' about your sister?"

His cheeks burned. *I said her name aloud, didn't I?*

"Is something wrong?" Professor Embre asked.

Yahshi stared at his hands, which no longer clutched a bloody log. "Sorry, Professor," he said in a shaky voice.

"Sit down."

He kept his head low as Professor Embre dove into her lecture. *I should be taking notes*, he thought. But instead, he scanned the room, paranoid Cal would appear in one of the vacant seats, watching him.

I'm not like you, Cal.

"No," she whispered into his ear, "but you should be."

A breeze tousled his hair despite the closed windows, sending a chill down his spine. He tapped his boot against the floor and bit at the end of his pencil. *She isn't real. She isn't real. She isn't—*

The bell rang, and he was the first trainee out the door.

"You're seeing things, aren't you?" Vell asked, catching up to him in the hallway.

"Hearing," Yahshi admitted. "Mostly."

"What are you hearing?"

"Voices."

"Voices?" she asked. "Or just one?"

Yahshi went quiet. Surely Vell was wondering why he'd hallucinate about the Belladonna Prodigy, but the last thing he needed was to obsess over Cal again. *I'm finally committed to the program. I shouldn't be thinking about the incident, and I certainly shouldn't be talking about it.*

"Well, whatever you're hearing, it's not unusual," Vell continued, accepting his silence. "Hallucinations are a side effect of belladonna intoxication. It started after the second dose, right?"

"Umm... yeah. I think so."

She shrugged. "That explains it then."

"Well I hope the effects wear off soon." Yahshi caught himself fidgeting with his vest buttons and shoved his hands into his pockets. "I miss relying on the morning bell to wake me up. Now it just mocks me."

After Medical class, Vell suggested they skip lunch to avoid sparring on a full stomach—and to get some extra practice in before the second phase. A smart move, Yahshi assumed, until they arrived at the training room early to find the pinless Brackle twins one step ahead of them. He and Vell lingered by the door, studying their potential opponents.

First, Limbo. He was arguably the sloppiest and most impulsive trainee of their cycle. Yahshi heard that he lost his match against Durlan Ouzo in the first phase because he'd tripped over one of his bootlaces. They were tied in triple knots today.

Second, Ceylon. His level-headed nature made him the better fighter of the two. As they engaged in a practice match against each other, Yahshi could tell that he was leading the fight, stringing his brother along and teaching him in the process.

Vell turned to Yahshi, her hair already up in a ponytail. "Shall we?"

Yahshi had only practiced with Vell the day prior, but she already held a much better chance now that she was getting a handle on the basics. Her stance was more stable, and she moved with more confidence—but that didn't make her a more challenging opponent than either of the Brackle twins. Getting paired with her was Yahshi's best-case scenario, but it was also the scenario he dreaded most.

"That's what happens when you get too close to people," Cal said. "You lose sight of what matters."

Yahshi ignored her voice, dodging one of Vell's punches. Perhaps if he pretended Cal wasn't there, she eventually wouldn't be.

They stopped practicing when Commander Roz entered, golden stopwatch in his hand.

Yahshi glanced at the clock, his shoulders stiffening. He'd expected Pinto's absence, but Sunna and two other pinless boys hadn't arrived either.

Commander Roz had no intent to wait for them. "Vell Patura and Limbo Brackle—you're up first. Please enter the sparring range."

"Good luck," Yahshi said.

Vell stepped forward without looking at him, joining Limbo in the green zone.

Click. "You may begin."

Vell's eyes darted to Limbo's boots, and his lips parted. As he checked his laces, she sprinted after him with a shove, leaving him stumbling.

Limbo regained balance near the end of the sparring range, and Vell ran forward to push him out of bounds.

He ducked under her arms and struck her in the side.

Yahshi winced. *Come on, Vell...*

"Good job, Brother," Ceylon whispered, folding his hands together.

Vell pivoted out of Limbo's view, jamming her foot into the back of his knee—the same move she'd tested on Yahshi. He nearly lost balance but crouched and pressed his palm to the floor, grounding himself.

She stepped away, and Yahshi sighed. *She was so close.*

When Limbo began to jog around the edge of the sparring range, Vell spun in place at the center, keeping her eyes locked on him.

He's trying to make her dizzy.

Vell reached the same conclusion and trailed behind him, maintaining an even distance between his back and face. They had each other in check, circling the edge at a matched pace.

After a few loops, Vell made the next move, speeding up to close the gap between them. She readied her arms to push Limbo out of orbit from behind.

He vanished before her palms could meet his back, stepping into the center of the green zone.

With his opponent near the edge and himself planted inward, Limbo had the upper hand. A single push left Vell falling out of the sparring range. She landed on the black zone with a single roll.

Ceylon sighed in relief, but Yahshi darted to Vell's side.

"That was impressive," he said, helping her stand.

She attempted to move her shoulder and winced. "*Great.*"

"Really, you almost had him," he added.

She shook her head with watery eyes, immune to his attempts to distract her from the defeat. They turned to see Commander Roz attaching a pin to Limbo's collar, declaring his victory.

"Vell, please see Blimmery in the infirmary," Commander Roz said.

"Sorry, Vell," Limbo muttered, but his eyes were on his newly earned pin.

Yahshi fished for Vell's gaze, and she finally looked at him.

"I'll see you at supper?" he asked.

"Good luck," she muttered.

Vell left the training room with a tight grip on her shoulder, but Limbo lingered to spectate his brother's match.

"Yahshi Konya and Ceylon Brackle, you're up next," Commander Roz announced.

Yahshi joined Ceylon on the green zone and raised his hands. They were trembling a bit, an occasional side effect he'd been experiencing since the first dose. *I'm not scared. It's just the belladonna*, he assured himself.

Click. "You may begin."

Yahshi waited for Ceylon's first move—a punch, which he dodged. Then he blocked his second attack and ducked under his third.

"Why haven't you struck back?" Cal asked.

Yahshi was too annoyed by the return of her voice to ignore it.

I hate fighting without a good reason to, he mentally replied.

"You have your reason. You want to graduate, don't you? To prolong peace on the island? That's what you wrote in that essay of yours."

He blocked another punch. *That's a different kind of reason.*

"How so?" Cal asked.

A knife-jabbing pinch in his ribs knocked him back to reality. His breath caught in his throat as he doubled over, clutching his torso.

"You're too soft," Cal whispered. "That's why you lose."

Ceylon knocked him off-balance before he could recover from the hit, and his head slammed onto the floor. The pressure of a bony knee against his chest made breathing impossible.

I can't win.

Yahshi tapped out because he couldn't bear another beating like last time.

Ceylon lifted his knee, allowing him to inhale a few gasping breaths.

"Are you okay?" he asked, helping Yahshi into a seated position.

He ignored the question, distracted by the sight of Commander Roz approaching them with a pin that—once again—was not for him.

Ceylon's concerned frown lingered just a moment longer before he abandoned his opponent on the floor, standing to claim his pin.

When Yahshi finally pushed himself to his feet, the metal door slid open to reveal Pinto and Sunna.

They wobbled into the room, their steps uneven, their faces red. Yahshi should have been pleased that Pinto magically showed up, or at least grateful to see Sunna for the first time in days—but he felt nothing.

"It's nice to see the two of you," Commander Roz said. "Pinto Dempsey and Sunna Rickabee, please enter the sparring range."

Ceylon gave his brother a high-five before leaving the training room, but once again, Limbo stayed behind to spectate. He smirked as Pinto and Sunna dragged themselves onto the green zone, facing each other with their shaky hands raised. It looked like they'd spun around a hundred times beforehand.

"Clever." With a grin, Commander Roz clicked a button on his stopwatch. "You may begin."

Yahshi wasn't in the mood to stick around, but leaving during the match might offend Pinto, so he stayed to watch. But he didn't *see*.

Our Research exam is the day after tomorrow. What are the odds I pass it and *earn my pin during the final phase?* He grabbed his collar, wondering what a pin would feel like against his fingers.

The match ended with Commander Roz attaching a pin to Pinto's collar while Sunna stood with one boot in the black zone.

Pinto smiled at Yahshi, who could only return a lazy nod. *Even he won his match today. What am I doing wrong?*

"Limbo, would you help Pinto and Sunna to the infirmary?" Commander Roz asked.

Limbo crossed his arms. "Fine..."

Yahshi nearly joined them, but Commander Roz caught his gaze and held it until the other boys left.

"Is something wrong?" Yahshi asked. The words came out sharper than he'd intended, but the last thing he wanted to do was endure another guardian lecture.

"Yahshi, do you know *why* you keep losing?

He thought of Cal, and her voice. "I'm not sure."

"During your matches against Quax, Keiyo, and Ceylon, you hesitated at every opportunity to strike." Commander Roz leaned in. "What are you afraid of?"

"I'm not afraid. I've just... seen what happens when people go too far. I wouldn't wanna hurt anyone like that."

"You know what hurts me the most in my field of work?" the guardian asked. "Trainees who neglect their potential."

Yahshi was dying to look away and break the tension, but he didn't want to appear ungrateful for a private critique. He forced his eyes to widen instead.

"You have more combat experience than most trainees here, but the moment you're in the green zone, it all goes down the drain. If you want to succeed here, that's a big problem."

Of course I wanna succeed. To succeed meant moving on, and feeling better, and doing good. He was done being the star student turned lowlife, the witness corrupted by trauma, the boy who never left the woods that day. *I'm ready to be selection material.*

"This *problem*... how do I fix it?"

Commander Roz smiled. "I want you to think about that moment in the courtyard. You had a strong drive, a fire within you, and I appreciated that."

"You mean, you like that I was dedicated to my investigation. That I protected what I cared about," Yahshi clarified. "But I shouldn't have punched him, right?"

He sighed. "Look, I was a lot like you when I was younger. I caused a lot of trouble getting into things I shouldn't have because I wanted to do something special, to be someone, but I didn't know what to do or who to be. The Academy changed that. I found my purpose here, and maybe you can too. That's why I'm rooting for you to make the final five. But to earn your spot in the Force, you need to light that match again. Can you do that for me?"

Yahshi lowered his head. It was true that he might have earned his pin by now if he'd fought to his full potential, but he'd been letting his memories of the incident interfere.

I can't graduate as the same boy who entered. If I truly want this, I need to change.

He raised his chin. "I can do that for you, Commander."

Yahshi stopped halfway up the staircase, noticing Limbo, who was on his way down. His tightly laced boots, melodramatic bird tattoo, and narrowed eyes made his blood boil.

"What the hell are you staring at?" Limbo asked, halting a few steps above him.

"How's Vell?" Yahshi asked.

"Well, she's not my sister, so why should I care?"

"She's hurt because of you."

"I didn't *choose* to fight Vell, did I?" He crossed his arms. "What's the real problem here?"

"She needs to win more than you do," Yahshi said, recalling what Ceylon had told him. Limbo was only here because his brother wanted to be a guardian, and by tagging along, he was directly threatening the success of trainees like Vell, who had much more to gain.

Limbo scoffed. "We're in a competitive program, not a charity group. Did you expect me to lose on purpose just because you fancy her?"

"I don't—"

"It's *your fault* you lost today," Limbo interrupted. "Don't take it out on me." He shoved his shoulder into Yahshi as he passed him.

"He's right," Cal said. "It is your fault. If only you'd listen."

Shut it. Yahshi gritted his teeth, resuming his way.

Pinto and Sunna were lying on two beds in the infirmary, Vell icing her shoulder on a third.

"Oh, Yahshi!" Doctor Blimmery was sitting at Sunna's bedside. "It's good that you're here. Ice your face, please."

As Yahshi scooped ice from the chest into a bag, Sunna began to cough.

Pinto looked over at him. "Hey, are you still—"

"I'm still breathing," Sunna croaked. "Sorry to break the news, but you didn't kill me yet."

Yahshi smiled briefly before sitting next to Vell. "That didn't go as planned," he muttered.

"It went horribly," she corrected.

"How's your shoulder?"

"Hurts."

"Do you think you can practice this evening?"

"No."

"That's fine. We should prioritize the history exam for now anyway." He raised the ice bag to his bruised cheek and flinched. *I'm glad Ceylon didn't land any brutal hits.*

"I guess." Vell's gaze dropped to her boots, and Yahshi frowned.

"Don't give up."

"I can't afford to."

"Then, what's wrong?"

"I'm just... considering the odds." She rose, her expression tightening. "I have to go."

CHAPTER 12

YELLOW MITTENS

I vow to sever emotional ties to those of my life
prior to guardianship.

♫ THINGS WILL GET BETTER · VIAN IZAK ♫

Yahshi skipped supper to get a head start on studying, which involved walking down library aisles, trailing his fingers along the spines of countless books. He felt like a droplet in an ocean of knowledge.

Rain began to pelt the windows in a storm, so he slowed his pace, gazing at the glass.

The sky weeps with us.

As he entered a new aisle, he thought of Selection Day Eve, the last day he and his father had muttered that phrase together. *Has he forgiven me by now?*

Yahshi scuffled to a stop, nearly tripping over a trainee who was reading on the floor. From his blue bandana alone, he identified him as Dice.

"Sorry," Yahshi said, stepping around him.

"The sky weeps with us," Dice muttered, stopping him again.

I didn't say it aloud earlier, did I? He peered back at Dice, who turned a page, eyes glued to his book. *No, I didn't. I'm sure of it.*

A few minutes must have passed, because Dice turned another page.

"That phrase," Yahshi said, breaking the silence. "You've heard it before?"

The rain intensified as Dice stood, slamming his book shut.

"No. I haven't."

He passed Yahshi and glanced at him from the end of the aisle, as though he might say something more, but he didn't.

He left.

Yahshi rushed after him, reaching the end of the aisle to spot him heading for the door.

"Where are you going?"

"Dining hall." Dice quickened his pace. "I'm hungry."

The slam of the door sent a vibration through the air, and Yahshi shivered.

When he returned to his quarter a few hours later, Pinto was at his desk, writing under the candlelight. He looked up with a smile before resuming.

"Have you been documenting *everything* in that book?" Yahshi asked, changing into his pajamas.

"Just the important parts," Pinto chirped, and the pin on his collar twinkled like a star.

After changing, Yahshi crawled into bed. The soft blankets and silk pajamas tried to coax him into slumber, but he fought his exhaustion and forced himself into a seated position. Pinto was finally in a good mood after being sick and grumpy for three days. *I should talk to him.*

"Congratulations on your match today." Yahshi tried to sound genuine, but the bitterness slipped through.

"Thanks," Pinto said. "I'm sorry you lost yours."

He forced a smile. "It's okay."

Pinto closed his journal as he stood, surprisingly stable. "Where were you during recreation time?"

"I was studying in the library," Yahshi said. "I'm gonna fail this exam."

He limped to his bed and took a seat. "At least you hardly reacted to the first dose. If you can get past the next few days, you'll be at a huge advantage."

Advantage? "I doubt that," Yahshi said. Pinto was the one with a near-photographic memory and a pin on his collar.

"Doctor Blimmery says that every cycle, there's a few trainees who can't fight the poison. I'm worried I might be one of them."

"Of course you're not. Two guys were filtered, remember?"

"And if it weren't for Vell, I would've been number three. She can train, and you can study, but I have no control over how my body reacts to the poison." He scoffed. "Out of all the things to get me filtered, I never thought it'd be a glass of juice."

"You're being too hard on yourself."

"You don't get it. I'm hanging from a ledge right now."

The raspiness in his voice made Yahshi lean back.

"I only earned my pin today because Sunna accepted my deal," he continued.

"What deal?"

"In our poisoned states, we'd surely lose against anyone else. We took a risk and arrived late, hoping Commander Roz would pair us together by default. That would at least give us both a fairer shot at winning."

Yahshi recalled how Commander Roz had referred to Pinto and Sunna as *clever.* Surely the guardian had caught onto their trick, but instead of disqualifying them, he honored their plan.

"The reality is, I keep getting lucky. Vell saved me, and Commander Roz spared me, but that won't last forever. Something *always* goes wrong eventually."

Someone knocked on the door. Pinto shot Yahshi a questioning glance before standing with a wince.

"I got it," Yahshi said. *Perhaps Doctor Blimmery wants to check on Pinto an extra time today.*

But when he opened the door, Vell stared back at him. Her eyes were bloodshot, and her long hair had been cut into choppy shards, each clump a different length.

"Can I come in?" she asked, her voice weak.

Yahshi stared, before stepping aside.

Vell rushed into the room, smiling briefly at Pinto before sitting on Yahshi's bed. She looked around as though she were searching for something.

Vell looked unusual in pajamas, and Yahshi realized that was because he'd never seen her past the night bell before. As far as he knew, she spent most of her free time alone in her quarter.

"What's that?" Pinto eyed a package of crackers in her hands, and she tossed it over. He tried to catch it with his fatigued arms but missed—the package hit his chest before flopping onto his bed.

"You raved about them during our first supper here," Vell noted.

"You have a good memory. Thanks." Pinto popped the package open. "It's nice to have real food again. Doctor Blimmery keeps bringing me porridge with *activated charcoal*. Yeah, right. For all I know, it's poisoned too. I've been pouring it down the drain."

Vell smiled. "If you ate the porridge, you'd be feeling better by now."

"Or I'd be dead." Pinto bit into a cracker. "Is it worth the risk?"

Yahshi cringed at Vell's hair. "How's your shoulder?"

"Not bad," she answered. "I'll be fine tomorrow."

He sat next to her. "And... your hair?"

"It looks awful," Pinto added with his mouth full.

"I know," Vell said, fidgeting with the ends of her pajama sleeves. "And I'm sorry for showing up like this. It's... stupid."

"It's not stupid," he argued. "It's just weird, that's all."

Yahshi glared at him, and Pinto raised his brows, oblivious.

"I-I didn't know where else to go," Vell explained, "and I was talking to Yahshi earlier, and I guess I just... I feel so displaced here."

Yahshi couldn't find the words to express that he understood exactly what she meant, but he did. Not a night had passed when he hadn't thought of his father in Sitra and the comfort of what used to be normal. The bright side was that he had Pinto to talk to, but every evening, Vell would isolate herself in her quarter.

Pinto was about to take another bite, but he set the package down when Vell reached for her hair.

"It's pretty heavy when I tie it up, so I thought maybe if I cut it, then

I'd—I don't know. I just—every night I think about what might happen if I don't get stronger." Her posture collapsed, and she fell forward, her face landing on her shaky fingers. "My mother needs the pension for her medicine."

Yahshi squinted at the floor. *So that's why she stole.*

He recalled Vell's reaction to hearing about his mother's sickness during the War. It seemed out of place at the time, but now that he saw the full picture, he wished he could go back and change how he responded.

I hardly remember her, he wanted to say, *but I still care. Of course I care. I'm not heartless.* He didn't say it, though, because Pinto was in the room, and there was a lot Pinto didn't know.

"I'm so sorry, Vell." He figured she wouldn't understand the extent of his apology, but she made eye contact and nodded. *She gets it.*

"How bad is her condition?" Pinto asked.

"With the money, I assume she's doing better now," Vell said, "but if I get filtered, my family would go back to scrambling for solutions. It'd be all my fault."

Pinto rolled his trembling fingers into a fist, pushed himself to his feet, and rummaged through one of his desk drawers.

"What are you doing?" Yahshi asked.

He turned around with a pair of scissors. "Fixing Vell's hair."

She ran her hands along the uneven strands. "You really don't have to—"

"Relax," Pinto said. "I used to cut my sister's hair all the time."

Vell glanced at Yahshi, who shrugged back.

"Well," she admitted, "I suppose it can't get any worse."

"No. It really can't." He pointed to a chair, which she dragged to the middle of the room and sat on.

Yahshi watched him as he separated clumps of hair, studying them before getting started. *He's an expert at breaking things down into steps.*

"I didn't know you had a sister," Yahshi said as Pinto made his first cut. "Is she young, or was she there during the"—he instantly regretted the direction he'd taken his question in—"you know, when—"

"She's thirteen, so yeah. She lost her eye." Pinto spoke in a tone so casual he could have been pointing out the weather. "Luckily she was only two during the War and doesn't remember a thing. We're quite close, actually. She's the only reason I feel awful about being here."

"Is that why you've been writing?" He glanced at the bamboo journal on Pinto's desk. "For her?"

He nodded with a grin, clearly impressed by Yahshi's deduction. "I plan to give her my journal eventually. It can't make up for the lost time, but it's the best I can do."

"She's lucky to have you," Vell said. "I always wished I wasn't the oldest."

Their conversation flattened for a while, but it wasn't an awkward kind of flat. They listened to the meditative snips of Pinto's scissors, which were spaced at perfect intervals.

"Sorry," he said. "It doesn't usually take me this long. The poison is still—"

"*Serum*," Vell corrected.

Pinto tried not to chuckle, but he did.

"It's okay," she continued, dropping the humor. "No one's expecting you to heal overnight."

"It certainly feels like it." He bit his lip, focusing as he made a final cut.

Vell reached for her hair, which now fell evenly above her shoulders.

"It looks better," Yahshi assured her.

She caught a glimpse of her reflection in the mirror. Her hair was lighter, and *she* looked lighter.

"Thanks, Pinto," she said.

"Consider it payment for the crackers." He waved the scissors in front of her. "And for punching me the other day."

Vell smiled.

After cleaning up, their conversation flattened, but this time it was an awkward kind of flat. Pinto eyed the clock while Vell eyed the door, but no one moved or said a word.

Yahshi cleared his throat. "You can stay... if you want."

Pinto raised his palms. "That's probably not—"

"I'll stay," Vell said.

She and Yahshi watched Pinto as he opened and closed his mouth a few times, struggling to argue. He gave up with a sigh. "Fine..."

Yahshi removed a blanket and pillow from his bed and arranged them on the floor.

"Sorry," Vell muttered.

"I don't mind," he replied.

She glanced at Pinto, who was watching with a befuddled expression from across the quarter. "You're not wearing your pajamas," she pointed out.

"Yeah," Pinto said. "That's fine."

"You're not gonna change?"

He frowned. "I'm not changing in front of you."

"I didn't expect you to." She gestured to the restroom door with her eyes, and Pinto's lips parted.

"Yeah, just change in the restroom," Yahshi said.

Pinto looked back and forth between them. "Forget it." His tone sharpened. "It's fine."

Yahshi tilted his head. "So you're gonna sleep in your uniform?"

He nodded.

"Are you sure?" Vell asked.

"Yes!" Pinto barked, his face reddening. "Seriously, why are you two so obsessed with my pajamas? I'm exhausted, okay? I can change in the morning." He threw himself into bed and pulled the blankets to his chin. "The world doesn't end if I don't sleep in silk."

Yahshi and Vell made eye contact.

"I—uh..." Yahshi swallowed a chuckle before it could escape. "I'll put out the lanterns then."

As Vell climbed into his bed, he blew out the lanterns and laid himself on the floor. His eyes were beginning to drift shut when Pinto said, "I got pretty mad there, didn't I?"

And soon enough, he was laughing, and Yahshi and Vell were laughing too.

"Quiet," Pinto warned. "The others could hear, and how the hell would we explain the noise?"

"Pillow fight," Vell muttered.

Yahshi laughed again, and Pinto shushed him in a panic.

"Stop that," he scolded, but the humor in his voice remained. "I'm serious."

"Don't *shush* me when you started it," Yahshi said.

Pinto didn't reply until silence filled the room again. "You know what?" he said, his voice softer. "I'm feeling better tonight."

"Really?" Yahshi asked.

"Yeah. I think it's about time I start showing up to class again. I've missed far too many lectures."

"I can lend you my notes," Vell offered.

"Are you sure?" he asked, and Yahshi realized exactly what she was planning.

"You can look through mine too," Yahshi said. "And in exchange, maybe you could help us study for the Research exam."

"What is this, some kind of alliance?" Pinto asked.

"Exactly," Vell said.

"If we combine our strengths, we can make the final five," Yahshi said. "All three of us."

"All three of us," Pinto repeated. "That doesn't sound too bad."

Yahshi could hear the smile in his voice.

"So, are you in?" Vell asked, and Pinto didn't miss a beat.

"Absolutely."

With nothing more to be said, the silence returned one final time, and Yahshi cherished the optimism of the night. He wouldn't allow his past to hold him back any longer.

When their breathing steadied, signaling sleep, he left the quarter with a lantern in one hand and a pair of yellow mittens in the other.

The front door to the Academy, he discovered, was locked every night with a metal bar much heavier than it looked. He held his breath and tightened his grip, setting it down without a sound.

The candlelight guided him across the field to the forested road, where he opened the lantern door and held the mittens over the flame. An orange dot marked the wool, growing until the heat seeped into his fingers, and the mittens were fully ablaze.

"Ah!" He flinched, tossing them onto the dirt before they could burn him.

I have to win. He glued his eyes to Alora's yellow mittens as they crackled in the night, brighter than ever. The fire left a trail of smoke puffs drifting toward the moon.

From now on, no more hallucinations. No more voices.

Footsteps approached him, but he didn't raise his chin to face the interrupter.

"You don't need my help anymore." Cal's black boots came to a halt next to his. "I'm proud of you."

Her tone was smug, but Yahshi lacked the energy to unpack why.

"Goodbye, Cal," he ordered.

"Good job, Yahshi."

He blinked, and her boots disappeared.

CHAPTER 13

FLAME WITHIN

I vow to submit myself to extreme mental or physical
correction if necessary.

♫ FEVER · BALTHAZAR ♫

Yahshi discovered that hair could make a miraculous impact on perception. Upon Vell's arrival to the dining hall for breakfast, trainees fell silent. Her long hair had once softened the features that now made her resting face menacing. By carrying herself with a newfound boldness, she redefined her haircut as a statement of dedication rather than an act of helplessness.

Vell sat across from Yahshi, slamming three history textbooks onto the table.

He flinched at the impact.

"Shall we?" she asked.

Pinto dragged her textbooks in front of him. "Impressive titles."

"Why these three in particular?" Yahshi asked. "I was in the library for hours yesterday, and I had no clue where to begin."

"Study smart, not hard. Remember?" She took a bite of oatmeal.

"Obviously the exam will cover the limited topics Professor Embre has lectured us on," Pinto elaborated, gesturing for emphasis. "That includes the formation of the Force, the Atherus War, and changes in the guardian divisions over time."

Vell swallowed. "I searched for a book on each topic in the library this morning."

Yahshi grinned, eyes darting between them. "Thanks for the explanation. Now I feel stupid."

"You're very welcome," Pinto said, and took a swig of watery coffee.

Throughout the remainder of breakfast and Research class, Pinto flipped through the textbooks, compiling a list of sections to review. He showed them his notes on their way to the lab.

"My study plan is failproof," he said. "If we review the information in these nine sections, we'll learn everything we need and nothing more."

Yahshi was so awed by his impeccable handwriting that he hadn't processed the information on the page.

"You could be a scribe," Vell said.

"Sure, if I get filtered." Pinto chuckled. "Scribe. Sure. That's now my pathetic backup plan."

They were the only trainees to study in the dining hall over lunch and supper—but when they arrived at the library during recreation time, nearly everyone was there, wandering through aisles, flipping through pages, reciting notes under their breath.

Pinto and Vell left with the other trainees after sunset—but Yahshi stayed behind. *Just one more hour*, he told himself. And then an hour turned into two, and three, and four, and more... And before he knew it, birds were making their morning calls outside, their squawking carrying through the walls.

Three critical events led to the formation of the Force, a pivotal shift in the Empire's security, he read. *The first was the belladonna poisoning of—*

The door swung open.

Yahshi glanced at Pinto and Vell before refocusing on the textbook page. *The first was the belladonna poisoning of Princess Pollena, which spurred leading botanists to study the plant, laying the foundation for tolerance training at the Academy program and the practice of lacing guardian tools.*

"Yahshi!" Pinto yelled. "Please tell me you didn't stay up all night."

"I didn't stay up all night," he said in a melodic tone. Surely they wouldn't blame him for spending extra time studying had they known how far he'd fallen behind academically over the past two years.

He skipped to the next paragraph. *The second was the attempted Vakoi Palace invasion. Although the anarchists were unsuccessful, their plan sparked concern regarding the Royal Family's safety and the security of the—*

"Stop," Vell said.

Yahshi's jaw dropped as the textbook slipped out from under his fingertips.

Vell slammed it shut. "You're being reckless. Without sleep, you won't think clearly."

"No need to scare him, Vell." Pinto appeared next to her, arms crossed. "It's too late now."

"I'm *fine*, really. Not sleepy at all." Yahshi sprang to his feet as the bell rang. "Let's get breakfast." He reached for another textbook.

Vell swatted his arm away. "Leave the books."

"But I need to—"

"Leave them."

Yahshi turned to Pinto, who shook his head. "Just leave the books, Yahshi."

With a sigh, his shoulders slumped. "Okay..."

They enjoyed a peaceful breakfast in the dining hall while the others continued their last-minute cramming. Yahshi wished he could join them, but perhaps Pinto and Vell had a point. *If I didn't soak up the information last night, I'm not gonna soak it up over a meal.*

He was pleased to discover Sunna in the lecture hall despite his absence during breakfast.

"I'm glad you're feeling better." Yahshi sat beside him for the first time in days.

"I'm glad to be back." Sunna offered a smile, which faded as Professor Embre passed out their exams—each containing one hundred multiple-choice questions.

Yahshi peered down at the first one.

Which three events led to the formation of the Vakoi Empire's Force?

After turning in his exam, the sleepiness kicked in. He had to pinch himself throughout Medical class to stay awake, and as he walked with Pinto and Vell to the dining hall for lunch, his eyes continually drifted shut.

"If you don't catch up on sleep, you'll die tomorrow," Pinto said.

The thought of sparring in the final phase made Yahshi's stomach churn, but he couldn't afford to make the same mistake of falling behind in one class for the sake of another. If he went to sleep now, he'd miss their field class, and for all he knew, they'd have a filtration involving horseback riding or plant identification next, and he wouldn't be prepared.

"I can't miss our afternoon classes," he said, fighting the urge to yawn. The tension growing between his ears made him feel like his head outweighed his body.

Pinto rolled his eye. "I missed *two days* of classes, and I'm alive, aren't I?"

"But I need to help Vell train."

"Pinto can fill in for you," Vell said.

His brows jumped. "I can?"

"Just go to sleep," she pressed.

It didn't take much convincing. Yahshi turned back for his quarter, where he slept for nearly fifteen hours.

The sun was long from rising when he woke up, so a book on natural remedies Vell had suggested kept him occupied until the morning bell.

After scarfing breakfast down with Pinto and Vell, he entered the lecture hall fully awake and bright-eyed. His days at the Academy were merging together, but at least he was well-rested. He couldn't remember the last time he'd felt so alert.

The pledge of allegiance ended with Professor Embre grabbing a stack of graded exams. She didn't waste time on an introduction before making the reveal.

"The trainee with the lowest score," she said, "is Durlan Ouzo."

A collective sigh filled the air.

Yahshi followed everyone's eyes to a boy with a crooked tie and shaggy hair. He could tell with a single glance that Durlan had been slipping.

He resembled Limbo's former roommate who'd filtered himself from the program the week prior.

What was that guy's name again? Yahshi tapped his fingers against his desk, trying to jog his memory. *I can't recall.*

"Durlan, you're filtered from the program," Professor Embre stated. "A guardian is waiting in the common room to escort you home."

Durlan held a stern expression. "Are you positive that you graded correctly?"

"Of course."

"Could you double-check?"

"There is no mistake."

Durlan looked around the room as though he expected someone to volunteer to leave in his place. His arms shook as he met Professor Embre's gaze again. "I can't go back."

"You're filtered. You have to go back."

You have to go back. Yahshi shivered at the thought of being told those words someday.

"But I already earned my pin, see?" Durlan burst to his feet, pulling his collar to show her.

As Professor Embre stared at his four-petaled pin, unimpressed, Yahshi realized they were not symbols of victory, but requirements. *To lack a pin makes one insignificant. To earn a pin makes one sufficient. Acceptable.*

"I bet I could win a match against any trainee in this room right now," Durlan continued, his voice rising to a shout, "and you're gonna filter me over a *history exam?*"

Professor Embre strolled down the aisle with a blank expression, her boots clacking against the floor.

"What if I retake the test?" Durlan pleaded, his voice breaking. "Really, just give me a new exam, and I guarantee my score won't be the lowest this time."

Professor Embre stopped in front of him, her gaze cold.

"Please!" His eyes began to water. "You know why I'm here. I need this. If I don't graduate, I—"

Professor Embre slapped him.

The trainees gasped, meeting each other's widened eyes.

Durlan stepped away with a palm cradling his red cheek.

"You've made a fool of yourself, Durlan." Professor Embre pointed to the door. "Fools don't belong in the Force."

Durlan bit his trembling lip and lowered his head. His bangs fell to shield his eyes as he took slow, measured steps down the aisle. Trainees looked away as though eye contact would infect them with his foolishness.

He left without shutting the door, and Professor Embre waited for his footsteps to fade before marching to her desk. She walked the same as she always had, but Yahshi couldn't shake the feeling that something had changed.

"For the remainder of class, I'll explain the correct answer for each question." She passed out their exams like nothing happened. "Pay close attention to your mistakes, and learn from them..."

Yahshi's exam displayed the circled number fifty-two in red ink, but he didn't mind the low score. All that mattered was that it wasn't the lowest.

When the bell rang, the trainees flinched. They were all a little on edge that morning as they rushed to the door, speeding up past Professor Embre's desk. Yahshi accidentally met eyes with her, and she held his gaze. *Dammit. Why did I look?*

He stopped by her desk because he knew better than to play ignorant. Pinto and Vell shot him concerned glances on their way out.

Once they were alone in the lecture hall, Professor Embre pulled his revised essay out of a drawer.

"It's perfect," she said.

He smiled. "Really?"

"Hold onto it as a reminder of what drives you." She handed him the pages, and he was certain he caught her flash a grin.

"I will," he said, tucking it into his bag.

"As for the exam, you cut it close. If you'd missed one more question, you and Durlan would be tied for the lowest score. The Research Division values attention to detail, so be more cautious when you read next time. You missed at least three questions because you chose *examples* instead of *exceptions*."

Despite the comparison to Durlan and his foolishness, a weight lifted from his shoulders. Professor Embre had done nothing but threaten him since his arrival, but today she'd given him a kind critique, a sign that part of her was rooting for his success in the program.

"Thank you, Professor. I'll be more careful."

She nodded. "You're dismissed."

Yahshi left to find Pinto and Vell waiting for him in the hallway.

Pinto stopped biting his nails, but the anxiety still marked his face. "What was that about?" he asked in a hushed tone.

"I think I may have"—Yahshi peered back at the door—"impressed her."

He sighed in relief. "I thought you were about to get filtered."

"Of course not." Yahshi headed for the staircase, and they caught up to him on either side. "Your study plan was failproof, remember?"

"So," Vell said, "what'd you get?"

"A fifty-two."

Pinto gasped. "*Fifty-two*? What the hell? You missed nearly half the questions! How is that possibly supposed to impress her?"

Yahshi leaned toward him. "Fascinating, isn't it?"

"Oh, come on! Don't just ignore me," Pinto said. "What was that meeting about?"

Doctor Blimmery had yet to arrive when they entered the lab. The waiting trainees were huddled in groups, muttering about Durlan's scene with Professor Embre.

As Yahshi walked down the aisle, he spotted Sunna's pinless collar and slowed to a stop, allowing Pinto and Vell to pass him. He hadn't considered the possibility of being paired against him in the final phase.

Anyone but Sunna.

He shook his head, correcting his statement.

Or Vell. Anyone but Sunna or Vell.

He was scanning the room in search of his other potential opponents when someone joined him in the aisle.

"So the three of you are friends now," Quax said. "Strange..."

Yahshi faced him. "Why is that strange?" It was Quax who didn't want to stay friends with him at the Academy. *Does he expect me to talk to no one, ever?*

"It's just weird timing. You spent two years pushing everyone away, and now you're suddenly making friends in the program?" He leaned in, lowering his voice. "I thought you didn't trust the guardians, remember? I thought you said that *not* getting selected wouldn't be so bad."

Yahshi took a deep breath. "I finally moved on," he said firmly. "Isn't that always what you wanted?"

Quax scoffed, his eyes darting to Pinto and Vell. They were at their shared lab table, reviewing a Medical textbook together. "So all the times I tried talking sense into you did nothing, but those two fixed you overnight?"

"That's not what happened. And it's none of your business, anyway."

"So my sister's your new role model? The old Yahshi's just... gone now?"

He narrowed his eyes, his fingers rolling into fists. "Why are you *so* mad that I'm here?"

"Because you never have to work for anything," Quax spouted.

"*What?*"

"I used to look up to you when we were younger, you know that? You were smart, and funny, and you had no problem getting people to like you. I was the whiny one. I had to *earn* people's attention, but you had it by default. And then you threw it all away after the incident like it meant nothing. I had to work my ass off to reach your level—and even at your worst, you still got everything I worked for."

He closed in on Yahshi, making a point to tower over him.

"You *always* win," Quax said.

Yahshi shoved him a few steps back, refusing to give in to his physical intimidation.

"Are you kidding me? After Cal got selected, you became rich and popular without having to lift a finger." Yahshi crept toward him, closing the gap. "And with the best tutor in town, *anyone* could be a star student."

Quax released a chuckle of disbelief, which escalated into laughter that grated on his nerves more than any insult ever could. With a shake of his head, he turned his back to Yahshi, intending to end their discussion there.

Yahshi gritted his teeth, stepping into Quax's trail. Then he took another step, and another, and before he knew it, he was grabbing his shoulders and shoving him down the aisle.

Quax stumbled sideways, nearly tripping over his own feet. He clung to a table to steady himself while Yahshi stormed toward him.

Right as Quax looked up, a fist met his face.

He groaned, clutching his nose. "What the *hell* is your problem?"

"Ooh, they're fighting!" Keiyo said.

"Cut it out!" Pinto shouted.

Yahshi threw another punch.

Quax ducked under it, retaliating with an uppercut that left Yahshi's jaw stinging. But his rage numbed the pain, and he sprang at Quax again.

Yahshi fought for every *Capital Weekly* article Quax had torn, every grudge he'd held against him, every baseless accusation he'd made. And suddenly the room was on fire, and his fists were on fire, and he was burning alive, but he couldn't help it.

Quax's cheekbone took a blow that cut off his edge, which made it easy for Yahshi to dodge his next attacks. He waited for an opening and kicked his knee, sending him to the floor.

The rain continued to strike the glass dome, but Yahshi didn't listen. He pinned Quax down and jammed his fist into the eye he'd blackened three weeks prior. He wanted to see it bruised and swollen again.

He needs to know that he can't win.

Shouting ensued as he brought his arms down over and over. There were footsteps and gasps and names called as blood dripped from Quax's nose.

Yahshi lost count of the hits before a group of arms dragged him away. He nearly fought their interference, but he cooled down by immersing himself in the sound of water splashing against the glass.

CHAPTER 14

WHAT COULD HAVE BEEN

I vow to abstain from sexual and romantic pleasures henceforth.

♫ YOU ARE ENOUGH · SLEEPING AT LAST ♫

"How could you possibly be so reckless?" Pinto paced their quarter, biting his nails.

"Quax spoke ill of me," Yahshi said.

"So? I don't like him either, but you went too far." He plopped himself onto his bed, running his fingers through his hair. "Honestly, Yahshi, you should be terrified. I wouldn't be surprised if the guardians filter you for misconduct."

"Doctor Blimmery called off Medical class over an hour ago," Yahshi argued. "If the guardians had plans to filter me, they would have done so by now."

"You don't know that."

"I gave Quax a black eye three weeks ago, and they still selected me." He leaned against the wall, arms crossed. "I doubt they'd filter me for giving him another one."

Pinto frowned. "That was... you?"

"What? You don't think I'm capable?"

"I just... didn't think you were the type."

"What type?"

"You know." He paused. "Aggressive."

Yahshi looked away, shaking his head. "I don't understand why you're making a fuss about this."

"Because you told Vell and I that we'd graduate together—the three of us. Remember that? I even helped you study for the exam, and then you go beating at Quax, sabotaging your spot in the program like you're in this alone? I thought we were gonna help each other make the final five. I thought we were"—he lowered his voice—"*friends.*"

"Oh." Yahshi lowered his head. "I wasn't thinking about it like that."

"Well, think about it a little more from now on, will you?" The bell rang, and Pinto stood. "Come on, let's get lunch."

They left Room 4 to find Vell flipping through a Medical textbook in the lobby. She joined them in walking downstairs, repeatedly trying to tie her hair into a ponytail despite it being too short every time. Her nervousness must have been contagious, because Pinto was biting his nails again.

All eyes were on Yahshi as he entered the dining hall.

Quax hadn't shown up for lunch.

The trio grabbed their trays and sat in silence for a few minutes, waiting for the attention to die down.

"Hey, Vell?" Yahshi asked.

She didn't look at him. "What?"

"We could skip lunch and practice if you want."

"I'll pass."

Pinto glanced at him, then at Vell. "I could practice with you instead," he offered.

"I'm eating," she said, stabbing her fork into a cherry tomato. The juice splattered against her cheek, and she wiped it away with her sleeve.

Yahshi hesitated to speak again. "Is your... shoulder better now?"

"It's fine." She popped the tomato into her mouth.

He couldn't tell if Vell was in a bitter mood because of the approaching final phase or the fight in the lab, but he didn't dare to ask. It wasn't until she sipped her beet juice that she perked up, her eyes widening.

"It's the second dose," Vell announced.

Yahshi grabbed his glass and brought it to his nose, testing its smell for something off. "How do you know?"

She took another sip and nodded. "The aftertaste. It's sweeter."

"You've got to be kidding me." Pinto scoffed. "Right when I'm feeling normal again."

Yahshi eyed a box of antiserum under the serving table, which Doctor Blimmery said they could help themselves to as needed. He stood to grab a vial for Pinto, but Vell stopped him by the wrist, shaking her head.

"Don't take the antiserum unless you think you may go unconscious," she said. "Otherwise, it's self-sabotage. Makes you throw up the serum before your body learns to tolerate it."

Yahshi retook his seat.

"So during our first dose," Pinto said, his brows knitting together. "My body didn't learn to fight the toxins? Not at all?"

"A little," she said.

He grabbed his glass and eyed the swirling fluid inside. "Then this dose will be awful too, won't it?"

"Definitely."

Yahshi expected the news to outrage Pinto, but it actually seemed to calm him. He understood precisely how to improve his tolerance—suffer helplessly. No antiserum, no relief. But a plan was a plan, and Pinto loved plans.

"You'll want to finish your food first too," she added. "It'll lighten the symptoms."

"Huh." Pinto narrowed his eye. "Look, as much as I appreciate the tips, I must ask—where does this knowledge of yours come from?"

"My brain." Vell took another bite.

"Yeah, Pinto," Yahshi teased, nudging him in the arm. "That's where thoughts are made."

"I'm serious! Normal people don't know this much about plants."

"None of us are normal," Vell said. "That's why we got selected."

Pinto leaned toward her. "You didn't answer my question."

She slammed her fork down, her tone sharpening. "It was for my mother, okay? If you read enough medical books, you'll stumble into all kinds of information."

Pinto grinned at his glass, satisfied, but Yahshi's gaze lingered on Vell. Her cheeks were red, and she'd raised her voice as though she had something to hide.

After a few measly sips, Pinto cringed.

Vell gulped hers down in one steady stream.

"What kind of monster are you?" Pinto asked. "Poison or not, it still tastes awful."

"Just hold your breath," she said.

While Pinto struggled to finish his glass, Yahshi squinted at his own. On one hand, consuming the dose might ruin his performance during the final phase that afternoon. On the other hand, skipping the dose meant falling behind in tolerance training, and his body might respond horribly to the next one—perhaps it'd leave him hospitalized.

"You're not drinking," Vell noted.

"I'm thinking." He tapped his fingers against the table.

"Try holding your breath." Pinto set his empty glass down. "Vell's right —it helps."

"I don't think I can risk feeling sick during the final phase," Yahshi decided. "I'll sneak the glass back to my quarter. If I win, I'll drink the rest later."

Vell leaned into a sigh, placing her forehead in her hands. "You could have been kind enough to share that idea before I chugged it all."

"You'll be *fine*, Vell," Pinto said, a fragment of jealousy in his voice. "You hardly react."

It didn't take long for the other trainees to realize that today's juice contained belladonna.

Keiyo was scanning the room with sudden twists of his head as though an invisible enemy were after him.

The Brackle twins left to rest in their quarters, their arms wrapped around each other to stay balanced.

Sunna only drank a third of his glass before bolting, snatching an antiserum vial on his way out.

When Yahshi turned his attention back to his table, Pinto was rubbing his temple.

"You should lie down before it gets worse," Vell said.

"I'll walk with you," Yahshi said.

"No, I'm fine." Pinto gripped the table, pushing himself to his feet. "It's just a headache for now. I'll bring your glass up too."

"Are you sure?" Yahshi asked.

"I can manage. The two of you should focus on getting your pins." He grabbed Yahshi's glass, and the beet juice trembled in his grip. "Sunna will likely be in bad shape, even after taking the antiserum. Amal is a planner but never has a backup when his first plan falls through. And Firn—well, he's small, but he can fight. Don't underestimate him." He stepped away from the table, marking his leave.

"Wait!" Yahshi called.

Pinto looked back at him.

"I just wanted to say thank you," Yahshi said. "For making these last few weeks bearable."

He sighed. "Oh, don't make this goodbye."

"We could lose today," Vell stated.

"I know," Pinto said.

"Then it could be goodbye," she said.

"Yeah..." His voice softened. "I know."

"You'd be a perfect guardian." Vell smiled. "I mean it."

Pinto smiled back, and Yahshi wondered if this would be the last time he'd see him. Perhaps the night he cut Vell's hair would be nothing but the start of what could have been a lifetime of friendship.

"Good luck," Pinto said, and with that, he left the dining hall.

By the time the pinless trainees gathered for the final phase, the redness in Sunna's cheeks had drowned his freckles. His hands were tucked in his pockets, but it was apparent they were shaking.

Yahshi studied Firn next, who was a bit shorter than him. His frailness gave the impression that a punch too hard might snap him in half, but when he met Yahshi's gaze, it was clear he had every intent to claw and bite for a pin.

Vell ignored Yahshi's stare with a gulp, locking her eyes on Commander Roz as they waited for him to commence the final phase. Despite her recent improvements, he surely wouldn't lose against her—but the thought of pushing Vell out of bounds or pinning her down sickened him almost as much as the thought of getting filtered.

Lastly, he observed Amal Travo, a stocky boy who'd beaten Quax in a casual arm-wrestling match a few days prior. He knew little about his fighting skills, but he had a feeling he'd be the most challenging opponent here. Thankfully, Amal was blinking slower than usual—an indicator of belladonna-induced blurry vision. *I'm glad I didn't take the dose yet.*

As Yahshi returned his attention to Commander Roz, his eyes widened with a realization. *There's five of us. How will he assign pairs with an odd amount of trainees?*

The bell rang, and Commander Roz cleared his throat. "This is the final phase. Anyone who does not earn their pin today will be filtered from the program."

The blood rushed to Yahshi's head when Commander Roz looked at him.

"Yahshi Konya, please enter the sparring range. Alone."

Pinto's right. He stepped onto the green zone. *I'm getting filtered for misconduct.*

"Today you acted in aggression without permission from a guardian," Commander Roz said. "The Academy is unlike Sitra Secondary, where instructors may turn a blind eye to behavior like yours. Here, you train responsibly, under guidance."

Just say it. Yahshi clenched his fists at his sides, bracing himself. *Just filter me already.*

"You have sixty seconds to state your case. After your outburst this morning, why *shouldn't* we filter you?"

His fists unraveled. *My case?*

Commander Roz clicked a button on his stopwatch. "You may begin."

Yahshi froze in the green zone. Any reasonable person would argue against violence in response to a verbal attack—but clearly, there was a way to pass this test. Commander Roz was seeking a specific answer. *All I have to do is find it.*

He closed his eyes, recalling the *Capital Weekly* articles he'd read and the messages they implied.

Guardians are honorable.

Guardians don't make mistakes.

Guardians are... perfect.

When he opened his eyes, he wasn't sure how much time had elapsed, but it wouldn't take long to make his point, because the right answer was simple.

"Commander, on our first day in the program, you paired me against Quax for a Defense demonstration."

Yahshi's bold tone made the guardian raise a brow.

"I lost to him because I considered him a close friend, and I would *never* hurt a close friend," he continued. "But he's been tormenting me about my selection ever since."

Commander Roz glanced at his stopwatch, so Yahshi cut to the chase.

"One of the Vows every guardian makes before joining the Force is to support their fellow guardians. A trainee like Quax, who shuns other trainees, will graduate to become a guardian who shuns other guardians. I fought him today because he disrespected me, and I knew that without correction, he would never change."

Yahshi stood tall, hoping his exaggerated confidence would sell the words if they hadn't sold themselves. He had argued *not guilty* because guardians were never guilty. They always did the right thing, even if it wasn't pretty. *And most importantly, guardians know how to tell a great story.*

"You're treading on thin ice," Commander Roz said. With a *click*, he checked his stopwatch and nodded at the time. "With that being said, you did state your case well."

Yahshi couldn't conceal his smile as Commander Roz attached a pin to his collar.

"Congratulations."

"Thank you, Commander," Yahshi said, returning to the sidelines.

Vell smiled grimly at his pin.

"Sunna Rickabee and Amal Travo, please enter the sparring range."

As much as Yahshi wanted to spectate Sunna's match, he knew who Vell's official sparring partner would be, and he had an idea. He led her away from the green zone—far enough so Firn couldn't overhear. He did, however, stare back at them with eyes so large he looked like an owl.

"Crazy eyes," she muttered.

"Vell," Yahshi said, drawing her attention, "Firn was sick during the second phase, so he didn't see your match against Limbo. This is the perfect opportunity to rush him and catch him off-guard. He won't expect you to take initiative."

"Rush him..." She nodded. "Okay."

They returned to the sparring range to see Amal facing Sunna, his face red. His initial plan must have fallen through, and as Pinto had predicted, he didn't have a backup.

Sunna grabbed Amal's wrists and pushed, drilling him into the black zone.

Yahshi wanted to cheer but contained himself.

"Amal, you're filtered from the program," Commander Roz said. "A guardian is waiting in the common room to escort you home."

After a moment of hesitation, Amal left without a word.

They all saw what happened to Durlan Ouzo.

"Congratulations, Sunna," Commander Roz said. "Please see Doctor Blimmery in the infirmary."

Sunna could hardly walk to the door in a straight line, but Yahshi smiled at the pin on his collar. *I wonder if he'll be in class tomorrow.*

Finally, it was Vell and Firn standing on the sparring range, their hands raised.

Yahshi twisted the buttons of his vest as he waited for Commander Roz to start the match. *You can do this, Vell.*

Click. "You may begin."

Vell rushed after her opponent as fast as her legs would carry her.

For a second, Firn froze, paralyzed.

But then he woke himself up.

No, don't do that! Yahshi wanted to shout. *Don't wake yourself up!*

Firn held his ground, refusing to backtrack closer to the black zone. He threw a jab and cross as Vell neared him, which she ducked under, maintaining her forward momentum.

Yahshi held his breath as Vell launched herself at Firn, wrapping her arms around his waist. Together they flew out of the sparring range, several feet off the ground.

Firn's back struck the black zone, and Vell landed over him, pinning him down, her breath racing. Although she didn't see Commander Roz smile, Yahshi did—and it made him smile too.

Vell was the first trainee to throw herself into the black zone along with her opponent. Perhaps many others could have won their matches had they worried less about touching the black zone and more about who would touch it *first*.

You're a genius, Vell.

"Firn Irvine, you're filtered from the program," Commander Roz said.

Vell jumped to her feet, and Yahshi mouthed Commander Roz's next line as he said it.

"A guardian is waiting in the common room to escort you home."

By the time the door slammed shut behind Firn, Vell's collar boasted a golden pin.

Commander Roz nodded at Yahshi and Vell before leaving the room next.

Fourteen trainees remained.

And we're two of them, Yahshi realized, a smile spreading across his face once again. He nearly congratulated Vell, but she embraced him before he could speak.

Yahshi's eyes widened.

"That could have been a disaster." Vell pulled away, her palms resting on his shoulders.

"Yeah." He chuckled. "It could have been."

When Yahshi returned to Room 4, Pinto was writing in bed, too immersed in his words to notice him.

"How are you feeling?" Yahshi asked.

Pinto's hand went limp at the sound of his voice, his pencil slipping onto the blankets. He stared at Yahshi for a few seconds before slamming his journal shut.

"Forget about me!" Pinto jumped to his feet, smiling as he gripped his nightstand to steady himself. "You're here?"

Yahshi flicked his pin. "I'm here."

"And... Vell?"

"She's here too."

Pinto leaned his head back. "Thank the stars! Where is she?"

"Lobby. Talking to Sunna."

Pinto rushed to the door. "I need to congratulate her. And thank her for the belladonna tips. And talk to her." He swung the door open, and Yahshi caught a glimpse of Vell and Sunna playing chess.

"I'll be back," Pinto said over his shoulder. "I wanna hear all about your match."

"I didn't have one."

"How mysterious," Pinto whispered, and left their quarter.

Standing alone in Room 4, Yahshi spotted a glass on his nightstand and laughed. *I never thought I'd be excited to drink poison.*

He stepped onto the balcony with his beet juice, taking in the view. A brief look over the railing made his head spin, but the fear was nothing compared to the fear of getting filtered.

With this realization, he managed to look down again—longer this time. *I can handle the Academy.*

A gentle breeze caressed his face, nature affirming his hypothesis. He raised the glass and took a sip of lukewarm juice.

And there it was—that sweet aftertaste. Belladonna wasn't all that bad. *The guardians only select the exceptional, after all.*

CHAPTER 15

NOT A BUNNY

I vow to guard the lives of those deemed worthy by the Empire.

♬ YOU ARE THE MOON · THE HUSH SOUND ♬

Two days passed before Quax showed up to class again. He had bruises on his face and a thick, white bandage over his nose.

Professor Embre paused her lecture to stare Quax down as he passed her, holding his head low.

"If you're going to show up, show up on time," she said, crossing her arms. "You're either all in or all out, understood?"

"Yes, Professor." Quax sat next to Vell in the front row. "Sorry."

Yahshi stared at the back of Quax's head, waiting for the moment he'd look over his shoulder with a fiery glare. But he never did.

"He's over it," Sunna whispered. "So please just... leave him alone."

Yahshi met Sunna's pleading eyes and gripped his pencil tighter. If anyone needed to leave people alone, it was Quax. But he didn't want to argue with Sunna, of all trainees, so he nodded and continued taking notes on the lecture.

For the next two weeks, Professor Embre introduced the many rules of

Guardian Protocol, the history of their creation, and the varying punishments for breaking them. Pinto quizzed Yahshi and Vell over supper every day, positive their knowledge of Protocol would be crucial for an upcoming filtration.

With Doctor Blimmery, they learned how to prepare belladonna serum and its two remedies—antiserum and neutralizer. Vell tested Yahshi's belladonna detection skills during lunches—and on days when their juice *didn't* contain belladonna, Pinto allowed her to lace his glass with a serum vial she'd stolen from the infirmary. He never felt well, but his tolerance strengthened every day.

Commander Roz began training them in hand-to-hand combat with the addition of daggers, every guardian's secondary tool. Classes ended with casual sparring matches, which Yahshi found himself enjoying now that there was no pressure to win.

The only stressful event of their Defense classes took place when Commander Roz requested they remove their pins. Yahshi braced himself for a filtration, but it turned out that Limbo had complained about having to detach and reattach his pin every day, and some trainees had lost theirs. They were an unnecessary hassle.

As time passed, Quax's nose healed. Yahshi stopped looking over his shoulder in anticipation of his impending vengeance because he realized it would never come. His little speech during the final phase had turned out to be more than a good story—it was reality. A little pain was all it took to eradicate their resentment toward each other, and maybe it was possible to graduate someday and support each other as fellow guardians.

As Professor Embre says...

He passed Quax in the hallway, and they greeted each other with the same emotionless gaze.

United in the Force, we are one.

Yahshi entered the lab to find equipment spread across their tables—beakers, mortars, pestles, and syringes, among others.

Dice hummed, slipping a pair of thick gloves on. "I guess the time has finally come, hasn't it?"

"The time for what?" Yahshi asked.

"Our next filtration, obviously," Keiyo butted in from across the room.

Yahshi flinched at the word *filtration*, and the slamming of Limbo's hands against a table made him flinch a second time.

"Oh, shut it, Keiyo!" Limbo yelled.

"What? Is *filtration* a bad word now?" Keiyo crossed his arms with a grin. "You know the drill. If something's off-routine, we're being tested."

The final phase had taken place two weeks prior, but it felt like a lifetime ago. Yahshi made eye contact with Pinto and Vell before the door busted open, drawing their attention to Doctor Blimmery. He wheeled a metal cart into the room containing fourteen wooden boxes—one for each of them.

"Filtration. I told you so," Keiyo muttered to Limbo.

Yahshi grabbed a pair of black gloves, trying to recall everything he'd learned during Medical lessons, but his thoughts continued to fly away, leaving a single word behind.

Filtration. Filtration. Filtration.

The panicked whispers and scoffs tapered off as Doctor Blimmery's explosive laughter filled the air.

"Oh, relax. Relax! This isn't a filtration, alright? Just a normal exercise to practice what we've been studying so far."

Limbo glared at Keiyo, and Yahshi sighed in unison with the others, his grip on the gloves loosening.

Doctor Blimmery rolled his cart down the aisle, sliding a box in front of each trainee.

Yahshi noticed fur poking through the coin-sized holes in the wood.

"We've covered plenty of Medical material in the past five weeks. It's about time you kids put that knowledge to use." The guardian stopped by his desk and faced them. "Gloves on!"

Yahshi slid his hands into the fabric, which was shiny and smooth on the outside but coarse against his skin. Judging by the equipment on their table, he figured the exercise would involve preparing a belladonna remedy, which Doctor Blimmery had demonstrated on several occasions—although the trainees had never participated before.

Antiserum was the safest remedy, which contained water, ground mustard seeds, and salt. Its purpose was to induce vomiting, but it needed to be ingested almost immediately after belladonna consumption to work, and the intoxicated person would have to be fully conscious while taking it.

The second remedy was neutralizer, used as a last resort if the intoxicated person lost consciousness, consumed belladonna too long beforehand, or failed to recover after taking the antiserum. It was made of calabar beans, a poisonous plant grown in the City Hospital's lab for its medicinal properties. Doctor Blimmery had explained how the toxins of one plant could serve as a remedy for the toxins of another plant with opposite side effects.

How strange it is that the same plant could poison one person but save another, Yahshi had thought. *What differentiates the poison from the cure? The killers from the saviors? The truth from the illusion? Does it all come down to... circumstance?*

"In your box, you'll find a rabbit injected with belladonna," Doctor Blimmery explained. "Your goal is to create a neutralizer out of calabar beans to heal it. I have a bowl of beans on my desk—help yourself as needed. Remember to use gloves, unless you find rashes fun. You're building a tolerance to belladonna, not calabar.

"Prepare the diluted mixture as we've reviewed in class. Don't change the concentration, but *do* change the dose for your rabbit. Like with humans, it should be injected into a muscle, but instead of the shoulder, it'll be the rabbit's front thigh. Be careful with the dose because it's possible to over-correct, in which case you'll poison your rabbit with the cure. You kids following?"

"Yes, Doctor."

"Once you save your rabbit, or *fail* to save your rabbit, find another trainee to shadow until the bell rings." He held his arms out. "Well, what are you waiting for? Those rabbits won't heal themselves!"

Yahshi took a deep breath and opened his wooden box. A white rabbit was lying inside, its stomach rising and falling sporadically, drool dripping from its open mouth. As it trembled, its feet twitched and hit the wood.

Poor thing...

He bit his lip and closed the box. Its life depended on his neutralizer. *But I can't remember the ratio for calabar beans to liters of water.*

On the way to Doctor Blimmery's desk, he glanced at Pinto, who held four fingers up.

One to four. Yahshi grabbed a single bean from the bowl and returned to his table. *Thanks, Pinto.*

He dropped the pea-sized bean into a mortar and smashed it with the pestle until it was fully ground into black powder.

I could throw this in a pepper shaker to kill someone over supper. He chuckled. *But today, I'm using it to save a bunny.*

After verifying that his beaker contained one liter of water, he sprinkled a quarter of the ground bean into it and stirred until the mixture was fully dissolved. One of Doctor Blimmery's previous lectures echoed through his head as he reached for a syringe.

"A human dose contains two milliliters of neutralizer. But for children, this number will be lowered, as it's based on weight."

Weight. I can work with that. He peeked inside the wooden box and estimated that the rabbit weighed about twenty times less than him. *It's not like I have a scale. One-tenth of a milliliter it is.*

He filled multiple syringes with his chosen dose of neutralizer and was the first to complete the preparation stage. Doctor Blimmery nodded in approval from across the room. *Perhaps I wouldn't be a bad fit for Medical.*

He opened his box and gagged as he lifted the drooling creature. When he was younger, he'd imagine catching one someday—but in nature, not a lab.

"I'm sorry, bunny." He held the rabbit down with one hand, gripping the syringe with the other. "It's going to hurt, but you need this."

Sticking the needle into the rabbit's front thigh, he injected the dose. The rabbit squirmed under his hand before settling down, but it wouldn't stop trembling.

Yahshi gritted his teeth and reached for another syringe. He injected a second dose into the rabbit's other thigh and waited for the shaking to stop.

This time, it intensified.

What did I do wrong?

His eyes widened as the rabbit began to spasm. Its stomach swelled under his gloves, which made him push down even harder, as though letting go might result in an explosion.

After struggling in his grip for several seconds, the rabbit stopped moving. Yahshi yanked his hands away.

"No. No, come on! You're okay!" He removed his gloves and held his palms against the rabbit's warm, unmoving fur. "Come on, breathe!"

The eyes of his fellow trainees burned through his skin as he lifted the limp rabbit onto its feet.

Its legs collapsed beneath it.

The bunny's dead. Yahshi slammed two fists against the table and lurched forward, his eyes shut. *The bunny's dead because of me.*

He could hear the clinking of pestles against marble and spoons against glass as the other trainees resumed their work. The noise was sinful. He needed the quiet back to bask in it and think about what he'd done. But everyone was ready to move on.

Everyone's always ready to move on too quickly.

A hand warmed his shoulder, followed by Doctor Blimmery's voice.

"Hey, you made a good effort, kid. You gave your rabbit too much neutralizer, that's all. After the first injection, it takes a few minutes for the effects to kick in. You should wait between ten to twenty minutes before injecting more. The second dose overcorrected, and the neutralizer overpowered the serum. But your estimated dose was excellent, and you did a wonderful job moving quickly—those are important factors when lives are on the line."

"I see." Yahshi opened his eyes and gently placed the rabbit in its casket of a box.

For the remainder of class, he shadowed Dice, watching him finish the preparation of his neutralizer.

After injecting the first dose, they waited a few minutes, and the rabbit miraculously wobbled back to its feet. Dice lifted the rabbit, placed it into his wooden box, and closed the lid so it couldn't escape.

Yahshi stared at the identical boxes, knowing one contained a dead rabbit while the other contained a living one—and that outcome was entirely a result of his error. He could still feel the haunting, ghostly fur against his palms.

To his dismay, he wasn't the only one to perform the exercise poorly.

Sunna mixed too much ground calabar into his beaker, and the first injection was enough to send the rabbit to permanent slumber. "I'm sorry," he said with a stiff upper lip.

Limbo's first dose wasn't enough, and the rabbit stopped breathing before he could inject another. "Oh, for the glory of Vakoi, wake up, you stupid thing!" he shouted.

Quax spent too much time on calculations to ensure the accuracy of his dose, and the rabbit died before he could fill a syringe. "Dammit," he muttered. "My neutralizer's perfect, and I didn't get to use it."

Yahshi sawed his knife through a piece of chicken, took a bite, and willed himself to chew. He'd taken a life that day, and here he was, eating the result of another.

"So, what's your assessment?" Vell pointed to his glass, but he wasn't in the mood to participate in her guessing game. His juice smelled too much like blood.

"We all make mistakes, Yahshi," Pinto said. "It's not easy to gauge how much neutralizer to use, but you'll improve with practice."

"It's dead," Yahshi spat.

"Huh?"

"I killed the bunny, Pinto." He scowled at his friend's oblivious expression. "I had the power to save it, but it died in my hands."

"We're only five weeks into the program." Pinto tilted his head. "We're not expected to be prodigies."

"You don't get it. This has nothing to do with—"

"Let's talk about something else," Vell said.

Before they could, a bout of laughter filled the dining hall. They turned to a group of trainees who were staring at the window in amusement.

Sunna was kneeling in the field, digging with a flat stone. At his side were four wooden boxes.

"Poor Sunna," said Vell.

"Wow. He's slipping, isn't he?" said Pinto.

Sunna stared back at them through the window. Tears streamed down his cheeks, but he wiped them away and resumed his digging.

I can't allow myself to slip. Yahshi raised his glass. *I need to pull myself together.*

His juice tasted like blood too.

CHAPTER 16

INFILTRATION

I vow to embody guardian ideals with a refined public image.

♫ FLICKERS · SON LUX ♫

It was forty-three days after the neutralizer exercise when Yahshi turned sixteen. He woke up thinking about his father, who was fading into a distant memory. Pinto and Vell were starting to feel like his real family, and the Academy more like his real home.

He frowned at the sound of blankets rustling from across the quarter.

"Yahshi?" Pinto whispered. "Do you hear that?"

Footsteps on the balcony made them jolt upright into seated positions. A silhouette loomed behind the glass door, but it was too dark to discern its face.

"Who's there?" Yahshi yelled.

The door slid open, inviting a gust of air into their quarter.

They jumped out of bed as the figure entered. Curtains billowed around it like ghosts.

"Happy birthday," said a familiar voice.

Yahshi sighed in relief, but his heart wouldn't stop racing. "Not funny!

You scared us."

"How the hell did you get up here?" Pinto asked.

"Balcony," Vell replied.

"Well, yeah," Yahshi said. "But... you climbed?"

"You could have knocked," Pinto added.

"Vell," Yahshi said. "*Why?*"

She shrugged. "I just wanted to see if I could."

"Ah, typical." Pinto shivered and gestured to the balcony. "Close the door, please. It's freezing."

Vell closed it, and Yahshi lit the lantern on his nightstand.

"Birthdays aren't a big deal here, you know." He looked up to see her sitting on his bed. "The program doesn't schedule time for cake."

"I know." She smiled. "But my family would always wish me happy birthday first thing in the morning. Feels wrong not to do the same for you."

He tucked his hands into his pockets, smiling back. "Well, if we're still here in three months, I'll be sure to return the favor."

She glanced at the balcony. "Minus the climb, of course."

"Why do you say that?"

"We've seen you climb during stealth exercises," Pinto chimed in.

Vell nodded. "You climb like a five-year-old."

"Oh, come on..." Yahshi said. "I'm not *that* bad."

"Admit it." Pinto pointed at him. "You're afraid of heights."

"I am *not* afraid of heights."

Vell burst into laughter.

"Alright, get out!" Yahshi gestured to the lobby door. "We need to get ready."

"Fine." She looked back as she left. "I'll see you in the dining hall."

He offered an exaggerated wave.

Over breakfast, Pinto and Vell discussed their theories about the next filtration. After two months of waiting, it was starting to feel like folklore.

Meanwhile, Yahshi focused on Sunna, who was smiling with Quax and Keiyo as usual. Ever since the neutralizer exercise, he'd been acting like the rabbit burial in the field had never happened, and everyone was playing along with it.

"Hey, Sunna?" Yahshi asked during Research class. "Have you been feeling better?"

"What do you mean?" Sunna replied.

"I mean, are you sure you're okay?"

He laughed. "I'm fine, Yahshi."

The bell rang, and they stood without thinking. It was all part of the routine.

"I pledge my allegiance to the Vakoi Empire."

It was what they did. It was what they said.

They retook their seats, and Yahshi continued. "If you ever want to talk about—"

"Yahshi," Professor Embre scolded, "enough mumbling back there."

He shut his mouth—not only because she'd told him to but also because she was holding a threatening stack of pages.

"I'll get straight to the point. We pushed you to your limits during your first month here, and since then, we've given you plenty of space to recover. Now it's time to get back to business."

The air thickened. The Academy had started to feel like an ordinary school, but now they were on that tightrope again.

"In today's filtration, you'll be handed various fictitious documents, including criminal profiles, interrogation transcripts, and witness reports. Your task is to assign three fictitious criminals to their punishments based on your memory of Guardian Protocol. You have one hour to make your matches with no reference to your notes or discussion amongst each other. Any trainee who fails to match all three criminals correctly will be filtered from the program."

It's a good thing I've been reviewing Protocol, Yahshi thought, and Pinto glanced at him as though he were saying, *You're welcome.*

Yahshi started by organizing his documents by criminal name. He read through each stack thoroughly before referring to his answer sheet, which listed three names on the left and three punishments on the right.

He had an easy time with two of the matches. According to Protocol, the first criminal was caught drug dealing and deserved ten years in detainment. The second criminal had insulted a guardian, earning himself three years of community service. Yahshi drew two lines, connecting their names to their corresponding punishments.

The third criminal, however, unsettled him. The fictitious guardian had broken a Vow by failing to report his brother's involvement with the Underground. Yahshi empathized with the guardian, who simply wanted to keep his brother safe. He wished he could make an exception to Protocol, just for him.

But there was no fourth option to draw a line to, so he matched the criminal to the death penalty and turned his paper in.

Twelve days later, Yahshi had already forgotten the name of the trainee who failed their criminal matching filtration. He had become a master of forgetting the unimportant.

"So..." Vell pointed to his glass. "What's your assessment?"

His beet juice tasted the same as it always did, so he checked to see if Pinto's face had turned red. Unfortunately, his roommate had yet to touch his glass.

"You're a cheat," Vell said, noticing his attempted shortcut.

"Your game's no fun," Yahshi said.

"Why? Is it too hard for you?"

He took another sip and analyzed the aftertaste, but he couldn't detect anything sweet.

"No serum," he concluded.

Vell said nothing.

"Well?" he prodded. "Am I right?"

She took a sip of her own juice. "I'll tell you in a few minutes. You may change your mind."

"How dare you?"

Yahshi's smile faded when he noticed Pinto scowling at his plate. He hadn't been acting like himself since a Defense class the week prior, when Commander Roz introduced them to the Force's three primary tools—bow and arrows, dual swords, and throwing blades. On an undisclosed date, they would need to excel with one tool of choice, and Pinto had yet to show an interest in any of them.

"You take this detection thing too seriously, Vell." Pinto sipped his juice like he knew he'd said something wrong and wanted to wash the words away.

But Vell wouldn't let it slide. "Detection is Yahshi's weakest skill, and at some point, we'll be tested on it."

Pinto looked away. They could never take any skill in the program too seriously, and he knew it.

"I was thinking we could help you with tools during recreation time today," she added.

"Why's that?"

"You haven't performed well with any of them."

"It's only been a few days," Yahshi said with a chuckle. "I'm sure he'll connect with a tool eventually. I mean, I didn't think dual swords were right for me at first, but they're growing on me."

"*Exactly.*" Pinto narrowed his eye at Vell. "You're acting like I'm the only one who hasn't chosen a tool yet."

"I'm surprised." She studied his defensive expression, her gaze softening. "You don't normally cut yourself any slack."

"We've had a busy few months," Yahshi argued. "I think he deserves a little slack."

"I'm not cutting myself slack, okay?" Pinto said, raising his voice. "You're biased—both of you. It's not my fault you picked your tools so quickly."

"True." Vell pointed her fork at him. "But it is your fault that *you* haven't."

Pinto glared at her before continuing to eat.

Yahshi was already brainstorming a new topic of discussion when Vell piped up again, reigniting the fire.

"I'm only trying to help," she said.

"Maybe that's the problem." Pinto slammed his fork down. "You're always getting involved when it's none of your business. Why don't you worry about your own performance?"

"Pinto," Yahshi warned through gritted teeth.

"Because that's not how the three of us work. We made a deal to look out for each other." She wiped her hands on a table napkin and stood, signaling her leave. "Would you rather I care about you, or your ego?"

Pinto looked up at her with a widened eye. "Wait, Vell..." He shook his head. "I'm sorry. I think the poison's making me irritable again."

"There was no belladonna today." She faced Yahshi with a nod. "Good job."

As she left for the door, Pinto covered his face with his palms.

"Hey," Yahshi said, leaning toward him, "remember when you were worried about me getting filtered for misconduct? You reminded me that we're in this together. She's just doing her part."

"I know," he said, hidden behind his hands.

"It's not shameful to accept help. Like you said, we're not expected to be prodigies."

Pinto sighed as he dropped his hands. "I know..."

The air was poisonous that afternoon. They practiced their tools on different sides of the training room and chatted with boys from other social circles. Yahshi knew Vell wasn't holding a grudge against him, but she also seemed to want nothing to do with anything related to Pinto.

They sat together as usual during supper, but the silence dragged on.

By the time they returned to their quarters, Yahshi had given up on the day, hoping they'd cool down overnight. He was about to get into bed when Pinto started tying his bootlaces.

"Where are you going?"

"Training room," Pinto answered.

"It's late."

"I have some catching up to do." He headed for the door.

"Wait!" Yahshi slipped his boots on. "I'll come with you."

"In your pajamas?"

"What? Is it against the rules?"

Pinto shrugged with a frown. "Hopefully not."

They entered the lobby, and Yahshi stopped when Pinto approached Room 1 instead of the staircase. He knocked on the door.

Vell was still in uniform when she opened it. Her bold stare demanded words, and Pinto seemed to break under the pressure. He stood frozen, speechless.

She looked to Yahshi for an explanation, and he tucked his hands into his pockets, diverting his gaze to establish himself as an innocent bystander.

"I..." Pinto sighed, finally gathering his words. "I want you to care about me, not my ego."

Yahshi cracked a grin, and Vell joined them in the lobby.

"Let's go," she said.

Yahshi dismounted a pair of swords from the wall. He'd grown used to their weight, and he cringed at the memory of nearly dropping them during his first practice session.

He demonstrated a sequence he'd been working on, swinging the blades in clean strikes. The moves were rhythmic and unexpected at times but always in perfect timing.

I bet it'd look beautiful with music, he thought, which made him cringe. He would never say such a thought aloud. Through observation he'd learned that guardians enjoyed the arts but never participated. It wasn't their place.

Yahshi ended the set of twenty motions in his starting position—one blade running down the right side of his back and the other pointing up toward his left shoulder.

"I never actually watched you perform a full sequence. It's incredible." Pinto raised a set of wooden practice swords. "But would you mind showing me an easier one?"

As they rehearsed the basic strikes and blocks, Vell sat cross-legged on the floor, spinning a four-bladed throwing star between her thumb and index finger. Yahshi was correcting the transition of Pinto's grip on the handle when the door slid open.

"You kids are up late," Doctor Blimmery said. "I was about to exercise."

"At this hour?" Vell asked.

"Insomnia," the guardian replied.

"Oh," Yahshi said. "Well, we can—"

"No, you should stay. Motivation is a fleeting gift. I'd never knock it down while it's flying." His eyes drifted to Pinto with a grin. "Swords, huh? Always thought you'd be an archer."

"*Hilarious*, Doctor," Pinto said.

He laughed. "Ah, that's good. You think I'm joking, don't you?"

"I have *one eye*."

Yahshi and Vell struggled to suppress their laughter.

"I would think that'd give you an advantage, considering how archers close an eye to aim." Doctor Blimmery retreated into the hallway. "Goodnight!"

The door slid shut, concealing him from view.

"Huh," Yahshi said after a moment of thought. "Well, he does have a point."

"I suppose I've never given the bow and arrow a fair chance," Pinto admitted.

Yahshi and Vell made eye contact before springing into action. While he mounted the swords, she fetched a bow and a quiver of arrows.

Pinto stared at the foreign tool in his hands before getting into position. With his eye on the target, he drew the bow, aimed, and released.

The arrow soared across the room before striking one of the smaller rims of the target.

Yahshi's jaw dropped, and Vell smiled.

"Wow." Pinto lowered his bow. "Maybe Doctor *Blim Blim* isn't all that bad after all."

Yahshi circled around him. "Look at you! One eye and a giant bow in your hands. Talk about intimidating."

"And still, somehow, childish." Vell kicked a tin of arrows toward him. "Finish these up. I need to quiz Yahshi on Medical."

"Have him quiz you on Protocol too." Pinto plucked an arrow from the tin. "Let's not forget how you nearly sentenced a man to three years of community service for drug dealing."

Her face drained of color. "I shouldn't have told you."

Pinto chuckled, but Yahshi questioned her strained voice.

"Would you mind fetching a book from my quarter?" she asked Yahshi in a softer tone. "It's the red one. It'll help you memorize bone names."

He nodded. "Got it."

Pinto shot another arrow, which struck even closer to the bullseye.

"Take that, target," he spat.

Yahshi stared at the arrow for a few seconds before leaving.

On his way to the staircase, he stopped to observe a speck of light through a hallway window. *Maybe it's fireflies. Are fireflies that bright?*

With a frown, he descended to the second floor and grabbed the red book from Vell's quarter.

He nearly headed back up to the training room, but the thought of that unusual glow stopped him again. *Could it be a lantern?*

He entered the common room instead and crept past the door to the guardian quarters. His eyes widened at a metal bar on the floor.

Through the window, he confirmed that the speck of light was a lantern. The trainee holding it stood at the outskirts of the field, dressed in identical pajamas. He was speaking to a cloaked figure on a black horse.

The Academy horses are white.

Yahshi set Vell's book on the floor and stepped into the chilling air. By the time he scaled the front steps to the courtyard, the trainee was heading back to the building, and the cloaked figure was galloping into the woods.

He ducked behind a bush and peered over it. The trainee entered the courtyard, his face partially blocked by his raised lantern, but his neon bandana gave him away.

The bush rustled when Yahshi lowered his head, and Dice's footsteps vanished.

He held his breath.

A few moments later, Dice resumed walking—but he was heading toward the bush, not the front door. It was clear he knew where Yahshi was hiding. *I guess our field lessons really do pay off.*

Knowing he'd find him eventually, Yahshi popped up from behind the bush.

Dice froze. "How long have you been out here?"

"We're not supposed to see outsiders," Yahshi stated.

Dice's lantern illuminated the horror on his face. They both knew the conditions in the contract they'd signed on Selection Day. Although the guardians hadn't explicitly outlined the consequences of breaking them, they were bound to those contracts in blood, and that implied enough.

"If you tell the guardians, I'll lie, and you won't have proof." Dice's voice trembled, and Yahshi could tell he was bluffing.

"Was that a relative?"

Dice looked away. "Yes."

"You're lying, aren't you?"

No response.

"Dice, what's going on?"

"There are things I can't tell you," he said, a chuckle slipping through his words.

Yahshi frowned at his misplaced humor.

"Listen," Dice continued, "you're not safe here. You need to get filtered for your own sake."

"Why?"

He stepped toward Yahshi, who resisted the urge to step back. "You should have listened to your father on Selection Day."

Yahshi stumbled as if the words Dice had thrown held real, physical weight. "How do you know about that?"

Dice hurled his lantern at the ground, and it shattered as many more questions piled up in Yahshi's throat, fighting each other to break free.

The air darkened, and Dice ran.

Chasing after him, Yahshi's boot snagged a piece of the broken lantern. He stumbled, crashing head-first onto the courtyard with his chin grazing the bricks. Shards of glass cut into his wrists as he pushed himself up.

I can't catch up to him.

He ignored the blood dripping down his palms and trudged his way up the front steps. A neigh echoed in the distance, followed by galloping, and when he looked back, a white horse disappeared into the woods.

"Help!" He bolted into the common room and pounded on the door to the guardian quarters. "Guardians! Help!"

He didn't stop knocking and shouting until the door opened.

Doctor Blimmery's jaw dropped. "Yahshi!"

"I-It's Dice."

"You're bleeding!"

"H-He's gone."

CHAPTER 17

JUST A BUNNY

I vow to treat Royal Family members with impeccable
manners and respect.

♫ SORROW - THE NATIONAL ♫

The Academy guardians called a meeting in the common room first thing in the morning. Some trainees eyed Yahshi's wrist and chin bandages or looked around for Dice, but no one said a word. Perhaps their fear of a surprise filtration outweighed their curiosity about a few minor peculiarities.

"We're granting you a day off," Professor Embre announced, "but it's not for a good reason." She gestured to Commander Roz, who cleared his throat.

"The entire Bayin family, including Dice, went missing last night," he said. "We believe they may be false converts spying for the Underground."

Trainees turned to Pinto, whose face drained of color. His intuition had been right all along.

"We're lucky Yahshi caught him meeting with a stranger last night," Doctor Blimmery said. "If he hadn't seen him, we'd still have a spy living among us."

Trainees turned to Yahshi next, whose throat tightened at the weight of the lie he'd told the Academy guardians.

"What did Dice say after you confronted him?" Commander Roz had asked the night prior.

"Nothing. He just panicked, and ran."

When the bell called them for breakfast an hour later, Pinto didn't show. Yahshi and Vell figured he needed time alone to process the news, but his absence from lunch forced them to search the grounds.

It took half an hour to find him. He was sitting outside on the grass, leaning against the stable, his eye locked on the woods Dice had fled through.

"I'm sorry," Vell said, sitting beside him.

Pinto nearly shuffled away but didn't, perhaps to spare her feelings.

"You can go," he choked out. "You can just—"

His trembling lower lip stopped him from saying more as he lurched forward, gripping his vest to fend off tears. The Underground had infiltrated the Force's military program, proving they were planning to strike again. It was eye-gouging last time. What next?

"You don't have to push us away." Vell wrapped her arm around him. "You can let us care."

Pinto inhaled a few stifled breaths before leaning into her shoulder. He sobbed as though he had lost his eye right then and there, as though he were reliving the memory. Vell ran her fingers along his curls.

But Yahshi could only watch.

For the following week, Pinto spent recreation time in the woods, shooting arrows at trees for hours.

When Commander Roz revealed it was time for their primary tool filtration, most trainees stepped back, but Pinto stepped forward, his chin high.

"I'll go first."

His voice was deeper now, and Yahshi didn't like it.

"You'll have three chances to hit the bullseye." Commander Roz pointed to a target across the room, then to a string on the floor.

Pinto positioned himself behind the string, drawing his bow. He stared at that target as though it were a traitor—as though it were Dice Bayin himself.

The arrow shot across the room, striking the bullseye on his first try.

Yahshi flinched at the impact.

"Wonderfully done," Commander Roz said.

A boy named Brasher Marz failed the filtration, butchering the moves in a dual sword sequence. Unlike those filtered before him, he smiled and said goodbye to the eleven remaining trainees, patting Yahshi on the shoulder as though they were friends when they'd only spoken once or twice.

As Brasher strode to the door, ready to leave a marvelous building he would never reenter, Yahshi wondered if he'd botched the sequence on purpose.

He practiced it flawlessly yesterday.

During supper, there was something different about Pinto—something unsettling about the way he dragged his knife through a piece of flesh that had once been part of a living, breathing cow.

Yahshi left the table without a word, racing to the library.

Instead of questioning where my parents were from, Dice asked where my father *was from.* He paced down an aisle, rubbing the scab on his chin. *He also said, the sky weeps with us.*

Yahshi slowed to a stop, eyes on his boots. *Strangest of all, he knows I didn't listen to my father on Selection Day. But how?*

The library door creaked open, followed by footsteps.

The only explanation is that my father has a connection to the Bayins. He thought of their criminal matching filtration and shivered.

"Yahshi?"

He took a deep breath and emerged from the aisle, entering the open study space.

"Is something wrong?" Vell asked, approaching him.

He held his hands behind his back, diverting his gaze. "Why do you ask?"

"You ran off during supper."

Right.

He could feel her searching for his eyes, but he refused to look at her. *If I look at her, I might tell her.*

"I understand why Pinto's been acting weird," she said, "but I never expected this from you. You've been so... *distant* lately."

"Well, I didn't mean to be," Yahshi said. "I'm just stressed."

"Stressed about what?" There was a pause, but he didn't fill it.

"Talk to me," she pressed.

I wish I could, Vell. But the information was too risky. He'd lied to the guardians about what Dice said. His father might have been a false convert. He needed to come clean to the Force about both of those facts, but he knew he wouldn't. And by sealing his lips, he made himself a criminal.

"Thank you," he said, hugging her. "But really, I'm okay."

Despite Pinto's daily inquiries, Professor Embre never provided any updates on the Bayins—because there *were no updates* on the Bayins. According to her, the case was still unsolved, efforts to trace their location had failed, and the Research Division was just as frustrated as Pinto was.

They should be working harder, Pinto would argue. *They should be searching every nook and cranny of the island. Actually, you know what? They should be searching the ocean. Send the boats! Lace the tools! What are they waiting for?*

He was so focused on the Bayin case that even the slightest diversion from the topic left him fuming—and at this point, everything was a diversion because no one was talking about the case but him.

Yahshi wished he would stop talking about it.

But he didn't. Day after day, Pinto brought up the case Yahshi secretly hoped would never be solved.

Thirty-two days of his complaining passed before Doctor Blimmery wheeled a second cart of rabbits into the lab.

"I know the recent weeks have been challenging for you kids." He slid a box in front of each trainee as he made his way down the aisle, Professor Embre trailing behind him. "It's clear the Underground is planning something, but moping around isn't going to fix that."

"In today's filtration, we'll be testing your restraint," Professor Embre said. "Guardians face challenges that require quick yet thoughtful solutions. To make the right moves under pressure, it's crucial to resist emotional interference."

Doctor Blimmery stopped by his desk. "Boxes open!"

Inside Yahshi's box was a rabbit—and a dagger.

"You kids know the drill. You fail this test, we send you home." He clicked a button on his stopwatch. "You have five minutes to kill a rabbit."

What?

Yahshi knew the Force dealt with the most dangerous criminals on the island, but he hadn't internalized the reality that as a guardian, he might sometimes have to kill.

It's just a bit of a shock, that's all, he told himself. *But it makes sense. It does.*

Limbo was the first to lift his rabbit out of the box. It was trembling and drooling, injected with belladonna for an effortless kill.

He raised his dagger, and after taking a breath, dropped the blade through its neck.

Yahshi's stomach churned as blood dripped from the table, forming a puddle around Limbo's boots.

Sunna turned away. "For the glory of—"

"I'm gonna be sick," Ceylon said, gripping his neck.

Limbo yanked the dagger out of the rabbit's body. "There!" His grip on the handle tightened as he turned to the guardians. "Is that what you want?"

"Thank you, Limbo," Professor Embre said in a monotone.

"You're welcome, *Professor*. You are *so welcome* for mindlessly taking a life!"

Doctor Blimmery looked up anxiously from his stopwatch, but he said nothing.

"Thank you, Limbo," Professor Embre repeated, sharper this time. "You're dismissed."

"Excuse me?"

"You're filtered from the program."

"I'm filtered? For what? Not killing a bunny with a smile on my face? I'm filtered for showing even an *ounce* of empathy?" He scoffed, staring at the blood around his boots. "This rabbit isn't a traitor to the Vakoi Empire. It's not like it's a spy for the Underground. It's just a bunny, Professor."

"That's true. It's just a bunny."

"You can't filter him," Ceylon protested. "He did what you asked!"

"Drop it, Ceylon," Keiyo warned.

"You know what?" Limbo shouted. "I'm out! I'm filtering *myself* from the program. If *this* is what it means to be a guardian, then I want no part of it."

"You've *been* filtered." Professor Embre pointed to the door. "A guardian is waiting in the common room to escort you home. Leave now, Limbo. Don't test me."

Yahshi held his breath, mentally willing him to comply. *Just leave already. Don't make her snap.*

After a moment of contemplation, Limbo grunted, tossing his dagger at the floor. He left a trail of scarlet footprints behind him as he stormed down the aisle.

"Please, Professor!" Ceylon pleaded.

"One more word out of you, and you'll leave with your brother."

Ceylon opened his mouth again, but Limbo stopped and looked back at him. "You heard her. Not another word. If *this* is your path, then by all means, follow it. But it's not mine."

And with the slam of a door, Limbo was gone. The dripping of blood from his table echoed in the silence.

"Three minutes," Doctor Blimmery said in a strained voice.

Yahshi held a blank expression, removing the rabbit and dagger from his box. Limbo's filtration had proven that to pass the test, they must not only complete the task but also remain calm while doing so.

He brought the blade to the rabbit's neck, but his arm stopped as though someone had snatched it.

Like Limbo said, it's just a bunny, and the bunny did nothing wrong.

But it's just a bunny. It's not like it's a living, breathing human, right?

It's just a bunny. What does that mean?

Yahshi loosened his grip on the handle, pausing to observe his fellow trainees.

Pinto decapitated his rabbit and cringed as blood spilled over his table. He searched for a rag to clean the mess.

Vell located her rabbit's heart and stabbed it swiftly, removing the blade with clean palms.

Quax punctured his rabbit's stomach. It struggled in pain, but a few extra stabs finished the job.

"Two minutes," Doctor Blimmery said.

As Pinto, Vell, and Quax headed for the door, Ceylon looked back at them. For a moment, Yahshi thought he was planning to filter himself and leave with his brother—but instead, he swiped the dagger from his table and impaled his rabbit.

Sunna dropped his tool on the table post-kill, struggling to steady his breaths. The task had visibly moved him, but not enough to fail. He left the room with Ceylon.

"One minute," Doctor Blimmery warned.

Yahshi held the rabbit down. Its fur was soft, and so, so warm.

Only five trainees will emerge as guardians, Yahshi reminded himself, gripping the dagger tighter. *I won't let a bunny stop me from winning.*

With a push, he brought the blade through its neck, and warm blood covered his hands like a pair of mittens.

Four trainees, including Limbo, had failed the restraint filtration.

So many empty tables. Yahshi looked around the dining hall. *So much empty space.*

Vell didn't bother testing Yahshi's belladonna detection skills. After a few bites of bread, she leaned back, watching droplets race down the window.

It was storming outside, the clouds darker than charcoal.

"Look." Pinto pointed to the glass. "He's out there again."

The rain made it hard to see, but in the distance, a trainee was dragging a cart of wooden boxes across the field.

Vell shook her head. "He's been slipping."

"It was only a matter of time," Pinto replied.

Keiyo's voice caught Yahshi's attention from across the dining hall. "Quax, we should talk to him. At this rate, he'll get himself filtered."

"Maybe it's better that way." Quax peeled his eyes from the window. "Let's face it—Sunna doesn't like the program. He never has."

Pinto and Vell called after Yahshi as he burst from his seat and bolted away. He slammed the dining hall door behind him and left the building as fast as he could, entering a battlefield of hammering rain that struck his skin with the force of a thousand tiny darts.

When he caught up to Sunna, he dropped to his knees and dug with his hands, helping him deepen the grave. The first dead rabbit they placed in the hole made Sunna's face contort, shedding tears.

It was missing its head.

That's Pinto's, Yahshi recalled, his stomach churning at the memory.

They added the other rabbits next, blood covering their calloused palms, but it had to be done. Someone had to do the dirty work.

Sunna didn't say a word to Yahshi until they were finished, covered in mud, standing by a heaping pile of dirt.

"Do you ever wonder if you'd be happier back home?" Sunna asked. His voice was hollow, and Yahshi was certain he was staring into the eyes of a ghost.

After lunch, Commander Roz called a meeting in the lobby to announce their updated living arrangements. With ten available quarters and only seven trainees remaining, there wasn't a need for roommates anymore.

Yahshi watched Pinto clear out his drawers and stack his fresh uniforms, preparing to move out of Room 4. *We've been drifting apart, and this is the grand finale.*

Pinto stopped at the door and sighed. "Yahshi, are you okay?"

Yahshi frowned, nearly convinced he'd heard him wrong. He couldn't remember the last time Pinto had spoken to him seriously.

"I'm fine," he said. "I felt bad for Sunna. That's all it was."

Pinto nodded before leaving their shared quarter for the last time.

After showering and changing into a fresh uniform, the bell called Yahshi to Defense class. He ignored it, waiting for the departing footsteps of his fellow trainees to disappear before sitting on a sofa in the lobby.

What do I do?

He plucked a pawn from a chessboard and rolled the piece between his thumb and forefinger. The Force could trace the Bayins at any time, and he couldn't shake his paranoia about their potential connection to Martu. *It's not like I can leave the grounds to ask Father about this.*

One of the quarter doors creaked open, and Yahshi looked up to see Vell leaving Room 1.

"Hi," she muttered. Her eyes were red.

He raised his palm in a brief wave.

She joined him on the sofa, her hands trembling as she folded them in her lap. He could tell she was trying to say something, so he set the pawn down.

"I can't..." Vell wiped a stray tear from her cheek. "I can't do this any longer."

He frowned. "What are you saying?"

"I'm filtering myself from the program." She leaned forward, her hair falling to shield her face. "I'm done."

"Hey, I-I know that the bunnies—"

"This isn't about that," she snapped. "Yahshi, there's a reason why I have so much knowledge about belladonna."

"You read about it in books," he said, more like a question than a statement.

"Not just books. Without enough money for my mother's medicine, my family took desperate measures."

"Belladonna only grows in the City Hospital's lab." He wanted to prove her story was false because he knew it couldn't be good.

"You can find it elsewhere if you know where to look, or who to ask. For a certain type, there's an element of thrill to the plant's effects." Vell traced a finger along the lines in her palm. "After I read about its medicinal benefits, my father bought some pots from a drug dealer. While he worked, I skipped classes to care for my mother and experiment with the plant. I got rashes at first, but eventually, nothing. I was unintentionally building a tolerance all that time."

"Vell…" Yahshi said, his voice shaky. "Why were you selected?"

"You can't speak of this." She leaned in, staring boldly into his eyes. "To anyone. Ever."

"I promise."

She looked away and took a deep breath. "Someone reported my father for possession. We never found out who," she began. "It was Selection Season at the time, so Doctor Blim was available to investigate. He burst into our home and caught me with belladonna berries in my hands.

"That should have been the end of the story. He was supposed to detain me, but when he saw my mother in bed, he started to ask about her condition, then about belladonna and general knowledge of medicine. It was like he was… testing me. He gave me this long stare and then he just… left. He broke Protocol that day, and a few weeks later, I was selected."

She met his gaze again, her eyes widening.

"I-I shouldn't…" Vell buried her face in her hands, muffling her voice. "I shouldn't have told you."

Yahshi wrapped his arm around her and pulled her closer. Unlike his choice to kill the rabbit, he'd done so without hesitation.

"It's okay. I'm on your side, alright?"

"Five years for possession," she said. "Death for Doctor Blim."

"What?"

"That's what we'll be sentenced to if the Force finds out." Her voice weakened. "Five years for me. Death for him."

Yahshi closed his eyes with a sigh. "Filtering yourself isn't the answer, Vell."

"There's no space here. You're either a guardian or a rabbit. You can't be both."

"Listen, you've made it this far without anyone finding out, and I won't tell a soul."

She sniffled. "Not even Pinto?"

He shook his head. "*Especially* not Pinto."

They sat in silence for a while, until Yahshi spoke again.

"I have something to tell you too. It's about Dice, and my father..."

CHAPTER 18

HAPPY BIRTHDAY

I vow to reject emotion when faced with moral quandary.

♫ SPARROW - THE HUNTS ♫

"I didn't see you in the dining hall today," Yahshi said.

"I'm not too hungry."

With a sigh, he sat next to Ceylon on the courtyard bench. They stared at the Emperor's statue, which was covered in dewdrops. Puddles on the bricks reflected clouds that were still dark and heavy after the night-long storm.

"I'm sorry about Limbo," Yahshi said, breaking the silence, "but do you remember what you told me, back when we first met?"

"I can't say I do."

"You told me that guardianship has always been *your* thing, not his."

Ceylon finally faced him. "It's true," he said, managing a small grin. "I bet he's much better off at home right now—writing stuff, painting things, not being angry all the time like he was here... But I wish he hadn't left the way he did."

Yahshi gulped at the memory of a hole packed with rabbits. He spotted a brown patch of dirt in the field and diverted his gaze.

"If he hadn't blown up over that *stupid* bunny," Ceylon continued, raising his voice, "maybe he'd end up liking—"

"You must be starving," Yahshi said, eager to change the subject. "Why don't you come to supper? You can sit with us."

Ceylon took a deep breath, his shoulders loosening. "Actually, I *am* pretty hungry," he admitted, and they headed to the dining hall together.

Pinto poked at his food, not bothering to acknowledge the newcomer, while Vell stared with an intensity that made Ceylon shift in his seat. He forced a smile, and when she didn't smile back, Yahshi had no choice but to jump in.

"So, what was it like growing up in Vakoi City?" he asked. "You saw guardians a lot, didn't you?"

"Oh, all the time," Ceylon replied, trying to catch Pinto's eye. "They practically run the capital."

Vell stabbed a piece of chicken with her fork and studied its flesh. "In Miranda, guardians only show up if there's bad news."

Pinto stood from his seat, and Vell continued eyeing the chicken while his footsteps echoed away.

"Sorry," Ceylon said, "I shouldn't have—"

"No, it's not your fault," Yahshi said.

"He does that sometimes," Vell added, finally taking her bite.

Six weeks later, Yahshi and Ceylon entered the training room to find Vell and Keiyo preparing for a casual competition. As the only trainees remaining with throwing blades as their primary tool, they'd started to spend a chunk of recreation time practicing together. Yahshi didn't enjoy the thought of Vell mingling with the other group. *But I still talk to Sunna on occasion, so I can't complain.*

"No spin technique." Keiyo tossed a dart into the air and caught it by its handle. "Let's go."

"Target Bird or Target Turtle?" Vell asked.

"You *named* the targets?" Ceylon said.

"After animals?" Yahshi chuckled. "What's wrong with you two?"

Vell smiled at their arrival, but Keiyo ignored them, pointing to the closer target.

"Bird," he answered.

"You first." Vell tied her hair into a low ponytail, which she could finally do now that it'd grown past her shoulders.

Yahshi and Ceylon sat on the floor, watching Keiyo as he aimed his dart, shuffling in place. He couldn't seem to find the right stance.

"What are you doing here?" Keiyo peered down at them and scoffed. "Go practice with your own tools."

"We're spectating your game." Yahshi leaned back and propped himself up with his arms.

"Yeah, I'd hate to miss the awesome shot you're about to make," Ceylon said.

Keiyo shook his head, refocusing on the target. With a swing of his arm, he threw the dart, and it struck just a finger's width from the bullseye.

"Hah!" He crossed his arms, facing his opponent. "Beat that, Vell. Let's see you try."

"I'll try." She plucked a dart from the bandolier across her chest and sent it flying.

Keiyo flinched when the tool landed next to his, striking the bullseye.

She faced him with a blank expression. "I win."

"*Yeah right,*" Keiyo argued, and his defensive nature made Yahshi laugh. "The challenge was to use a *no-spin* technique. Your dart definitely spun."

"It definitely did not," Vell said.

"You were watching, right?" He turned to Yahshi and Ceylon. "Did it spin?"

"Oh yeah, it spun." Yahshi forced his grin away. "Many times."

"Probably a thousand times." Ceylon twirled his finger. "So quickly the spins couldn't be seen by the human eye."

Vell laughed, and Keiyo rolled his eyes. "Your friends are assholes, Vell. Let's start a new game."

As they prepared for another round, Yahshi's gaze wandered to the wall.

Somewhere outside, Pinto was aiming arrows at tree trunks, unable to move on from the unsolved Bayin case. And here he and Vell were, enjoying their time without him, shouldering the guilt but giving up on relieving it.

"Hey, I have an idea." Ceylon nudged his side. "Let *me* talk to Pinto."

Yahshi raised his brows. He didn't consider Ceylon a particularly close friend, even after eating meals together for weeks, but there were moments that tried to prove him wrong.

"That's nice of you, but even Vell can't talk any sense into him."

"Just give me a chance, Yahshi. What do you have to lose?"

He considered the offer before raising his voice. "Hey, Vell! We'll be right back."

"Oh, take your time," Keiyo said, spinning a throwing star in his hand. "*Please.*"

On their way out, Ceylon slung a bow and a quiver of arrows over his back. He rushed down the staircase so quickly that Yahshi could barely keep up with him.

"What's your plan, exactly?"

Ceylon slowed his pace, glancing back at him. "I realized that you and Vell are too soft."

"What?"

"You and Vell. You talk to Pinto like you're coaxing a little boy out of bed. But the boy is tired, the blankets are warm, and the air is *so* cold. Sometimes you have to rip the blankets off."

"I'm not following."

"Pinto is stubborn, okay? You can't baby him." Ceylon chucked an imaginary object across the common room. "You have to throw common sense at him like a rock to the skull."

"How do you come up with those analogies on the spot?"

"It's an art form. Years of practice."

As they stepped outside, Yahshi folded his arms. The weather had been getting even colder, and the wind amplified the chill.

"While we were in the training room, I remembered this one time when Limbo got second place in an art competition. He wanted to get first, so that sent him into a slump. He had nothing but horrible things to say about his paintings for weeks. I kept arguing, saying his work was great. He didn't listen, of course."

"That sounds like Limbo," Yahshi said. "What'd you do?"

"Well, one day, I got really fed up. Instead of begging him not to criticize his art, I agreed with everything he said. When he called his work trash, I offered to throw it out for him. You should have seen the look on his face. It did the trick overnight."

"What makes you think a tactic like that would work on Pinto?"

"He's stubborn, just like my brother. They both have a lot to say and not much to listen to. It takes a different kind of approach to help people like that. You have to use their own words against them."

Yahshi pondered this idea as they combed through the surrounding woods. *He might have a point.*

When they found Pinto, he was aiming at a distant tree.

A twig snapped under Yahshi's boot, and Pinto froze with his bow drawn.

"What are you doing here?" Pinto asked.

"You need to rest," Ceylon said.

"I can't. The Bayins are *still* missing, which means the Underground is more clever than the Force. We're going to war, and we're not prepared." He finally shot his arrow, which skimmed a branch, missing the trunk entirely.

"Dammit," he muttered. "I'm slipping."

"You really are," Ceylon affirmed.

Pinto faced him with a widened eye, and Yahshi cringed. *This won't end well.*

"I'm sure you're a big fan of Professor Embre's worst-case scenario mindset," Ceylon continued.

"Of course I am," Pinto said.

"Then tell me your worst-case scenario."

He gripped his bow tighter. "The Underground strikes again. It's inevitable."

"I can think of something worse than that."

"What?" Pinto asked dryly.

"The Underground strikes"—he stepped toward him—"and you're not in the Force because moping around got you filtered. So you have to watch another war unfold from the sidelines, just like before."

Pinto pursed his lips, and Yahshi waited for the moment he'd lash back with a snarky remark. But he said nothing.

Yahshi leaned in. *Nothing?*

Ceylon plucked an arrow from his quiver. "Look at the moss," he said, drawing his bow.

His arrow pierced a patch of moss on the tree Pinto had missed.

"I remember your famous shot during the primary tool filtration," Ceylon said, lowering his bow. "You hit the bullseye on your first try, and look at you now. You really are slipping."

Pinto's red face threatened to explode, but as a gust of wind swept over him, his gaze softened. He looked to Yahshi, and it seemed he actually cared what he had to say for a change.

"Please, let this go," Yahshi said. "Without rest, you won't improve. And those are your words, not mine."

Pinto looked at the arrows scattered about the ground—results of his failed shots. "I'm not gonna let the case go," he said, "but I guess it's time to ease up a little."

Yahshi smiled at Ceylon as Pinto headed for the building, leaving them behind. They watched him disappear through the trees.

"It reached him," Yahshi muttered. "I can't believe it."

"You're welcome," Ceylon said, taking a few steps in Pinto's trail.

"Wait!"

He stopped, looking back at Yahshi with raised brows.

"While we're out here, could you help me with something?"

"What is it?"

"I need to practice climbing up the side of the building," Yahshi explained. "Just to the second floor—high enough to reach the balconies."

"What?" Ceylon frowned. "Why would you do that?"

"I need to sneak into Vell's room."

"Why?"

"To wish her happy birthday."

"It's her birthday?"

"It will be, in about a week."

"Now I'm the one who's not following."

"Just help me out, will you?"

He winced dramatically. "That's a big favor to ask. I've seen you climb."

Yahshi leaned forward with pursed lips, urging him to help.

"Fine," Ceylon said, shaking his head. "But you'll have to start small." He pointed to a short tree with branches that hung lower than most, making for an easy climb.

As Yahshi began his ascent, Ceylon watched from the dirt, shouting for him to grab certain branches or to stop looking down.

Yahshi trembled as he hoisted himself up. *I hate this.*

When he reached his goal branch, he gripped the trunk to balance himself and looked down with a smile.

Instead of congratulating him, Ceylon drew his bow, aiming at Yahshi's head. "Jump."

"What?"

"I said, *jump.*" He pulled his bowstring tighter. "Jump, or I'll shoot!"

Yahshi held his smile. "You're joking, right?"

"I'm shooting on *one.*"

His smile shattered. "Are you *crazy*?"

"Three!"

"Stop that!"

"Two!"

"This isn't funny!" he yelled, tightening his grip on the trunk.

"One!"

Yahshi leaped from the branch, hearing an arrow strike the tree as he flew from it. Leaves around him rustled, singing their praise.

But soon enough he was no longer flying, but *falling*, hurtling toward the ground. His heart raced as he reached for branches, his fingers grazing some and snapping others.

The impact of his hip against the ground knocked the air out of him. He squeezed his eyes shut and rolled onto his back, clutching his side.

"Nice jump."

Yahshi forced his eyes open to find Ceylon peering down at him.

"What the hell?" he croaked. "You actually shot!"

Ceylon smiled. "I knew you'd jump."

"How could you possibly know for sure?"

"Well, you jumped, didn't you?"

Yahshi groaned, propping himself into a seated position. When his breathing settled, he met Ceylon's eyes.

"I jumped."

"And you're fine, right?"

"Yeah," he said with a chuckle. "I'm... fine."

Ceylon offered a hand to help him up, and Yahshi took it.

Despite the lingering pain from his jump, he scaled the side of the building ten days later, gripping vines and window trims to climb up as he'd practiced. He reached the balcony of Room 1 in less than a minute.

And now, the finale.

He hopped over the railing, landed softly on his feet, and slid the glass door open.

Vell was sitting in a chair she'd dragged to the middle of her quarter.

"Wow," she said. "You did it."

"Indeed I did." He stepped inside, curtains rippling around him.

She smirked. "Were you scared?"

He lifted his shirt to reveal a stubborn bruise stretching from his waist to his hip. "Not after this."

"Yahshi!" She jumped to her feet. "What happened?"

He laughed as he dropped the fabric.

"Happy birthday, Vell."

CHAPTER 19

GUESSING GAME

I vow to guard classified Royal Family information
with lifelong discretion.

♫ BITE - CHARLIE CUNNINGHAM ♫

Nearly a month after Vell turned sixteen, the trainees were remeasured for new uniforms. Their delivered sets arrived the following week with an additional item—winter coats lined with fur.

Yahshi smiled as he tried his on for the first time. There was something rewarding about lasting at the Academy long enough to witness a change in season. *And it's nice to have Pinto back to normal again.*

Yahshi could tell he hadn't stopped thinking about the Bayin case, but he'd stopped talking about it, and that was enough. Pinto had even thanked Ceylon for knocking some sense into him.

On their way to the dining hall that morning, Pinto's trembling fingers struggled to button his coat. "Worthless, flimsy thing," he muttered.

"If it's worthless, get rid of it." Vell shivered. "I'll gladly take another layer."

"Ugh!" Pinto said, still fumbling with his buttons.

"You should be grateful we have coats at all," Yahshi said.

"Yeah, Pinto." Ceylon jabbed him in the side. "And at least with your coat on, Professor Embre won't point out—"

"*Don't* say it," Pinto warned.

"At least she won't point out how tight your shirt is," Ceylon said through a smile.

Yahshi laughed, and Vell looked away to hide her grin.

"That was *one time*, okay?" Pinto gave up, leaving his coat half-buttoned. "I have larger shirts now."

"I'm surprised you didn't get smaller ones to show off," Yahshi said. "Now that you've finally put on some muscle."

Pinto rolled his eye. "Don't be gross."

"Come on, Pinto," Ceylon teased. "Show us your arms."

"Do you have abs now?" Vell asked.

"Shut it, all of you!" Pinto shouted, shooting glares at them. "I hope I get filtered soon. I could use the peace and quiet."

Over lunch, they bonded over how much they hated their recent field classes. Yahshi didn't say it, but he actually enjoyed vault driving. He'd been picking it up surprisingly fast.

After clearing their plates, they drank their beet juice together.

Yahshi scrunched his nose. "The taste never gets any better."

"So," Vell said, "what's your assessment?"

Pinto turned in his chair, crossing his arms to ensure Yahshi and Ceylon couldn't cheat by watching him—he still suffered from mock-sunburn and shaky arms.

"There's... belladonna," Yahshi said.

"Is that a statement or a question?" Vell asked.

"Statement?"

"Wrong."

"Really?" Pinto faced them again, revealing his red cheeks. "Because I'm certain there's a dose in mine." He held his hands up to demonstrate their shakiness.

Vell squinted at him. "Are you sure you're not cold?"

"Of course I'm cold. But I'm definitely poisoned too."

"You know how Doctor Blim feels about—"

"Fine. I'm definitely *in-tox-i-cat-ed*. Is that better?"

Ceylon smacked his lips together. "I have a feeling there's serum in mine too," he added, "but I can't tell for sure."

"Vell!" Keiyo called from across the dining hall. "Is there belladonna or not?"

"Everyone seems to think so," she replied. "I-I don't know."

"But you always know," Keiyo said.

"Are you feeling okay, Vell?" Sunna asked.

Quax set his glass down. "There's belladonna today. I'm sure of it."

Vell shook her head, eyes on her juice.

"Oh no," Pinto muttered.

"What?" Yahshi asked. "What is it?"

His eye darted to the door. "It's a filtration."

And as though it were on cue, the door swung open, and Doctor Blimmery wheeled a cart inside.

"Congrats on completing seven months in the program, kids! Even if you get filtered today, I bet you'll always have the coolest stories to tell over supper."

Silence.

Complete, utter silence.

"Alright, here's the deal. Half of you had serum in your drinks, and half of you didn't. If you think yours had *no* belladonna, move to the left." Doctor Blimmery gestured to the window. "And if you think yours *did*, move to the right." He gestured to the opposite wall.

Vell stood first, peering down at Yahshi and Ceylon before walking to the left side of the room.

Pinto headed to the opposite side, claiming his juice *did* contain belladonna.

Yahshi and Ceylon leaned toward each other because they both couldn't be sure.

"We're shaking," Yahshi pointed out, raising his palms.

"But our symptoms never show up this quickly anymore," Ceylon countered, staring at his own hands. "It could be the nervousness—and the cold."

"Unless we were given a higher dose than usual." If that were the case, their symptoms would appear earlier. *What if every glass with belladonna has a different dose?*

"Make your choice!" Doctor Blimmery sang. "Left or right?"

Sunna joined Vell on the left. His face wasn't red and his hands barely shook, so Yahshi was positive he'd made the right choice.

"Okay, let's think this through." He leaned over the table. "There's seven of us, but Doctor Blimmery said *half.*"

"So three drinks had belladonna, and four didn't," Ceylon said, "or four drinks had belladonna, and three didn't."

"Vell and Sunna are correct. Left is solid."

Quax and Keiyo joined Pinto on the right side of the room.

"We know Pinto's correct too," Ceylon said. "I also trust Quax—he seemed confident earlier. Keiyo, though? He's a wildcard."

"It doesn't make a difference," Yahshi said, visualizing an alternative layout. "If Keiyo's wrong, the room would still be split with three on one side and two on the other—only flipped. It doesn't affect our odds."

They took another sip in unison. Yahshi still couldn't decide, and when he met Ceylon's blank gaze, he knew he couldn't either.

"So," Ceylon said, "what now?"

Yahshi mentally replayed the possibilities, hoping he'd spot something different, but he didn't. Their reality was simple.

"There's four potential combinations," Yahshi explained. "I go left and you go right, you go left and I go right, we both go left, or we both go right. I'm on the left in two of those options, and in two, I'm on the right, so..."

"There's a fifty-percent chance one of us wins," Ceylon concluded.

"And a twenty-five percent chance both of us do," Yahshi added.

"Is that all we have to work with?"

Yahshi clenched his jaw and nodded slightly. "At this point, it's a guessing game."

If only I put more effort into honing my detection skills. He gripped his glass tighter. *Now I'm betting my spot on the flip of a coin.*

"Hey." Ceylon mustered a smile when Yahshi met his gaze. "I go right, you go left?"

Yahshi smiled back. "Deal," he said, his voice hardly more than a whisper.

Doctor Blimmery's voice filled the room. "Make your choice now, please."

Yahshi joined Vell and closed his eyes, bracing himself for the worst-case scenario.

"One of you kids is incorrect," Doctor Blimmery announced.

The blood rushed to Yahshi's head, leaving him faint. He couldn't move, breathe, or think, and for a moment he feared he was falling because he could no longer feel the floor beneath his feet.

Vell took his hand and squeezed it, grounding him. Her warmth lingered in his fingers for only a moment before Doctor Blimmery's voice extinguished it.

"I'm sorry, Ceylon," the guardian announced, "but you're out."

"No," Vell whispered, releasing his hand.

Yahshi opened his eyes to see Ceylon frozen, his face ghostly.

Quax and Keiyo sighed in relief before glancing across the room at Sunna, who smiled back.

Pinto leaned over Ceylon's shoulder, whispering what must have been goodbye. And just like that, it was game over, and the dread of everything Yahshi had been pushing away came hurtling back.

He thought about his father's potential connection to the Bayins. He thought about Vell's criminal background. He thought about the matching filtration, the rabbits buried outside, and Pinto's arrow striking the bullseye. Breathing was no longer automatic—he had to walk himself through the steps.

"A guardian is waiting in the common room to escort you home," Doctor Blimmery added.

Ceylon didn't move for what felt like a lifetime, and Doctor Blimmery was kind enough to allow him the space. But even Ceylon knew he couldn't stay forever, and he eventually headed for the door.

This isn't fair. He deserves to be here as much as I do.

The only way to make this right would be to filter himself too. The others would automatically secure their positions in the final five, making this the last filtration. He could do everyone a favor.

But instead, Yahshi wallowed in the knowledge that luck had favored *him*.

He waited until Ceylon shut the door before leaning forward with his hands on his knees. *The program isn't fair. It never has been. But I don't wanna play dirty to win. I don't wanna win like this.*

He wasn't sure how much time had passed before Doctor Blimmery broke the silence.

"The final filtration will take place two months from today. There will be five spots and six of you left, so expect this to be your most competitive test yet."

No, don't give us a date. Let me sit with this. Let me process this. Let me breathe.

"We're removing afternoon field classes to extend your recreation time. Use it wisely." Doctor Blimmery took a single step away, stopping with a sigh. "I-I'm sorry, everyone."

When the guardian left, Yahshi forced his spine to straighten. His breaths were shallow, his throat tightening to the size of a straw.

Vell wrapped her arms around him.

"I made a guess," he choked out.

"I know."

As time passed, the guilt faded. Yahshi was, quite literally, *lucky* to have made it this far into the program, and he was not set on taking that luck for granted—nor did he spend another second considering the absurd idea of filtering himself for the sake of equity.

In Research classes, Professor Embre introduced floor plans of the essential guardian buildings in Vakoi City. Yahshi studied them until he could sketch each room by memory.

"You finally did it," Pinto said, flipping through his floor plans.

Yahshi massaged his cramping hand. "It only took me three weeks longer than you."

In Medical classes, their focus shifted to the development, crafting, and lacing of guardian tools. One day, they entered the lab to find arrows awaiting them at their tables. Keiyo smirked as he inspected his.

"What's so amusing to you?" Doctor Blimmery asked.

"This arrow," Keiyo said. "It's stupid."

"How so?"

"It's too long, too heavy, too"—he bent the arrow to demonstrate—"flimsy."

Doctor Blimmery gestured for him to continue.

"I'd shorten it for sure." He ran a finger down the shaft, stopping where he'd make the cut. "Maybe down to two-thirds of its current length."

Doctor Blimmery stroked his beard. "Why?"

"It'll wobble less in the air, obviously."

"Meaning?"

"It'll fly farther—and faster. More precise too."

Doctor Blimmery nodded with puckered lips. "Good job, kid."

Keiyo looked around to find the other trainees staring.

"How the hell did you know that?" Quax asked.

He shrugged. "It's only common sense."

With time, Keiyo's natural talent with tools proved undeniable. The other trainees began to flock to the lab, competing to catch up to his level. Pinto, Vell, and Quax eventually diverted their energy toward their other deficits, but Yahshi and Sunna carried on.

Over the course of a month, Yahshi crafted twelve daggers with progressively straighter blades. Sunna crafted sixteen, all sharper and stronger than his. He even carved designs into the handles that grew more intricate with every piece.

"Yahshi, please stop wasting your time with Sunna." Vell tugged his arm, trying to drag him out of the lab. "I doubt the final filtration will test our crafting skills."

Yahshi pulled his arm free. "How can you be sure? It's a crucial skill in the Medical Division." He adjusted his crafting glasses and hammered at a piece of metal, but Vell didn't leave his side.

"Hey," she said after a few minutes, "can you still draw those floor plans from memory?"

Yahshi froze, hitting a blank as he tried to recall the fourth floor of the Investigation Office. He leaned over with a gloved hand on his forehead. "Oh, for the glory of—"

It was a balancing act. Improving one skill meant getting rustier with another, which left the six trainees walking the same tightrope, waiting for one to slip and leave the other five victorious.

Vell's right. Yahshi removed his gloves, then his goggles. *I can't afford to get rusty with anything.*

So he went to the library, and he studied those awful plans until he memorized them again.

Defense lessons were a different kind of challenge. Although primary tool sequences were easier to pick up and remember, they pushed him to his physical limits. The repetitive swinging and slicing of his swords felt like he was slowly ripping his arms from his body. Every morning he woke up with his shoulders screaming, begging him to slow down, but he couldn't.

About three weeks before the final filtration, Sunna accidentally swung a sword into Keiyo's shoulder.

With a shriek, Keiyo collapsed to his knees, and Yahshi gasped at the sight of blood oozing across the green zone. He sheathed his swords and inched toward Keiyo's wriggling body.

As Sunna entered a state of hysterical panic, Commander Roz kneeled beside Keiyo, insisting on transferring him to the City Hospital.

"No!" Keiyo yelled, kicking back against the guardian's attempts to lift him. He looked like a child throwing a tantrum. "I'm staying! You can't take me there!"

Commander Roz released Keiyo and stood, staring at him with a rare look of uncertainty. After a moment, he whispered something to Quax, who dragged Sunna away.

"I'm sorry!" Sunna yelled. "Keiyo, I'm so sorry!"

Quax guided him to the door. "Just shut your mouth already."

Yahshi leaned toward Vell and whispered, "Should we get Doctor Blim?"

"I'll go," she muttered. "Stay here."

As Vell left the scene, Pinto approached it, crouching by Keiyo's side with a forced look of concern.

"You're injured," he said. "You need help."

"Oh, shut it, Pinto!" Keiyo yelled through gritted teeth. "You want me gone, but I won't go that easily!"

They knew getting transferred to the Hospital meant getting filtered, and Keiyo was in the program to win.

They were *all* in the program to win.

The night before the final filtration, Yahshi stepped onto his balcony. The weather was beginning to warm up, reaching that perfect temperature between hot and cold.

As he gazed up at the full moon, Ceylon popped into his head for the first time in weeks. *Has he found a new career path yet?*

He gripped the dewy railing and shivered at the thought of losing another friend—but even more terrifying was the possibility of being the one to leave. If he were to return to Sitra, he'd lose not just one friend, but all of them.

Close to graduation, and close to each other. That's a recipe for disaster, isn't it?

"Hey!"

"Yahshi!"

He looked to his left, then his right. Pinto and Vell were standing on their own balconies, dressed in identical golden pajamas.

"Really?" he asked. "Both of you?"

"Can't sleep," Vell said.

"Tomorrow feels like my death day," Pinto said.

"Oh, don't be dramatic," Yahshi said. "We've worked hard for this."

"So have they," Vell said, hoisting herself onto her balcony railing. The wind picked up, sending tendrils of hair whipping around her face, but she easily held her balance.

Yahshi followed her lead, climbing onto his own railing. When he looked to his left, Pinto was already perched on his—and together they walked the Academy tightrope, admiring the glittering sky, and making it their own.

"The past two months have been... tough," Yahshi muttered.

"The worst," Vell corrected.

"If only Sunna brought that sword just a *little* bit to the left." Pinto swung an imaginary sword in front of him. "Right through Keiyo's head."

Vell chuckled. "You're horrible."

The stars twinkled a little brighter that night.

"You know, I'm really glad we went through this together." The words left Yahshi's mouth before he could filter them, but he didn't mind. He wanted them to know how much he cared tonight—just in case.

"I love you too," Vell said.

"Final five, right?" Pinto asked.

"Final five," Yahshi and Vell echoed in unison.

CHAPTER 20

LOSING A FRIEND

I vow to embrace my division and unit placements
without question.

♫ MADNESS - TRIBAL BLOOD ♫

The Academy guardians and trainees gathered in the courtyard at the crack of dawn.

"Please know that if we could accept all six of you into the program's second half, we would do so in a heartbeat." Professor Embre glanced at the statue beside her and smiled. "But Emperor Vakoi's orders restrict us to five."

"For the final filtration, each of you will wear one of these." Commander Roz reached into a box at his feet, retrieving a leather belt with three evenly spaced dove feathers attached. He fastened it around his waist—one feather dangled from each hip, and the final one hung behind him like a tail.

"The first trainee to lose all three feathers will be filtered from the program." He pinched a feather, and with a tug, it popped free.

Doctor Blimmery wiped his eye, prompting a passing glare from Professor Embre.

"This filtration will take place on the Academy field," she explained. "There are three rules, but breaking them will automatically disqualify you, so listen closely.

"One: You must only remove feathers from the belt of your assigned target.

"Two: You must stay on the field exclusively. The surrounding woods, courtyard, and main building are no-go zones.

"Three: No tools, and no horses."

Doctor Blimmery tucked his hands into his pockets, eyes on his boots. "Those are... the only rules."

Which means we can even use force. Yahshi's fingers seemed to roll into fists against his will.

"If you have any tools on you, remove them now." Professor Embre held her hands out.

Vell and Keiyo retrieved a few throwing stars from their pockets. They grinned at each other before handing them to Professor Embre.

"Now it's time to announce your targets," Commander Roz said. "Pinto Dempsey, your target will be Quax Avarium."

The trainees faced Pinto, knowing he couldn't win a fight against Quax with brute force alone. He pulled at his curls, devising a plan, and Quax watched him brainstorm with narrowed eyes.

"Quax, your target is Keiyo Pickett," Commander Roz continued.

Quax looked away from Pinto with a dropped jaw. "What?" he and Keiyo asked in unison.

"Keiyo, your target is Sunna Rickabee."

Quax's frown softened. He gestured for his friends to lean toward him and began to whisper.

Yahshi was too far away to make out their conversation. *What are you telling them?*

"Sunna, your target is Yahshi Konya."

Sunna glanced at Yahshi with a grim smile, and despite the circumstances, he smiled back.

"Yahshi, your target is Vell Patura."

His smile vanished. He faced Commander Roz, who nodded in confirmation.

Me, tracing Vell?

She avoided his gaze.

"Vell, your target is Pinto Dempsey," Commander Roz finished, and the clouds darkened as he passed out their belts.

"On the field, you'll find six red dots painted on the grass," Doctor Blimmery said. "Claim one and stand on it until Roz blows his whistle."

Commander Roz slipped a golden whistle between his lips, and they rushed to fasten their belts.

The guardians remained in the courtyard while the trainees scattered across the field in search of the red starting points. They were so far apart that once Yahshi claimed one, he could barely see the other trainees' faces.

There's two bridges between our groups, he realized. *Me and Sunna. Pinto and Quax.*

There was only one way for him to win alongside Pinto and Vell.

Quax needs to leave today.

He crouched into a running position. *It's simple. I need to outrun Sunna long enough for Pinto to pluck all three of Quax's feathers.*

A high-pitched whistle pierced the air.

Sunna bolted after Yahshi, Keiyo trailing at his side to facilitate his success.

I can fight Sunna, but not both of them. Yahshi pivoted and ran toward the trees. *If they catch me, it's over.*

He turned right and ran parallel to the woods, glancing over his shoulder. Keiyo parted from Sunna's side, sprinting in the direction Yahshi was heading in. *He's trying to cut me off.*

Changing directions, he nearly lost his footing as he avoided their attempts to tackle him. Adrenaline took over, and he quickened his pace.

While Keiyo and Sunna fell behind, Vell appeared at Yahshi's side and ran with him.

"Don't stop. No matter what."

"I know," he said.

"No matter what," she repeated, leaving his side.

He watched Vell rush at Quax from behind while Pinto had him distracted. Launching herself forward, she wrapped her arms around him, replicating the move she'd used to earn her pin eight months prior.

Although she didn't knock Quax down, she stunned him enough for Pinto to swoop in and pluck a feather.

Nice one, you two.

When Yahshi looked back at his pursuers, Keiyo wasn't running at Sunna's side anymore. He scanned the area as he ran, anticipating a surprise attack. But instead, he spotted Keiyo coming to Quax's aid, tackling Pinto to the ground and landing a fist to his face.

Yahshi stopped, wincing as Keiyo punched him again.

Only Vell could pluck Pinto's feathers, but nothing was stopping the others from hurting him.

"Yahshi!" Vell shouted. "Keep running!"

Pinto grabbed Keiyo's shoulder and squeezed, aggravating the wound that hadn't healed completely. He wailed and struck him back with a blow stronger than the first two.

Pinto grimaced, releasing Keiyo's shoulder.

Yahshi studied Sunna's approach, trying to decide if he had enough time to intervene.

"Yahshi!" Vell shouted. "Go!" She tried to stop Keiyo, but Quax grabbed her from behind, locking her in a chokehold. As she struggled for air, Keiyo struck Pinto again.

Yahshi's focus flew back and forth between the two fights. *I have to do something.*

Without escaping Keiyo's grip, Pinto couldn't pluck Quax's remaining feathers, which would send the game into free-for-all chaos. On the other hand, he knew nothing was stopping Quax from choking Vell until she could breathe no longer.

Before he could make a decision, Vell dug her nails into Quax's arms. He pulled back and winced, freeing her.

Vell wheezed as she ran after Pinto, resuming her effort to help.

A light popping noise stole Yahshi's attention. He turned to find Sunna standing next to him, feather in hand.

As he stumbled back, he looked down at his belt. It was missing a feather.

"I'm sorry," Sunna said. "We all know it's either you or Quax."

Yahshi lunged with a jab, but his tracer dodged it and countered with a punch of his own. He ducked, and as he ran past Sunna, a finger skimmed one of his remaining feathers.

Fighting is too risky. Instead of facing him with another attack, he bolted away. *I need to keep running.*

Sunna's footsteps trailed close behind him as he circled the field again and again. His stamina was waning, but luckily, so was Sunna's. After a few more loops, he looked back to see him doubled over, panting.

Yahshi halted to catch his breath too. As he wiped the sweat from his forehead, he returned his attention to the other four. Vell had managed to distract Keiyo, creating an opening for Pinto to face Quax without interference. And with Sunna still resting afar, Yahshi had a perfect opportunity to step in. *We can end this now. Together.*

He had almost arrived at the scene when Quax delivered a blow to Pinto's jaw, leaving him reeling.

"Pinto!" Yahshi shouted.

Quax charged forward to finish him off—but just as he was about to punch, Pinto grinned, dropping his exaggerated act. He ducked and slipped past him, plucking a second feather.

Quax's cheeks turned red, and he froze when Yahshi arrived to offer Pinto support. He'd have to take on both of them with only one feather left.

Rather than fighting against the odds, he swerved around them, making a beeline to the other group. Vell was still keeping Keiyo busy, so Quax had no problem plucking a feather from him as he darted past.

A bolt of lightning split the sky. Quax had grown tired of waiting for Sunna to pluck Yahshi's feathers to win, and by taking fate into his own hands, he had changed the game.

Keiyo gasped, and Vell's jaw dropped as she backed away. With a chuckle, Pinto ran after them, still hunting his target.

Yahshi had yet to fully process the betrayal when two hands struck his back. His feet slipped out from under him, and he fell forward onto the dirt. A popping noise signaled that Sunna had plucked another feather.

"Dammit." Yahshi rolled onto his side, locking his last feather between his right hip and the grass. He nailed himself down, resisting Sunna's attempts to flip him over and get him filtered. He heard Pinto and Vell crying out—something bad was happening—but he could do nothing to help.

Another set of footsteps approached, and he gritted his teeth, preparing to resist two boys instead of one. *Keiyo's here, isn't he? He's joining Sunna to end the game. It's over.*

But then Sunna stumbled away.

Keiyo was in a fighting stance, facing him. "Leave Yahshi alone!"

Sunna frowned. "Why—"

"Quax plucked my feather," Keiyo said. "I won't let him win."

"What's your plan, then, huh?" Sunna countered. "Pinto's down."

"Down?" Yahshi hopped to his feet and spotted Pinto lying in the distance, Vell kneeled at his side. Rain began to fall as he left Keiyo and Sunna arguing behind him.

On his way to his friends, he crossed paths with Quax, who was still pursuing Keiyo's feathers. He spotted blood on his knuckles and stopped, glaring over his shoulder.

"What the *hell* did you do?"

Quax ignored him, continuing to run.

Yahshi sprinted and kneeled by Vell, cringing at the sight of Pinto's body. Blood gushed from his crooked nose, running down his cheek and staining the grass scarlet.

"After Keiyo ran off, Quax panicked." Vell sniffled. "I tried to stop him, but..."

He leaned closer, noticing the cuts that marked his neck, jawline, and hands.

"We have to do something." She clung to Yahshi's shoulder. "We need Doctor Blim."

He could hardly hear her. The rain dripped into his eyes, blurring his vision, drowning him. With Pinto unconscious, Quax was immune to the game. Keiyo would have to defend his last two feathers from Quax, freeing Sunna to pursue Yahshi, who only had one left.

I'm the closest to getting filtered. He gulped. *Unless...*

Vell was struggling to pull Pinto up. "Yahshi, help me carry him."

He eyed the feather at her hip.

If he were to return to Sitra, what would he do with himself? What career path would he pursue? What would be the point of everything he'd worked for in the program? The beatings, the studying, the poison, the pain—it would all be for nothing. It would all be a waste.

But it didn't *have* to be a waste.

Yahshi grabbed her feather and pulled it.

Vell looked back at him, her red eyes widening. "He's hardly breathing! And your *first move* is to pluck my feather?"

"I didn't have a choice." He dropped the feather as though it'd erase what he'd done. "I could easily get filtered!"

"My mother's life is on the line!"

His eyes watered, and he softened his tone. "I understand that."

"Your mother's dead," said Vell. "What could you possibly understand?"

The lump in his throat made it hard to speak. "I'm sorry," he choked out, "but I need this too."

As he reached for another feather, Vell turned and plucked one from Pinto's belt. Tears streamed down her face, and Yahshi's hand retreated.

Footsteps approached them from behind, and they looked back at Sunna's pale face.

"What happened?" he asked in a quivering voice, scanning Pinto's wounds. "Quax really hurt him this bad?"

Vell ignored him, gripping a second feather.

One more move from Sunna, and Yahshi wouldn't hesitate to pluck another feather from Vell. One more move from Yahshi, and Vell wouldn't hesitate to pluck one from Pinto.

"What kind of madness is this?" Sunna stepped back, shaking his head. "I should have left this place a long time ago."

Thunder roared as Sunna plucked his feathers, filtering himself from the program.

After showering, Yahshi didn't leave his flat until the evening, when his stomach started to rumble. He entered the dining hall to find only one five-seater table, leaving him no choice but to sit with Vell, Quax, and Keiyo for the first time.

A band played a jumpy, celebratory tune as Professor Embre wheeled a cart of cake slices to the table. "Congratulations on securing your spots as Academy graduates in the Force." She slid a plate in front of Yahshi first, but he didn't look at it.

He couldn't take his eyes off the empty seat.

"I'm sure you're all worried about Pinto, but he's in excellent hands at Vakoi City Hospital. He'll return as soon as he's well enough." She served Quax and Vell their slices next. "As you know, the second nine months in the program include shadowing real guardian units in the City, or on expeditions into Eastern Territory. Yahshi Konya—you're up first."

He nodded once, numb to the news.

"Your first assignment is tomorrow morning. Meet your shadow unit leader in the common room at 6:00." She set the final plate down, and with a swoop of his arm, Keiyo sent it flying.

Yahshi peeled his eyes from Pinto's chair, watching the plate shatter against the floor, cueing an explosion of chocolate.

The music took an off-pitch track to silence as the band members looked over.

Professor Embre glared at Keiyo before leaving the dining hall, and that jumpy tune picked up again.

As Quax devoured his cake, Vell stabbed a fork into hers and left it there. Yahshi took a bite, which he promptly spit out. *Too sweet.*

He closed his eyes and focused on each instrument, one at a time. When he reached the violin, he convinced himself the long notes were distant screams.

Is this what winning feels like?

He allowed the music to drown him for a few minutes before returning to his quarter. Throughout the entire night, he imagined how Sunna's return to Nominner had played out.

In one scenario, Sunna's family hugged him, cried, and cooked his favorite meals. He told them marvelous stories over supper, and they laughed until they lost their voices.

In a second scenario, Sunna returned home regretting his choice to filter himself. His family scolded him for getting so close to success and pouring it down the drain.

Yahshi chose to believe the second—for his own sake.

When the sleepiness caught up to him, it was nearly 6:00, and he no longer had time to rest. He changed into a fresh uniform and made his way to the common room, where his shadow unit leader stood by the door, waiting.

She turned to face him, and he froze at the sight of Cal Avarium.

"Hi, Yahshi. Congratulations on making the final five."

As we stand on the cusp of the Return, we prepare to step back and watch the sprouting of a new era, a time where peace embraces our Empire, nurtured by the Principles of Unity we have all held dear.

THE PROVISIONAL COUNCIL

PART 2
REDEMPTION

THE INTERRUPTER

We reject unnecessary violence, seeking peaceful resolutions
even in turbulent storms.

♫ ABSENSE · ANTITHEMICS ♫

Yahshi flinched as Cal reached for his messy hair.

"You'll be a guardian soon," she said. "Look the part."

In his hallucinations, Cal had never touched him before. He'd heard her voice and seen her face, but he'd never felt her breath against his forehead as she leaned in, adjusting his bangs.

"Cal?" he choked out, clinging to the chance that she wasn't real. He imagined her saying, *Cal? No, Cal's not your shadow unit leader.* Then he would look closer, and someone else's face would replace hers.

She stepped back, her smile fading. "It's *Commander* to you."

Yahshi's eyes widened—and she burst into laughter.

"I'm kidding!" She tucked her hands into her pockets. "*Relax.*"

He couldn't bring himself to laugh with her. Cal had never been a talker growing up—not even a smiler, and certainly not a *jokester.* In this one conversation alone, she'd given him more attention than she had in his entire life.

"I'm confused. You're my unit leader?"

"Your *shadow* unit leader." She winked and headed for the door. "But do well on your assignments, and perhaps you can join my unit officially. My members are lovely, but they've outgrown my leadership."

He caught up to her, eyeing a Defense Division badge on her shoulder. "So it's decided then? I'll be a commander?"

"Nothing's *decided*," Cal said.

Yahshi squinted. It seemed like every word of his sparked Cal's commentary, and he couldn't tell if she was being playful or not.

"You're still a trainee," she explained. "The Defense Division is currently considered your best match, which is why you're my shadow, but that could change in the next nine months. You'll be joining my unit on monthly expeditions until graduation, when your official placement will be announced."

Cal opened the door, and a gust of cold air struck Yahshi's face.

"Wait!" he called.

She looked back at him.

"Shouldn't you see Quax?"

She blinked.

"He's upstairs," Yahshi added.

"Is Quax my shadow?"

"No, but—"

"Then we'll have our reunion when it's time to."

And for just a moment, the Cal he remembered was back. He'd seen her avoid Quax like this countless times before. *I'm studying, Brother*, she'd say. *Maybe after my run. You can work on that puzzle while you wait.*

But Yahshi pushed his bitterness aside when he realized that she was a guardian sent to the Academy to pick up her shadow, not to socialize. *And after what Quax did to Pinto, why should I care whether she visits him?*

Without another word, he joined her outside, and they made their way across the field together.

I hardly knew her back then. He slipped his hands into his pockets, mirroring her posture. *And it's been three years. People can change a lot in three years. I know I have.*

"You look exhausted. My friend Evaris was the unlucky trainee too—shadowed the day after our final filtration. You'll meet her in a minute." A pause. "She's my best friend."

Yahshi raised a brow at her reluctant final sentence. The thought of Cal having a best friend was about as awkward as she'd made it sound.

"Did you sleep?"

"No," he replied.

"Who needs sleep, anyway?" She shrugged with a chuckle. "There's coffee in the vault if you want some. It's good stuff. Not the watered-down bean juice they serve in the program."

"It's fine. I don't drink coffee."

"Well, you should," Cal said, nudging his arm. He didn't like the nudging thing.

"It'll be an easy day in terms of shadowing," she continued, "just a lot of driving around. We're heading to Vori, a town about two and a half hours from here. It's barely in Eastern Territory, right past Border Control."

When they arrived at the vault, she yanked the passenger box door open, revealing two commanders inside.

A man in his mid-twenties shook his head at Yahshi. "I-I knew we weren't st-stopping for breakfast."

"Don't be silly," Cal chirped. "We never stop for breakfast."

"Who's the kid?" asked another guardian. Yahshi assumed she was Evaris.

"He's our shadow."

"You're kidding," Evaris spat. "For how long?"

"Until I don't want him anymore." Cal hopped inside. "Galler, you're driving."

"G-Got it." He left the box as Yahshi entered.

"You didn't tell me about a shadow," Evaris said.

"Because I knew you'd make a fuss about it the entire ride here," Cal said.

"He'll slow you down."

"Aw." She pouted. "Well, that'll make two of you."

Yahshi sat beside Evaris as Cal shut the door, darkening the air. She cupped her palms around her mouth and shouted, "Ready!"

The horses began to trot, and dirt crumbled under the box's wheels as they set into motion.

"Yahshi, meet Evaris." Cal sat on the opposite bench and gestured to her unit member. "For someone who also shadowed the day after the final filtration, you'd think she'd have more sympathy for you."

"I do have sympathy for him." Evaris crossed her arms. "That's why I don't want a shadow. I don't like shadows. I never liked *being* a shadow."

"Oh, don't be dramatic. He'll be just fine." Cal grabbed a canister and took a swig of coffee.

Yahshi faced Evaris. "Why didn't you like being a shadow?"

She looked away with a shake of her head.

"Don't let her get to you. Today's target isn't a big deal." Cal smoothed the wrinkles out of her overcoat with a scowl. "The man's been accused of treason, so we need to search his place and detain him for questioning. That's all there is to it. Ninety percent of the work is traveling in this hell of a box." She banged a fist against the wall, and Yahshi flinched. "We'll have you back in time for lunch, supper at the latest."

"What kind of treason?" he asked.

"The East runs on a rationing system," Evaris started.

"Oh, Evaris, he knows that already," Cal said. "Yahshi, you remember studying ration tickets with Professor Embre, right?"

He nodded.

"And you remember how to decipher the numbers on the tickets?"

He nodded again.

"So I'm sure you know it's not hard to forge them with practice. Unfortunately that means rebels in the East are putting together fake ones to claim extra goods. That's what our target's been accused of."

"There's enough goods to go around, right?" Yahshi asked. "Why would they forge tickets?"

"Greed, that's one thing." Cal's voice deepened. "But the second is worse."

"The Underground?"

"Bullseye. Most of the ration forgers we've detained—real ones, not false reports, mind you—well, they've admitted their affiliation to the Underground. So of course, we bring them in for questioning because—"

"Protocol," Evaris finished with a sigh. "And you know how the Force is about Protocol."

Cal glanced at her before continuing. "As I was saying, most ration forgers feed us misinformation and waste our time. I'm starting to think it's more dangerous to lock them up for questioning than to get rid of them."

Evaris plucked an arrow from her quiver and spun it between her fingers. Her face was pale.

"Luckily, most reports like this are complete flukes," Cal continued. "Easterners are nasty, you know. They'll frame each other over the pettiest things. Jealous of your neighbor for being more attractive than you? Boom! Send an anonymous report of treason with their name. Stress them out and waste the Force's precious time."

"So if the search is meant to confirm or deny his forgery," Yahshi said, "what kind of evidence are you looking for?"

"The stolen rations," Cal answered.

"But if he's stealing goods, wouldn't he eat them? Use them?"

"If he's a basic thief. But if he's a member of the Underground, he'll be storing the surplus in bulk. Sometimes we open a closet to find it filled with bread, or blankets, or coal... And don't get me started on the floorboards. They think hiding stuff under them is revolutionary, but it's one of the first places we look."

"Why doesn't the Force make the tickets more complex?" Yahshi asked. "It wouldn't eliminate foul play, but it'd cut it down significantly, right?"

"Finally, some common sense!" Evaris shouted, her voice echoing through the box. "Seriously, what the hell? Why do smart people always end up in Defense? We need people like you in the Research Division."

He blushed.

"Our unit has been nagging professors to switch up the rationing system for months," Cal said. "But *apparently*, they have bigger fish to fry. Like searching for the Bayins."

"Oh. Right." He thought of his father and gulped. "I thought the Research Division moved on from that case."

"No, but they should. I think he's a damn waste of time, another one of the Underground's tactics to distract us. I mean, seriously, what will finding the Bayins do? Unless they're leading us astray, it's not like they'll talk. At most we can lock them up, maybe execute them, but that's just pride, a way to say, *In your face, targets! We traced you!* But how much closer will it bring us to the Underground? Well, not close at all. Professors never stop to ask themselves what's essential to pursue, and then commanders like us have to do their pointless bidding."

"Those preppy bastards," Evaris said. "At this rate we should label it the Blockhead Division."

"Hey, *language*," Cal scolded. "Support your fellow guardians, remember?"

"Constructive criticism is the best form of support."

For the next hour, they told Yahshi stories about various traitors they'd encountered on expeditions. In this giant game of predator and prey, he'd assumed the guardians were the cat, searching for rebel mice in hiding. But despite the Underground's sneaky nature, they were the real cat, keeping the Force running around in constant confusion and fear.

"We should be passing through Sitra right about now," Cal said.

"Really?" Yahshi asked. "Are we stopping?"

She scoffed through a smile. "Why would we stop?"

"I-I don't know. Just, since you mentioned it, I thought—"

"They aren't your people anymore."

"I know."

"And the Force organizes visitation opportunities. You know that too."

He searched her eyes for a hint of yearning. "How often do they let you see your parents?"

"I haven't seen them in a long time."

"How long?"

"A long time."

"So that's it?" he asked. "You don't think about them?"

"I think about my job," Cal said, her tone sharpening, "because this is so much bigger than me."

Evaris sighed. "Cal—"

She held a palm up, muting her unit member, and Yahshi stared at his boots.

It was silent for the next hour and a half.

Yahshi jumped from the vault last, landing solidly on the road. He wandered a few steps off while his shadow unit chatted, taking in the outside world for the first time in nine months.

The town of Vori was unlike anything he'd seen before. He knew Eastern Territory had three times the population of the West, but he'd never imagined how crowded it'd be.

Narrow alleyways and roads formed a network of tightly packed houses, and by every door hung a lantern that reminded him of the one back home. He wished he'd talked to his father more when he had the chance. *Where did you grow up? Where was I born? Why did you convert after the War?*

A group of children passed the vault, waving at the guardians and eyeing Yahshi's trainee uniform. He waved back, but his smile faded when he noticed a few curtains drawn shut. Then he saw a man, who had been smoking on his porch, glance at his watch and rush down the stairs as though he conveniently had somewhere to be.

"Yahshi, focus," Cal snapped, pointing to a house across the road. "That's the one."

Evaris unslung her bow, and Yahshi frowned as Cal pressed a dagger handle to his chest.

"Are tools necessary for a check like this?" he asked, taking it from her.

"No, but they make the job easier." Cal's voice was stiff, lacking its earlier warmth. "Galler—ready the vault for detainment. You two—follow me."

"You g-got it." Galler hopped into the box.

"Let's hope he didn't run," Cal muttered, leading Yahshi and Evaris away. "I *hate* when targets run."

The house was the most run-down on the block. Its roof was rotting—in dire need of replacement—and its broken windows were boarded up. *It must leak when it rains.*

They stopped on the porch, and Cal turned to Yahshi. "Don't speak unless spoken to."

He nodded, and she knocked on the door.

A middle-aged man and his son greeted them. The boy looked around seven, and he clung to his father's legs at the sight of their tools.

I'm not gonna use it, Yahshi wanted to say—but he wasn't allowed to speak.

A woman organizing a bookshelf glanced at the door and fumbled, nearly dropping a stack of books in her arms.

The man cleared his throat. "Do you need something?"

"Yes," Cal said. "A quick search."

He nearly spoke again, but when Evaris gripped her bow tighter, he stepped aside.

Yahshi lingered in the doorway as they searched the room, careful not to get in their way. While Cal nudged the floorboards with her boots, Evaris removed a mandatory portrait of Emperor Vakoi from the wall. She verified there was nothing behind it before shuffling through the bookshelves. The woman stepped aside, watching with quivering eyes.

Eventually, Cal looked at the sofa.

Yahshi's hands went tense when he noticed the boy's jaw drop. *They're hiding something.*

Cal met eyes with Evaris, who helped her push the sofa aside. The man wrapped an arm around his son, pulling him closer as Cal dropped to her knees and pressed her palms against the floorboards. A few slid against each other, and she removed them to reveal a hidden ditch.

Yahshi was too far away to see, but he knew Cal found something inside because she smiled.

"Please, ma'am," the man said. "You can take me, but leave my wife and son out of this."

"It's *Commander* to you," Cal said, lifting a can of black beans. "There are definitely more of these than your rations have allotted for a household of three." She pulled more cans out of the ditch, and the family's faces drained of color.

The boy tugged the man's shirt. "Father, what's going on?"

"It's okay," the man said, stroking the boy's hair.

Evaris reached for an arrow. "Are you a member of the Underground?"

"No." The man stepped back, dragging his son with him.

"No, of course not," his wife echoed, tossing her stack of books onto the floor.

The impact made Cal grit her teeth. "Then what are these stolen goods for?" she shouted. "You must *really* love beans."

"We do," the man said, maintaining his calm tone. "Right? Don't we?" He shook his son by the shoulder, cueing the boy's tears.

"Father," he cried, clearly knowing something was wrong.

Cal stood and kicked a stack of beans. As they rolled, the man stormed after her, raising a lantern over his head.

She dodged, throwing a star from her bandolier. It slit his cheek and struck the wall before Yahshi could blink.

The man's lantern shattered against the floorboards.

He shot after Cal again as the boy cried and the woman yelled for him to stop. Yahshi glanced at his dagger. *What should I do?*

It was only when Evaris raised her bow, aiming at the little boy, that the man stopped. He raised his palms, breathing heavily. "Don't hurt him."

"Then don't move," Cal said, plucking another star. "You resisted detainment and attacked a guardian. You violated Imperial Law."

Yahshi's heart skipped a beat when she met his gaze. "Call for Galler," she ordered.

He ran onto the porch, where the weight of a pair of eyes stopped him. He looked around to spot its source—an old woman leaning against a neighboring house. She had dark eye bags and curly white hair that drifted in the wind.

"Look at you." The old woman crossed her frail arms with a smirk. "A baby Nightshade. What a pity."

Yahshi frowned before snapping back to his senses and bolting down the steps. "Help!" he yelled, waving his hands at the vault.

Galler jumped through the open door and ran to him. "N-Never use the word *help* during an e-expedition, no matter the st-stakes, alright, Shadow?" He spoke in a soft tone, but the critique struck Yahshi like a throwing blade. "It's unprofessional and f-fuels the enemy."

"Right. Sorry."

Galler raised his voice. "D-Did they find anything?"

He nodded.

"D-Did he resist?"

He nodded again, and Galler drew his swords. "W-Wait here. Evaris and I will se-secure the wife and child"—he eyed the dagger in Yahshi's hand—"and then you're g-going to finish the job."

He gulped. "Finish—finish what—"

"You know what I mean."

Galler slammed the door behind him, leaving Yahshi alone on the porch, gripping Cal's dagger. He had accepted that someday, he might have to kill. But he had never imagined *who* he might kill.

He looked for the old woman, but she was gone.

"No!" the boy screamed at the top of his lungs. "Let me stay with him!"

The door burst open, and Galler dragged the sobbing boy down the steps.

"I hate you!" the boy said, meeting Yahshi's gaze. "I hate all of you!"

You think I'm a monster, but I'm doing what's right. Yahshi turned his back to him. *Your father committed treason. He smuggled goods and resisted detainment. He's not a good role model for you. Don't you see that by following Protocol, we're helping you? We're making this right.*

He entered the house to find Cal on her knees, pinning the criminal down. As he approached them, he adjusted his grip on the handle. He didn't want to kill the man, but it had to be done. *Someone has to do the dirty work.*

"You don't want to kill me," the man said. "What if I know something?"

"We'll have an easier time getting your wife and son to talk," Cal said.

The man tried to break her grip, but the serum from her laced star had weakened him.

"Do you ever stop and ask yourself why you're doing this?" the man asked in a shaky voice. "Just once, think for yourself. Think with your own mind."

Yahshi crouched and held the blade to the target's neck. He thought of the blood that spilled over his hands in the lab. He thought of Sunna's tears in the rain. He thought of those rabbits in the dirt. He had a ridiculous urge to bring them flowers.

Flowers? He closed his eyes. *Have some restraint.*

"What are you waiting for?" Cal said.

Yahshi took a deep breath. *He's just a traitor*, he reminded himself, and with a swift motion, yanked the blade.

His eyes burned against their lids as the man audibly spilled out and died.

The dagger fell from his grip as he stood and turned his back to the corpse. When he opened his eyes, he gasped at the sight of Cal in front of him. He wondered how long he had been crouched on the floor, listening to Death speak.

"Good job, Yahshi," Cal said.

Good job?

The young boy flashed through his mind. The Force would grant Yahshi rare visitation rights to see Martu after graduation, but that boy had no chance for a reunion. He would never see his father again. *And it's all my fault.*

Yahshi raised his hands. They were tainted with the blood of a traitor who was also a father—a criminal who fought to protect his son.

Cal offered him a scarlet handkerchief. It took a moment to process that it was for wiping his hands on. He brushed the cold fabric against his palms, watching the blood clear away like it had never been there.

When he offered the handkerchief back, she shook her head. "Keep it."

And as though Alora's yellow mittens had revived from the ashes, it all came back to haunt him. He had a souvenir again, a reminder of the evil he couldn't escape no matter how far he traveled.

Yahshi tucked the handkerchief into his pocket, wishing he could cry because to cry would make him human. But when he touched his cheeks, they were dry.

Their walk to the vault was a blur. He followed Cal like a ghost, a shell of a living boy who was now only a shadow of Death.

Cal took the exterior driver's seat while Yahshi joined Evaris and Galler inside the passenger box. The traitor's wife and son were restrained, their mouths gagged, and they stared at Yahshi with a hatred that made him wish he could run.

But he wasn't allowed to run, so he slammed the vault door shut, confining himself to the darkness.

They left the beans under the blood-soaked floorboards and drove away.

NOT HUMAN; PERFECT

We hold ourselves accountable and learn from our mistakes,
like shaded flowers growing toward sunlight.

♫ MONSTER - HALF MOON RUN ♫

Yahshi traveled with Cal's unit three hours to the Detainment Facility, where a group of Defense guardians isolated the wife and son in separate interrogation rooms.

"Professor Famir," Cal said, greeting a Research guardian who seemed to be in his thirties. He had a mustache curled at the ends and hair so short it might as well not exist. "Meet Yahshi, my shadow. He'll join us in sitting in on your interrogations."

Yahshi's blood ran cold as Famir smiled at him.

"Cal!" Evaris laughed. "It's your shadow's first time in the Facility. Surely he deserves a tour."

Cal narrowed her eyes at Evaris for a moment before nodding. "Good point. Show Yahshi around. Galler—you're with us."

Evaris guided Yahshi down a dark corridor, dropping her smile. She didn't give him a tour.

Instead, she sat with him in a torch-lit watchtower, and they gazed silently at the outskirts of Vakoi City.

Yahshi felt like a criminal in a cell for the half-hour trip to the Academy. He didn't realize the vault had stopped until Galler opened the door.

"You're fr-free to go now, Shadow."

Yahshi hopped from the platform to see Commander Roz slip a notebook and pen into his overcoat.

"Thank you for the report."

Cal shook his hand with an iron grip. "It's my pleasure, Commander." She patted Yahshi's shoulder on her way to the driver's seat. "I'll see you next month."

No. Yahshi crossed his arms. *I won't be seeing you next month.*

He avoided Commander Roz's gaze as Cal drove the vault away, heading back to Vakoi City.

"I heard the story." Commander Roz led Yahshi toward the main building. "She said you had impressive restraint for your first—"

"Kill?"

"I was going to say *assignment*." He sighed. "Look, I know it wasn't easy, but you should be proud of yourself for following Protocol."

"As if I had a choice," Yahshi muttered.

"What was that?"

He eyed the traces of blood on his boots. *I need to clean them before the others see.* How ironic that he felt the need to bury evidence he'd followed Protocol.

"You returned with perfect timing," Commander Roz said after a moment of silence. "Everyone was just getting seated for supper."

"Wonderful."

"Yahshi, why the attitude?"

"I killed him, Commander." He stopped on the field, and the guardian faced him.

"You followed Protocol."

"I followed Protocol, *and* I killed him. Don't use one truth to cover another."

He stepped toward Yahshi, lowering his voice. "I understand this was a new experience for you, but you did what you had to do."

"He was a father."

"He was a *traitor*."

"I slit his throat like it was nothing!"

"Hey," Commander Roz snapped. "I'm not responsible for your feelings. If you're choosing to be angry that he died, be my guest, but don't take your anger out on me. I'm not the one who killed him."

"I didn't want to kill him."

"Yet you killed him anyway. That is the burden every guardian must carry." He continued walking, and Yahshi had no choice but to follow him.

"Every two years, we select twenty exceptional students for the program, and only the *most exceptional* make the final five. The fact that you're still here proves you can handle immense pressure—much more than the average person. If someone as strong as you isn't willing to get his hands dirty to keep our people safe, who will? Certainly not Sunna."

Yahshi gulped at the memory of yesterday's filtration. It was clear to him now that Sunna hadn't thrown away his future by filtering himself—he had saved it.

"Don't shame him. He was the best of us."

"He was the *sixth* best, and that's a fact. Most people are weaker than you would imagine, Yahshi. The nature of humanity requires the minority strong to protect the majority weak. If strong people like you turn weak, our people will fall victim to greater evil time and time again."

"Well if our job is to kill fathers, maybe we should redefine what it means to keep people safe."

Commander Roz locked a hand on his shoulder, and Yahshi maintained eye contact, refusing to succumb to his intimidation.

"Apologize."

Yahshi leaned in. "For what?"

Commander Roz shoved a fist into his gut, releasing him with a shove. He stumbled back, wheezing.

"Yahshi, let's go inside."

He followed him across the courtyard with a slight limp, clutching his stomach, struggling to steady his breaths—but his rage outweighed the discomfort. *I hate you, Commander*, he thought, tears finally welling in his eyes.

When they entered the common room, Yahshi rushed for the staircase, but Commander Roz grabbed the back of his vest, stopping him.

"Don't touch me!" Yahshi pried himself from the guardian's grip. A tear slipped down his cheek, and he wiped it away with his sleeve.

Commander Roz stared with hollow eyes. "Is it out of your system now?"

He bolted for the staircase again.

"Enough!" Commander Roz shouted, and Yahshi turned around, his face aflame.

"Fine!" The volume of his voice strained his throat. "Fine, you win! I'll finish my damn supper!" He stormed into the dining hall and slammed the door.

His fellow trainees watched from the table, their eyes wide. It was clear they heard everything.

Yahshi sat and grabbed his spoon. He expected the utensil to shake in his hand and prove that he still had some humanity left—but his grip was steady.

When he looked up, Quax was staring at Keiyo, who averted his gaze with a shake of his head. Rage crackled inside Yahshi too, but he put out the flames. How could someone like him judge Quax for injuring Pinto? *It's not like he killed him.*

"So," Keiyo said, breaking the silence, "how was your assignment?"

"Fine," Yahshi muttered.

"Apparently we're not allowed to ask for details, but... are you okay?"

"Drop it, Keiyo," Vell said. "He said he's fine."

"But he's not, obviously."

Yahshi burst from his chair, realizing he hadn't washed his hands.

I don't care what Commander Roz does. I'm not finishing my supper.

He rushed to the sink in the infirmary, where he emptied a bottle of alcohol over his palms. He scrubbed his fingers with soap and water until they bubbled so much he couldn't see his skin. He washed and rinsed and washed again, but he never felt clean. There was a film he couldn't remove, no matter how strong the soap or how pure the water.

"A baby Nightshade." Yahshi rubbed harder as the old woman's voice echoed in his head. *"What a pity."*

He still had soap on his hands when he fetched a vial of yellow fluid and fumbled to pop the stopper off.

The antiserum tasted rotten.

He gripped the sink, vomiting what little food remained in his system. The stench made his nose wrinkle as he looked up at his reflection in the mirror. His porcelain skin, marble eyes, and midnight hair only mimicked the boy he had once been

I'm not human.

Cal's reflection appeared behind him in the glass.

"No," she said, "but you're perfect."

For the second night in a row, Yahshi couldn't sleep. On several occasions, he slipped out of bed to scrub his hands in the restroom, and by the time the sun rose, his skin was cracking, and his eyes stung with every blink.

His mouth watered at the sight of an omelet in the dining hall, but he didn't grab his spoon. *I don't deserve to fill the void in my stomach.* He scooted his chair away from the table, watching the others eat. Quax and Keiyo occasionally looked at him, but they said nothing.

After breakfast, Yahshi caught up to Vell on his way to the lecture hall out of habit. She quickened her pace, leaving him behind.

He took his usual seat and glanced at Sunna's empty chair. *Will I ever see him again?*

"Professor," Quax said after the pledge of allegiance. "How's Pinto?"

Vell scoffed.

"A Medical unit stopped by this morning to update us on his condition. He should be well enough to return next week." Professor Embre leaned back in her chair. "Listen, I know this isn't an easy time for any of you. Not only are you dealing with the aftermath of the final filtration, but you're also adjusting to changes in the program's curriculum, like the addition of shadow assignments."

She made eye contact with Yahshi, and he pursed his lips. *Do you know, Professor? Do you know that I killed?*

"Trust me when I say that I understand exactly how you feel. I was a trainee in your shoes once. Everything gets easier when you realize that the pressure is gone. There are no filtrations. There is no competition. You are all on the same team. The program's second half is a time for learning, but most importantly, it's a time for *healing*."

The other trainees exchanged glances, considering the guardian's advice, but Yahshi stared her dead in the eye. How could this be a time for healing when he had been forced to kill a man? *That father will never heal from the blade to his neck, just as I will never heal from placing it there.*

"Yahshi, you weren't here yesterday, so let me bring you up to speed." She offered a smug grin. "Now that you've reached a baseline of standardized knowledge, classes will be less formal with an emphasis on individual learning. You're encouraged to explore the topics that interest you most and develop unique skill sets. We'll be monitoring your progress in class and on your monthly shadow assignments to determine your official division and unit placements."

He studied her face, trying to read whether she'd been the one to assign him as Cal's shadow. The Academy guardians knew he had witnessed the incident. They had not made that decision by chance.

"Speaking of which," Professor Embre continued, "Vell, your first assignment is tomorrow morning. Meet your shadow unit leader in the common room at 6:00."

Yahshi folded his dry hands together under his desk. "What's her shadow unit's division?"

"Vell's placement is none of your concern," Professor Embre said.

"It's a Medical unit, right?" Yahshi raised his voice. "Or do you purposefully force trainees to shadow units they'll hate, just to make them miserable?"

"Yahshi, you're obviously bothered." Professor Embre pointed to the door. "Get out."

"What?"

"You're making rude implications about our judgment, and I won't stand for it. I don't want you back in this room until you regain composure."

"So you're not gonna answer my question?"

"Out!" She slammed a fist against her desk. "That's an order."

Yahshi marched to the door, looking back at his fellow trainees, who avoided his gaze. He shook his head before leaving the lecture hall.

He spent the day alone in his quarter, skipping over classes and meals. His stomach was devouring itself, but he wasn't in enough pain to face Commander Roz or Professor Embre again, so he lay in bed early to sleep off the hunger.

Except the hunger stayed, because sleep never came.

I'm a monster. If I had done the right thing, I would not be this sleepless and hungry and angry. My hands would not be cracking and bleeding. My boots would not be damaged from the lye soap I rubbed on them. I had followed Protocol, but I had not done the right thing.

After a third restless night, he glanced at the clock and jumped out of bed. It was nearly 6:00.

Vell's leaving on her assignment soon.

He burst into the lobby to find Keiyo tossing a throwing blade into the air. The star came whirling down, and he caught it with a pinch of his fingers.

"You haven't been eating," he noted. "Something bad happened on your assignment."

Yahshi didn't reply.

"Do you think Sunna was right?" Keiyo tucked the star into his pocket. "That this is all... madness?"

Yahshi nodded as the door to Room 1 swung open. Vell entered the lobby, her eyes locking on Keiyo—but not Yahshi.

"Hey," Keiyo said. "Just wanted to wish you good luck on your assignment."

She walked over and hugged him. "Thanks."

"Have fun out there," he muttered, cloaking the concern in his voice with a chuckle. "And I know you're a badass, but remember—serum vials aren't for recreational use."

Vell pulled away, smiling with a shake of her head before finally meeting Yahshi's gaze. She and Keiyo waited for him to speak, but the words clotted in his throat. *Surely she wouldn't appreciate my concern after everything I did in the filtration.*

He headed for his quarter.

"Wait," Vell called.

Yahshi stopped with his hand on the doorknob.

"You were gonna say something." She frowned. "So say it."

He opened the door. "It's nothing you'd wanna hear."

"Yahshi," Vell said, stopping him again. "Why are you bleeding?"

His eyes widened at the sight of his hand on the doorknob. Trails of blood spilled from his flaky knuckles, inching toward his wrist.

"I just wanted to tell you to stay safe on your assignment," he said, his voice hardly more than a whisper. "That's all I was gonna say."

He fled to his restroom and ran his hands under a forceful stream of water. The stinging cracks in his skin reminded him of the punishment he deserved. The only way to avenge the Eastern man's death was to destroy the monster who had taken his life.

I will never murder for the Force again.

Yahshi breathed through his teeth to keep from wailing as he lathered soap into his wounds.

With my own blood staining my boots, I will leave behind the heartless killer I've become.

CHAPTER 23

HEARTLESS

We honor the ebb and flow of empathy, finding reflections
of ourselves in every lake we encounter.

♫ SWIM · NICK KINGSWELL ♫

A few hours after Vell left with her shadow unit, Keiyo knocked on Yahshi's door. "Doctor Blim wants you in class. And I know you're mad at the guardians for some reason, but this is Blim Blim we're talkin' about. He means well. So come out, will you?"

Yahshi tucked his hands into his pockets and joined Keiyo in the lobby.

With Pinto hospitalized and Vell on her assignment, the lab was exceptionally empty. Yahshi searched for blood on the floor as he walked toward an open table, but the tile was spotless—as though teenagers had never spilled poisoned rabbits over them. *Guardians are experts at cleaning up their messes. They wipe their hands and pretend a bad thing never happened.*

"Yahshi, I'm glad to see you here," Doctor Blimmery said. "What are you interested in working on?"

"Nothing." He lifted his gaze from the floor. "Is that an option?"

"I'm afraid it's not." Doctor Blimmery turned to grab something from his desk, and Yahshi slipped on a pair of gloves.

"You've missed a few lunches, so you have a tolerance dose to catch up on." He brought him a glass of beet juice, which Yahshi grabbed with his gloved hands.

"Why the gloves?" Doctor Blimmery asked.

"I think I'll work with calabar beans, actually. Don't want my skin to flare up."

He took a sip, and Keiyo glanced at him from across the room.

"Wonderful." Doctor Blimmery approached Quax next. "And how about you? Is there anything in Medical you're interested in exploring more deeply?"

"Not really," Quax said with a shrug. His hair was messy, his eye bags dark.

"Think on it for a minute." He turned to Keiyo last, who was already standing at the cabinet where they stored their tools.

"I'll be crafting today," Keiyo said without the guardian's prompting.

"Perfect," Doctor Blimmery replied. "Yahshi, I'll fetch those beans for you."

Keiyo hesitated to open the drawer labeled with his name before opening Sunna's. Doctor Blimmery had only taken a few steps toward the door when he slammed the drawer shut.

"Where did they go?" Keiyo turned around, his face red. "I wanted to study them!"

"There would be nothing to study," Doctor Blimmery said. "You were always superior at crafting."

"But I wanted to keep them," Keiyo said in a softer tone.

"I'm sorry, but when Sunna left, his things did too."

Yahshi watched Keiyo's shoulders loosen, the redness dissipating from his face. He returned to his table with his own crafted tools, and Doctor Blimmery nodded in approval before leaving the lab.

It's human nature to choose who we surround ourselves with. Why is it necessary to keep us from our friends and families? It's not about our ruthless schedule, is it? The rules are in place to control our emotions. Because if they control our emotions, they control our actions. And if they control our actions, they own us completely.

Doctor Blimmery returned a few minutes later with calabar beans, which Yahshi pretended to work with for the remainder of class. When the bell rang, he headed to the common room and gazed through a window, staring at the field. He continued to stand there, even after the bell rang for lunch and another bell rang for Defense class.

Eventually, Doctor Blimmery appeared next to him. "Hey, kid. What are you doing here?"

Yahshi tucked his hands into his pockets, eyes glued to the window. "I'm waiting for Vell."

"Alright. Why don't you wait with me outside?"

"I'll wait here."

"Yahshi," the guardian said with an unusual firmness to his tone, "wait with me outside, please."

Not wanting to antagonize the last Academy guardian he liked, Yahshi followed Doctor Blimmery through the door, and they crossed the field together.

"I heard about your assignment," Doctor Blimmery said. "What you did wasn't easy, but you need to understand that the Force doesn't tolerate this kind of behavior. You do understand that, right?"

"What kind of behavior?"

"You're acting out, Yahshi."

"I'm not acting out."

"Yes, you are. And I'm not saying this because I'm angry at you—I'm not. I'm simply worried about what could happen if you don't get your act together."

"If they hate me so much, I can leave. I can go home, and Ceylon can take my spot instead."

"That's not how it works." Doctor Blimmery sighed. "Yahshi, it's not easy to run this program. It takes time, money, creativity—and these resources are invested with the expectation that the graduates' contributions will be worth it. Do you really think that if you piss them off enough, they'll send you home? The Force won't pour a valuable investment like you down the drain over a bit of unruly behavior. Even if it requires heavy correctional measures, they'll do whatever it takes to fix you and get their money's worth."

"What kind of correctional measures?"

Doctor Blimmery hesitated. "During Selection Seasons, I work part-time in the City. Sometimes that involves writing articles for *Capital Weekly*, a responsibility of mine dating back to graduation."

They stopped on the forested road as Yahshi recalled the handwritten article he'd found in Doctor Blimmery's quarter. It wasn't hard to believe the Force would entrust him with writing for the press. He had a talent for making people feel safe.

"There was... a graduate from my cycle. Maelin. I wrote an article about her many years ago." Doctor Blimmery smiled, his eyes shimmering. "The Force sure knows how to tell a good story."

Yahshi nearly asked about the article, but the sound of approaching horses drew his thoughts back to Vell. He smiled when he noticed that the guardian driving the vault had Medical badges on his shoulders. He parked and hopped from his seat as Doctor Blimmery retrieved a notepad from his overcoat.

"Should he be here for this?" the guardian asked, eyeing Yahshi.

"Go ahead," Doctor Blimmery said.

Vell's unit leader stared a moment longer before clearing his throat. "Well, she's exceptional. We met with a Research unit to discuss the development of a less risky form of neutralizer, and she caught on like *that*." He snapped his fingers. "She even pitched a few ideas of her own."

He paused as Doctor Blimmery scribbled a few notes down, giving him time to catch up.

"And she's got a way with darts," he continued. "We had a competition over lunch break, and she beat every one of us. We haven't seen precision like that since—well, since Commander Cal." He was about to share more, but Doctor Blimmery stashed his notebook, cutting the discussion short.

"That's all," he said.

The unit leader nodded and shouted, "Ready!"

A guardian inside the passenger box opened the door, and Vell hopped out. She made her way toward Doctor Blimmery with a grin that faded at the sight of Yahshi.

"Great job today, Vell," Doctor Blimmery said. "You're a bit late, but we saved supper for you." He headed for the field as the vault drove away, leaving Yahshi and Vell alone on the road. They lingered, the distance between them expanding, before heading for the field next.

"I'm glad you're shadowing a Medical unit," Yahshi said.

She scoffed, staring directly ahead. "Don't do this."

He fished for her gaze. "Do what?"

"*This*. I don't want you trying to... fix things."

"Why not?"

She finally faced him, glaring as though he was trying to murder her mother.

"I'm sorry," he said, his eyes burning.

She looked away. "Leave."

"Vell—"

"If you're sorry, then *leave me alone*."

Yahshi lowered his head so she couldn't see his pathetic attempt to hold back tears, but it probably came through his voice anyway.

"Okay, if that's what you want," he choked out. "But before you push me away, let me say this. Please."

He didn't pause to gather the right words because they were all there, and they were all true.

"You have no idea how much I regret what happened. I wish I helped you carry him. I wish I didn't pluck your feather. I was selfish and immature, and you were right—I didn't need to stay in the program like you did. Actually, staying in the program was the last thing I needed, and I finally see that now. So if I could go back and make everything right, I would do so in a heartbeat, even if it meant getting filtered. But I can't. It happened. And I know you hate me for it, and maybe there's no way you could ever trust my word again, but I want you to hear me say that I'm sorry, and... I miss you."

"I miss you too," Vell said. "You're different now. You're something else."

One week later, Yahshi showed up to Research class. He'd been avoiding Professor Embre due to suspicion that she'd assigned him to shadow Cal, but deep down, he knew he couldn't blame anyone but himself for taking that man's life, so into the lecture hall he went.

Professor Embre scowled at him as he approached an empty desk. She was about to address his prolonged absence when the door busted open, diverting her eyes.

Yahshi froze when Pinto entered, back from treatment at Vakoi City Hospital. His good eye was swollen, and his arm was in a sling—but despite his battered state, he offered Yahshi and Vell a smile.

They both looked away. *He doesn't know what happened after Quax knocked him out.*

Pinto limped to Yahshi's desk and took the empty seat beside him. "What did I miss?" he whispered.

Yahshi shook his head, gluing his eyes to Professor Embre as she began her lecture. Pinto started taking notes a few minutes later, and Yahshi noticed that his nails were shortened to jagged stubs, his cuticles red. *He's been biting them.*

"Yahshi?" Pinto whispered again, his pencil pausing on the page. "Is something wrong?"

He bit his lip, ignoring him.

When Pinto joined Vell's lab table during Medical class, which they'd shared for the entirety of the program thus far, she left his side and found a new place to work.

By lunch, Pinto was glaring at Yahshi and Vell, his lips twitching.

Keiyo cleared his throat. "So, Pinto, are you feeling better?"

"I'm feeling great," Pinto grumbled, his glare shooting to Quax. "Just great."

Quax took another bite, eyes on his plate.

"But you know what would make me feel even better?" he continued. "If there was more than one table left in the dining hall. Then I wouldn't have to watch Quax eat like a pig."

Quax set his fork down and gulped.

"And then Yahshi and Vell could sit at their own table, pretending I don't exist. It'd be perfect." Pinto leaned back in his chair, shaking his head. "I don't know what's going on with you two, but I don't care. Whatever you *think* you're angry about is *nothing* compared to what I've been going through at the Hospital. I'm the only person who deserves to be angry here, and I deserve an apology."

"I'm sorry," Quax said.

"Look at me," Pinto ordered, and Quax slowly raised his chin, his face wrought with guilt. "You did this to me." He pointed to his face. "I had to spend a week in the Hospital because of you. My one good eye was swollen shut. I couldn't see anything for *three days*. Do you have any idea how awful that was?"

"I didn't mean to go that far," Quax said, looking him in the eye this time. "I got carried away. I'm sorry."

"Oh, save it, Quax." Keiyo shook his head. "You turned your back on me by plucking my feather. No one had to get hurt, but you chose not to stick to our plan. You *chose* this!"

"I was scared, okay? What was I supposed to do? Get filtered without putting up a fight? The game was set up to pit us against each other from the start."

"True, but you didn't have to butcher my friend," Vell said.

Pinto frowned, clearly confused by her mixed behavior.

"I know that, okay?" Quax said. "I messed up. I didn't mean to go that far, and I'm sorry."

"Apologies don't change the past," she argued. "You nearly killed him."

"I hurt him, yes, but I wasn't trying to kill him." His eyes watered. "I messed up, and I admitted that, and I said that I'm sorry. What more could you possibly want from me? How do I fix this if my apology means nothing to you?"

"Quax is right," Yahshi said. "There's nothing he can say or do to make you feel better, so we should put our energy into moving forward."

"Oh, I'm sure you'd love that, wouldn't you?" Vell narrowed her eyes at him. "You're just as guilty as Quax. You had no problem letting Pinto *die*."

"He wasn't dying," Yahshi said.

"What does she mean by that?" Pinto asked, but Vell answered for him.

"After Quax knocked you out, I asked Yahshi to help me carry you. But instead, he plucked my feather."

"And then she plucked yours," Yahshi added.

"Don't you dare pin this on me!" Vell shouted. "I wouldn't have done that if you hadn't turned your back on him."

"But you still did it." Yahshi cowered at the memory of Cal ordering him to kill. "Just because you were pressured into something doesn't mean you don't have to take responsibility for it."

"I can't believe you," she said. "You're heartless."

"Yahshi, is that true?" Pinto asked. "You had no problem letting me die?"

"Yes!" he yelled. "*Yes*, is that what you wanna hear? I had no problem letting you die because I'm heartless, and I don't care who I hurt! I'm an awful, irredeemable monster who can't be trusted. I'm *poison*, and all of you should hate me forever."

"You're being mean, Vell," Keiyo muttered, gripping his fork tighter.

Yahshi's frown loosened at the sight of Keiyo's dry, flaky hands.

"Excuse me?" she asked.

"Yahshi doesn't deserve this." Keiyo slammed his fork down, making her flinch. "You're not any different from him. You turned your back on Pinto because of Yahshi, but Yahshi only turned his back on Pinto because Quax beat him up in the first place. It all traces back to Quax. If he hadn't betrayed me and attacked *your* target, we wouldn't be arguing right now. There's only one heartless person here, and it's *him*."

Quax stood so quickly that his chair fell over. He left the dining hall without a word.

IT CAN'T BE GOOD

We listen cautiously, allowing whispers of the wind
to guide us closer to our destiny.

♫ DRAINED · DEATH OF HEATHER ♫

That night, Yahshi knocked on Keiyo's door for the first time. It'd taken a fleeting glimpse of his hands over lunch for him to wonder if he'd gone through something similar.

Keiyo opened the door and rubbed his eyes. "It's late..."

Yahshi leaned toward him, lowering his voice. "Cal's my shadow unit leader."

"What?" Keiyo asked, his eyes suddenly alert. "Quax's sister?"

He nodded.

"There's no way..."

Yahshi pulled his hands out of his pockets, and Keiyo gulped at the sight of them.

"She scares me, Keiyo. She ordered me to kill."

Keiyo crossed his arms and lowered his chin as though he were trying to shield himself.

"And the traitor was a man with a wife and a son," he continued. "The boy was crying, but I killed his father anyway. Cal's unit detained the wife and son for questioning, but I wouldn't be surprised if they killed them too. And I-I think I finally have the answer to the question I've been asking myself for a long time. The Force—well, I'm not sure if I'd call it evil. But it can't be good."

He paused, choking on a breath. "Something horrible is going on here, and Sunna saw it before any of us, and Limbo saw it even earlier than him. And now I'm seeing it, but it's far too late for me, so I can't do anything but wish I never pricked my thumb on Selection Day."

Keiyo stepped aside, summoning him into his quarter.

In Yahshi's previous attempts to converse with Keiyo, he'd always dismiss him. He never would have guessed that someday, he'd be the only person at the Academy to listen.

Keiyo tossed a dagger across the room, and Yahshi caught it by the handle. He recognized the sloppy carvings.

"This was Sunna's. One of his earlier pieces." Yahshi trailed his fingers along the handle's flower designs. "I thought Doctor Blimmery cleared out his drawer."

"It wasn't from the drawer," Keiyo said with a sigh. "The night of the final filtration, I went into Sunna's quarter after supper, before the guardians cleared his stuff. I don't know why, really. I was just angry, although that's probably obvious 'cause I threw a plate of cake across the dining hall." He chuckled. "Which is a shame looking back on it 'cause I bet it was pretty good cake. And I guess part of me... *missed* Sunna. Well, that's stupid. He had just left the grounds, but—"

"It's okay to miss him," Yahshi said.

Keiyo shrugged before continuing. "So I was walking around his room, right? It was getting dark, and I could hardly see a thing. Ended up stubbing my toe on his bed frame—which hurt like hell, by the way—and I realized I should probably light his lantern, but I couldn't figure out where he kept his stupid matchbox. And at this point my toe was throbbing and I was really pissed off, so I started chucking his pillows across the room and slamming his drawers, and... when I looked back at the blankets, that's when I found it. Sorry, not the matchbox. The dagger. He kept it under his pillows."

Yahshi offered the tool back. "Why?"

"I think he's been scared for a while now." Keiyo grabbed the handle, and for a moment, their cracked hands were exposed next to each other. *Maybe we're more alike than I thought.*

"Scared of the guardians, the trainees, or all of us. Who knows?" Keiyo tossed the dagger from hand to hand. "We're a violent bunch, aren't we? I'm just realizing that now. The longer we last in the program, the more messed up we become, and let's be honest—we were all a bit messed up at the start." He caught the dagger a final time and studied its handle. "You know, I like to think Sunna looks back on the past nine months and remembers me as a friend, but part of me knows he thinks of me as a monster."

"I doubt that," Yahshi said. "He wouldn't have spent so much time with you if he didn't consider you a friend."

"Or it was all a game of survival to him. Befriend the strongest boys so you don't have to watch your back. Be nice to the others because you secretly wish you were friends with them instead."

Keiyo stashed the dagger in his desk.

"You know," he said, facing Yahshi, "I never really wondered if I'd like being a guardian. I didn't think about stuff like that. I only started training 'cause I didn't have any friends, and it's what people with lots of friends were doing. So I lost weight, got stronger, and suddenly I was funny, not annoying. People started to like me. But I never asked myself what *I* liked."

Yahshi gulped. "On your first assignment yesterday, you shadowed a Defense unit, didn't you?"

"I don't mind fighting in practice, and I know I'm pretty good at it," Keiyo said without confirmation. "But I like tool crafting the most. You know, developing new styles, making them look cool—stuff like that."

Yahshi grinned. *He's a crafting prodigy. I won't deny it.*

"Last night, I started to think about what you asked Professor Embre in the lecture hall—about whether the Academy guardians want us to suffer. I thought you'd gone mad at the time, but I get it now. The guardians know I'm the best at crafting and enjoy it most, but they're still making me shadow a Defense unit. It's like they think my muscles are all I'm good for. Like it's a shame that I came here as one of the best fighters, with tons of private combat experience, and they thought it'd be a waste to let me tinker with metal.

"But it's also confusing because accusing them of something like that is wrong. We're supposed to trust their judgment because that's what we do, but sometimes I want nothing more than to ask, *Why are we doing this? Why do I need to kill her? Is there any other way?* But I don't ask because that's *not* what we do, you know?"

"I'm sorry," Yahshi said.

"My unit leader told me it would be nothing. He said it was most likely a false report."

"Cal told me that too."

"Do you think they lied? Do you think they were ordered to make us kill right from the start?"

Yahshi blinked. "I don't know."

Keiyo plopped himself onto his bed. "I guess it doesn't matter. Confronting the guardians will only make everything harder for us."

"That's no reason not to."

"It's every reason not to," he argued, raising his voice. "You've really pissed them off, Yahshi. All those days you didn't show up to Research class, Professor Embre couldn't stop mumbling under her breath about you. And Commander Roz came to me in Defense class a few days ago to ask how many meals you've been skipping. They won't shut up about you. You're giving them trouble, and I can tell they're ready to give it back. I'm not gonna put myself through that too."

Keiyo rubbed his temple. "I need to snap out of this, and so do you. *Especially* you. So what if they're lying? So what if they want us to suffer? If we don't learn to manage our emotions, we'll spend the rest of our lives screaming at each other and making our hands bleed, and I don't want that for myself. This isn't sustainable."

Keiyo had jumped onto Yahshi's deserted island, but now he was threatening to leave just as quickly.

"No." Yahshi frowned, stepping toward him. "I want to feel how I feel for a change. I want to live as I am. Don't you?"

"But restraint is *how* we live, Yahshi." He looked up at him with tears welling in his eyes. "Don't you see that? There is no other way."

And in that moment, he pictured Keiyo hopping into his boat and paddling from the shore, because he knew he had lost him.

Over the next few weeks, Yahshi couldn't take his eyes off Keiyo. He watched him start to smile again. He watched him go from moping around during classes to actively participating and learning with excitement. He watched the skin of Keiyo's hands heal completely.

But Yahshi's hands never healed. He wouldn't allow them to because letting them heal would mean forgetting what he'd done—that he would learn to put it past him, just as Keiyo had, and he wouldn't lose himself like that. *I won't let the monster inside me win.*

On the last day of their tenth month, Professor Embre greeted Yahshi with a smile at the start of Research class. "Your second assignment is tomorrow. Meet your shadow unit leader in the common room at 6:00."

He rushed toward an open seat, but she snatched his wrist, stopping him. "Awfully dry weather this time of year, isn't it?" she asked, raising his arm to observe the cracked skin.

Yahshi pulled his wrist free. "Awfully dry."

"Go see Doctor Blimmery in the infirmary. He should take a look at your hands." She pointed to the door, and he left the lecture hall, lacking the energy to protest.

Doctor Blimmery was reading a novel when he arrived. He set the book down and smiled.

"Hey, kid. Do you need something?"

"Professor Embre wants you to look at my hands."

"Sure, have a seat."

Yahshi sat on a bed, and Doctor Blimmery dragged his chair in front of him. His eyes widened at the sight of his skin.

"How long has this been going on?"

Yahshi shrugged and looked away.

Doctor Blimmery shook his head before standing and rustling through a cabinet. He smiled when he found the bottle of cream he'd been looking for.

"Doctor?" Yahshi muttered. "What does it mean to be a Nightshade?"

"It's another word for the belladonna plant, that's all." He retook his seat and plopped a helping of cream onto Yahshi's hands. "Why? Did someone call you that?"

"Yeah, on my assignment." Yahshi rubbed the cream into his skin. "It sounded bad—the way she said it."

"Some Easterners use it to insult guardians. It's their way of shaming us, because in their eyes, we're the enemy."

"Why do they view us as the enemy?" Yahshi asked. "*Are* we the enemy? Is that what Maelin realized?"

Doctor Blimmery pressed a finger to his lips. "Don't say her name."

The cream sparked a burning sensation in Yahshi's hands. It was strangely soothing.

"Doctor, I don't wanna shadow Cal's unit tomorrow."

"I know," he said in a warm tone, "but you were assigned to shadow Cal's unit."

"By who? Them, or you?"

"*Us*. We're the Academy guardians. We're a team."

"But you're different. You've always been different from them. I know that. You're willing to bend the rules more than they are. So please, Doctor. Please don't make me shadow her tomorrow. I can't see her again after what happened last time. I told myself I'd never... I just *can't*."

"I'm sorry, kid, but it's out of my hands."

"Please, help me." Yahshi stared into the old man's eyes, searching for a hint of empathy. "Help me like you helped Vell."

Doctor Blimmery gripped Yahshi's arms. "You will *never* speak of that again."

Yahshi winced. "I'm sorry."

He tightened his grip, his nails pinching Yahshi's skin. "You could get me killed. You could destroy Vell's family."

"I said, I'm sorry!" Yahshi yelled.

"Promise me that you won't speak of that again."

"Okay! I promise!"

He released him, and Yahshi stared with heavy breaths, his arms aching.

"Listen to me very closely, kid. You only have monthly assignments with Cal until graduation. A handful of days with her is nothing compared to *years*, agreed?"

Yahshi nodded.

"So if you'd like to avoid being assigned as her official unit member on graduation day, here's what you're going to do..." Doctor Blimmery leaned toward him. "You're going to do everything she tells you to, but you're not going to do those things well. You're going to get vaultsick, even though you don't get vaultsick anymore. You're going to accidentally drop your dagger and blame it on your sweaty palms. And if she tells you to kill someone again, then for the glory of Vakoi, you're going to do it, but it will visually pain you. You will lack restraint. Do you hear what I'm getting at, kid?"

"Is there no way to avoid them completely?"

"You know the answer to that question." Doctor Blimmery burst from his chair. "I'm trying to help you in the only way I can. There is no other way. As long as you're physically able to shadow Cal's unit, you will shadow Cal's unit, understood?"

Yahshi lowered his head, standing without a word. Instead of returning to the lecture hall, he made a beeline to his quarter, where he washed the cream from his hands and crawled into bed.

Later that evening, Commander Roz knocked on Yahshi's door. They hadn't spoken to each other since their discussion after his first shadow assignment.

Commander Roz didn't bother with pleasantries. "You haven't been eating enough. You're losing muscle."

"That's not true," Yahshi argued.

"Do you need proof? Do you need me to bring out the scales so I can show you the evidence in numbers? Everyone can see it. Your uniforms were tailored to fit you perfectly, but now your sleeves are all baggy."

He glared at the guardian, his anger simmering just beneath the surface.

"We're putting you on a specialized meal plan. Come downstairs. *Now.*"

He followed Commander Roz to the dining hall, where a plate of steak, cheesy potatoes, and nuts awaited him. While the other trainees picked at their salads, Yahshi cut into his meat. Commander Roz watched from a distance, ensuring he finished every morsel before allowing him to leave.

The sudden increase in intake left his stomach aching. He held an arm around his waist as he climbed back to his quarter and stepped out onto the balcony. It felt like his insides were sore.

Yahshi hoisted himself onto the railing and balanced on it. The sun was setting on the horizon.

As long as I'm physically able to shadow, I'll shadow, huh? He glanced at the two-story fall with a gulp. *I understand, Doctor.*

With a deep breath, Yahshi stepped off the railing. The wind washed over him while he sank through the air, disappearing into the gathering darkness.

CHAPTER 25

BURIED ALIVE

We hold honesty sacred, bringing dark truths to light
regardless of the discomfort it may bring.

♫ NOTRE DAME · PARIS PALOMA ♫

Yahshi lay on an infirmary bed, his right leg throbbing, his vision blurry.
When he tried to sit up, a searing bolt of lightning shot through his body,
burning through his abdomen and forcing him to collapse. He allowed the
blankets to drown him, submitting himself to the pain.

"You're lucky you didn't land on your back, kid." Doctor Blimmery
leaned over him. "From a height like that, you could have ruined your
spine."

Yahshi nearly screamed when Doctor Blimmery moved his leg without
warning. The pain spread through every muscle in his body, almost replicating
the point of impact.

"I can't shadow tomorrow," he said through gritted teeth.

"Of course you can't," Doctor Blimmery spat.

After a few minutes of excruciating examination, the guardian sighed.
"You'll miss at least a month of training." He helped Yahshi into a seated

position, elevated his leg on a stack of pillows, and brought a cup of hot tea to his lips. "Drink this. It'll help with the pain and inflammation."

Yahshi took a few sips before smiling weakly. "Willow bark?"

"I've taught you well." He slipped on a pair of gloves before drenching a rag with alcohol and dabbing the cuts along Yahshi's arm. *There must have been pebbles in the grass.*

Next, he applied a coating of paste made of crushed willow bark, water, and other medicinal herbs. "The setting and bracing process for your leg will take a few hours. I'm addressing the smaller injuries first so they don't get infected during the lengthy leg treatment, causing further complications. Sometimes what seems like the priority is not the priority. Timing is key."

"I can't believe you're turning this into a Medical lesson," Yahshi muttered.

"I can't believe you jumped."

"I fell."

"Okay." Doctor Blimmery began to wrap Yahshi's arms in thin bandages. "But don't fall again."

When he finished, he rushed to the door and looked back. "I'll put together a brace. In the meantime, don't even *think* about leaving that bed. And finish your tea. You'll thank me later."

After he left, Yahshi lay in silence. His eyes watered, half in pain and half in frustration. He had worked so hard to make the final five, and now that he was here, he wanted to leave more than anything. But the guardians would let him die long before they'd set him free.

I can't live like this. I need a way out.

Over the many days that followed, Yahshi trudged his way through the recovery process. The brace Doctor Blimmery had constructed for him was padded with hay, which made it itchy, and despite how much he complained, the guardian never volunteered to fix it.

Professor Embre occasionally visited to slam a few textbooks on his bedside table. He strangely looked forward to her appearances, as the books curbed his boredom and distracted him from his aching back.

Commander Roz's visits, however, were the bane of his existence. He brought him food three times a day, insisting he continue his specialized meal plan to regain strength as soon as possible. Yahshi almost wanted to get weaker to spite him. *The Force wants us healthy so they can get more use out of us. It's all about investments and returns.*

The program's first nine months had flashed by, but every day he spent in the infirmary seemed to last years. He only confirmed a mere week had passed when Keiyo visited him with news about his second shadow assignment.

"It does get easier," Keiyo explained. "It's not always so bad."

"But sometimes it is," Yahshi said.

"That's true about anything though. Any job. Any hobby. And with people too—instructors, friends, parents. Nothing is perfect. That's just the way it is." He nudged Yahshi's brace, making him wince. "How's the leg?"

Vell and Pinto never visited. He didn't expect them to, but he wished he could see them. He wished he knew if they were okay.

It might have been a few days after his talk with Keiyo when Quax entered the infirmary, ransacking the cabinets for bandages. His left sleeve was rolled up, revealing a shallow cut across his upper arm.

"Bottom right," Yahshi said.

Quax glanced at him before opening the cabinet and locating the bandages. "Thanks," he muttered, securing one over the wound.

"What happened?"

"I was sloppy." Quax leaned against the cabinets. "How are you?"

"Surviving."

"Yeah?" He squinted. "Why the hell did you jump?"

"I fell."

"Do you really think I'd believe that? You're terrified of heights. There's no way you'd get close to *leaning* over that railing unless you had bad intentions."

"I got over that fear, actually."

"Why did you jump?" Quax asked, softer this time.

"Will you tell?"

"Not a word."

Yahshi closed his eyes. "I wanted to get out of my second shadow assignment."

"That badly? Bad enough to jump?" Quax asked. "You've been up here for ages."

"I don't like my shadow unit leader."

"Why not?"

"It's Cal."

"What?"

"Your sister."

Quax dragged a chair and sat at Yahshi's bedside. "How is she? Was she happy to see you? It's been three years!" A smile spread across his face.

"She made me kill someone."

His smile faltered. "Who?"

"A smuggler. He resisted detainment."

"Oh." Quax lowered his chin with a gulp. "Well, that's Protocol."

"She didn't wanna see you." He shuffled in bed, struggling to find a more comfortable position. "I told her you were upstairs, but she said it wasn't the time."

"Well, I-I mean, that makes sense. She had an assignment to complete. It wasn't the right time."

"She hasn't changed. She acts happy and social now, but it's an act. She's the same girl under that mask."

"Yeah? What girl, Yahshi?"

"The girl who never cared about anyone but herself."

"That's not true."

"She never ate supper with you and your parents. She didn't have any friends—and that was a choice because people tried to get close to her. All she cared about were her books, and her puzzles, and whether she could run around the lake faster than she did the day before, and—"

"That's because she's focused. She takes her work seriously."

"More seriously than she could ever love you."

Quax was quiet for a moment. "Don't act like you know her."

"She's cold, Quax."

"You're delusional." He burst from his chair and headed for the door.

"Wait!" Yahshi called.

"What?" Quax snapped, pivoting to face him.

"Before the selection ceremony began, you were gonna tell me something."

His gaze softened. "You still remember that?"

Yahshi nodded, pressing for an answer, and Quax turned his back to him again. It wasn't until his hand was on the doorknob that he finally spoke.

"I didn't want to get selected." He opened the door and looked back at Yahshi. "I just wanted to see her."

He closed the door behind him, and Yahshi wiped his eyes.

"Today's the big day." Doctor Blimmery attempted to pull Yahshi into a seated position. "Up, up, up! You've got an assignment to complete."

"Assignment?" Yahshi glued himself to the bed. "No. I can't, Doctor. I'm—"

"You're reassigned to shadow a Research unit," Doctor Blimmery said with a wink. "Can't have you on your feet too much, and professors have a talent for sitting around all day."

He gave up on lifting Yahshi and gestured for him to stand. "Up! Out of bed. For the glory of Vakoi, it's been a month! You've been cooped up long enough."

"But I like it here." He swung his legs off the bed. "I like it a lot."

"Oh, shut it, you." Doctor Blimmery tossed him a pair of crutches. "Give these a try."

Yahshi caught them and used one to hoist himself up. His right leg dangled heavily, but it didn't hurt. He pulled the second crutch under his free shoulder and took a step forward.

"Thanks, Doctor. But I'm disgusting. I haven't showered in days."

"You're not getting out of this one, kid." He held the door open for him.

"Fine. How do I get downstairs?"

"Hold the railing and lead with your good leg." Doctor Blimmery chuckled. "You'll figure it out."

When Yahshi reached the common room, Professor Embre stood by the sofas with crossed arms. "You look embarrassing."

"I didn't know I'd be shadowing," he said.

"They're waiting outside. You're joining Pinto so he can keep an eye on you. It's not the shadow unit's responsibility to babysit the injured."

"Got it," Yahshi said dryly, heading for the door.

"But before you go, I'd like to have a quick word with you." Professor Embre appeared in front of him, blocking his path. "I've been told that you'll be given access to the archives today, and I think it'd be beneficial for you to look through the correctional profiles."

"Why do you say that?"

"I just think it might interest you." She stepped out of his way with a smile, and Yahshi frowned before passing her. His arms were shaking from carrying his weight by the time he reached the vault.

"I'm Famir," said the mustached unit leader. "We met briefly in the Facility, remember?"

"I remember," Yahshi said.

Famir opened the vault door to reveal Pinto and two professors.

With a blank expression, Pinto helped Yahshi into the vault. They sat next to each other on a bench and made brief eye contact before their shadow unit leader hopped inside.

"It's a pleasure to have a second shadow," Famir said. "Although to be frank, I can hardly handle my official unit members alone."

One of them leaned forward, hands on his knees. "Oh, *haha*, Professor."

"Today we're heading to the Investigation Office to gather and discuss information about the Underground," Famir explained. "Pinto, you'll take meeting notes like last month. Those were excellent, by the way. Especially considering how your arm was in that cast."

Yahshi glanced at Pinto's arm, which had fully healed.

"Thank you," Pinto said, his smile so radiant that it overshadowed the faded bruises on his face.

"Yahshi," Famir continued, "your job is to sift through interrogation transcripts in the archives. Look for any commonalities between detained members of the Underground—recurring phrases, locations, etcetera. Let's see if you spot anything my unit missed."

"Yes, Professor," Yahshi said, and Famir left to drive the vault.

They traveled half an hour to the City. Pinto helped Yahshi off the platform, handing his crutches back before distancing himself.

With a glance, Yahshi could imagine the Investigation Office's interior based on the plans he'd memorized. It contained four expansive floors, which included the common room, archives, conference rooms, and private offices.

Famir unlocked the front door with an oddly shaped key and gestured for them to follow. Yahshi struggled to keep pace as they crossed a room of lounging areas, overflowing bookshelves, and dining tables.

"This is the Office common room," Famir explained. "It's where everything converges. We have books. We have food. Shelter. Water. Air. All the necessities of life." He led them to the staircase.

Thankfully we're only one flight of stairs from the archives.

"Can you handle it?" Pinto whispered.

Yahshi raised his brows, surprised he'd bothered to ask. "Yeah, I can. Thanks." He lagged as he followed them upstairs, and Famir was tapping his boot against the floor when he finally caught up to them.

The archives were far grander than the Academy library—so extensive that Yahshi couldn't see the walls. What stood out most was the addition of file cabinets and wooden desks for individual study, fit with comfortable rolling chairs.

"Today's meeting topic is the Underground's hideout," Famir said. "We need to figure out where those smuggled goods are being funneled to."

"Do you think that's where the Bayins went?" Pinto asked.

"I think it's likely." Famir straightened his tie, and Yahshi concealed a grin—it hadn't been crooked in the first place. "Yahshi, the files I need you to go through are in that section there. Start with interrogation transcripts from the past month."

"Got it." He swung himself toward the file cabinet Famir had pointed to.

"We'll fetch you for lunch," Famir said. "Pinto, follow us."

As they headed upstairs, Yahshi's eyes widened at the stuffed drawer. *How could the Force detain* this *many traitors in one month?*

He leaned his crutches against the cabinet, hopped to the nearest desk, and flipped through the hefty stack until a file caught his eye—it was labeled with the date of his first shadow assignment. The report inside was signed by Cal, and under her signature were the names *Galler Ashen of Miranda, Evaris Starfall of Vakoi City,* and *Yahshi Konya of Sitra (Shadow).*

The report contained a summary of events after Cal knocked on the door. Yahshi saw a brief mention of his name and, knowing it would describe the murder, closed his eyes. He turned the page before opening them again to find an interrogation transcript between Famir and the target's wife.

> [LOCATION: Detainment Facility, Interrogation Room 2]
>
> PROFESSOR: Why were you and your husband stealing rations?
>
> WIFE: Because we were hungry.
>
> PROFESSOR: If you were hungry, you would have eaten them.
>
> WIFE: [No response]
>
> PROFESSOR: We have reason to believe that your family is affiliated with the Underground. Is that true?

Yahshi gripped the page tighter.

> WIFE: What do you want?
>
> PROFESSOR: I want you and your son to live, and I can arrange that. Just tell us where those goods were going.
>
> WIFE: I don't know.

PROFESSOR: Surely you know, since you've been hoarding them. Tell us where they were going, and we'll let you and your son go.

WIFE: You're evil.

PROFESSOR: Your people gouge our eyes out, and you call us evil?

WIFE: Oh, is that what they tell you? They tell you the Underground did it? We had nothing to do with the raids. Your own emperor did that to you as an excuse to infiltrate our land.

PROFESSOR: Smugglers like you love to lead us astray. You love to lie to us. You love to waste our time.

WIFE: I'm not lying. I'm not lying.

[Wife begins to cry, and Professor injects serum into her neck]

Yahshi's eyes burned as he turned the page.

SON: You killed them!

PROFESSOR: You must understand that your parents were involved in something horrible. They were not good, and I'm sure you know that because they would sneak around a lot, wouldn't they?

SON: I think so. But they love me.

PROFESSOR: Yes, of course. They love you dearly. They've been keeping secrets from you to protect you. They didn't want you to know what they were involved in. They didn't want you to know that they were doing very bad things.

> SON: Are you gonna kill me too?

> PROFESSOR: No, we don't have to do that. If you help us, maybe we can help you.

> SON: Okay.

> PROFESSOR: Why don't you start by telling us what they were doing with those beans?

> SON: I don't know.

> PROFESSOR: Did you eat them?

> SON: Not often.

> PROFESSOR: Then surely they were going somewhere, right?

> SON: I don't know where they go. Sometimes they disappear.

> PROFESSOR: What do you mean?

The following line was underlined twice.

> SON: The beans. They disappear.

The interrogation continued without any further reveals—until the final note.

> [Professor reaches a dead end with Son and injects serum into his neck]

Yahshi slammed the file shut.
Thank you, Commander Evaris. I'm glad I wasn't there.

As he continued to read the transcripts, he met all kinds of Eastern characters—families, friends, coworkers, neighbors. They claimed the guardians were missing something, that they weren't listening—only to be injected in the end.

This was not the commonality Famir had told Yahshi to look for, but it was the one he found nonetheless. And the more he read, the more he wondered if the Underground had nothing to do with the raids. If Famir had the heart to murder a little boy after saying he'd help him, what did that say about the Force's values?

What if Emperor Vakoi conducted the raids? Yahshi reached the end of the file stack and raised his chin, staring blankly at the wall. *What if everything we're told is a lie?*

After organizing the files in order of date, he hobbled to the cabinet and returned them. He was conjuring a surface-level report for Famir when he spotted a drawer labeled *Correctional Profiles*.

A lonely folder rested inside.

> Doctor Maelin Vandros of Frontal, 21, attempted to save the life of a patient who, during treatment, was revealed to have an affiliation with the Underground. The Force canceled the operation, but Maelin fought to continue the procedure on the criminal's life despite his background, injuring three of her fellow guardians. Following the criminal's death, Maelin resisted correctional measures to the point of insanity and was

Yahshi looked away.

> executed.

The next page was a *Capital Weekly* article signed by Doctor Blimmery. *The Belladonna Savior*, it called her. The story claimed that Maelin was assisting a Defense unit on a special operation into Eastern Territory. A vicious group of Underground rebels murdered her as she was tending to an injured unit member. The article thanked her for her service and selfless sacrifice.

At the end of the article was a note from Doctor Blimmery justifying its publication.

> I wrote this narrative to protect the hearts of Maelin's friends and family in Frontal and to avoid raising concerns about weakness within the Force. We must remain strong in the face of conflict to instill comfort and confidence in those we protect.

Yahshi returned the file to its rightful place, leaned against the cabinet, and slid to the floor.

It's a warning. The Force doesn't keep the truth about Maelin a secret from guardians. Everything is right there in that drawer, a warning for all those intuitive enough to find it.

Doctor Blimmery was trying to protect him, and Professor Embre was trying to threaten him. But despite their differing intentions, their advice resulted in the same outcome—Yahshi Konya becoming another perfect puppet. How ironic that keeping him safe also kept him under their control.

I am not the first. Maelin defied the Force, and perhaps there were more who remain undocumented.

Yahshi could either play the game or die resisting it. He could either live a guardian or die a traitor.

He thought of Cal, whom the Force had given a second chance. Except that wasn't what it was. They didn't show her grace—they saw an opportunity to use her. They pretended to save her to ensure her absolute devotion to their cause. And as wrong as it was to kill Chima Fernis, her crime suddenly paled in comparison to the atrocities the Force had committed.

Now I know what determined our selection. The Force searched for talents to exploit, but most importantly—motivations to twist. They targeted Cal's criminal status, Yahshi's desire for a grand future, Pinto's childhood trauma, Vell's concern for her mother, Quax's longing for a reunion, Keiyo's need for approval. *They take advantage of our weaknesses and strengths alike.*

Each guardian was both a victim and an aggressor, caught in the insidious game of survival orchestrated by the Force. The unsuspecting teenagers who entered the game with good intentions were quickly ensnared, and as they grew into young adults, they found themselves unable to leave while the Force lured in their next prey. And thus, the cycle continued, over and over, until the humans became monsters, and the monsters destroyed anyone who stood in their way.

Upon his return to the grounds, Yahshi ran into Vell and Keiyo in the lobby. They were aiming blades at a target again.

Vell hesitated to throw a star, her eyes drifting to Yahshi's crutches, but she said nothing.

"How was your assignment?" Keiyo asked.

Yahshi had nothing to say either. He swung to Room 4, slammed the door behind him, and tossed his crutches away. They clattered against the floor as he fumbled into his bed for the first time in a month, relishing in its familiarity.

But the comfort of his quarter vanished quickly, and the silky sheets buried him alive.

FOREVER A NIGHTSHADE

We cultivate the resilience of a mighty oak, weathering natural disasters while standing firm in our values.

♫ FALLING INFINITE - BLACK MATH ♫

In the few weeks that followed, Yahshi began to attend Research and Medical classes again. During lectures he would gaze through the windows, silently brainstorming ways to leave the Force without suffering the same fate as Maelin. He knew nothing about her, neither her personality nor how she looked, but he felt he could understand her. And as strange as it was, he wished to share a conversation with her more than anything.

He eventually ditched the crutches and brace, replacing them with a bandage around his leg. He was healing, and with healing came the fear of being reassigned to his original shadow unit.

On the three-month anniversary of his first assignment, he readied himself for the announcement that he'd be joining Cal on a surprise expedition—but when he entered the lobby, Professor Embre had news for all five of them. His fellow trainees were scattered about the lobby sofas, and she gestured for him to join.

He sat beside Vell, who didn't meet his gaze. They hadn't spoken a word to each other in two months.

"Congratulations, everyone," Professor Embre said. "You've officially completed one year in the program. As per Academy tradition, today is the day you earn your marks."

She walked to the staircase without allowing the news to linger, and the trainees followed her.

Yahshi stood last, knowing that today he'd be permanently marked with the symbol that united all members of the Force. His weak leg wobbled with every step.

Vell wrapped an arm around him as they walked down the staircase. She didn't say a word, and he didn't ask her why she helped.

When they reached the common room, she left his side, joining the others by the Academy guardians. Next to them was a gong, stove, and metal chair with locks and chains. Yahshi spotted a branding iron in Doctor Blimmery's grip.

The trainees inched closer to each other, seeking mutual support. It became clear to Yahshi how immature they'd been, fighting over a game the Academy guardians had set up when the actual conflict was larger than they'd ever imagined. They were all victims, yet they had treated each other as enemies.

"Yahshi," Professor Embre said, "you're first."

As he stepped toward the chair, Pinto and Quax patted his shoulders reassuringly. He flinched when Vell grabbed his hand, meeting his gaze before letting go.

Yahshi managed a weak grin.

"You took a broken leg like a champ," Keiyo said, playfully punching his chest. "You can handle it."

He nodded before leaving them behind, his remnant smile fading. His eyes watered more with every step, and he bit his lip, trying to keep from panicking before the branding iron had even met his head.

When he reached the chair, he stopped, and all was still. He turned to the Academy guardians, trying to devise an excuse to escape this, but then he remembered the file about Maelin and knew he had no other choice. He would find a way to break free from the Force, but it would not happen now. He would need to be patient, and in the meantime, he would need to play along.

So he sat in that cold metal chair and closed his eyes as Commander Roz secured the locks that held his wrists, ankles, and neck in place.

"Recite the Guardian Vows," Professor Embre ordered.

Yahshi gritted his teeth and tugged at the locks, but he was chained down too well. With time, he settled and whispered, "No."

"What was that?" Commander Roz asked.

"No," he said, bolder this time.

"Yahshi," Doctor Blimmery warned, "please recite the Vows for me."

He inhaled a deep breath.

"That's it," Professor Embre encouraged.

"It's going to hurt," Commander Roz said. "But you need this."

Those words sounded familiar.

"I-I vow… to serve the Empire with absolute devotion. I vow to partake in Imperial ceremonies when called upon. I vow to complete forty…"

"Keep going," Professor Embre said.

"I vow to complete forty consecutive and obedient years of service."

Yahshi pressed his head against the rigid backrest until he ached, punishing himself for signing away four decades of his life. But then he remembered that words were only words, and this ceremony was a form of emotional control. If he wanted to break the Guardian Vows someday, he would do just that.

With renewed strength, he resumed his recitation to the final Vow.

"…I vow to embrace my division and unit placements without question."

One of the guardians rang the gong, and the ringing pierced Yahshi's ears, silencing his thoughts. He opened his eyes as Professor Embre tucked his bangs back with a band and wiped his forehead with a damp cloth.

A fire crackled nearby, but he couldn't see it. Commander Roz gestured for him to open his mouth, offering a rolled cloth. Yahshi bit the fabric harder as Commander Roz stepped aside, Doctor Blimmery taking his place with a hot branding iron in his gloved hands.

He couldn't help it. His arms and legs pulled at the restraints again, pinching his skin. *They want me to believe that I've caught onto them too late.*

"Stop struggling and close your eyes," Doctor Blimmery said.

Yahshi opened his eyes wider, his face hot. *They want me to believe there's no way out, no matter how hard I try.*

Doctor Blimmery shook his head before leaning in, bringing the branding iron closer.

Yahshi's willpower faltered, the panic taking over, and he clenched his eyes shut. *They want me to believe I'm forever a Nightshade.*

The branding iron pressed into his forehead, searing his skin. Heat dripped over every part of his body as he pulled and shook, desperate for the pain to knock him out, but it didn't. Tears flooded down his cheeks, and silent screams filled the fabric in his mouth.

But I will never *let them win.*

After the ceremony, the Academy guardians left the trainees alone in the common room. Yahshi tried to focus on his breathing, but the throbbing pain in his forehead only worsened.

Keiyo broke their prolonged silence with a groan. "What the hell was that?"

"An advance notice would've been nice." Pinto adjusted his eye patch out of habit and yelped.

Quax was lying on the floor, staring at the ceiling. It took him a minute to catch up before he chuckled. "I can't believe you forgot the Vows."

Keiyo smiled at him for the first time since the final filtration. "I didn't think they'd be *this* important."

"Professor Embre was furious," Pinto added.

When Yahshi smiled, the skin on his forehead swelled and pulsed, followed by unbearable itchiness. He rubbed the tender skin, sending a wave of pain through his head.

Vell pushed his hand away from his face. "Don't touch it."

He nodded, folding his hands in his lap as he studied the identical wound on Vell's forehead. The guardians had managed to lure her because she wanted to help her mother. And now she was trapped for the rest of her life, only to see the person she loved most when granted permission.

His gaze drifted to Pinto, his old roommate and the most driven boy he'd ever met. He had joined the Academy to prevent tragedies like the Eastern raids, but what if the smugglers' claims were true? What if he was fighting *for* the people that gouged out his eye, not against them?

He looked at Keiyo next, a boy far more introspective than he ever would have thought. A boy who saw through the lies but chose to live them because it was the path of least resistance. And maybe he was brighter than Yahshi because by not fighting his circumstances, he was happy. But he would never be honest.

Finally, he turned to Quax, his childhood friend from Sitra. He'd sacrificed everything to see his sister again. He took that branding iron to his forehead for her, and Yahshi wondered if Cal could ever understand and reciprocate her little brother's love.

They were a group of sixteen- and seventeen-year-olds who had joined the Academy without knowing any better. Now they were marked as property of Emperor Vakoi, fated to live a life of luxury and confinement. And at that moment, all the pain Yahshi had felt over the past few months came hurtling back, and he lurched forward, gripping the fabric of his vest. The air grew thinner the harder he gasped.

"It's okay." Pinto stood and sat next to him. "We'll heal."

Yahshi nodded, and Vell wrapped her arms around him.

"I'm sorry," she whispered. "You're not heartless."

CHAPTER 27

BETWEEN THE LINES

We seek collective liberation, mindful of the delicate balance among all living things.

♫ DIVINE LOSER · CLEM TURNER ♫

Yahshi approached the lab rabbits' burial spot, a daily habit he'd developed in remembrance of Sunna. The weather had warmed up in the two months since the branding ceremony, which came with blooming flowers and luscious trees in a landscape he wished Sunna could see. And then he realized Sunna *could* see it, because Sunna wasn't dead.

I keep forgetting there's a life outside of this program.

Sunna had returned to a world Yahshi would never be part of again, while Yahshi had remained in a world Sunna would never reenter. They had lived under the same roof for nine months, and now they were dead to each other.

"Do you ever wonder if you'd be happier back home?"

I do now, Sunna. Yahshi kneeled and set his hand on the grass, which had fully grown over the mound of dirt, evened into flat land by the rain. *Are you happier now that you're home? Are you as happy as I could have been, had I left instead?*

In the rare times Sunna popped up in conversation, the other trainees agreed that he'd never been fit for guardianship. They claimed he'd worked through the program with sheer willpower, and the final filtration had pushed him too strongly against his nature. It was actually a blessing in disguise, because if he hadn't filtered himself, he could have made the final five. He could have been committed to forty painful years of service, his fate bound in blood through the contract he'd signed on Selection Day, reinforced with a mark on his forehead.

Yahshi trailed a finger along his four-petaled brand. It was fully healed but still sensitive to the touch. *He could have turned out like me.*

"Hey!"

He spotted Pinto in the courtyard, waving him over. With a sigh, he crossed the field to reach his friend.

"What are you doing here?" Yahshi asked.

"Today's not the day to show up late for breakfast. We have good news." Pinto led him up the steps. "Hurry!"

Doctor Blimmery was standing by the dining hall table with a white briefcase. "There you are, Yahshi! I wanted to make sure you were here for the announcement."

He took his usual seat next to Vell. Quax and Keiyo smiled at him, and he smiled back because acting bitter wouldn't make leaving the Force's grasp any easier. He had learned that the hard way.

"And you're still on that meal plan, remember?" Doctor Blimmery added.

Yahshi took an exaggerated first bite, and Vell concealed a grin.

Pinto shot her a scornful glare as Doctor Blimmery continued. "I'm pleased to announce that you've reached the baseline tolerance level required by the Force, which means... no more beet juice!"

Keiyo clapped and cheered alone.

"These are called maintenance vials." He plopped his briefcase onto the table and opened it to reveal five vials, each about the size of a thumb. "Guardians drink one every morning to maintain tolerance. You first, *Pin*."

Pinto snatched a vial and studied its red fluid through the glass.

"Don't take all day."

He scowled at Doctor Blimmery before popping the cork stopper off.

Everyone watched as he chugged the fluid in a single gulp.

"Wow," Pinto said, smacking his lips together. "It tastes...sweet."

Doctor Blimmery laughed and passed out the remaining vials. The others drank theirs, proud of reaching the milestone, but Yahshi drank his because he had no other choice.

"Yahshi? Pinto?" Doctor Blimmery called. "You're shadowing together tomorrow."

"Great," Yahshi said, and he meant it. Sifting through documents in the archives never bored him because he knew that somewhere in that room was the answer to his question.

How do I leave the Force alive?

"Yahshi, I'd like you close today," Famir said.

"I'm sorry?"

"You've spent two assignments cooped up in the archives. I think it's time to get you in a real meeting."

"No," Yahshi said, cringing at himself immediately. He couldn't deny orders from Famir, but perhaps he could prompt him to change his mind. "Sorry, I didn't mean that. I've just been... I feel like I've been making progress. I think I'm onto something."

"You don't mind staying in that stuffy room?"

"Not at all. I'm happy to keep looking."

"Very well," Famir said. "Pinto, you'll join our meetings like usual, but don't worry about taking notes. We want your voice today."

Pinto gasped. "Really?"

Yahshi left the staircase to enter the archives. He waited until he could no longer hear his shadow unit's footsteps before rushing to a file cabinet of trainee contracts. He flipped through the most recent ones, expecting to find only the contracts of guaranteed graduates. But he also found those of Sunna, Ceylon, Limbo, and every other filtered trainee from his cycle.

Why would the Force keep them? He extracted Durlan Ouzo's contract at random and read its five points. Commander Roz had gone through them so long ago that he hardly remembered what they were about. His eyes widened at number four.

> Should you be filtered from the program, yet the Force later encounters a situation that demands an augmented guardian presence, your acquired training, albeit partial, may obligate you to a mandatory service call. It is the inherent responsibility of every individual trained under the Empire's military resources to rise to the occasion in critical times. Your commitment to this program signifies your pledge to uphold this duty if needed, regardless of your graduation status.

He stuffed Durlan's file into the drawer, wanting to ignore the discovery that even filtered trainees were not free. They could be summoned back into their cages with a snap of the Force's fingers.

What if I move to a random town? Change my look and identity? He reached for his forehead. *Right, I'm marked. That makes it all a bit harder.*

But he would not give up, because the moment he'd give up, he'd lose the game. There had to be a smarter play.

Yahshi rounded up the files that had piqued his interest during his last assignment. They each included a detainee claiming that Emperor Vakoi and the Force were behind the raids.

He was studying the transcripts at a desk when a girl entered from the staircase, distracting him. She had silky black hair, tan skin, and eye bags that made her blue irises pop. But most importantly, she looked too young to be a guardian, and her clothes didn't fit right. The fabric was too loose in some places and too tight in others.

"I've never seen you in the Office before," Yahshi said.

"You're a shadow. You don't know everyone yet." She pointed to the badges on her shoulders, marking her as a Medical Division member. "And I'm not here often."

As she walked toward him, Yahshi decided there was no way she could be any older than Cal, who only had one other girl in her cycle—Evaris. He was preparing to run to the staircase and report the intruder when she stopped at his desk and flipped through a pile of transcripts.

"Quite the curated selection. I've been wondering how long it'd take to get another one."

"Another what?"

She crossed her arms and smiled. "Another Maelin."

"I don't know who that is," Yahshi said.

"Sure you do." She glanced at the cabinet labeled *Correctional Profiles.*

"Who are you?"

"Just a tool, like you." She turned her back to him, sauntering around a nearby desk. "Our only freedom is with the enemy."

"What enemy?"

"The Underground," she replied. "We can't get them to talk. We can't figure out what they're planning. We can't understand them. Sometimes we can't even trace them. So if we join them, we're free. Like Dice."

"You know about him?"

"I know about everyone, including you." She opened a cabinet drawer and flipped through the files, but he could tell she wasn't reading them. "I know you're that little investigator the Academy guardians took a chance on. They like to do that sort of thing. I think they get bored when the kids are too... obedient... so they pick a challenge and see who can mold them the most. Don't ask for evidence. It's just a theory."

Yahshi frowned. It was dangerous for a guardian to share a treasonous thought like that aloud. But then again, she wasn't a guardian, was she?

"Do you have contact with anyone affiliated with the Underground?" she asked.

Yahshi thought of his father and shook his head. "Of course not."

"Hmm. Shame."

He flinched as a panting guardian burst into the room. "Your Highness," the commander said. "What the hell is wrong with you?"

Your Highness? Yahshi looked at the girl, who rolled her eyes.

"I wanted some fresh air," she said.

"Oh, yes," the guardian mocked. "There's nothing fresher than the smell of rotting documents in the archives." He tapped his foot, waiting for a reply—but she stared at him silently, smirking.

"Oh, for the glory of Vakoi—"

"Thank you," she interrupted. "I'm glorious. I know."

She's... Princess Kia, isn't she? Yahshi narrowed his eyes, recalling her Royal portraits. She was always portrayed with longer hair and softer features that made her look sweet and approachable. In reality, she didn't meet the golden standard of beauty the press implied, nor did she disappoint the eyes.

"Shadow." The commander made eye contact with him. "Not a word of this, alright?"

"He can report you if he wants to," the Princess sang.

"I won't," Yahshi said.

She offered him a smug grin.

"Great." The guardian headed for the staircase, but she didn't follow him. "Please, Kia..."

"Addressing me by name?" She tucked her hands into her pockets. "Doesn't that violate a Vow?"

He sighed. "Please follow me, Your Highness."

"That's more like it." She finally followed him.

"And take that damn uniform off," he added. "It's disrespectful."

"It's cute."

When they left the archives, Yahshi sat in silence, his thoughts racing. What was that guardian's role in Princess Kia's life? Where did she get that uniform, and how did she get into the Investigation Office? Why didn't she look like her portraits?

But one question trumped them all, shoving its way to the front of his mind.

She has a point. He faced the transcripts. *What if my only way out is to join the enemy?*

Yahshi and Pinto returned just in time for supper. They smiled at Vell as they sat next to her.

"How was it?" she asked.

"Amazing!" Pinto replied.

Yahshi thought of his odd encounter with the Princess and shrugged. "Same as always."

"I don't know why you insisted on staying in the archives, but I'm not complaining." Pinto glanced over his shoulder. "Look, I know we're not supposed to discuss what goes on during our shadow assignments, but today, I got to see the Detainment Facility. My unit leader had me transcribe the interrogation. It was wild!"

"What?" Yahshi frowned. "I thought you were at a meeting."

"There was a change of plans. It's a long story."

"Why didn't you tell me?" His question came out harsher than he'd intended.

"We were in the vault, Yahshi. I'd be an idiot to break the shadow confidentiality rule in front of Professor Famir. Plus, it's no big deal. I only wrote the transcript. It's not like I did any interrogating myself."

"How'd it go?" Vell asked.

"The suspect was guilty of treason, so... you know, Protocol." Pinto took another bite as though he'd pointed out the weather, not implied that he'd witnessed an execution.

Yahshi lost his appetite. If he hadn't argued with Famir, pushing to stay in the archives for another assignment, *he* would have been in that interrogation room.

Keiyo made eye contact with him and shrugged as though he were saying, *Well, what can we do about it?* Quax's oblivious expression gave the impression that he hadn't been listening, and Vell raised her brows, confused about why Yahshi was staring.

He wiped his hands on a table napkin and stood. "I'll be in my room for a bit."

"Yahshi, wait," Pinto said. "You should finish your supper."

"Oh, not you too..." He laughed, but Pinto held his stern expression.

"Commander Roz asked me to make sure you're eating enough. It negates the whole point of the meal plan if you're not finishing your plate." Pinto looked at the others, who nodded in unison. "And we've been meaning to discuss something with you anyway."

A heavy weight filled the dining hall as Yahshi retook his seat. His fellow trainees looked around at each other, silently deciding who should speak first.

Eventually, Vell cleared her throat. "Yahshi, we should talk about your hands."

"My hands?" He folded them under the table now that he knew they were observing him. His hands hadn't healed since his first shadow assignment, but no one had mentioned them in weeks.

"And how you keep going to the field every morning," Keiyo added. "To that spot where the rabbits were buried."

Yahshi's eyes widened.

"And how you always show up late to meals," Pinto said. "That way we finish our plates first, and you can leave the room with us after taking no more than a few bites."

"And how you jumped," Quax said with a sigh.

Yahshi narrowed his eyes at him. "You said you wouldn't—"

"We're not stupid," Pinto said. "We all knew you didn't fall. He didn't have to tell us."

"And we know it's because you were avoiding Commander Cal," Vell said.

Yahshi glared at Quax and Keiyo, knowing that extra detail was something one of them *did* tell.

"So we wanted to ask what we can do," Pinto said. "You know, to help you feel better."

"Nothing," Yahshi replied. "No, I'm fine. Everything's fine."

Vell snatched his hand out from under the table, examining his skin. "Yeah?"

He yanked his hand free, shaking his head. He thought he'd been playing along, but they'd all read between the lines.

"I wish you would talk to us," Pinto said. "I hate that you feel like you have to keep secrets."

"We're trying to be your friends," Vell said, "but you won't let us."

"Yahshi..." Keiyo leaned forward, setting his hands on the table. They were so smooth. "How can we help you?"

Yahshi looked at Quax, who nodded, urging him to talk.

Their confrontation proved that he'd inched closer to Maelin's fate than he'd realized. If he were to worry them any more than he already had, they would do the only thing they believed was right—ask the guardians for help, which could only end with him getting sent to correction. *And I don't want to find out what happens in correction.*

It was clear he could afford to sulk no longer. If he wanted a way out of the Force, he needed to play perfect long enough to find one.

"I think..." Yahshi trailed off, staring at his hands. "I-I want to be strong again. But I don't know how. And... maybe it'd be good if you could help me get out of... whatever *this* is."

Pinto's warm embrace took him by surprise. "We'll be here for you," he muttered, "no matter what, okay?"

Yahshi stiffened in his friend's arms. He had to let them believe he was open to their support—that they could change him. But in reality, he was still alone on that island, surrounded by a dark, raging sea.

CHAPTER 28

HEROES LIVE IN STARS

We cherish the memory of our heroes, who live in stars,
and celebrate their unwavering courage.

♫ DEAR DOUBT · MICHAEL SCHULTE ♫

"Read this book," suggested Pinto. "A commander wrote it decades ago after retiring from active service. He reflects on the difficult choices he faced during expeditions. Perhaps you can relate." So Yahshi agreed and read the book.

"Talk to me," suggested Vell. "Don't bury what happened. Tell me everything about your first assignment from start to finish." So Yahshi agreed and told her everything.

"Let's play chess," suggested Quax. "Emotions are quicksand. If you linger in them too long, you'll sink. You have to stay busy." So Yahshi agreed and played chess with him.

"Practice tool crafting," suggested Keiyo. "It seemed like you enjoyed it when Sunna was here, and if you don't anymore, practice something else. You gotta find things you like doing again, you know?" So Yahshi agreed and practiced tool crafting.

As the weeks flew by, he became a master of playing along. His fellow trainees could no longer read the pain between the lines because he ensured there were no lines at all—he would not drop that fake smile, even when he believed they were no longer looking.

Despite the exhaustion his acting caused, he pushed himself to return to his routines. He finished his meals, attended classes consistently, and regained his prior strength. He applied cream to his hands in the infirmary until they healed. And as the weeks rolled into a month and a month rolled into three, he earned back the trust and respect of the Academy guardians and soon-to-be graduates.

That's how you dodge correctional measures. Yahshi grinned as he adjusted his tie, staring into the eyes of his reflection in the mirror. *That's how you live in fire without getting burned.*

He was seventeen years old now, and he appeared to be healthier and happier than he'd ever been. He was in the best physical shape of his life, his brand was prominently displayed—which he faked having pride in by styling his hair in a manner that wouldn't cover it—and when he smiled, he nearly convinced himself he was looking forward to his graduation into the Force.

I'll have access to more information in the City, so I'll come up with an escape plan then. For now, I need to lay low.

He entered the lobby to find Keiyo lying on a sofa with his legs over the backrest and his head dangling off the cushions.

Yahshi crossed his arms. "What are you doing?"

"Manifesting." Keiyo closed his eyes and chanted, "Medical, Medical, Medical..."

As he continued chanting, Yahshi sat next to Quax, who was watching Keiyo in disapproval. *I wonder what division I'll be officially placed in.* He willed it to be any division but Defense and any unit but Cal's.

Vell entered the lobby right as Keiyo swung his legs off the couch. He rolled onto the floor and lay there, his eyes closed, gasping for air.

"Manifesting again?" she asked.

Keiyo gripped his head without answering, immersed in his dizziness.

Yahshi frowned at her. "How did you know?"

"He always does that when he's procrastinating on tool development." Vell kicked Keiyo's legs aside and sat on the sofa. "Thinks it'll solve his problems."

"While I'm *brainstorming* for tool development," Keiyo choked out. "Big difference. It's part of the process, okay?"

Quax leaned back with a sigh. "I don't get why you're so stressed about your placement. You'd be a good fit anywhere."

"That's exactly the problem," Keiyo said. "I'm not like you guys with your limited talents. I wanna be a doctor, but I'm good at *everything*. They need me *everywhere*. What are the chances they choose what I want? Well, the answer is simple—thirty-three percent!"

Quax threw a blunt end of a dart at him. "Shut it."

Yahshi laughed. "Maybe you'll be the first guardian with multiple division placements. All three badges on your shoulders."

Keiyo shot up into a seated position, facing Yahshi with a smile. "Oh, that'd be epic. *I'd* be epic."

Footsteps from the staircase turned their heads to Doctor Blimmery. He rushed into the lobby and threw his arms out, yelling, "They're here!"

"There's no way!" Keiyo shouted, jumping from the floor. He and Quax ran after Doctor Blimmery, who was already racing downstairs.

Yahshi and Vell met eyes with a chuckle before standing and trailing long behind them.

A few weeks prior, the final five had discussed their fashion preferences with a team of designers from the City. Although guardians wore standardized uniforms daily, their formal wear allowed their individuality to shine on special occasions. One of them was their graduation ball—an Imperial ceremony that'd be held at Vakoi Palace.

When Yahshi and Vell reached the common room, Quax and Keiyo had wooden boxes in their arms labeled by name. Yahshi spotted three more on the sofas for him, Vell, and Pinto.

"Doctor, can we try them on?" Keiyo pleaded, tossing and catching his box repeatedly.

"Of course! Take them back to your quarters." Doctor Blimmery scanned the four trainees before sighing. "And someone get Pinto up! Damn kid's been sleeping his life away."

"I'll get him." Yahshi stacked Pinto's box onto his and lifted them both. He was about to follow Vell to the staircase, but Doctor Blimmery set a hand on his shoulder.

"I'm proud of you, kid," he whispered. "We're *all* proud of you. These past few months, you've been doing so well."

His grip on the box tightened.

"Fitting in here..." Doctor Blimmery continued, releasing him. "It's worth the effort, alright?"

Yahshi looked back at a man who, at one point, might have been like Maelin too.

He forced a smile. "Alright, Doctor."

The guardian smiled back, and Yahshi headed upstairs.

Vell and Quax were chatting in the lobby when he arrived, boxes on their laps as they waited for Keiyo to finish changing in his quarter.

Yahshi set his boxes down and knocked on Pinto's door. When he didn't answer, he cracked the door open to find him wide awake, writing in his journal.

"You were just gonna ignore me?" Yahshi said. "How rude."

Pinto set his pencil down. "They're here, aren't they?"

"They're here."

As Pinto joined him in the lobby, Keiyo's door burst open, and he rushed into the room wearing a dirt brown suit that screamed all forms of subtlety —with the exception of a bright yellow bow tie. He spun around and held his arms out to ask, *What do you think?*

"It's awfully dull." Pinto sat next to Vell, who frowned at him.

"You look great," Yahshi said, eager to distract him from Pinto's comment. "But I'm surprised you didn't request something flashier."

"Well, I'd say my plan worked flawlessly," Keiyo replied, "because your eyes are on my tie."

Yahshi pried his eyes from the pop of yellow.

"While the rest of you show off, I'll play the charming, modest type. The ladies won't be able to look away." Keiyo flicked his tie, and Pinto rolled his eye. "Oh, what are you on about? Just because we can't get married doesn't mean we can't dress to impress."

Quax playfully bumped into Keiyo on the way to his quarter.

A few minutes later, Quax returned wearing the formal wear he'd been dreaming about—a white suit with golden embroidery. Every cufflink and button matched the emblem on his forehead, and the shimmering square of silk in his breast pocket waved with every step as though it had a will of its own.

They stared in awe as Quax trailed his fingers along his upturned blazer collar. The fabric was stiff, lined with diamonds, and his skin glowed against the bright material.

"Wow, you look..." Keiyo crossed his arms, studying his formal wear with a nod. "Arrogant. Yeah, you look like a complete asshole."

"You're just jealous because a yellow bow tie was the best you could do." Quax grinned and pointed at Pinto. "You're next."

"Yahshi can go," Pinto said.

Yahshi entered his quarter and changed into a suit that matched the nostalgic green shade of his Sitra Secondary uniform. The cloth felt foreign against his skin after wearing nothing but his trainee uniform and silk pajamas for the past seventeen months.

He smiled at the mirror. The designers had embellished his tie with a faded zigzagging pattern—a detail he hadn't requested, and most would never notice. Their passion shined through the piece, and he wondered if there was any field of work he could care about like them.

Wow. He straightened his shoulders and stepped back. *I look like a different person.*

His smile faded, realizing they were entering a new phase of life together, but he wasn't planning to stay.

"What is that?" Quax squinted as Yahshi reentered the lobby. "Is that a Sitra Secondary student I see?"

Keiyo laughed. "You aged two years in that suit!"

"Green?" Vell asked. "Interesting."

"Sage green," Yahshi corrected, taking a seat next to her. "Why is that interesting?"

She ignored his question and turned to Pinto, urging him to show off his formal wear next.

"I'm not trying it on," Pinto announced.

"Why not?" Yahshi asked.

"It's obvious they fit you three perfectly. The designers know what they're doing, so there's no point in a test run."

"This isn't about testing our clothes for design flaws," Quax said, a hint of humor in his tone. "Graduation is less than a month away. Can't we have some fun?"

"Fun?" Pinto asked. "For the past three weeks, we've had more etiquette lessons than actual training. It's like everyone forgot that we're in a massive conflict with the Underground. We still have no clue where Dice went. He could be living under the Academy floorboards for all we know. This isn't the time to learn how to waltz for our graduation ball or practice holding utensils."

Quax went silent.

"You're overreacting," Vell said. "We all deserve a break from training, including you."

"You can cry if you want to," Keiyo teased. "We don't judge."

Pinto's face turned red, and Yahshi sighed. *This won't end well.*

"Oh, you think I'm being dramatic, do you? In a perfect world—yes, we deserve a break. But we don't live in a perfect world. What we deserve isn't always what we get." He headed to his quarter, box in hand.

"Are you trying it on?" Keiyo asked.

"Go run laps!" Pinto yelled.

Keiyo grinned at Quax. "That's a new one."

Pinto slammed the door behind him, and Vell stood. "I'll talk to him."

"Maybe don't?" Yahshi said. "He needs to cool off."

Vell paused, then nodded. "Blade-throwing?" she asked Keiyo.

"Sure." Keiyo pointed to her box. "But you're gonna try that on first, right?"

She grinned as she hugged it. "Secret."

"Oh, come on, Vell!" Keiyo said. "Humor us."

"Your patience is my birthday present."

"It's not even your birthday," Yahshi said.

"Well, it almost is." She tossed the box into her quarter and headed for the staircase. "I'll be in the training room."

"Wait! I need to change first!" Keiyo ran into his quarter to put his uniform back on, and Quax left soon after to do the same.

Sitting alone in the lobby, Yahshi analyzed a chessboard on the table ahead of him. Its pieces formed a completed game.

The king was knocked over, lying on its side.

On Vell's seventeenth birthday, the Academy guardians granted the trainees a day off. Pinto shut himself in his quarter while the others strolled down their favorite spots on the grounds, reminiscing. They were beginning to say goodbye to the program, and it was surprisingly therapeutic. Yahshi hated how he enjoyed it. He hated how he loved the Academy.

As they walked around the field, their conversation drifted to filtered trainees.

"Do you guys remember Durlan?" Keiyo asked.

Quax chuckled. "The one Professor Embre slapped?"

Vell and Keiyo laughed at the memory, but Yahshi didn't.

"I wonder how Sunna and Ceylon are doing," Yahshi said, changing the subject.

"Oh, I bet Sunna's having a blast, you know?" Keiyo ran ahead of them and walked backward, hands in his pockets. "He always missed his friends and family back home. Talked about them all the time when we were roommates."

"He wouldn't shut up about them," Quax added.

"And Ceylon's with his brother now," Vell said. "He's happy."

"His *lunatic* brother." Keiyo smirked. "Limbo was like a devil on his shoulder, you know?"

"I don't know," Yahshi said. "I'm starting to think he was nice. I mean, he wasn't *nice*, I guess. But he always spoke his mind when something bothered him. He didn't... hide."

Quax's smile faded. "Right. Like with the bunnies."

"Yeah," Yahshi said. "Like the bunnies."

The conversation died, and Yahshi cursed himself for bringing the mood down. He patched his mistake up with an exaggerated sigh, saying, "When's Pinto gonna get over this?"

Quax shook his head. "He's being such a baby about it."

"Hey, let him be. He'll move on," Keiyo said. "Trust me—on graduation day, he'll be all chirpy as if he hadn't spent the last month moping under an imaginary raincloud."

"*Can you believe this?*" Vell said in a low tone, impersonating Pinto. She spun around with her eyes on the clouds. "*Isn't this building incredible? The ceilings are so high!*"

That night, the Academy guardians kindled a bonfire in the field, which the trainees huddled around to get warm. Every breeze sent a shiver down their spines, and it didn't help that the grass was damp from the evening rain.

Vell tossed a few packaged chips and sweets around the fire. "Doctor Blim snuck these onto the grounds for me." A chocolate bar landed by Yahshi's boots, and he grabbed it with a grin. They'd eaten nothing but circulated meals for the past eighteen months, and it was nice to have cheap snacks from the outside world again.

"I don't get it. How did you manage to win his favoritism?" Quax chuckled. "I doubt Doctor Blimmery would bring me snacks even if I were lying on my deathbed."

Vell made eye contact with Yahshi before shrugging. "Not sure." She hastily unwrapped a bite-sized package of chocolate and tossed it into her mouth.

"Where's Pinto?" Keiyo gestured around them, smiling. "He's not gonna join us out here in this miserable weather?"

Yahshi sighed. "I tried to talk him into it, but he told me he's gonna sleep early, which is Pinto language for *I'm in a bad mood.*"

"Oh, forget about him," Quax said, nudging Vell's side. "You're seventeen now."

"I'm seventeen," she echoed. "Weird."

"We were fifteen when we got here," Yahshi said. "I can't believe it."

"I know." She tossed her chocolate wrapper into the fire and watched it burn. "Time's gone by so fast."

"Too fast," Quax said.

Keiyo reached into his pocket and left his hand there. "Vell, I know we don't do the whole birthday thing at the Academy, but you knew I was working on this anyway, so…" He removed his fist and opened it, revealing a handful of throwing stars. They were shaped like the Academy emblem.

"Keiyo, you didn't!" Vell took one and raised it, smiling as the fire's reflection sparkled on the metal. "I love the stars best."

Yahshi smiled.

"Thank you, really." She grabbed the others and stood. "Can we test them?"

Keiyo stood next. "Of course."

Vell took a single step away before turning with raised brows. "I almost forgot." She pulled a shiny marble out of her pocket and tossed it over the fire at Quax. He snatched it from the air and frowned.

"It was time to return it," she said.

Keiyo's jaw dropped. "There's no way…"

Quax squinted as though he believed it might be a replica, his face turning red. "What the hell?"

Yahshi laughed as Vell took Keiyo's hand and fled the scene, racing toward the building.

"There, there," Yahshi said, patting Quax's shoulder.

He looked up, his eyes wide. "*How*?"

"Honestly? No clue."

Quax shook his head and slipped the marble into his pocket. They sat together by the bonfire, watching the flames crackle and dance as they nibbled on their snacks.

They nibbled for a long time.

"I feel gross," Quax muttered.

"Is this my third or fourth chocolate?" Yahshi asked.

"Fifth, I think."

"Yeah, right." He met eyes with Quax, who smiled back, and for a moment it felt just like old times. He nearly expected him to say, *Yahshi, follow me! Look what I made today!* And then he'd lead him into the woods to demonstrate his latest contraptions.

Yahshi's smile faded. "Did you mean it?"

"Mean what?"

"What you told me in the infirmary after I broke my leg. About how you did all of this to see Cal. Did you mean it?"

Quax took a deep breath before nodding. "Yeah."

"Why? I mean, she saved you, but—"

"Yahshi, I know what you think of her. You don't have to repeat it. She wasn't the nicest to me when we were younger, and you always saw that. But she had her sweet moments too. Sometimes she'd sit next to me and read, and I knew she could read anywhere else, but she chose to sit next to me, and that had to mean something. And every once in a while, when I was struggling with a homework assignment, she'd snatch the worksheet and fill it out for me. And you know what she told me one night, when she was half asleep?"

He gulped. "What?"

"She told me I have a way of making people comfortable. She told me she wished she had that too."

Yahshi wanted to believe those were signs Cal loved him, but he couldn't shake the feeling that they were somehow part of her master plan.

"And I-I miss her," Quax continued. "And I know you can't wrap your head around that as an only child, but she's my sister. Of course I love her."

"Why didn't you tell me the truth back then?"

"Because the moment I brought up the idea of training for my selection, you had nothing but horrible things to say. You thought it meant I was giving up my dream, that it wasn't what I wanted." His voice was raspier now. "And you were right, Yahshi. You were. But the thought of never seeing my sister again for the rest of my life hurt more than leaving my silly projects behind. So I did everything I could to get here. I gave up my dreams, and I crushed my parents. They weren't okay with losing *both* of their kids. They begged me to stop training, so I had to lie to them. I had to tell them

I wanted this, and they eventually believed me. And now I'm not even sure if it'll be worth it, because maybe you've been right all along. Maybe she didn't save me because she loved me. Maybe I made all these sacrifices to see someone who doesn't want me in her world, and now there's no way out."

They sat in silence for a few minutes.

"They weren't silly," Yahshi muttered.

"What?"

"Your projects. They weren't silly."

"Thanks."

Yahshi faced him, his brows knitting together. "Listen, I shouldn't have said that she didn't wanna see you. I shouldn't have mentioned her at all— you weren't supposed to know who my shadow unit leader was."

"But you told me, and I know it now," Quax said. "I didn't wanna believe you at first, but it—it really does sound like her."

"Ignore everything I said, okay? She had a job to bring me on my assignment, not to see you. Of course she couldn't say hi. Actually, saying hi would be a violation of Protocol. It simply wasn't the time, but graduation *is* the time. You'll get the reunion you've been working for."

"You really think so?"

Yahshi nodded because Quax would be safer living a lie. Safe from correction and the darkness that killed Maelin.

"Thanks, Yahshi."

He forced a smile.

"You know, it's unbelievable how much we've fought over the past few years." Quax chuckled. "Think about how excited our younger selves would be if they knew we'd graduate from the Academy together."

Yahshi burst into laughter. It was ridiculous how they'd only been at each other's throats—all because the Force turned them against each other. They had fallen for the trap as many had before them.

I know you're up there, Maelin. He fell backward onto the grass, his laughter fading as he gazed at the glittering sky. *I promise to find a way out of here, and it will all be thanks to you.*

CHAPTER 29

MARVELOUS CAGE

We discount the allure of superficiality, seeking beauty
within the earth, body, and spirit.

♫ WE HAVE IT ALL · PIM STONES ♫

After putting his trainee uniform on for the last time, Yahshi took in every detail of his quarter—the empty bed where Pinto used to sleep, the nightstand that once held a pair of yellow mittens, the balcony he had jumped from to avoid shadowing Cal.

I'll never see this room again.

He grabbed his formal wear box on his way out. Today, he could finally leave Room 4 behind. He almost felt free but woke up from the Force's illusion. *I'm simply moving into a new cage.*

"Yahshi, it's graduation day!" Pinto was beaming as he paced the lobby. "Can you believe it?" He threw a dart and struck a target in the bullseye.

Vell shot Yahshi a look that said, *I told you so.*

Quax and Keiyo were yawning, their eyes red.

"What happened to you two?" Yahshi sat across from them.

"We kind of like it here," Keiyo answered. "We're like, the *best* here, you know? But in the Force, we'll be like everyone else. Actually, it's worse than that. We'll be the fresh five. The newbies." He closed his eyes and began to chant, "Medical, Medical, Medical..."

The Academy guardians appeared, bright-eyed with broad smiles.

"I guess I can't call you kids *kids* anymore," Doctor Blimmery said. "You're guardians now!"

"We're proud of you," Professor Embre said. "Really, we are."

Yahshi chuckled at her need to emphasize.

"Breakfast first," Commander Roz said, "and then we're off."

The trainees followed them to the dining hall, where their singular table was replaced with a longer one. The Academy guardians shared a meal with them for the first time. They were no longer guardians and trainees but guardians and guardians.

"I hope you placed me in Medical," Keiyo said.

"Patience, Keiyo," Professor Embre replied.

Doctor Blimmery frowned before taking a bite.

After breakfast, Professor Embre and Doctor Blimmery traveled on horseback while Commander Roz led the graduates to a vault parked on the road. Quax entered the passenger box last, shutting the door behind them and yelling, "Ready!"

Commander Roz began to drive the vault, and Quax took a seat.

"Look at you!" Keiyo jabbed him in the side. "Such a commander already."

Quax smirked. "We'll see about that, *Doctor*."

Keiyo closed his eyes. "Medical, Medical, Medical..."

While the others watched Keiyo in amusement, Yahshi leaned his head against the aluminum wall. His thoughts drifted to when he'd sat in a vault just like this one while the man's wife and son stared him down.

Pinto shook his shoulder. "Are you vaultsick, Yahshi?"

"A bit."

"Ah, boring!" Keiyo shouted. "Come on, don't be sick on the big day!"

Careful not to soil his act, he chatted with them for the rest of their half-hour ride.

When the vault stopped, they grabbed their boxes and hopped out.

"Leave them," Commander Roz said.

They slid their boxes back inside.

What came next was a multi-hour tour. They saw public parks with abstract gardens, sculptures taller than trees, and murals on the sides of buildings. They gawked at men in neon suits and top hats and women with makeup incorporating gems and feathers. They heard children singing and dancing and playing instruments to greet them, bicyclers ringing their bells in congratulations, and cheering from windows. They smelled smoke from restaurants cooking fish and meat on grills, a salty breeze from the nearby shore, and bold perfumes and colognes of residents walking by.

Yahshi found himself waving back at children and smiling at the art of those passionate about their work. And when they sat in a famous rooftop restaurant, and he took his first bite of a dish he'd never tried before, he closed his eyes and savored it.

If freedom was a taste, he decided, *this would be it.*

He forgot he killed a man. He forgot he sold his soul to the Empire.

But after lunch, when they arrived at their final destination and were told to bring their formal wear out of the vault this time, reality struck again.

"Welcome to the Guardian Complex," said Commander Roz.

"Your new home," said Professor Embre.

They stood at the front steps of a sixteen-story building containing one hundred and fifty flats. It was only now that Yahshi wondered why there were fifty extras, as there were only one hundred guardians on active service at once. *Are they anticipating the need to call filtered trainees back into the Force someday, using the loophole in the contract?*

"Come along now," said Doctor Blimmery, gesturing for the graduates to follow them into the Complex common room.

"Recent graduates always start on the highest level," Professor Embre explained as they began their ascent to the sixteenth floor. "Perform well in service, and you'll earn your right to the convenience of lower floors."

When they reached the highest level, the graduates were winded. Yahshi set his box down to catch his breath.

There was no lobby—just a narrow hallway with windows on the right and ten doors on the left.

Professor Embre passed out their keys.

"The graduation ball begins at 5:00 this evening," Commander Roz said. "You have a few hours to rest and get ready before then. Please—do not leave the Complex. You should be wearing your formal wear when you meet me in the common room at 4:45. We'll head to the Palace together."

Doctor Blimmery clapped his hands. "Congratulations, *guardians*."

As the instructors headed downstairs, Yahshi grabbed his box and located the door to his flat—Room 148. With a bit of fidgeting, he unlocked it, and the door swung open.

What a marvelous cage.

Yahshi entered the common room at 4:45 sharp to find the others already there.

Pinto was dressed in black pants and a vest adorned with golden buttons. His blood-red blazer and dress shirt complemented the fiery shade of his eyepatch and tie. Yahshi noticed his hair was greasy, as though he'd tried to style it but the curls refused to cooperate. Despite his hair, he looked more than classy—he lit the room like wildfire.

Next to him stood Vell, wearing a silky violet dress that fell to her calves, barely grazing the tips of her boots. Multi-layered sleeves flowed around her arms like petals, and a silver flower pendant rested between her collarbones. Her hair was tied up in a messy bun with a lavender ribbon, a few loose strands framing her face.

"You two look surprisingly flashy," Quax said.

Keiyo rubbed his chin as he looped around them. "Pinto looks like a devil, and Vell looks like a girl." He pointed to her hairdo. "Bonus points for the ribbon."

"Wow." Vell glanced over her shoulder at him. "Thanks."

Keiyo pulled at his bowtie with an awkward chuckle. "I have to admit —I'm starting to feel brutally underdressed."

The other four turned to Yahshi, expecting a comment, but he couldn't gather enough excitement to praise their formal wear. All he could think about was the upcoming announcement of their division and unit placements. *Any division but Defense. Any unit but Cal's.*

Realizing they were still staring, he cleared his throat. "Very red," he told Pinto. "And very purple," he told Vell. They looked disappointed, but luckily, Commander Roz's entrance distracted them.

"It's time!" he announced.

The graduates exchanged smiles at the sight of Commander Roz's formal wear. His suit hugged his broad shoulders, and the golden flower pin on his lapel caught the chandelier light. His sharp eyes swept across the graduates as he observed their outfits from afar.

"You look marvelous," Commander Roz said. "All of you."

They filed into a vault and traveled to Vakoi Palace, only a few minutes away. When the box door opened, Yahshi jumped out, finding himself at the base of the Palace Wall. The brick structure filled so much of the sky that there was no room to look at anything else. *How did Princess Kia get past it that day? Surely she didn't climb.*

Commander Roz greeted a Defense guardian by the gate who opened the barred doors, allowing them through.

Of all the art in Vakoi City, the Palace was by far the grandest. It took up more than half of the space within the circular Wall and featured towers that stretched nearly as high. Each of its intricately carved pillars and stained-glass windows radiated a unique style, yet the designs blended together in perfect harmony.

Commander Roz led the graduates through a garden of mossy rocks, lush greenery, and serene water fountains. The front steps were embedded with jewels that stole their eyes until they entered the Palace.

Professor Embre and Doctor Blimmery greeted them in the common room.

"Remember what you practiced," Professor Embre said. "I refuse to see any fumbling on stage." She was wearing a sleeveless black dress with a high neckline that emphasized her toned arms. Seeing that her hair was just as unruly as usual, Yahshi sensed that she'd thrown her formal wear on at the last minute.

Next to her, Doctor Blimmery flaunted a navy-blue suit with striped pockets and a polka-dot tie. "Follow us there, and don't get lost!"

The Academy guardians led them so quickly through the twists and turns that Yahshi had no time to observe the paintings, portraits, and framed paperwork on the hallway walls. Before he knew it, they were standing by a pair of wooden doors, and he could hear muffled chatter from the other side.

Professor Embre and Doctor Blimmery swung the doors open, and the band's opening number exploded in Yahshi's face. Guardians and guests clapped and cheered as the graduates filed onto the ballroom stage.

As instructed, they formed a line facing the crowd. Yahshi took a deep breath at the sight of Famir's and Cal's units. *Let's get this over with.*

Commander Roz cleared his throat, and the ballroom fell silent. "Over the past eighteen months," he began, projecting his voice, "these five individuals have grown from gifted children into skilled guardians. Throughout the program's first half, they trained and studied relentlessly to make the final five."

"And throughout the program's second half," Professor Embre continued, "they gained hands-on experience by shadowing guardians on monthly assignments. Let's take a moment to acknowledge the shadow unit leaders who helped our new graduates learn the ropes."

Applause. A few eyes turned to Cal and Famir. Yahshi didn't know the other shadow unit leaders, but they were somewhere in the mix feeling prideful. *Why don't they see the damage they've done?*

"Words cannot describe how proud we are," Doctor Blimmery said. "We wish they could stay at the Academy forever, but it's time to let them spread their wings, marking the official start of our next Selection Season."

Spread our wings. Yahshi chuckled, and Pinto shot him a questioning stare. *Funny choice of words, Doctor.*

As the crowd cheered again, a realization struck Yahshi like a punch to the face. Another Selection Season would begin tomorrow. The Academy guardians would spend six months evaluating fifteen- and sixteen-year-olds in the West before revealing their next twenty victims. There had been so many in the past, and there would be so many to come. More to fight.

More to suffer. More boys and girls would enter the program and leave, never the same.

Yahshi stared down the line, observing his peers.

Keiyo closed his eyes as he dropped his head, mouthing the word *Medical.*

Quax locked his eyes on Cal in the crowd, waiting for her to look at him.

Vell gulped at the sight of her shadow unit leader, possibly hoping to join his unit—or perhaps not to. She hadn't told Yahshi anything about her assignments, so he couldn't be sure.

Pinto tapped his boot against the stage, anticipating his assignment to the Research Division but perhaps a bit anxious that, for some ridiculous reason, he might be proven wrong.

"We've been observing their strengths and weaknesses and analyzing reports from their shadow unit leaders," Commander Roz explained. "After careful consideration, we've finally decided on their official division and unit placements."

Doctor Blimmery held up an embroidered Medical badge. "Keiyo Pickett of Miranda."

Keiyo opened his eyes with a gasp. "Yes, Doctor?"

He grinned. "Welcome to Medical."

Keiyo exhaled through his smile before wrapping his arms around Doctor Blimmery. "Thank you! Thank you! Thank you!"

"You've been assigned to Doctor Larin's unit at the City Hospital," Doctor Blimmery added, his voice strained by Keiyo's suffocating embrace.

The crowd cheered as he pulled away, taking the Medical badge into his hands. A group of guardians shouted louder than the rest.

"Go Keiyo!"

"Welcome to our unit!"

"We're happy to have you!"

Keiyo reclaimed his spot in the line of graduates, and Professor Embre raised a badge next. "Pinto Dempsey of Frontal," she called—to no one's surprise. "Welcome to Research. You've been assigned to Professor Famir's unit at the Investigation Office."

"Professor Famir? Really?" Pinto took the badge from her outstretched hand.

"We had three different units fighting for you!" Famir yelled. "I had to arm-wrestle to win your spot."

Pinto laughed, stepping back into line.

"Quax Avarium of Sitra," Commander Roz said. "Welcome to Defense."

Quax grinned as he took the badge into his hands, and the room fell silent in anticipation.

"You've been assigned to Commander Cal's unit. Give a hand to the first siblings in the Force in guardian history!"

Cal finally met her brother's gaze from the crowd, waving with a light smile. Tears welled in his eyes, and he stepped back into line.

"Yahshi Konya of Sitra," Commander Roz started.

Yahshi's eyes widened at a Defense badge in his hand.

"Welcome to Defense," he finished.

The crowd cheered as Yahshi snatched the badge from Commander Roz. He tried to smile because he needed to keep his act going until he could find a way out of the Force. That was his plan. That was what he'd been working toward. But his lips wouldn't budge.

They hate me. They want me to suffer. They want to break me. This is all part of their plan.

Commander Roz leaned over his shoulder as Yahshi failed to restrain his scowl. "I know you've been struggling."

He held his stiff expression, perplexed, as Commander Roz raised his voice for the final part of his announcement.

"You've been assigned to Commander Lim's unit at Vakoi Palace."

Yahshi said nothing before stepping into line, refusing to thank him even though he *was* grateful. Being in a Palace unit meant he wouldn't have to go on expeditions unless the Force launched a special operation, which was rare.

The boys turned to Vell last, who stood at the end of the line. Her eyes were on Doctor Blimmery.

"Vell Patura of Miranda," Commander Roz continued.

"What?" Keiyo blurted, clutching his Medical badge.

Doctor Blimmery looked at his boots, and Vell's face drained of color.

Yahshi glared at Commander Roz, urging him to laugh it off as a joke—

but Commander Roz *never* joked.

"Welcome to Defense."

The boys exchanged confused looks as Vell passed them, accepting the badge from Commander Roz. She forced a smile before returning to her spot in line, the crowd roaring in excitement.

Yahshi locked eyes with Vell. He wished he could scream and cause an uproar. He would do anything to reassign Vell to Medical, the division she belonged in.

But they had all vowed to accept their division and unit placements without question.

Commander Roz cleared his throat. "You've been assigned to join Quax in Commander Cal's unit."

That was the final straw. Yahshi choked on his breath as the cheering picked up again. He stepped forward, but Vell grabbed his arm and shook her head. "Don't."

"Any other unit," he muttered. "They could have put you in *any—*"

Pinto elbowed Yahshi in the side, and he finally shut his mouth.

The band played another song as the graduates and Academy guardians filed off stage, standing at the sidelines. In their place, five guardians in their late-fifties stood, retirement speeches in hand. Yahshi didn't listen to them as they spoke of their undying devotion to the Force and appreciation for their fellow guardians.

Vell was supposed to be in Medical with Keiyo. Why does everyone else get what they want while she has to suffer? What kind of thought went into such an unfair decision?

And then he remembered the day he walked with Doctor Blimmery across the field, waiting for Vell to return from her first assignment. Her shadow unit leader had shared that she'd beaten them in a dart competition, and it was more apparent now than ever that they never considered personal opinion.

They didn't show me grace. They placed me in a Palace unit because they knew I wouldn't function on expeditions, and they want me to function. Because if I can function, I have value. It's all about them. It's never about us.

Yahshi turned to Vell, who smiled at him. He could almost hear her saying, *Get your act together. Don't cause any drama. There is nothing we can do.*

After the retirement speeches, the band played a waltz, followed by guests inviting each other to dance. Yahshi watched the room fill with motion.

Famir held a hand out for Cal, who was wearing a knee-length dress of vibrant colors swirling into muted tones, a blend of contradictions. Her chunky bracelets and black boots clashed with her pearl necklace and earrings. Yahshi saw different versions of her flash by as she spun, and he couldn't decipher which was authentic.

He flinched when Vell took his hand by surprise. She led him to an open space, and as they faced each other, he could see a familiar hatred brewing in her eyes.

Vell guided his hand to her waist and stepped closer. "Smile," she whispered.

"What?"

She grinned as she placed her free hand on his shoulder, sending a chill down his spine. "They've been watching you."

Yahshi peered past her, spotting the Academy guardians muttering by the stage. He inhaled a shaky breath as he returned his gaze to Vell.

"Smile," she repeated, and this time, he did.

The music intensified as they danced through the pain. This was their life now. The glamor, the fancy clothes, the extravagant ceremonies—this was all theirs, and they had earned this, and it was a tragedy.

They were puppets of the Empire, dancing by strings controlled by a greater Force. Dancing because they were placed in a ballroom, and that was what to be expected. They were not their own people. They had never been, from the moment they pressed their thumbs against those contracts. And they could not speak their minds because speaking their minds meant breaking Imperial Law, the Guardian Vows, or Protocol. And they could not fight because fighting meant tangling the strings and suffocating themselves in the process.

So instead, they danced as they were told. They faked their smiles and laughter, listening to the frustrated flickering of torches and pounding of shoes against the marble floor. They buried the truth between the lines and pushed the lines so close together that no one could see the space between them.

What would it take to cut these strings? Yahshi led Vell into a twirl. Her dress rippled around her until she faced him, her hand meeting his again like clockwork. Moves they had practiced. Moves they had been trained to make. *What would it take to really, truly dance?*

A final violin note ripped through the air as they embraced each other.

"Congratulations," Vell said.

He hugged her tighter as the world seemed to crash and crumble and burn around him. He knew he couldn't stay with her, but he couldn't leave her either.

"Congratulations," Yahshi whispered.

POISONED APPLES

We emulate the strength of a beehive, collaborating in harmony
to achieve our shared purpose.

♫ BEAUTIFUL CRIME - TAMER ♫

Yahshi jolted awake with gasping breaths, his pajamas drenched in sweat. It took him a minute to realize he was in his Complex flat, not a stranger's bed.

I can't live like this.

He opened the curtains to reveal the bustling center of Vakoi City, a world most could only dream of living in. With a sigh, he yanked the curtains shut.

A golden envelope on the floor caught his attention. It'd been slipped through a slot in his door. He opened it to find a bill of exchange for his first week of service. *No amount of money could pay me to stay.* He slammed the bill onto his nightstand and began to change into his guardian uniform.

Vell knocked on his door. "Yahshi?"

"Give me a minute." He tied his bootlaces and slipped his overcoat on.

"I'll be in the hallway. You're running late."

Yahshi parted one side of his overcoat, shaking his head at the abundance of pocketed supplies. "So at the Palace," he said, strapping his dual swords to his back, "do you really think I'll need my primary tool, serum, antiserum, neutralizer, *The Guardian Handbook*, lock busters, rope, and—"

"Yes, all of it." Vell did not sound amused.

Yahshi scoffed at the full-length mirror. He used to wonder what this moment would feel like. The answer was simple.

Heavy.

He opened the door to find Vell with her arms crossed. She was wearing an identical uniform, but instead of dual swords, her stars and darts were secured in a bandolier across her chest.

"Hurry," Vell said, turning to rush down the hallway.

Yahshi locked his flat and caught up to her.

"You look good," she said, "but your hair's getting oily again."

"Oh, great." Yahshi ran a hand through his hair. "I don't know why it does that."

"I told you. You need a hat."

"No thanks."

"You'd look cool in a hat."

"Guardians don't wear hats."

"You could be the first." She paused. "I'll buy you one."

"And I'll throw it out," he muttered.

They made their way down the seemingly infinite staircase.

"How are you feeling?" Vell asked.

"I'm good." Yahshi glanced at the Defense badge on her shoulder. "What about you?"

"We're in the same division." She made the statement cheerfully, but he knew what she meant.

"I have a feeling you didn't take one," she added, pulling a spare maintenance vial out of her overcoat.

Yahshi rolled his eyes, grabbing the vial.

"Yahshi," she warned. "We signed the contract. We made the Vows. We graduated."

"I know."

"Watch yourself. I can't do that for you."

"I know."

"It doesn't seem like you do."

"I get it, Vell." He popped the stopper off and chugged the mandatory poison.

"I'm worried," she said.

"Why?" He tucked the empty vial into his overcoat.

"You're slipping. I thought you were doing better. I thought you got past this."

Yahshi didn't reply, and they scaled the remaining steps in silence.

When they reached the common room, he spotted Cal chatting with his fellow graduates. He wanted to hate her but couldn't because his uniform was identical to hers.

"Morning, Vell," Cal said as they approached her. "Ready for your first day?"

Vell looked at Yahshi. He could almost see everything he'd told her about his first assignment flash through her eyes.

"I'm ready," she said.

"And Yahshi, I'm so glad you found a unit that suits you." Cal smiled as though it were an insult, which made it one.

"Let's go, let's go!" Quax clapped and headed for the door. "I've *been* ready."

As Cal and Vell trailed behind him, Keiyo cupped his palms around his mouth and yelled, "You better keep that girl away from poison, Quax!"

"I'll miss you too!" Vell shouted back.

"Stay safe," Pinto said.

Quax spun around, flashing an eye roll. "Don't be sappy."

Yahshi had too much to say. The words clumped together, forming a knot in his throat. Watching them leave with Cal felt like watching them die.

Pinto chuckled, resting an arm on Yahshi's shoulder. "We made it."

Keiyo appeared by his other side. "I know it sucks," he whispered, "but they're gonna be fine."

"I know," Yahshi muttered, and that was the harshest knowledge of all.

Cal closed the door behind her unit.

"Hey, Yahshi?" Pinto said.

"Yeah?"

"You're supposed to be at the Palace right now."

He glanced at the clock and sighed.

Emperor Vakoi looked nothing like his Royal portraits or the Academy's courtyard statue. His shoulders were less broad, his face less proportional, and his body less muscular. *Actually, he's not muscular at all.*

"I'm sorry for being late, Your Majesty," Yahshi said, clenching his fists under their table in the Palace tea room. "No one told me I'd be meeting you."

"So you're only punctual when you expect to meet someone important?" Emperor Vakoi asked.

Shut it. "I apologize."

Emperor Vakoi's arm trembled as he poured Yahshi a cup of tea. He wasn't strong. *It'd be so easy to kill him.*

Yahshi accepted the warm teacup. It was decorated with the same four-petaled flower branded into his forehead. *How humiliating it is to be marked in the same way as a cup.*

He took a sip and puckered his lips. "Your Majesty, there's—"

"Belladonna?" Emperor Vakoi smiled, every tooth in his mouth on clear display. "Impressive."

Yahshi forced a grin. *What the hell?*

"Commander Yahshi, may I be frank?"

No. "Of course."

"The Vakoi Palace is the safest building on the island. If I thought my daughter was in danger here, I would have hired a guardian with at least ten years of experience. Yet I chose you." He leaned forward. "Why?"

"I thought I was assigned to Commander Lim's unit."

"Officially, yes. You work for him on paper, but in practice, you report to me."

Just get to the point. "Your Majesty, I'm not following."

"Starting today, you're Princess Kia's bodyguard," Emperor Vakoi said. "The truth is, there is no greater danger in this Palace than my daughter herself. Her brother Kodo has no problem staying within the Wall, but she's wreaking havoc with her plans to sneak out every week. In the past year, I've assigned five different Defense guardians as her bodyguards, and they managed to keep her under control, but none of them solved the root problem."

"What's my role, exactly?"

The Emperor pressed his stubby finger to Yahshi's chest. "The Underground is a dangerous organization, and we must prevent their advancements, no matter the cost."

Hidden behind his close-lipped smile, Yahshi was gritting his teeth. He wanted to swat the Emperor's finger away but couldn't because he owned him—and they both knew it.

"My daughter likes to talk nonsense about joining the Underground." Emperor Vakoi finally pulled his finger away. "It's only a matter of time before she leaves the Palace one day and never comes back. I fear they could get their hands on her. It would change the game. Are you following?"

I hate you. "I believe so, Your Majesty."

"I'm looking for a *final* bodyguard," Emperor Vakoi said. "I want you to help my daughter understand that her recklessness jeopardizes our people's safety. So make her trust you, and make her change. If you fail like the others have, I may have to resolve the matter myself. And I'd rather not. Is that clear?"

Are you seriously threatening to kill your own daughter?

"It's clear," Yahshi said, crossing his arms. He could feel his dagger handle pressing into his waist, but he shook his head, breaking the thought away.

"And if you can manage," the Emperor added, "find out how the hell she gets past my Wall."

Princess Kia's fingers soared across the keys of a white piano, playing a haunting tune. Her bangs blocked her eyes, and her uncombed hair draped over her shoulders. She was wearing a simple green dress, its only embellishment being a strip of silk tied around her waist with a sloppy bow at the back. If she were to stand among a crowd of Vakoi City teenagers, Yahshi would not have assumed her royalty. Wealthy, yes—but not royalty.

She continued playing as Yahshi made his way across a dark room of bookshelves, musical instruments, and heavy chandeliers.

When he stopped by the piano, Princess Kia pressed her bare foot against the dampening pedal. The notes blurred together, leading into the chorus. He watched her play for a minute before clearing his throat.

"Excuse me, Your Highness."

She continued to play, so he raised his voice.

"I'm your new—"

Yahshi flinched when she pounded the keys. Despite her jagged movements, she still played the right notes in the right order. He waited until the piano returned to its original volume before speaking again.

"I'm your—"

She played louder in response to his voice. The song sped up to the point where it was no longer recognizable, her fingers moving so quickly he couldn't catch them with his eyes. When he took a step closer, she jammed her foot against the pedal, and the sheer volume of the merging notes left him with his palms over his ears.

Then the music stopped, dropping dead to the floor.

"I know my father had a little talk with you." Princess Kia stared at the keys, refusing to look at him. "But you should know that you're not gonna change me. I will *never* listen to a Nightshade. You're all the same. My father's pawns. Overtrained pushovers with muscles instead of brains."

The Princess resumed playing, softer this time. The song came to an unsatisfying stop a few minutes later, ending one note too early.

"Really, no response?" she muttered. "Don't be boring. I hate boring."

"It seemed like you didn't want me to speak," Yahshi said.

She faced him with a jolt, and her blue eyes widened. "You're the shadow, from the archives."

"That's right, Doctor."

She stared at her lap with a grin. "Surely you have questions for me. Perhaps you're wondering how I entered the Office without a key? Or how I got a doctor's uniform?"

"I don't really care," Yahshi said, harsher than he'd meant to. "Sorry."

"Don't apologize if you're not sincere. I detect lies better than you detect poison."

"Serum," he corrected.

"Oh, is that what they teach you? Cute." The Princess eyed his swords. "And what do you call those?"

"Tools."

"Not weapons?" She chuckled. "You know, I find it hard to believe you don't have *any* questions. Perhaps you're wondering why I'm so insistent on leaving the Canister?"

"Canister?"

"That's what I call the Palace. If the Force can rename things, so can I." She stood and smoothed her dress out, staring at his overcoat. "Hand me that mango, will you?"

Yahshi parted one side of his overcoat, and she snatched his dagger from its holding strap.

"Careful," he said. "It's laced, and you have no tolerance."

"You're right. I have no tolerance for you." She squinted at the blade before handing his secondary tool back. "Cool toy. Any questions yet?"

"I'll listen to whatever you wanna tell me."

The Princess leaned forward, lowering her voice. "I know you're like Maelin."

"I'm not sure what you mean."

"I'd be an idiot not to notice the transcripts you were studying. You want a way out of this hellhole, and so do I."

"Why? You have everything."

"And wannabe guardians say the same about you."

Yahshi stashed his dagger.

"You think I have everything, but I have nothing. Even Nightshades have more freedom than me, and that's saying something because you're practically slaves. Your flat and utilities are covered by the Force, which means you get a huge payment every week with nothing important to use it for. My father's like the rich parents in the capital who throw pocket change at their kids to buy candy after school. So yeah. We're very similar —me and you."

"Because we're both nothing but Palace accessories?" Yahshi asked.

"I'm a bit worse than an accessory. At least my father has a use for you." She smiled at the term he'd chosen before continuing. "My brother will take the throne someday—he's the asset. And then there's me, a fifteen-year-old who's too worthless to make use of but too important to lose. He knows if I run away, someone will use me as leverage to get what they want from him—I'm the liability. My brother secures a future for the Empire, and I threaten it. That's no way to live, but it's the role I was born into. What makes us different is that you *chose* to tangle yourself in my family's mess. So, money or ego?"

"Excuse me?"

"Why'd you sign the contract? If you're not happy as a guardian, it has to be one or the other. So was it money, or was it ego?"

Yahshi thought about his choice in the office on Selection Day. He'd pricked his thumb because he wanted a grand dream. He wanted to believe he could be someone bigger and better.

"Ego," he admitted.

"And look at you now, sitting in the Palace with the Princess. You've secured the *dream*. Am I wrong?"

"You're right."

"And yet you reject it."

"I do." He held firm eye contact.

"I read a marvelous story last night." The Princess moved her hands through the air, flipping through imaginary pages. "A young boy bites into a shiny apple, only to realize he's being poisoned. And yet he takes another bite. Does that sound familiar?"

"I can't tell if it does."

"Then perhaps you can tell me this." She grinned. "If you were that boy, at what point would you stop eating?"

Yahshi pursed his lips. He'd been trying to escape the Force for months, but it wasn't easy. He had to be patient, find more information, and wait for the right time.

"Just because you take a bite doesn't mean you have to finish the apple," she continued, pushing him for a reply.

"Of course not. But there are other factors to consider, like—"

"What? Your fellow graduates?"

"We've gone through so much together. It feels wrong to... leave them in the dark."

"I don't doubt that you're unhealthily attached to them after all that Academy trauma, but are they like Maelin? Do they hesitate to kill? Do they question the morality of the Force, and most importantly, do they resist it? Or is that only you?"

Yahshi gulped.

"I have a proposition for you, Commander." Princess Kia leaned against the piano and crossed her arms. "Let's leave together."

"What?"

"Let's leave together."

"No."

"Commander—"

"You realize how ridiculous that sounds, right?"

"It's not ridiculous. It's efficient."

Yahshi scanned the room, ensuring they were truly alone. "We shouldn't be talking about this," he whispered, but she continued.

"I'll be honest. I have a secret way out of the Canister—one my father doesn't know about. I could easily head east alone, yes, but I wouldn't last a day. That's why I need your help."

"I can't help you."

"I have *zero* life skills. I've never left the City." She chuckled. "Who am I kidding? I hardly leave the Palace Wall. I can't fight. I can't cook. I don't even know if I can climb a tree. But you? Well, you grew up in society. Like, *real* Western society. And you're a convert, so you have a history in the East."

"I was young. I don't remember the East."

"And you're a Nightshade," she continued, "so I know you can fight.

And I know you can kill if you have to. You can survive out there. I'll simply tag along."

"You'd make me an easy target. It'd be a suicide mission."

"No one will recognize me. My family's fancied up for the public eye. We both know I look nothing like my portraits. That's how I got into the Investigation Office—I slipped behind someone who had a key. Put me in a Nightshade uniform, and I'll blend in with the Nightshades. Put me in Eastern clothes, and I'll blend in with the Easterners."

"It's not about being recognized. It's about increased security. Imagine how much the Force would panic if a guardian were to go missing. It'd be a hundred times worse if a Royal Family member disappeared too. I'm sorry, Your Highness. I can't help you."

"But unfortunately, it's too late to decline, because I already know about you and Vell."

"Huh?"

"Vell Patura, another commander from your cycle."

"What about her?"

"Well, you're awfully close."

Yahshi frowned. "Who told you?"

"It was a guess, but now I know it's true." She faked a pout. "And I hate to ruin what you have, but breaking a Guardian Vow is a serious offense that I, as the Princess, am obligated to report to my father."

"What Vow?"

"You and Vell are in love, and a guardian can only love the Empire."

His face went hot. "Why would you say—"

Princess Kia burst into laughter.

"It's not funny," he snapped. "And it's not true."

"To be frank, Commander, I don't care if it's true. All I care about is that it makes a good story. And we both know how much the Force loves a good story."

"You're bluffing," Yahshi said. "You can tell Emperor Vakoi whatever you want, but he won't believe you. He knows you're out to make chaos."

"And yet he takes my word as fact, time after time. He sends my body-guards to correction when I get bored, not because he trusts me but because he's smarter than he is kind. So if I make a bold enough accusation, he'll take action because it's safer to trust the liar than risk calling my bluff. *The boy who cried wolf* doesn't apply to a man who despises wolves with every ounce of his being."

She stepped toward him, landing her final jab. "Leave without me, and I'll report you and Vell. You might not be here to get sent to correction, but Vell? Well..."

"Don't be cruel. She has nothing to do with this."

"And yet... I don't care."

He glared at her, and she raised her brows, holding a finger up.

"Oh, I almost forgot. You do know what happens during correction, don't you?"

"No," Yahshi spat.

"So it usually starts with mental correction."

"Stop," he said, but she wouldn't.

"To be honest, it sounds rather pleasant. They sit you down in a posh room and encourage you to talk about your feelings. They act like they understand you, take notes, and give you tasks to complete as homework assignments. They continue this process for a pre-established period, and sometimes, it works wonders. But if it doesn't, they move on to physical correction."

He shook his head. "Don't—"

"They restrain you, beat you up, lock you in isolation for days," she said, her words accelerating. "They use poison and drugs you've never heard of to manipulate and control you. They won't stop until they own your mind completely. And if you resist their efforts, they may decide they can't fix you. So instead, they'll cut their losses, get rid of you, and cover it up with a good story. Because no matter how much of a mess you are, they won't *ever* let you win."

Yahshi dropped his head, his blood boiling.

"Threats aside," Princess Kia continued, "I'm not a monster out to ruin your plans. I hear things in the Palace and know things most Nightshades don't. I'm clever. I can help you come up with a plan. I won't lie to you. I won't be stupid. I won't be dead weight. So why don't we end this back-

and-forth blabbering and throw our apples out together? What do you say?" She held her hand out.

And Yahshi took it.

CHAPTER 31

QUITE THE JUMP

We adapt to change like a flowing river,
carving our unique path toward unity and progress.

♫ THE BREACH · DUSTIN TEBBUTT ♫

"Oh, Yahshi!" Pinto said. "I'm so glad you're back from the Palace! I have big news. *Huge* news. Just come in. Come in!"

With a forced smile, Yahshi stepped into his flat.

"I only have a minute." Pinto glanced at the clock. "My unit's meeting me in the common room to get supper, but as soon as I'm back, I wanna hear all about the Palace, alright?"

"Sure," Yahshi said.

"Okay, big news. Ah, how do I say this quickly?" He paced the room. "Where to begin?"

Yahshi sat on Pinto's bed and looked around for a ring of keys, but they were likely in his overcoat.

"Okay, I've got it." Pinto sat next to him. "Remember when we were shadowing together, and Professor Famir would have me join his unit meetings?"

Yahshi nodded.

"Those were to discuss time-sensitive cases that the entire unit was responsible for. But professors also have individual cases to work on in their own time. They're usually related to petty crimes. Or big deals that died down."

"So, you got a case of your own?"

"Not just any case." Pinto hopped to his feet and did a twirl. Yahshi had never seen him do a twirl before.

"What case?" he asked.

Pinto shook his shoulder. "Guess whose case it is. Guess!"

Before Yahshi could speak, Pinto bit his lip in excitement, his face reddening until it finally burst from his mouth.

"The Bayins!"

Yahshi imagined Pinto in the archives, flipping through interrogation transcripts to discover that the Bayins had a connection with Martu Konya. And once Yahshi's father was in trouble, Yahshi would be in trouble, and the Force would send him to correction before he'd have the chance to leave, and—

"Professor Famir knows I'm the perfect guardian to take this case on. Not only was I in the program with Dice for months, but I've also known him since I was seven! I remember *so much*."

"That's amazing, Pinto."

"Right?" He stood tall. "I'm gonna find that spy, and once I do, guess what?"

Silence.

"Guess what?" Pinto asked again.

"What?" Yahshi said.

"I find Dice, I find the Underground. I find the Underground, I *end* the Underground. I'd change the course of guardian history. If I crack the case fast enough, I might even get promoted to unit leader at a younger age than Commander Cal. By a matter of months, but it's possible."

"Wow," Yahshi muttered.

Pinto glanced at the clock again. "Great, there I go rambling. Now I'm late. I'm never late." He rushed to the door, reaching into his overcoat to grab a ring of keys. "Let's talk more later, okay?"

"Here." Yahshi held his hands out. "I'll lock up for you."

"Thanks." Pinto tossed him the keys and left.

When Yahshi entered the hallway to lock up, Pinto was already near the staircase.

"Be somewhere I can find you, alright?" Pinto yelled over his shoulder. "And if Vell returns while I'm gone, tell her hi for me!"

"He needs a duplicate?" Keiyo asked, observing the key to the Investigation Office. Yahshi had easily recognized it among Pinto's other keys—it was oddly shaped like the one Famir had.

"I don't know why he needs it," Yahshi lied. "But it's probably best not to ask Commander Lim too many questions on my first day."

As Keiyo ran his finger along the key, Yahshi scanned the Complex common room, ensuring it was still empty.

"He told me to find a locksmith to make a duplicate, so I looked all over. No luck," Yahshi continued. "But I know you're good at tool crafting, so maybe you'd be able to—I don't know—help me out somehow? Is that something you could do?"

"Fascinating," Keiyo muttered.

"What?"

"This key, obviously. I've never seen anything like it." He flipped it over in amusement. "I bet it's impossible to pick the Office lock, even with buster tools like ours."

There goes Plan B...

"But you found the right man for the job." Keiyo removed the key from Pinto's ring. "I can handle it."

"You can?"

"I'm a genius, remember? A multi-talented and versatile master of all trades."

Yahshi smiled. "How long will it take you?"

"I don't know. Half an hour, maybe? I'll have to head back to the

Hospital for the right equipment."

"I can come with you," Yahshi offered.

"Don't worry about it." He was already at the door. "I'll bring the duplicate back soon. Hang tight."

So Yahshi hung tight. He sat on a sofa, hoping Keiyo would keep quiet about the task and hurry up. Hoping the doctors at the City Hospital wouldn't pay attention to what he was doing. Hoping Pinto and his unit would take their time at supper so the original key would be back on the ring in time.

When the door opened, Yahshi stood, but it was Vell and Quax who entered, not Keiyo. Quax was whispering something to Vell, who continually shook her head.

"Vell?" Yahshi called.

She left Quax behind, passing Yahshi without a glance.

"Wait!" Yahshi stepped after her.

"Yahshi," Cal snapped, stopping him.

He turned to see Cal emerge next to Quax in the doorway. They looked more alike than ever.

"Leave her be," she said.

"Why? What happened?" Yahshi asked.

Cal patted Quax's shoulder, and he didn't flinch a bit. "We leave tomorrow at 6:00. She better not flake."

Quax smiled. "She won't."

Yahshi cringed as Cal wrapped her arms around Quax. He'd never seen her hug him growing up, and he wondered if she only did so now to keep him under her control.

When she pulled away, Quax offered Yahshi an awkward wave and headed for his flat.

Yahshi waited for Cal to leave, but she lingered in the doorway as Quax began his ascent.

"It looks like you're healed now," she said, studying his leg. "I heard it was quite the jump."

"Fall," Yahshi corrected.

"Hmm..." She made eye contact with him. "I don't think you've healed yet. I think your leg is just as broken as it's always been."

"I'm not sure what you mean."

Cal took a single step into the common room. "You're a bad influence on Vell. You told her everything about your first assignment, breaking the shadow confidentiality rule and messing with her head. You made her think that acting out is normal—that it's tolerated. Your carelessness is jeopardizing the productivity of my unit and my reputation in the Force." She spoke to him differently now, like he was storing beans under his floorboards. "You have everyone fooled, but you haven't changed at all."

"I could say the same about you."

"Listen, I'm happy here. People respect me. They don't give me trouble like they did in Sitra. Things are better now, and you're not going to ruin that. You're going to stay out of my unit members' lives, and in exchange, I'm going to stay out of yours."

"Fine," Yahshi muttered.

"Look at me and say it."

He met her gaze. "*Fine*. I'll leave them be."

"Leave *who* be?"

"Quax and Vell," Yahshi said, his tone sharpening. "I'll leave them be."

"Perfect." Cal smiled. "Be more careful, Yahshi."

He waited for the door to shut before plopping himself onto the sofa. Cal had read between the lines when no one else could. She could get him sent to correction, and considering her implication that he was broken, that was precisely what she'd threatened to do.

Still, he had the urge to run upstairs and knock on Vell's door.

Leave her be? Yahshi eyed the staircase. *How could I leave her be?*

And yet he stayed where he was, waiting for that key.

Princess Kia stood behind the Investigation Office, dressed in baggy black clothes. Her hat clung to her head like a mushroom top, and the moonlike lenses of her sunglasses shielded her eyes. If they hadn't agreed to meet here at midnight, Yahshi wouldn't have recognized her.

"I think I finally have a question for you," he said.

"About time."

Yahshi crossed his arms. "How do you get past the Wall?"

"I chop my body up, toss the pieces over, then reassemble myself on the other side."

"I'm serious. How do you do it?"

"That's classified." Princess Kia dropped her chin, peering at him over her lenses. "I only have one safe way out of the Canister. I'm not trusting you with top-secret information like that."

"Yet you're trusting me with your life."

"Not yet. Until we leave, it's *your* life in *my* hands." She slung a bag off her shoulder and tossed him a set of clothes from inside. "Put these on."

Yahshi caught the foreign fabric and ran his hands along it, trying to recall the last time he'd worn something the Force hadn't told him to.

"Ew. Don't fondle them," Princess Kia snapped. "They're my brother's."

"I'm not—"

"Did you get the key?"

Yahshi pulled the duplicate out of his overcoat. Keiyo had brought it back only ten minutes before Pinto's return, which had been far too close for Yahshi's comfort. But he had the key, and that was all that mattered.

"You called Doctor Keiyo a prodigy." Princess Kia snatched the key. "Why does it look so weird?"

"Don't worry. It's supposed to look weird."

"If it doesn't work, I'll end him." She tossed Yahshi her bag and faced the wall. "Now hurry up and change. Be careful not to drop any knick-knacks the Force could use to trace the break-in back to you. No mangos, or trumpets, or—"

"Okay, I get it." Yahshi slipped the overcoat off his shoulders, and the fabric thumped against the ground. *I wish I could do that more often.*

After changing into Prince Kodo's clothes, he stuffed his uniform into the bag and slung it over his shoulder. "Ready."

She turned and removed her sunglasses. "You look so... normal."

Yahshi shrugged. "I always look normal."

"No. You're a guardian, and guardians look perfect." She slipped her sunglasses back on and led him to the front door.

Yahshi scanned the road as she jiggled the key, struggling to find the right angle.

"Is it working?" he asked.

"Your friend needs a tutor."

"Give it to me."

Princess Kia handed over the key, and with a bit of maneuvering, Yahshi popped the door open. He pocketed the duplicate as he walked softly into the pitch black common room.

Yahshi flinched as Princess Kia took a few clunky steps inside and slammed the door behind her.

"Shh!"

"What?" she asked in full volume. "There's no one here."

"We don't know that," Yahshi whispered. "There could be guardians working late on the higher floors."

"I can't see a thing."

"I'll get a lantern. Don't move. Don't talk. Don't breathe."

"There's no way I'm holding my breath."

It didn't take long for him to run into one of the dining tables, where he found a lantern and a box of matches. He lit it, filling the common room with a warm orange glow.

"Take off your shoes and follow me." He headed for the staircase.

"I'm not *that* loud."

"Just do it."

She rolled her eyes, leaving her boots behind. The archives were empty when they arrived.

"I'm wearing socks for no reason," Princess Kia said. "Thanks, Commander."

Yahshi held a finger to his lips. "There could be someone upstairs."

"How do you live with yourself?" She made a beeline for the nearest file cabinet and shuffled through its files.

"I know where they're stored." He rushed toward the opposite side of the room.

"Oh." She slammed the drawer shut and caught up to him.

Yahshi pulled a few rolled maps out of the drawer and partially unraveled them to confirm their titles. "Border Control Towers, Eastern Officer Patrol Routes, and... Eastern Trade Routes."

"Perfect," Princess Kia said. "Let's leave."

Halfway to the staircase, Yahshi spotted a drawer labeled *Bayin*. He diverted from their path to open it and found a few old files inside. *Nothing new.*

"What are you doing?" Princess Kia asked.

"I'm taking these too." He grabbed the files and shoved his hip into the drawer to close it.

"The Force will notice the missing Bayin files *much* sooner than a few maps."

"I know," Yahshi said.

The Princess smirked. "This case means something to you."

He stepped toward the staircase, but she blocked his way.

"Why else would you protect the Bayins?" she asked.

He said nothing, and after a moment, her face lit up.

"Your father!"

"What?"

"Your father, Martu. Oh, this is perfect! You have a lead, a direct contact to the Underground."

"How do you know my father's name?"

"I read about him in your selection files."

"What selection files?"

"You know, the stuff Academy guardians flip through during Selection Seasons—plus their annotations. There's a few days every Season when they meet at the Palace, and I get peeks here and there."

Yahshi frowned.

"I read lots about your father," Princess Kia continued. "Like how he kept you busy at the market and trained you in combat. It makes perfect sense now. He has connections to the Bayins, which means he has connections to the Underground. Of course he wouldn't want you to get selected. I wouldn't be surprised if he *encouraged* your questioning of the Force."

He froze.

"Am I wrong?" she asked.

"I don't know if he has anything to do with the Underground. It's just a theory."

"Ah, so that's why you insisted we take a route through Sitra. You want to confront him for answers. And in the meantime, just in case your theory's right, you're tampering with information to keep both of you safe."

Yahshi's grip on the files tightened. "You can never be too careful."

"There's a fine line between careful and naive. The Force has been on this case for over a year, and there's no way it would all come together *now*. But if those files go missing, they might put even more energy into the case, so your efforts would have a negative—"

"I'm taking the files," he stated.

"Fine. I'm not the one in danger."

They left the Office the same way they'd come. Princess Kia put her boots on as Yahshi put out the lantern, and they locked the door before regrouping behind the building.

"You should keep everything." Yahshi held the maps, files, and duplicate key out for her. "It'd be too dangerous to bring these to the Complex."

"That's *your* problem, not mine." She swerved around him, walking away. "Keep the clothes for tomorrow night."

Yahshi's blood ran hot. She was forcing him to keep the incriminating evidence to gain more leverage against him.

"How will you get back to the Palace?" he asked, frustration seeping into his voice.

"That's classified." Princess Kia spun around, walking backward into the shadows. "See you tomorrow, Commander."

CHAPTER 32

BECAUSE YOU'RE HERE

We stand in solidarity with those who suffer injustice,
clinging together like leaves in a gust of wind.

♫ IF I LEAD · KILTRO ♫

After a discussion over tea, Emperor Vakoi led Yahshi to a Palace dining room, where Princess Kia was reading as she ate. Yahshi sat across from her, and the Emperor left without a word.

"Hungry?" There was a sharpness to Princess Kia's tone. "I can ring that gong, and some loser will bring you a plate."

"I ate at the Complex."

"Yeah, but what do they feed you there? Dog food?" She slammed her fork down and turned a page.

"Is something wrong?" Yahshi asked.

"You told him everything, didn't you?"

"Emperor Vakoi called the meeting, not me."

She glared at him over the novel. "You told him I threatened you into leaving with me."

"It's been a week, so he asked for an update. I didn't say anything about our plan."

"I guess I'll have to tell him about everything we've done—breaking into the archives and gathering supplies and planning a travel route. I'll have to tell him about your father's connection to the Bayins."

"Your Highness," he said through gritted teeth. "Calm down."

"I'll have to tell him about Commander Vell too."

He snatched her book. "I told him *nothing*."

"Good." She cracked a smile. "I just wanted to make sure."

Yahshi flopped the book onto the table.

"So I feel like everything's moving along smoothly," she continued, dabbing her mouth with a napkin. "Let's leave tonight."

"No. We're not ready. We've gathered maps, tools, *poison*." He thought of the daily maintenance vials he'd been stashing in his getaway bag. "But we still need food."

"You have plenty of money. We can buy food on the run."

Yahshi thought of the second bill of exchange he'd received from the Force that morning. They'd have nearly 4,000 coins for the journey, enough to buy food and water for months. "But we don't know what security will look like in Eastern markets, especially after news breaks out. Shopping could be dangerous."

Princess Kia rolled her eyes. "Fine. We'll get food tonight, but we leave tomorrow. No backing out."

"I'm thinking dried goods—filling and light to carry."

"We'll buy anything. I don't care."

His stomach rumbled at the sight of her plate. He'd eaten breakfast at the Complex that morning out of curiosity and finally learned why guardians preferred dining out whenever time allowed. The free food wasn't close to Academy standards—he hadn't finished his plate.

To distract himself from hunger, he studied the dining room's stained-glass window. The shards were arranged to form beautiful flowers at first glance, but the beauty faded when he realized that each petal was pointy enough to pierce.

"The Bayin files," he blurted. "No one's mentioned them. Silence about the maps, I can understand, but the files? It doesn't make sense."

"You must be lucky."

"No, it's too convenient." He tapped his fingers against the table. "Actually, our entire plan is too convenient. I'm just realizing that now. Everything we've done is based on our assumption that the Underground is safe."

"I'm not assuming it's safe. Just better."

"But how do you know? What if my father has nothing to do with them? What if they kill us instead of letting us hide? What if, in some ways, they're just as evil as the Force?"

"As evil as the guardians who kill families at my father's bidding?" she countered. "The guardians who kill for the man who gouged out the eyes of his people and blamed it on his neighbor?"

Yahshi's throat clotted as he thought of the commonality in the transcripts. "So it's true?"

"I hear things in the Palace, Commander." She lowered her voice. "Thirteen years ago, my father initiated the raids with a small group of guardians sworn to secrecy. He blamed the violence on the East to justify killing the Atherus family and taking over their Empire. Did you know that Prince Runix was two years old when he was burned alive in his home? He would have been fifteen today, the same age as me, but I'm alive and he's dead because my father is a *very bad man*."

Yahshi shook his head. He and his fellow guardians had been following orders from a heartless tyrant, working like rabid dogs. *We are all evil through association.*

"After the war," Princess Kia continued, "my father allowed a single migration of Easterners to move West under the condition that they pledge their allegiance to him. They're known as converts, like you. Do you wanna know *why* he allowed such a thing?"

"Why?" Yahshi asked.

"My father's only desire is to keep Easterners fearful and productive. He doesn't care about earning their loyalty—he never did. He only allowed the migration because it made for a wonderful story. By letting all the smart, moral Easterners convert to his Empire and live on his land, he framed himself as a generous leader and the entirety of the East as evil. *All the good ones are among us, and all the bad ones are out there*—I'm sure you've heard *that* before."

Princess Kia gripped her fork tighter as lightning struck.

"It's all a giant farce. A story," she said. "Everything we're told is purely fiction."

She continued to eat as Yahshi sat there, processing her words. His gaze drifted to the stained-glass window again.

"You're right," he said. "It's practically dog food."

She rang the gong, and they ate breakfast together.

That evening, the Force granted the recent graduates a shared block of time off to discuss their first week as guardians. They dined on the highest floor of an entertainment complex, where abstract sculptures stood between tables, and swirling pillars pretended to hold the ceiling in place.

"We were only ten minutes into our journey"—Vell strengthened her voice, building anticipation—"and Quax had already slit his hand. Cal was furious."

Quax winced as he raised his arm, revealing a bandage around his palm. "It was a stupid accident. I nearly fainted."

"From one cut?" Pinto's jaw fell into an open-mouth grin. "Have you been taking your maintenance vials?"

Vell made eye contact with Yahshi, silently asking him the same question. He nodded.

"Of course I've been taking them." Quax pointed at Keiyo, who lowered his head. "But this idiot tried to overdose me."

"Keiyo laced our tools that morning," Vell explained, "and for *some reason*, the dagger Quax slit his hand on had *much* more than the usual dose."

"I was nervous, okay?" Keiyo said. "My unit leader says he'll give me a role in the tool crafting and development department if I do well during my first month. But I never laced that many tools before, so I accidentally mixed up the count of boxes and forgot which ones were already laced and..." He trailed off with a sigh. "Yeah, I laced some of them four or five times.

I'm sorry."

"It's alright, Keiyo." Quax's smile faded. "We're just messing around."

Vell studied Keiyo as he twisted his spoon, observing the candlelight's reflection.

"Is that my kids I see?" Doctor Blimmery slammed his hands onto the table, making their utensils jingle.

The spoon slipped from Keiyo's grip, and he raised his chin with an instant grin. "Doctor!"

"Doctor!" the Academy guardian shouted back, nudging Keiyo in the arm.

Yahshi wanted to ask, *Did you know, Doctor? Did you know the truth about the Eastern raids this whole time, just as you knew the truth about Maelin?*

Vell waved from across the table. "Hi, Doctor Blim."

"And hello to you too, *Commander*." He dragged a chair between Quax and Vell and took a seat. "I won't intrude for long. Just wanted to check in. What's it like being a real unit member?"

"It's intense," Keiyo answered.

"It's incredible," Quax said.

"It's not much different from shadowing," Pinto admitted.

"It's okay," Vell muttered in a monotone. Yahshi had no time to question the lack of enthusiasm in her voice before everyone was staring at him.

"Umm... it's good. Yeah. Really great." He cringed as they turned back to Doctor Blimmery because he hadn't spoken a word to his unit leader in person. As Princess Kia's bodyguard, he was practically unitless.

"I heard Vell and Quax have been filling in for Evaris and Galler quite nicely," Doctor Blimmery said, smiling at them.

Keiyo chuckled. "You mean, G-G-G-Galler?"

Doctor Blimmery flicked him on the forehead. He was still smiling, but his voice came out like a warning. "Don't go there."

"Alright, alright." Keiyo avoided eye contact as he took another bite. "My bad, Blim."

Pinto cleared his throat. "How's Selection Season?"

"Boring!" the old man yelled, catching the eyes of a few well-dressed Vakoi

City residents. "I'm no fan of reading through instructor reports and score sheets. Thankfully, the selection process doesn't require our full attention. So, in addition to the boring stuff, Roz, Embre, and I are working part-time in our prior roles."

So you're writing propaganda for Capital Weekly again, Yahshi wanted to say. *You're spreading lies to the public because you know. Who else knows? Would anyone tell me the truth, or would I unknowingly kill the innocent for the rest of my life?*

"It's been a nice change of pace for us too," he continued. "Keep in mind that we were almost as trapped as you were during the program's runtime."

"Do you still feel trapped, knowing what you know?" Yahshi wanted to say, except he *did* say it, and the table fell silent.

Doctor Blimmery stared at him sternly for a minute before bursting into laughter, spreading smiles around the table. "With knowledge comes freedom, Yahshi. I could never be trapped." He didn't pause before standing. "Well, alright! I'll leave you kids to it then."

As he left, a server in a suede suit arrived with their orders. Yahshi had chosen fish from the menu expecting a fillet, not the creature in its entirety —eyes, tail, bones, and all. *Someone caught this fish from its home and killed it. What did the fish do to deserve this, besides being the fastest and smartest of its kind—the first to reach the bait?*

Pinto took a bite of pasta before dabbing his lips with a napkin. "Other than the tool incident, how have the expeditions been?"

"Oh, they're nothing special," Quax answered. "We just knock on doors and search for goods all day."

"All day?" Pinto asked. "If you're busting that many smugglers, I can't imagine how many Underground members there actually are. We're not gonna identify all of them unless we change our strategy." He straightened his tie, which hadn't been crooked in the first place.

Keiyo chuckled, pointing his fork at Pinto. "You did the tie thing."

Pinto frowned. "What *tie thing*?"

"We're only one week in, and you're already adopting preppy Research habits." Quax ran a hand through his hair, and Yahshi noticed he'd trimmed it shorter than usual. "Bet it won't be long before Vell starts wearing her hair in a slick bun like my sister."

Vell rolled her eyes. "In your dreams."

"As I was saying," Pinto continued, "we're too reactive. Busting smugglers is only treating the symptoms of a deeper wound."

"Professors and their metaphors!" Keiyo teased.

"That's why my goal is to trace the Bayins," Pinto said. "Wherever they went, I bet it's where the leaders are."

"You?" Quax asked. "Singlehandedly tracing a family of spies to shut down the Underground?"

"I'm onto something. I really am. I just need to crack the case before my rival does."

"Ooh, a rival!" Keiyo said.

Yahshi narrowed his eyes. "What rival?"

"Well, I moved last month's Bayin files to my desk since I hadn't read them yet. The next time I checked the archives, all of the older ones were missing. Some professor took information from my case to solve it first and steal my promotion."

Quax chuckled. "You're assuming that cracking the case will automatically earn you a promotion."

"The Bayins disappeared over a year ago. Of course finding them would earn me a promotion! And I bet it'll happen in a matter of days."

"Days?" Vell teased.

"I bet!"

"How much are you betting?" she asked. "A thousand coins?"

"Well, that's a bit..." Pinto trailed off. "I don't know. Maybe."

Vell raised her brows, impressed.

"But enough about me!" Pinto met Yahshi's gaze. "We've been so busy. I never had the chance to ask you about the Palace."

"Oh, right," Yahshi said. "Well, being in Professor Lim's unit is more of a formality. I work as a bodyguard."

"For who?" Vell asked.

"The Princess," Yahshi answered.

Pinto gasped. "Why didn't you tell us?"

"It's not a big deal."

"It's a *huge* deal!" Keiyo said. "What the hell? How'd you land a job like that?"

"What are your responsibilities?" Pinto prodded.

"Forget that!" Keiyo pushed his plate away from him. "I've seen the illustrations. She's even prettier in person, isn't she?"

"She—she's really smart." Yahshi's eyes wandered between his fellow graduates, hoping that was all he'd have to say to end their interrogation, but they were far from finished.

"So she's... not pretty?"

Vell frowned. "Shut it, Keiyo."

"Have you spoken with Emperor Vakoi personally?" Pinto asked, eye wide.

Yahshi nodded. "We had tea a couple of times."

"You're kidding." Quax scoffed. "Yahshi Konya, having tea with the Royals before me? And I thought the Empire wasn't corrupt."

Pinto and Keiyo laughed.

"Guys," Vell said, "I don't think he's in the mood right now." Her eyes were on his untouched fish.

"No need to be all protective, Vell," Pinto said.

Keiyo followed her gaze to Yahshi's plate, his humor fading.

Yahshi grabbed his fork, preparing a bite as Vell and Keiyo watched him. *It looks like I'm slipping. I need to get my act together again.* He shoved the bite into his mouth.

"Hey, Pinto..." Keiyo said, an odd seriousness to his tone. "When did those files go missing?"

Yahshi nearly choked on his bite.

"The night of our first day in service, when Professor Famir assigned me to the case," Pinto said. "Why?"

"Oh." Keiyo stared at Yahshi, who avoided his gaze. "No reason."

Yahshi gulped the bite of fish. *He knows.*

The story came together so clearly. Keiyo would report him. The Force would find the getaway bag in his flat. Cal would chime in, revealing that he'd broken the shadow confidentiality rule. And it would be apparent to the Force that Yahshi was a mistake, a flaw in their system, and for the system to run smoothly again, they would need to eliminate him.

Yahshi stood from his seat. "Restroom," he muttered before speed-walking away, dodging tables and statues. He ran down the staircase to the main floor and left the building, taking a seat on the front steps.

The Force is closing in. He stared at the street as horses trotted past. *There is no going back now. I can either suffocate or flee.*

A couple walking down the sidewalk smiled and waved at Yahshi. He pushed the hair over his forehead in response, not wanting to be seen as a Nightshade, but with such a bold uniform, there was no way to hide.

A hand landed on his shoulder. He nearly jumped.

"Relax. It's me." Vell sat next to him on the step. "Is it all in my head, or were you avoiding me this week?"

"I've been busy."

"With what, Yahshi?"

He sighed. "I'm sorry. It's just... everything's changing. I'm not really sure where to go from here."

"It's okay." Her fingers twitched as she extended them. "I get that."

"Vell, did you..." He paused, his breath wavering. "On our first day in service, did you kill?"

"What? That's not what I mean."

"Sorry," he said. "What do you mean then?"

"Quax and I had a visitation right yesterday."

"You saw your families?" His eyes widened. "How was it?"

"My mother, she..."

He bit his lip, bracing himself to console her.

"She's fully recovered." Vell pulled the ends of her hair, avoiding his eyes. "The pension from our time at the Academy was more than enough for her medicine. She even volunteers at Miranda Hospital. The town calls me *Doctor Vell* as a joke, because my selection saved her life."

"Vell!" Yahshi's jaw dropped. "That's—that's great news!"

When she shook her head, his smile faded.

"What's wrong?" he asked.

"I don't know. I guess I..." Her eyes watered. "I guess I'm starting to realize that I don't have anything to work for anymore. Pinto made it through the filtrations because he wants to prevent the Underground from attacking the innocent again, but I was always in it for the money. Now my mother's healed. My father and I were never caught for our crimes, and I don't see why we ever would be. My family's fine. So what am I doing here? What's the point?"

Yahshi took her shaky hands into his. "You're right. You do understand how I feel," he said. "I don't know what comes next, but you'll figure it out. You always do."

"We'll figure it out together," she corrected.

"Right." His entire escape plan flashed through his head.

"You promise?"

He interlaced his fingers with hers. "I promise," he said, and he was sure of it then—Vell's hands were bloodied too.

She isn't happy here. It was so obvious, and part of him had known since graduation, but he had been pushing that fact away. He'd tried to convince himself that he was leaving the Force—not her. But both were true. He had been using one truth to cover another.

I'm a coward. To run means to find a key to the cage and unlock it, but only for my own benefit. How could I leave her behind in this place? How heartless could I possibly be?

Vell leaned her head on his shoulder. "If we made it through the Academy together, we can make it through the City. We don't have to stay trapped anymore."

Trapped. She feels it too.

The clouds darkened, and a gentle mist encased them.

"The sky weeps with us," he whispered.

"What was that?"

He shut his eyes. "Nothing."

The humidity intensified, warming his face.

"Vell?"

"Hmm?"

"Do you like the capital?"

"I do," she said, "because you're here."

CHAPTER 33

TELL HER

We work to uproot oppressive systems with the power of truth,
clearing the path for a better future.

♫ TOKI DOKI - TAKÉNOBU ♫

"How do you keep getting past the Wall?"

"I whistle three times to summon a dragon, and it lifts me over with its talons."

"As dragons do," Yahshi said, joining Princess Kia by the door to a convenience store. "You're never gonna tell me, huh?"

"I'll tell you at your grave once you're dead," Princess Kia replied.

"How do you know I'll die first?"

"Just a hunch."

He noticed she was wearing a beige trench coat and light pants instead of her usual nightly attire.

"Why the new look?"

"Trying to blend in with the commoners tonight," Princess Kia said.

Yahshi scanned the deserted road for *commoners*, and she rolled her eyes.

"I'm not wearing all black into a store," she said. "It's suspicious."

"*I'm* wearing all black."

"Yeah, but you can pull it off."

He frowned.

"Capital humor. You wouldn't get it." She eyed his bag. "Did you stop at a bank?"

Yahshi reached into it, feeling for a coin pouch under his uniform. "I exchanged my bills after... *supper*." He handed her the pouch.

"Why'd you say it like that?"

"Huh?"

"Supper. You said it like it's a bad word."

He shook his head.

"Commander," she continued, smirking at his silence, "what happened at supper?"

"Nothing." He turned to enter the convenience store, but she held her arm out, stopping him.

"Your mark."

Oh, great. Yahshi felt his forehead. *I hope no one saw me on the way here.*

Princess Kia reached into her bag and pulled out a thick, black headband to cover his brand with.

"It's embarrassing," he muttered, securing it under his bangs.

"No. It's part of you now."

"I wish it wasn't."

"But it is, so own it. If you don't, the Force will."

Yahshi smiled lightly, and they walked in together.

It was one of several tiny stores scattered about the City, a haven of warm lanterns in the darkness, always open to justify its overpriced items. The offerings were numerous, ranging from candy to toiletries to items with no perceivable purpose at all. A lone, greasy-haired attendant was reading a magazine behind the counter, his feet propped up on a stack of boxes.

"Ooh, look at this." Princess Kia held a miniature duck figurine to her cheek. "What's it for?"

"No clue." Yahshi grabbed another and stared into its rubbery eyes.

"I like it." She returned the duck and disappeared around the corner.

"If you're not gonna buy, don't touch," the man behind the counter scolded, shocking Yahshi into dropping his duck. It squeaked when it hit the floor, and he frantically picked it up.

The man glared at him over his magazine. "It's just for decoration, punk."

"Right, sorry. Decoration." His hands fumbled as he set it with the other figurines, almost knocking another one over in the process. He could feel the man's eyes watching him as he turned the corner.

Princess Kia was in the next aisle, a palm over her mouth.

"Punk?" Yahshi whispered. "What does that mean?"

"Just capital slang," she choked out between giggles. "You wouldn't get it."

They wandered the aisles in search of nonperishables, but all they could find was a modest selection of dried meat, fish, and fruit.

"Small bags," Yahshi said.

"Would it be suspicious to buy everything?" Princess Kia asked.

He narrowed his eyes. "I'm not bringing all these packages to my flat. It's too risky."

"I'll bring them to the Canister."

He raised a brow—she'd never offered to hold onto supplies before. "You're planning to keep the food so you can starve me, aren't you?"

"Shut it. I'm doing you a favor." She grabbed an entire row of dried apricots.

"I know," he said, grabbing a row of jerky.

The cashier's eyes widened as they neared the counter with towering stacks of packages in hand. He grabbed a notebook and pen to calculate the price, but Princess Kia plopped the coin pouch onto his table, interrupting him.

"Three hundred," Yahshi stated, already waiting at the door. "Should be enough."

"It's enough, alright," the man mumbled, opening the pouch to verify. "These capital brats with their parents' money..."

Princess Kia swiped the goods into her bag and followed Yahshi outside.

As they walked down the empty road, oil lamps on poles illuminated their path. It wasn't too active at night in this area of the City, but they could hear the distant buzzing of live music, cheering, and laughter.

"That noise. I wonder what it's from," Princess Kia said. "Lots of parties at night. Live performances too. Midnight stage plays and award ceremonies. Never been to any. Is there stuff like that in the East?"

Yahshi stared at his boots. "I doubt it. We certainly didn't have any in Sitra."

Part of him wished he could stay longer. There was so much in the City he would never have the opportunity to experience again. He would never go to any parties, or live performances, or midnight stage plays, or award ceremonies. His routine as a guardian would end tomorrow—along with the privileges that came with it. And he had no clue what kind of life he was trading it for.

"Are you scared?" Yahshi asked.

"What the hell do you think?" Princess Kia turned to him. "Commander—"

"Don't call me that," he said. "It's what the Force named me."

"Okay"—she leaned toward him with a smile—"*Yahshi.*"

"Sorry. What were you gonna say?"

She pointed into the distance, far beyond Vakoi City. "Do you think there's anything good out there?"

"I think there's good everywhere."

"But is there something good, purely good, right down to the core?"

After a moment, he shook his head.

It was silent for a long time.

"So, tomorrow morning," Princess Kia said in a chirpy tone. "During your shift at the Palace, we'll go over the plan again. Then you'll head back to the Complex."

"Right. And then we'll meet at—"

"Midnight."

"I'll bring a horse, and the getaway bag."

"I'll bring the food, and then we'll head east."

"East," Yahshi echoed, tucking his hands into his pockets. It was such a loaded word. East. And with the word, he thought of Vell. He thought about leaving her.

Dammit. She was like a pebble in his boot he couldn't ignore no matter how hard he tried.

"You're making that face again," Princess Kia said.

"I had a terrible supper," Yahshi admitted. "Horrible, horrible, *horrible* supper. All this planning, this sneaking around with you, is... making a mess. And now everything's spinning out of control."

"Slow down. What happened at supper?"

"Keiyo knows I took the Bayin files."

"Okay. And?"

"Pinto is completely, utterly blind." Yahshi's face went hot. "I mean, he's trying to trace the Bayins to impress the Force. And he's *so* excited about it. He can't keep his mouth shut. And to think it was the Force that —that did that to him."

"And?"

"Quax might as well have puppet strings tied to his limbs. He loves his sister *so much*, and Cal takes advantage of that. She's even faker than I imagined."

"And?"

"Vell..." Yahshi trailed off, recalling their earlier conversation.

"I need to tell her," he decided, his eyes widening. *I need to tell her, because maybe—just* maybe*—she'll want to leave too.*

"Tomorrow," Yahshi continued with conviction, "I need to tell her."

"Then tell her," Princess Kia said, and for a moment, their footsteps fell in sync. "I trust you."

The time was 4:13 in the afternoon. Yahshi secured his horse in a Complex stable, back from what only he and Princess Kia knew to be his final day at the Palace. The clomping of horse hooves turned his head to the open door, where he spotted Cal parking a vault outside. His pulse quickened. *This is my chance.*

He left the stable, raising his brows in false surprise.

"Hi, Yahshi," Cal said, hopping from the driver's seat.

He returned the fake smile. "Back from an expedition?"

"Back from a tea party?" she asked, and he forced himself to laugh with her as Vell and Quax emerged from around the passenger box.

"If it isn't the bodyguard!" Quax greeted him with a few slaps on the back. "Wanna get breakfast with Vell and me tomorrow? We know a good place."

"You won't have time, Brother," Cal stated. "Early start. We'll eat at the cafeteria."

"I hate Complex food," Vell muttered.

Quax elbowed Vell with a chuckle. "That's fine," he said, turning to Yahshi. "Next time, then."

Cal set a hand on Quax's shoulder, leaning in with a smile. "You did amazing today," she said, and Yahshi caught Vell rolling her eyes. "Take care of the vault, will you?"

"Of course." He saluted his sister before skipping off to secure the horses.

Cal lingered, waiting for Yahshi to leave. If he stayed any longer, she'd figure out that he'd run into them intentionally.

The wind picked up, shuffling his hair, and he combed the strands back into place with his fingers. "With weather like this, a hat would be nice." His gaze landed on Vell for a moment before he headed for the Complex. "I should go."

"Bye, Yahshi," Cal said. He could hear the crooked smile in her voice.

As another gust of wind rushed by, he looked back to see a strand of hair fall from Cal's bun. She poked it back into place—and for the first time, as she seemed to break character, Yahshi realized there must be something good in her too.

While he waited for Vell in the common room, Evaris caught his eye. She was sitting on a sofa, reading a novel.

"So you joined a new unit, huh?" Yahshi asked, approaching her.

Evaris closed her book and smiled at the cover. "Hey, Shadow."

"Hey." He sat next to her.

"Yeah, a new unit. It's been a breath of fresh air, to be honest." Her smile faded as she met his gaze. "I'm sorry about what happened, by the way."

"You don't miss your old unit?"

Evaris shook her head.

"Cal says you're best friends."

She frowned at Yahshi, and he knew what she meant. *We can't talk about this.* But he talked anyway.

"When you met her at the Academy," he whispered, "was she always like this? All charming on the surface?"

"No," she whispered back.

"What changed?"

"Shadow…"

"I won't tell a soul."

Evaris stared deeply into his eyes, calculating his intentions.

"Okay," she said with a sigh, scanning the room before leaning in. "We were roommates at the start of the program. I was scared of her at first—we all were. She'd just spent four months in the Detainment Facility, and we knew about the incident that got her there. I kept having this nightmare of her strangling me in my sleep."

Even under his heavy overcoat, goosebumps sprang across his arms.

"But every morning I woke up alive, I trusted her a bit more," she continued, her voice quaking. "I chose to believe she was simply a shy, protective older sister. And then I figured, as the only two girls at the Academy, we should stick up for each other, you know? So I helped her get along with the other trainees—gave her tips on how to be more… normal. In exchange, she helped me study and train. She had my back, and I had hers, and we made the final five together. We became best friends."

"Then why didn't you like being her unit member?" Yahshi asked.

"Because my best friend isn't real," Evaris said. "It took me a long time to realize that. A lot of observation. A lot of tiny, fleeting moments where she seemed just a bit off. And once everything clicked—and I realized that she only kept me close because I was useful to her—I was no longer her friend by choice."

"What do you mean?"

"I see her," Evaris said, her eyes widening. "You don't make an enemy out of Cal. It's much safer to be her pawn."

Yahshi thought back to the woods when Chima's blood splattered across his face. He imagined Cal untying him from the tree and handing him the log, telling him to finish the job. He imagined everything Evaris had been told to do.

"I'm sorry," Yahshi muttered.

Her brows inched closer together. "You're a good one, Shadow." She pulled him into a hug. "We're lucky to have you."

Her overcoat smelled like lavender.

Goodbye, Commander. Yahshi closed his eyes. *I wish you the best.*

He wanted to hate the Force but couldn't because good people worked in it too. It was bad, but not purely bad. Not down to the core.

Evaris hugged him tighter before letting go.

"Yahshi?" someone called.

They looked up to find Vell in front of them, hands in her overcoat pockets.

"Ah, you're my replacement," Evaris said.

"Commander Evaris," Vell deduced. "Cal speaks of you endlessly."

She grinned. "Going somewhere?"

"I'm buying Yahshi a hat," Vell said.

He stood, and Evaris looked up at him with raised brows. "Guardians don't wear hats."

Yahshi shrugged. "I could be the first."

Nods from City residents rained upon them as they strolled along the bustling sidewalks. Vell returned each greeting with a smile, and when a Defense unit of unfamiliar faces trotted by on horseback, she called the commanders out by name, her comfort in the Force growing with every interaction.

"It's hard, but I'm trying," she said, as though she could read Yahshi's mind. "If this is our life now, we might as well make peace with it." Her fingers grazed his, but she didn't hold his hand, and Yahshi had a feeling she might never do so again.

With a sharp turn, she ascended a flight of stairs to a quaint shop, leading him inside.

They wandered around the room, studying glass cases featuring designer hats varying in style and color. He eyed a top hat covered in fluffy feathers and purple stones.

"I think it would suit you," Vell said, and he rolled his eyes.

They parted ways, occasionally meeting each other's gazes to silently share their findings.

Yahshi was staring at a modest newsboy cap when a weight fell onto his head. He removed a green top hat that was far taller than it should have been.

"Boo," Vell whispered into his ear.

He turned to face her. "Stealthy approach. A-plus."

"You'd look cool in this one." She pointed at the hat in his hands. "And you like *sage green*, so…"

"You don't want me to make new friends. Is that it?"

"As if you have time for that anyway, *Your Highness*."

"I'm a bodyguard, not royalty."

"You're a royal bodyguard. Pretty much the same thing." She held her hands behind her back and nodded, prompting him to put it back on.

Yahshi donned the hat, and her cheeks puffed up as she burst into laughter. He yanked it off his head, cheeks hot.

"I'm buying it for you." Vell plucked the hat from his hands and wore it herself.

"Don't you dare."

"You're wearing it out," she said, and that's what he did, sparking laughter from a group of Vakoi City Primary students. He smiled at their amusement.

When they entered a public park, he removed his hat. The air was thick with the scent of freshly trimmed grass as gardeners tended to colorful flower beds. Joggers weaved between picnickers, and children played tag, disrupting the flow with sudden sprints and turns.

"Yahshi? Vell?" a familiar voice called.

They turned to face the Brackle twins, who were dressed in the Vakoi City Secondary uniforms they had entered the Academy wearing on orientation day.

Limbo scowled at the hat in Yahshi's grip, but Ceylon smiled and jumped. "Yahshi!" He grabbed him by the shoulders and shook him. "It's been ages!"

"Yeah, almost a year." Yahshi laughed, relieved he didn't seem to hold the detection filtration against him.

"And Vell!" Ceylon said, wrapping his arms around her. "Oh, I'm so glad the three of you graduated together."

As they hugged, Limbo approached Yahshi with narrowed eyes, reaching for his brand. He pressed his thumb against the raised skin.

"Did it hurt?"

"Like hell," Yahshi replied, glancing at Ceylon. "How's he doing?"

"He's ruined. He won't shut up about the Academy. It's like he never left." Limbo lowered his voice, his eyes glued to Yahshi's mark. "What an amazing program, right?"

He saw something close to concern in Limbo's face. Or maybe it was hatred. He couldn't be sure.

"Listen," Limbo whispered, leaning in, "if you're ever in trouble, you let me know. Okay?"

"Sorry, we're running late," Ceylon interrupted. He walked backward away from them, light on his feet. "See you around, huh, Commanders? I can't wait to hear *everything*."

Limbo followed his brother away, hands in his pockets. He looked back when Ceylon didn't, and Yahshi smiled grimly. *Thank you.*

When the twins were out of sight, Vell sat on a bench, and Yahshi joined her, resting the hat on his lap. Many people passed—some older and some younger, but all ordinary.

Yahshi stared at two girls sitting on a bench across the park. They looked to be around the same age as him and Vell. One of them was laughing as the other told a story, her expressions animated. He wondered what their lives were like. *I guess I'll never know.*

"Maybe it's weird," Vell said, watching the girls, "but sometimes I wonder what my future would look like if my mother never got sick. I was a decent student once. Maybe I'd be working for a modest pay back in Miranda. Maybe I'd get married someday, have a family. Would that be so horrible?"

"I don't know," he said. "I never really thought about it."

After a moment, she faced him. "What's this really about, Yahshi?"

He gulped, gluing his eyes directly ahead. *No, I can't tell her.*

Vell was struggling to adjust to her new life, but that was normal, and she was handling it. She was coming to terms with the sacrifice of guardianship, and by doing so, she was giving herself a chance for a happy life in the Force. She was not like Maelin, and she was not like Yahshi. *She doesn't have to leave to be okay.*

And even if she'd insist on leaving with him, it would be reckless to allow her to. He knew nothing of the dangers involved in reaching the Underground's hideout. He didn't even know if he'd live to get there.

"I just miss you," Yahshi said, meeting her gaze.

Vell smiled. "I miss you too."

Her eyes pulled him in, and everything he'd decided shattered and rearranged itself again. Vell was so kind, so understanding. He couldn't allow her to leave with him, but he could trust her with his plan, and she deserved to hear it.

I need to tell her, he confirmed, and that was final. He would shake that pebble out of his boot, and he would do it now.

Yahshi took a deep breath. "Actually, Vell, there *is* something I have to say."

She waited for him to gather his words, her smile vanishing.

"Yahshi!" Pinto yelled, running toward him. His face was bright red, and when he reached the bench, he was panting with his hands on his knees.

"Are you okay?" Vell asked.

"Yeah. Fine, fine." He gathered himself and stood tall, looming over them. "There was a breakthrough in the Bayin case. We need you to report to the Office for questioning in three hours." He handed Yahshi a golden ticket.

Vell's eyes widened.

"What for?" Yahshi asked.

"It's confidential," Pinto said.

The ticket included Yahshi's full name, hometown, division, unit leader, and instructions to report to the Office that evening at 8:00. The possibilities clashed against each other in his head.

Does this have to do with the real Bayin case, or is this about the missing files? Did Keiyo or Cal report me? Did the Force find the getaway bag in my flat?

What if the meeting isn't for questioning at all? What if it's a trap to send me to correction? Why else would they set up a meeting after hours? They could be giving me advanced notice so I underestimate the dangers and show up voluntarily. They could avoid making a scene by keeping the public and most of the Force in the dark. Why drag me into a cage when they can lure me in?

"I don't understand," Yahshi said. "Why am I involved?"

Pinto set a hand on his shoulder. "Listen, everything's gonna be fine. Just tell them the truth."

The truth, Pinto? He couldn't tell if the boy in front of him was a close friend or a blind puppet of the Force. *What truth are you talking about? What does the truth mean to you?*

"It'll be quick and painless, okay?" Pinto continued. "I'll see you there."

"Okay," Yahshi muttered.

Pinto offered Vell a nod of acknowledgment before rushing away, leaving Yahshi with a ticket that would lead him to an unknown destination. *But wherever it goes, it can't be good.*

He watched Pinto like a hawk until he turned a corner and disappeared. That's when the role he'd been playing broke away. He crumpled over, gasping for air, the walls of the world closing in. Vell's hand on his shoulder reminded him to breathe, but he couldn't. All he could do was—

Leave. Yahshi stood from the bench, and his hat tumbled onto the grass. *I need to leave.*

"Yahshi!"

He sprinted across the park and down the sidewalk until Vell's yelling faded into the distance. Soon enough he was mounting his horse by the stable and riding it away and realizing that his ticket for the meeting was no longer in his hand—he had dropped it somewhere.

When he neared the Palace, he stopped and gazed up at the Wall. The Defense guardians stationed at the gate would demand an explanation for his return—and without knowing Princess Kia's secret way out, he had no secret way in.

So he carried on alone, leaving behind the Princess, their supplies, and countless unspoken goodbyes.

CHAPTER 34

HOMECOMING

We bear the burden of making necessary sacrifices,
nourishing new growth as our ancestors did.

♫ BLOOM - SAINT MESA ♫

As Yahshi rode past Sitra Market, he felt like he'd been selling bread with his father only days ago. He could nearly smell the food stands, hear the chattering of gossip, see children shooting around, engaged in a game of tag...

A few minutes later, he spotted a glowing lantern in the distance and sighed in relief. *He still lives here.*

He checked his pocket watch as he galloped toward the house. The time was 7:02.

It won't take long for the Force to realize I left Vakoi City. Yahshi stopped his horse in the backyard and dismounted it. *Sitra will likely be the first place they look.*

After hitching his horse to a tree, it took him a moment to locate the concrete training platform, which was overgrown with shrubs. He stepped onto it and imagined his father in front of him, saying, *Show me your stance.*

He raised his hands. "Stop and Go?"

Martu mirrored him, then vanished into the darkness.

Yahshi sighed, and his horse whinnied as though it understood him.

"Shh!" he said, passing the horse. He didn't hop from stone to stone on his way to the front porch.

It's been eighteen months. Yahshi stood at the door, the lantern lighting his face in scattered shapes. He raised his fist, freezing before it could meet the wood. *What if he doesn't forgive me?*

The ticket Pinto had given him popped into his head. *I don't have time to worry.*

He knocked, and silence greeted him. There was no rustling of bedsheets. No footsteps. No voices. He leaned his forehead against the door, his breath bouncing off the wood and heating his cheeks as he knocked again.

Still, nothing.

Yahshi retrieved his lock busters and stuck a tension wrench into the keyhole, followed by a pick. He wiggled them in search of the lock's binding pin, but before he could unlatch it, the door swung open.

Martu stared at the wrench and pick in his hands.

"Father..." Yahshi stashed his lock busters. "I'm home."

A lump formed in his throat at the sight of Martu's sharp face and slender body. He looked so much smaller than he remembered, not because he'd grown frailer, but because Yahshi had grown stronger. He was taller than his father now and realized how much muscle he must have put on during the program. He didn't feel like the boy he used to be, and maybe he didn't look like him either.

Martu studied Yahshi's uniform—his shiny boots, white pants, tool-packed overcoat, and back-strapped swords.

Finally, he met his gaze. His grip on the doorknob tightened.

"Please don't close the door," Yahshi spouted. "I-I'm so sorry, Father."

Martu didn't close it, but he didn't let go either.

"I shouldn't have left you," he continued. "Now I've become someone I never should have, and I've..." He tucked his trembling hands into his overcoat pockets. "I've done things that no one should ever do."

The emptiness in his father's expression made his legs weaken.

"Please," he said, his voice quaking, "say something."

Martu's face twisted into a frown as he shook his head.

Why did I come here? Yahshi clenched his eyes shut. *I don't deserve his forgiveness.*

The air around him darkened as his father stepped forward, blocking the lantern light.

"Oh, Son." Martu pulled him into his warm embrace. "How I've missed you."

Yahshi opened his eyes, releasing tears.

Martu squeezed him before pulling away. "You've grown so much." His eyes watered as he trailed a finger along his brand.

Yahshi smiled and wiped his cheek.

"Come inside," Martu said.

He followed Martu into his childhood home, his eyes flying in all directions as he soaked in its familiarity. He saw the table from the Avariums, bread baskets on the countertop, and a crackling fireplace. Unlike the backyard, the house hadn't changed a bit.

Martu squatted to add more wood to the fire.

We don't have much time. Yahshi kneeled next to him and cut to the chase. "Father, are you a false convert?"

Martu added another log.

"Are you affiliated with the Underground?" he continued, prying for an answer. "Do you have a connection to the Bayins?"

Martu nodded once.

Yahshi stared at the flames. "So that's why you moved to Sitra after the War. It was known for having a low selection rate. That's why my high scores never pleased you and my low scores never concerned you. That's why you were so upset on Selection Day. You tried to reach me through Dice, but I didn't listen."

He took Martu's silence as a blatant confirmation.

"Were you ever gonna tell me?" He faced him with raised brows, and Martu sighed.

"Yahshi, I hid the truth to give you a normal childhood. I didn't want you to end up like Dice. He grew up believing his only purpose was to get selected and infiltrate the Academy. I didn't want to use you—I wanted to raise you. I wanted you to think with your own mind, your own reasoning. And then I was going to tell you everything once you turned eighteen, and I planned to bring you home."

"Home?"

"To Headquarters."

Yahshi nearly gasped. "You know where it is?"

"No, but your mother does."

"What?"

"I'm sorry." Martu set a gentle hand on his back. "Your mother was never sick. She's been working for the Underground in Atherus City. She helped the Bayins disappear and can do the same for us."

"She's been alive, all this time?"

"I brought you West to give you a better childhood, and your mother stayed behind to support the cause. There's more to the story, but once we get to safety, I'll explain everything." He stood and shuffled through a dresser. "It won't be an easy trip. We'll need to get past Border Control, and I bet security's tightened since the Bayins disappeared. Once we cross the border, it's a long journey to reach your mother, and I'm sure the Force will have every Nightshade after us. How long until they're at our tail?"

Yahshi blinked a few times, struggling to catch up. It took a minute to redirect his thoughts from his mother to their escape plan.

"A couple of hours, I suspect," he answered. "But passing Border Control shouldn't be a problem. I memorized their patrol routes."

Martu found what he was looking for—the family pension slips. Yahshi stood and took one. It was a bill of exchange for 1,000 coins.

"You didn't spend them?"

"Honestly, I thought about exchanging the bills, heading East alone, and finding your mother, but I couldn't leave if there was even a slim chance you'd come home. So I've stayed here, and I've saved the money. And now you're home."

Yahshi returned the bill. "I'm sorry, but we can't use them. Banks are closed for the night, and once the Force confirms we're on the run, they'll have our names red-listed by sunrise. It's Protocol."

Martu tossed the bills into a drawer. "That's alright. We'll make do without them." He shuffled through Yahshi's old clothes. "You'll have to change out of that uniform, but you won't fit these, will you?"

"It's okay. I should keep the coat for a while," Yahshi said. "We might need my tools."

Martu raised a shirt and shook his head. "We're not bringing your *tools.*" He tossed the shirt back into the drawer and searched for another candidate. "Everyone will know you're a Nightshade. The Underground won't help us, and the Force will spot you instantly."

"But even without my uniform, they could spot us anyway. How would we put up a fight then?"

"We wouldn't. If the Nightshades spot us, we've already lost. So we don't let them see us, Yahshi. From now on, this is hide-and-seek, and every guardian in the Force is playing tracer."

Martu continued rummaging through the drawer as a faint clip-clopping sound echoed in the distance. Yahshi closed his eyes, trying to pinpoint the horse's direction, but the air was silent. *Perhaps I imagined it.*

"Here, this should work." He held a wadded ball of clothes out for Yahshi. "Get changed. I'll find something to cover your mark."

A horse neighed, and they froze.

Perhaps a wild animal spooked my horse. Or maybe it smelled the smoke from the chimney, and it—

Yahshi flinched when a slap filled the air. His horse in the backyard whinnied as it galloped away, stranding him.

Someone's here.

Martu stuffed the clothes away before Yahshi could grab them. "Hide," he ordered.

Yahshi stared at him blankly.

"Now," Martu snapped.

The intruder knocked, sending Yahshi to his father's bedroom. With a steady hand, he shut the door behind him and pressed his ear to the wood. The front door creaked as his father opened it.

"Martu Konya," a guardian said. "You're being detained for questioning in Vakoi City."

Yahshi held a hand over his mouth. It was Commander Roz who'd struck his horse. *He knows I'm here.*

"Detained?" Martu asked. "For what?"

"Explain to me why there was a guardian horse in your backyard, property of the Force," Commander Roz said.

"I wasn't aware there was."

A pause. "Yahshi's here, isn't he? Did he run after receiving his ticket?"

"What ticket? Is he okay?"

Commander Roz paused even longer. "Lie to my face one more time," he warned.

Yahshi heard Martu stumble, followed by the front door slamming shut.

Commander Roz's steps were long and slow as he sauntered through the main room, searching for Yahshi.

I can't hide for long. Yahshi stepped away from the bedroom door, reaching for his sword handles. A floorboard creaked beneath his boot.

Knowing the instructor heard, he unsheathed his primary tool. The bedroom door opened as he readied his swords ahead of him.

Commander Roz's bold silhouette filled the doorway, a dull glow from the fireplace flickering behind him. His swords were drawn too.

"You're supposed to be in the City right now," Commander Roz said.

"I have a visitation right."

"I'm no fool, Yahshi."

As he entered the bedroom, Martu rushed him from behind. The collision made Commander Roz stumble briefly before he pivoted and brought a sword down. A bold gash through Martu's bicep left him wailing.

Yahshi's face burned as he ran after Commander Roz, who blocked his first swing, and his second, and his third. The combinations he'd practiced in the program were useless against the man who had taught him them.

Commander Roz countered with strikes of his own that Yahshi blocked —but slightly sloppier. Even with all his strength, every clash of their swords pushed him farther from the door. It wouldn't take long for Commander Roz to have him against the wall.

Yahshi's heel struck the bed frame, breaking his flow. A sword met his lower leg.

He winced as he parried Commander Roz's next attack, feeling warm blood seeping through his pants.

"You're sloppy this evening," Commander Roz muttered. "If you don't use your surroundings, they'll be used against you."

Yahshi caught a glimpse of Martu swaying in the doorway, clearly intoxicated. *I have emergency neutralizer in my overcoat.*

Another blade came pummeling toward his face. He swung his swords over his head, trapping Commander Roz's at their crossing point.

Commander Roz applied more pressure to break the blockade, and Yahshi's arms began to shake. He gritted his teeth and shoved his swords to the right—taking his opponent's sword with them.

Commander Roz's footing wavered, a brief flash of surprise in his eyes.

Yahshi swerved around him and bolted to the doorway, sheathing his swords. *Commander Roz has a horse outside. We just need to get to it first.*

He swung an arm around his father, whose breath was racing, his face bright red. "I can help you," he muttered, practically dragging him, "but we need to hurry."

As they neared the door, a force shoved them into it. Yahshi's cheek struck the wood in a blow that made his teeth buzz, a metallic taste filling his mouth. His ears rang, and the warmth of his father's body disappeared from his arms.

He turned around, spitting a mouthful of blood. Commander Roz was holding Martu from behind, and the sword against his throat glimmered in the firelight.

"Run," Martu choked out.

Yahshi glared at Commander Roz. "Let him go."

"If you both cooperate and return to the City for questioning, maybe we can work something out."

"Don't listen to him," Martu said. "They'll kill us both. You know that."

Yahshi tuned out his father, locking his eyes on Commander Roz. "You can take me, but leave him out of this."

"Yahshi, go," Martu said. "Travel by lantern."

Yahshi stepped toward them.

"Don't get any closer." Commander Roz applied more pressure to the blade, and Martu winced. "We know your father is a false convert, a liar, a traitor—that's why I'm here to detain him. But Yahshi, you still have a chance. You can plead your case to the Force. It doesn't have to end this way."

"Maybe I'll talk," Yahshi said, "but my father won't. He didn't tell me anything for years. So if it's information you're after, take me *alone.* You can lock me up, send me to correction, execute me—whatever you want. I don't care. You can use me, but leave him out of this."

Commander Roz's lips parted in disappointment. "I agree." He gripped his sword handle tighter, and Martu closed his eyes. "If your father won't talk, let's leave him out of this."

"Commander!" Yahshi screamed.

He slashed Martu's neck.

Yahshi froze as his father collapsed to the floorboards. Martu choked, thick blood oozing down his neck and pooling around him. When he tried to push himself up, the life left his body, and his arm collapsed beneath him. His fingers twitched a few times before going limp.

As the red pool expanded, Yahshi's eyes dried up because he could no longer blink. Martu might move, and he needed to see it. He couldn't miss the split second his father's fingers would twitch again, proving he hadn't left.

Please don't leave me. The world was still, like time itself had frozen. *Don't leave me when I've just come home.*

Commander Roz stepped forward, his boot landing in Martu's blood. "Yahshi, you're coming with me."

And at the sound of his voice, the clock began to tick again. Yahshi blinked. The chirping of crickets returned. His heart resumed its pumping. That's when he remembered that he was closest to the exit, and that Commander Roz's horse was somewhere outside.

He opened the door and ran.

"Stop!" Commander Roz yelled.

Yahshi soared over the front steps, a white horse near the woods catching his eye. He landed and bolted toward it, retrieving a dagger from his overcoat. Commander Roz trailed a few paces behind.

He sped up, summoning every ounce of his energy to reach that horse before Commander Roz could reach *him*.

He'd gained some distance when he arrived and started cutting the rope that secured the horse to a tree.

Come on!

Finally, the thinning rope snapped and fell. He stashed the dagger, mounted the horse, and whipped the reins—shooting forward just as Commander Roz brought his swords down, barely missing.

He galloped through the woods, glancing over his shoulder to see the guardian chasing after him on foot. *It won't take long to lose him.*

And when he finally did, the adrenaline faded, the pain kicking in. His leg throbbed, and his chest tightened at the thought of his father's blood soaking the floorboards.

Tears fell in a burning stream, and the rapid wind against his face couldn't blow them away as fast as they came.

CHAPTER 35

THE SKY WEEPS WITH US

We believe faith, patience, and initiative can plant
seeds of change that will blossom and flourish.

♫ YOU ARE A MEMORY · MESSAGE TO BEARS ♫

The forest was dense, with branches interlocking to form dead ends and alleyways. Yahshi's overcoat did little to shield him from the rain as he navigated his stolen horse through the maze.

He shivered as a gust of wind made the pummeling droplets fall harder, drenching his hair and blurring his vision.

About twenty minutes after leaving Sitra, Yahshi emerged through the outskirts of a neighboring town. Nominner residents smiled and nodded at him as they enjoyed late-night smokes on their front porches. It was too dark for them to notice his wound, but the uniform, guardian horse, and primary tool were flashy enough to draw eyes from all directions.

He slowed his horse to maintain stamina as he reached a forested zone on the opposite end of Nominner. His pocket watch told him the time was 8:14—the guardians in Vakoi City were likely realizing that he wouldn't be attending the meeting, or whatever mystery they had called him for.

The next few hours are crucial, Yahshi concluded, picking up speed. *I need to travel as far as possible before the Force sends Defense units searching for me.*

He galloped until he reached a cobblestone Border Control tower. It looked more menacing than in the illustrations he'd studied with Princess Kia in the Palace. Light seeped through the windows, and lanterns of officers on patrol traveled left and right.

Yahshi steered his horse behind a few bushy trees, concealing himself from their view as he rechecked his pocket watch. It was 8:36—Border Control officers would be surveying this area for another hour or so. He could travel along the outskirts of the woods to reach an unpatrolled area between towers, but he couldn't risk losing too much time with Commander Roz on his trail.

"My father would know what to do, wouldn't he?" Yahshi asked the horse, stroking its mane. "He should be here, not you. This isn't right."

He imagined his father's body on the floorboards. *What if he isn't dead? I should go back for him. I can still save him, and we can travel past Border Control together.*

But the logical killer in Yahshi knew that his father had already left. He had lost too much blood, and if the bleeding hadn't killed him, the belladonna had.

The image in Yahshi's mind shifted, and he no longer imagined his father on the floor but Commander Roz with his swords. *He didn't have to kill him. He chose to end my father's life.*

Yahshi peered at the wound on his leg. He remembered Commander Roz handing him his division badge on the ballroom stage. He remembered Commander Roz punching him after he talked back following his shadow assignment with Cal. He remembered Commander Roz attaching a pin to his collar for beating up his childhood friend. He remembered that meeting in the Sitra Secondary office when Commander Roz began to walk away, pressuring him into making a choice. And finally, he remembered that day in the courtyard, when Commander Roz had stopped him by the wrist to praise him.

He had been there from the start, watching and manipulating him.

Tonight was his finale. Tonight was the night he took everything away so Yahshi would have nothing left, and he would be under his ultimate control.

If Commander Roz cared about him, he would never have killed his father. But all he cared about was turning him into what he wanted him to be. In his eyes, Martu was Yahshi's final crutch.

"We won't let him win." Yahshi noticed the horse was shaking in the cold, just like he was, and on its shoulder was a brand that matched his own. "I have an idea now. Are you ready?"

The horse snorted, and Yahshi gripped the reins. "I won't let you catch me, Commander. I won't even let you *see* me. From now on, this is hide-and-seek, and I'll leave you playing tracer forever."

Yahshi whipped the reins, rushing toward the tower. The Force had stolen his life once, and he would not allow it to steal him again. He would fulfill his father's dying wish and reunite with his mother in Atherus City. There were so many mysteries left, and he would live to unfold them.

I graduated from Belladonna Guardian Academy. If anyone can beat the Force at their own game, it's me.

He stopped near the tower, and an officer rushed outside with an umbrella. "Where's your unit, Commander?"

"What do *you* think?" Yahshi spat. "I don't have a unit. I was visiting family in Sitra when a violent fugitive attacked me. He stole a horse and headed east."

"Are you sure he came this way?" the officer asked. "We didn't see anyone pass the border."

"Are *you* sure? Were you actively on watch, or were you sitting around reading a novel while a dangerous individual snuck his way through?"

The officer leaned back, his grip on the umbrella handle tightening. "If he was on a horse, we would have heard him, Commander. But we—"

"The Force doesn't hire you to *listen*—it hires you to *watch*." Yahshi scoffed, bringing the horse a few steps forward. "I don't have time for this."

The officer speed-walked alongside him. "You're not with a unit. It's Border Protocol, Commander, for us to verify the identities of the units passing through."

"Yahshi Konya of Sitra. Defense Division. Is my uniform not enough verification for you?" He stopped and peered down at him. "Listen, if I don't catch this man *tonight*, who do you think the Force will blame for his successful escape? Me, the guardian who tried to stop him and now has a gash in his leg to show for it?"

Yahshi gestured to his wound, which the officer cringed at.

"Or do you think he'll blame the lazy Border Control officer who let him sneak past the towers without batting an eye?" He waved his finger at the man. "If it weren't for your irresponsible behavior, I wouldn't be searching for him right now. You had one job, and you failed it, so don't you dare tell *me* that I'm not doing mine right."

The officer gulped. "I apologize, Commander."

"I want double the eyes on patrol tonight. Alert the other towers."

"I don't think—"

"That's an order," Yahshi snapped. "Understood?"

He took a deep breath before nodding. "I'm on it."

As the officer returned to the tower, Yahshi galloped into Eastern Territory. It only took about twenty minutes to reach a few scattered structures on the outskirts of the nearest border town. Despite the hour, a few residents were still on their porches, smoking or chatting with neighbors. They all stopped to glare at him. A Nightshade in Eastern Territory in the middle of the night had to mean trouble. *With a uniform like this, I might as well leave literal breadcrumbs.*

He traveled to a less populated area and dismounted the horse by a laundry rack. In the shadows, he changed into a linen shirt, a pair of trousers, and a scratchy wool sweater. A tied cloth around his wound slowed the bleeding, and a scarlet bandana hid his brand from sight. His hair fell over the fabric as an extra layer of protection.

The horse neighed as he jogged away from it, heading eastward in his new attire. Left in the mud were the guardian uniform and primary tool he'd worked so hard to earn.

The rain began to ease up as he jogged through the night. Despite his bleeding leg and the ache in his chest, he couldn't think of pain. All he could think of was the moment Commander Roz knocked on the door.

If only I arrived sooner. If only I didn't tell Princess Kia that we needed food.

We could have left the night before. And if we had, Father would be alive. He would have been here with me and Princess Kia, and everything would've been fine.

It didn't have to end this way.

As he reached the center of town, a few older adults smiled and waved at him. It was strange how comfortable he felt dressed in Eastern clothing with his mark fully covered, but with that comfort came the guilt of being a fraud. If they knew everything he'd done, they wouldn't be smiling and waving. They'd be pulling their curtains shut or rushing away, glancing at their watches as though they conveniently had somewhere to be.

He stopped to check the time, but he'd left his pocket watch in his overcoat. *I think it's around 9:30 by now.*

He turned right at the end of the residential road and immediately halted. A familiar house caught his eye—it was the most run-down on the quiet block, with a rotting roof and boarded-up windows.

I'm back in Vori.

Yahshi scaled the steps and placed a palm on the door, remembering both the murder he'd committed and the one he'd witnessed.

I should've left the Academy when Dice told me to. I should've left the contract unsigned. I should've known that Chima would come after Quax in the woods that day. I had so many chances to avoid this outcome, but I didn't.

He stared at the dead family's lantern. *It has no flame because of me.*

His father's last words echoed through his head.

"Travel by lantern," Yahshi muttered with a frown.

"Your mother adored these kinds," Martu had told him once. *"Her father was a lantern-maker."*

He had lied to Yahshi about his mother getting sick, and he had lied to him about her death during the War. He didn't find it hard to believe he had lied to him about much more, including her love for lanterns.

"Travel by lantern," Yahshi repeated. "What does that mean?"

Perhaps he was telling me to travel at night. He paced the porch, studying the lantern from all angles. *No, that's too abstract. If he wanted me to travel at night, he would have said that.*

Nothing about the lantern stood out. It was made of brass like his father's, but so were most of the other lanterns he'd seen in the East. The shapes in the brass didn't match those of the one at home either.

Yahshi opened its door. *A perfectly normal wax candle.*

His gaze followed the chain connecting the lantern to a hook in the porch overhang. His eyes narrowed when he noticed that the highest chain link was slightly larger than the rest.

He observed the other lanterns in the area, soft on his feet to avoid making his presence known. All the chains they hung from had links of even sizes. *It means nothing.*

When he turned a corner, he stopped when he finally found one— another lantern with a top chain link slightly larger than the rest. *It's probably a coincidence. I'm wasting my time.*

He knew he should be running at top speed, gaining as much distance as possible. *But a few burned minutes won't kill me.*

Yahshi approached the front door and knocked. A long silence passed before he heard footsteps approaching from inside.

When the door swung open, he faced an old woman with long frizzy curls that seemed to glow in the dark. He recognized her instantly as the woman who'd called him a Nightshade nine months ago. *Does she remember me too?*

"What's your business here?"

"I-I noticed your lantern."

"Password," she ordered.

Password? If she was asking for a password, the larger chain link was indeed a code for the Underground. *But Father never gave me a—*

Yahshi's eyes widened. "The sky weeps with us."

The old woman stepped aside, inviting him in.

She gave him no time to process what he'd discovered before slamming the door and leaning against it. "I know you're the shadow I saw that day. How does a Nightshade know our code?"

"My father's a false convert." The sentence came out shaky, and the woman's eyes softened. He could tell that she knew. *He* was *a false convert.*

She gestured for Yahshi to sit at the dining table and kneeled next to him. "Who did this to you?" she asked, rolling his pants up to reveal his cloth-bound wound.

"The commander I trained under," Yahshi said. "How did you know?"

"You have a limp." She headed for another door. "Wait here."

While she was gone, Yahshi unraveled the cloth he'd tied around his leg. She returned with a box of first-aid supplies and winced at the sight of his wound. "That's a nasty-looking thing."

"I've seen worse." He took the box. "Thank you."

She watched him as he used her supplies to clean and mend his wound. His stomach churned as he wrapped a fresh bandage around it. *Why should I live when Father did nothing wrong, and I made mistake after mistake?*

The woman offered him water. "So, what's your plan?"

"The Force will be after me soon. I need to get to the Underground's hideout." He took a few sips, curing the dryness in his throat. He didn't deserve it.

"Good, because that's your only option. I hope you know a courier."

"A courier?"

"Collectors like me hoard goods, but only a few couriers deliver them. They're the only ones who know where the hiders are. So to join the hiders, you need to find a courier who trusts you completely."

So that's why the Force can't get smugglers to talk. They genuinely don't know where their goods are going.

"My mother's a courier," Yahshi said. "Her name is Tonna, and she lives in Atherus City."

"The Eastern capital..." The woman looked away, squinting. "That's a long journey, but if you follow my instructions, I think you can manage."

Yahshi bit his lip. He stared at his glass of water, then his mended leg. "Why are you helping me? I'm a Nightshade, a killer, your enemy."

"My son's a Border Control officer, and my daughter teaches a twisted curriculum at Vori Primary. I don't think we're any different from Westerners. We lose good people to Vakoi's control too."

"I'm sorry," Yahshi said.

"It takes a strong person to break free, and I respect that. Plus, if there's anything that'll piss Vakoi off the most, it's a traitorous guardian on the loose." Her eyes welled up. "That's why I'm helping you, but for this to

work, you need to follow my instructions exactly."

She leaned in with a grin. "So, are you ready or not?"

342

CHAPTER 36

READY OR NOT

We shed our coldest regrets, basking in the warmth
of tomorrow's sunrise.

♬ RUN RIVER · SOUTHEY ♬

After a few minutes of instructions, the old woman shoved him outside and slammed the door.

Thankfully, the rain had stopped. His breaths filled the chilly air in white puffs as he tucked a coin pouch into his pocket. The collector had been kind enough to supply him with a modest amount of money, which made him think about the coins in his getaway bag. *Has the Force found it yet?*

He faced the North Star and turned right to continue eastward.

"Atherus City is located north of here, but you should travel east before heading north," the old woman had explained. *"It takes Nightshades ages to reach the East Coast from their capital—they have to cross the entire island. If anything goes wrong, being near the shore buys you extra time to wiggle out of it."*

Yahshi quickened his pace to a jog, thinking about the boy who'd watched him take his father's life. *I gave that child my own worst nightmare.*

He'd convinced himself that by leaving the Force, he could destroy the heartless killer inside him and start anew, but if he couldn't forgive Commander Roz, how could he forgive himself?

I am no better than the evil I witnessed tonight.

He ran until his lungs were on fire, then ran some more.

Hours passed. The pain in his leg, the parchedness of his tongue, and the stitch in his side couldn't stop him no matter how hard they tried.

He slowed to a walking pace when he saw a building labeled Heston Primary School. He'd finally reached another town.

I need water.

Yahshi scanned the lantern chains of homes along the road, his desperation growing. He was about to give up and continue traveling when he finally spotted one with a larger top link. He tightened the sweaty bandana around his forehead before knocking on the door.

"Collectors can provide you with food, water, and shelter, but remember that not every Underground member is tolerant like me. Some believe that once you're a Nightshade, you're forever a Nightshade. So keep your mark and prior affiliation to the Force hidden."

A young woman opened the door. She had bushy hair that grew in all directions, and she stared at him with narrowed eyes that warned him to run, but he didn't because his throat ached too much.

"The sky weeps with us," Yahshi croaked.

Her gaze softened, and like clockwork, she stepped aside.

It was a quaint, blandly furnished home, but whittled figurines charmed the space. Yahshi smiled at a wooden rabbit.

"A hobby of mine." The woman gestured to a table. "Have a seat."

He inhaled the glass of water she gave him, prompting a refill.

"You must be hungry too." She emptied a can of beans into a pot and ignited the stove. "Why are you running?"

Yahshi hesitated, recalling the old woman's instructions.

"From now on, you're a collector on the run."

"I'm a collector on the run," he said.

"Tell every collector you meet a different story."

"My father and I were forging ration tickets in Vori," he continued. "A neighbor reported us, and the Nightshades came to investigate, and..."

The final sentence clotted his throat, because unlike the others, it wasn't a lie.

"One of them killed my father, so I ran."

The unwelcome image of Commander Roz slicing his sword through Martu's neck flashed through his mind. With a flinch, he closed his eyes.

He wasn't sure how much time passed before he opened them again. The woman was looking back at him as she stirred the beans.

"What's your name?" she asked.

"If they ask for your name, make one up."

"Rugan," he said, stealing the name of the first boy who'd left the Academy. How strange that he remembered it now, after months of it being forgotten.

"I'm Denya." She spooned the beans into a bowl and placed it in front of him.

"Thank you." Yahshi took a bite.

"You look awfully young to be running alone." She sat across from him, and her eyes glimmered with a kind of sympathy Yahshi hadn't seen in a long time. It felt strange to be viewed as a teenager again. At the Academy he'd been nothing but a body to mold and a mind to control.

"I'm seventeen," he said, the truth slipping through his lips before he could alter it.

"Really?" Denya asked. "I would have guessed younger."

He pondered her words, taking a few more bites of bland beans. *If Father lied about Mother's death and her love for lanterns, could he have lied about my age as well?*

"What does your family do?" Yahshi asked.

"My older brother and I work with coal," Denya said. "After Vakoi took over, you couldn't find any other job around Heston. It's all they taught us about in school. Coal, coal, coal—we might as well breathe it."

"They taught you about coal in school?" Yahshi asked.

"You learned about your trade too, didn't you?"

He recalled his knowledge of Eastern curriculum and forced a chuckle. "Oh, of course." *I need to watch my mouth.*

"They teach coal here just like they teach fishing in Arinoma," Denya said, walking to a mandatory portrait of the Emperor. "Vakoi only cares about getting as much labor and resources out of the East as possible."

She pulled the portrait frame to reveal a secret compartment filled with bags of coal. "As much as I hate packaging, the hiders need to set things on fire too, so I'm glad to know I'm supporting the cause."

Yahshi nodded. "And your brother?"

"He works in the mines." She closed the compartment and glared at Emperor Vakoi's face. "That's where he is right now. Night shift. Has it much worse than me."

Yahshi glanced at a clock. It was a few minutes past midnight—the time he and Princess Kia had agreed to meet. He wondered how she was handling the news of his runaway, and then he remembered her threat.

"Leave without me, and I'll report the truth about you and Vell. You might not be here to get sent to correction, but Vell? Well..."

He shook his head. Princess Kia was bright, and he was confident she'd deduce that he'd left her out of circumstance, not to betray her. Knowing Yahshi had no other choice, could she possibly be cruel enough to direct her frustration at Vell?

He stared at his half-eaten bowl because he couldn't be sure.

Is that all I do? He dropped his spoon into the beans. *Hurt the people I love?*

He was on a mission to outrun the Force and find his mother, but what if she didn't *want* to see him? His parents separated so he could have a better upbringing, and he repaid them by joining the Academy, involving himself in the Force that killed Martu. He destroyed his family. How could his mother forgive him for the damage he'd caused?

"What's wrong?"

Denya was sitting at the table again. Yahshi wondered how long he'd been staring at his beans.

"You're not eating," she added.

What gives me the right to lie to collectors, abusing their kindness? What gives me the right to seek refuge with the hiders? His eyes burned. *What gives me the right to keep running?*

"Rugan?" Denya prodded.

"I don't deserve this," Yahshi said, avoiding her eyes.

"Hey," she said, leaning toward him. "*Everyone* has done bad things."

Yahshi shook his head. "Not like me."

"Just like you. We all make mistakes, but life isn't about erasing them. It's about changing the future."

Yahshi looped her words in his head. He wanted to agree that life wasn't about erasing the past because his past was indelible. The graphite was too dark, and erasing it would mean smudging and smudging until there was no paper left.

"You're young. You have an entire life to live. What are you gonna do with it?" Denya sighed. "You can do so much good, but only if you let yourself."

Yahshi finally met her gaze, and she smiled at him.

"Does that make sense?" Denya asked.

He nodded and took another bite.

While he finished his bowl, Denya told him more about her and her brother's jobs in Heston. He wondered what they'd do if they could do anything. *What did they dream about as children before Emperor Vakoi replaced those dreams with nightmares?*

Yahshi stood from the table. "Thank you for your hospitality, but I should get going."

"You can rest here if you'd like."

"I'm racing the clock, and you've helped me enough." He limped away.

"Wait," Denya called.

He stopped with a hand on the doorknob, looking back at her.

"I'm not sure how far you're traveling, but if you're in a rush, try hitching a ride with a trader. They can get you far from here much faster."

"Where can I find them?"

"They should be at the market right now. A few blocks that way." She pointed.

"Thank you. I'll do that." He opened the door and looked back at her again. "Oh, and if I were you, I'd find a new place to hide that coal."

Denya tilted her head. "Why? It's clever, isn't it?"

"Clever, but not enough. Those portraits are one of the first places Nightshades look."

"How do you know?"

"Just find something better, will you?"

She nodded, and Yahshi offered a smile before leaving.

Near Heston Market, he spotted a horse carriage with three bearded men laughing behind it. He forced his limp away and approached them with even steps.

"Good evening," Yahshi said.

"Evening? It's the middle of the night, lad," one of the men replied. "What do you need?"

He eyed the carriage. "Could I hitch a ride?"

"A ride?" a second man asked before bursting into laughter. "Oh, you're a little rebel, are you? Got in a fight with your mommy?"

"Or maybe he pissed off the Nightshades," said the third.

More laughter as the first replied, "What could a boy like him do to piss off the Nightshades?"

"What's the ride for?" asked the second man. "You causin' trouble?"

"And what's with the bandana?" asked the third. "You makin' some kinda statement?"

"The bandana's nothing." Yahshi stepped back, fearing they might snatch the fabric from his head. "And my reason for a ride is my own business."

"Ooh, his own business!"

The men looked at each other and laughed again.

Eventually, the first man settled down. "What's your offer, lad?"

It took a moment for Yahshi to realize he was negotiating a bribe. "I'll pay you fifteen."

"Fifteen coins..." the man said, stroking his beard. He turned to his friends, who laughed even louder this time.

Yahshi nearly scoffed, but he restrained himself.

"You're gonna have to pay a bit more than that," the first explained. "If you're not traveling for work, you're a criminal—and if you're a criminal, and you're in my carriage, that's not a good look for me, you see?"

"Twenty," Yahshi countered.

The man leaned toward him. "I'll take thirty-five."

He stared at the open back of the carriage. "Where's your next stop?"

"Arinoma," the first replied.

That's the fishing town Denya mentioned.

Reaching a town on the East Coast would buy him a significant amount of time. The Force would assume he'd be traveling on foot, so their search would begin in Nominner, Vori, and the surrounding towns.

"Deal." Yahshi pulled out his pouch and counted thirty-five coins.

"Get in before anyone sees you," the man said, pocketing the bribe.

He stepped onto the platform, squeezed between two stacks of bags, and sat concealed behind them. He could still peer through the gap to see the road.

The bearded men talked for a while longer before it was time to go. As the horses trotted, Yahshi allowed his eyelids to close, but the sound of another set of horses forced them open again. He peeked around a stack, his eyes widening.

Commander Roz and two Border Control officers were riding brown horses, scanning Heston for the rogue guardian.

I'll kill you, Commander. Yahshi yanked his head back, holding his breath and clenching his teeth. He could run out of the back of the carriage, using the element of surprise to kill his father's murderer.

Except he couldn't because he didn't have his tools. He could run out the back of the carriage and attack the guardian, but he would lose that fight. Commander Roz would kill him or drag him back to the capital— and either way, his life would be over.

Yahshi folded his hands and pressed them against his waist, pinning himself to the carriage wall. He feared one bump in the road was all it'd take for him to open his mouth and release an agonizing shout.

Killing Commander Roz won't bring Father back to life, he reminded himself. *It won't revive the collector I murdered, his family, or the bunnies that died of my doing. It won't fix anything.*

He couldn't erase the evils he'd committed, but he could at least prevent more blood from spilling over his hands.

Yahshi recalled the vow he'd made after his first shadow assignment.

I will never murder for the Force again.

While he sat in the rumbling carriage, waiting for Commander Roz and the Border Control officers' trotting to fade, he decided to revise that vow. He didn't care whose blood was on his hands anymore—or for what reason. He didn't want the blood at all.

I will never murder again.

He unraveled his fists, unclenched his teeth, and allowed himself to breathe.

You can't corrupt me, Commander. Gazing between the stacks of coal, he watched the guardian look everywhere but directly ahead. *No matter what you do, I will never again be the heartless killer you want me to be.*

Commander Roz pulled the reins, and his horse turned, disappearing from view. The Border Control officers followed his lead, and a few minutes later, the only hooves Yahshi could hear were those of the horses leading the carriage.

I may not deserve mercy—he leaned against a stack of coal—*but I will live to spread it.*

Closing his eyes, he drifted into a deep slumber.

CHAPTER 37

HERE I COME

We aim to become the embodiment of kindness,
inspiring a ripple of positive change.

♫ TRYING TO KILL THE MOON - MOTHERFOLK ♫

> UPDATE: The Belladonna Traitor

Yahshi halted by the door to Erenford Market, where a *Capital Weekly* article was pasted. News of his desertion had spread across the East a few days after he ran away, but the articles had always started with the word *WANTED*, not *UPDATE*.

He stepped closer, studying his revised portrait. The Force now depicted him in casual clothes rather than his uniform, but the most striking change was the addition of a bandana around his forehead.

> The Force is offering a reward of 100,000 coins for information leading to the successful tracing and detainment of Yahshi Konya of Sitra, 17, a fugitive guardian wanted for desertion.

Nothing new there.

> An update from the Research Division states that the target is a
> suspect of several other heinous crimes, including the murder of
> his father and fellow convert, Martu Konya, two weeks ago near
> the outskirts of Sitra before entering Eastern Territory.

Yahshi's eyes widened. "What?"

> The target is considered dangerous and should not be approached
> by civilians. Contact your local officers immediately if you have
> information regarding his whereabouts.
>
> The Force acknowledges and addresses this isolated incident with
> utmost concern. Rest assured, the actions of one individual do
> not represent our collective Force. Your continued trust is valued
> as we further investigate this matter to prevent such occurrences
> in the future.

Yahshi ripped the article from the wall.

"Thanks a lot, Roz," he spat, crumpling the page. "Did you lie to the
Research Division, or did they cover up your murder willingly?" He chucked
the wad of paper toward the distant shoreline, imagining the waves tearing
it to shreds.

Instead, the article landed in a bush, but the ocean roaring with a strike
of thunder was satisfying nonetheless.

He took a deep breath, remembering that he was only a few towns from
Atherus City. He shouldn't allow the Force's dedication to break his morale.
I am the cat, and they are the mice, he reminded himself. *I am the cat. They
are the mice. I am—*

"The Belladonna Traitor," someone said. "I don't believe it."

Yahshi turned to see a boy around his age, dressed in warm fishing attire
with a wool watch cap on his head. In his hands was a *Capital Weekly*
article, which he smirked at before eyeing Yahshi's bandana.

He tried to sprint away, but the boy ran into his path, blocking him. "Hey, hey," he said, sidestepping every time Yahshi tried to dodge him. "I'm not here to report you, alright? Any enemy of the Force is a friend of mine."

He settled down when the boy removed his hat. "Here, take it." He pressed the watch cap to Yahshi's chest. "I'll trade you."

"For what?"

"Your bandana."

"Why would you want my bandana?"

"Are you kidding?" the boy asked, and the genuine enthusiasm in his voice convinced Yahshi to take the hat. "You're a legend around... some circles. And the Force posting this article only proves that you're winning." He held his palms out, urging Yahshi to hand over his bandana.

"I didn't kill my father," Yahshi stated, holding a blank expression.

The boy laughed, emphasizing his outstretched hand. "Damn right, you didn't!"

Yahshi smiled and untied his bandana. If a stranger distrusted the Force enough to believe him, perhaps there was a chance his friends hadn't fallen for the lies either.

He handed the boy his bandana and put the watch cap on. The floppy fabric covered his brand, ears, and the back of his neck, cradling his head.

"Rather comfy," Yahshi said. "Thank you."

"I think it'll fool them." The boy looked back and forth between Yahshi and his portrait. "Nightshades don't wear hats."

"They don't, do they?" Yahshi chuckled. "Now I just have to hope you won't report my new look."

"Report you? Money from Vakoi is *blood money.* I wouldn't take the reward even if someone paid me to." He winked as he took a few backward steps. "Don't get caught, alright? It'll ruin the integrity of my souvenir."

"Thank you," Yahshi said, but the boy was already jogging away.

Despite the hat, he entered the market feeling exposed without his bandana. He hadn't removed it once, even during occasional opportunities to shower. *They see right through me.*

But they didn't. Erenford residents zoomed around him without batting an eye.

He slowed to a stop in the middle of the market and scanned the floor, searching for something to eat. His stomach rumbled at the sight of rice dishes and fruit smoothies—but a simpler wooden stand caught his attention and held it.

Yahshi approached a mother and daughter selling bread. "I'll take a sourdough." He pulled a velvet pouch out of his pocket to discover that he only had two coins left—the sign called for three.

"Two is fine," the mother said with a smile.

He smiled back as he paid, and the daughter wrapped his loaf in brown paper.

"Have a nice day," the girl chirped.

Yahshi thanked them before leaving the stand with a sourdough loaf. For a moment he questioned why he'd ordered a plain one instead of a cheese-filled bun—something more filling. But then he remembered that sourdough was Vell's favorite.

I hope she's okay.

He headed for the town center, where he'd search for an Underground member's home to rest at for the day. Tonight he'd leave for the final stretch of his journey to Atherus City, and for such a momentous occasion, he wanted to be well-rested.

In less than twenty-four hours, I'll be there, Mother.

As he walked, he questioned whether Keiyo and Cal had reported him. He theorized what Pinto did or didn't know when he delivered that ticket. He wondered how Quax reacted to the news about Martu, a man who had almost been an uncle to him.

He had left the Force but clung to the people. It hurt to know they would likely remember him as the lying monster who murdered his father. They would learn to see his heartless side and disregard his heart.

My worst regret is getting involved with them. Yahshi unwrapped his bread. *I entered their lives only to hurt them in the end. I wish they hadn't been cursed to know me. I wish I could erase what we've gone through together —for their sake.*

Before he could take a bite, he spotted a man sitting on the roadside. His frail body shivered in the morning air, and in front of him was a metal tin for people to throw coins into. It was empty.

Yahshi crouched by the man, holding out his bread.

The man stared at him, his eyes bold. A youthful glow filled his face when he smiled—he seemed to age ten years backward.

"You're a kind young man," he said, taking the bread. "People are quick to judge my past."

"I'm not one to judge pasts." Yahshi watched the man take a bite before walking away.

I can still do good. I'm not heartless.

When he reached the center of Erenford, he slowed to a stop. The view stole his breath away, and thoughts of the mess he'd left in Vakoi City disappeared. For the first time, he wasn't thinking about who to trust or which lantern chain had a larger top link. For the first time, he saw an Eastern town for what it was.

He saw a little boy throw his fishing rod at the ground because he hated fishing.

He saw employees sharing alcohol from a tin can, exhausted from a night shift.

He saw women whispering about the Underground as they passed him on their way to work.

He saw a teenage girl blabbering about Selection Season, only for her peers to scold her. "You can't be a guardian," they said. "The Force doesn't select Easterners."

Yahshi straightened his posture, listening to the heartbeat of Erenford as seagulls called out into the air. He was not safe, but he was free, and perhaps that was even more valuable.

"The Belladonna Traitor." Yahshi smiled. "Has a nice ring to it."

Like every night, Yahshi woke up on a stranger's sofa. He habitually reached for his head to ensure the bandana had stayed in place, but his fingers met the uneven skin of his brand.

Jolting into a seated position, he scanned the area until he found the watch cap resting on the floorboards.

Right, I wear a hat now. Must have slipped off while I was sleeping. He tugged it over his head and stood, eyes on the clock. The time was 1:04 in the morning.

He gulped at the sight of the collector reading at the table. The man looked up from the pages with a grin.

"You're still awake?" Yahshi asked in a shaky voice. *What if he saw my mark while I was sleeping and reported me?*

"I'm a night owl," the man replied, setting his book down.

"I should get going." Yahshi put his coat on, wrapped a gray scarf around his neck, and raced to the door.

"Wait!" the collector called.

He froze.

"Take this for your journey." He brought a jar of water to Yahshi, who sighed as he took it.

"Thank you."

"If you're hungry, I'll fry a fish."

"It's okay. I don't eat meat, and you've done enough for me already."

The man nodded. "Be safe out there."

Yahshi thanked him again and was on his way.

Atherus City was only a few hours north of Erenford, but he didn't know how long it'd take to find his mother after arriving. He speed-walked through town, devising a plan as he followed the North Star. *Surely the collectors in the City will know each other. At least one of them should recognize Mother's name. I'll use their knowledge to guide me.*

He quickened his pace to a jog down the eerie main road. It was always strange for him to arrive at a resting point during the lively hours of early morning only to wake up to find the streets nearly deserted. The bustling dirt road where fishers and schoolchildren conversed and traveled was now desolate. He could hear nothing but chirping crickets, croaking frogs, and the distant cries of a baby.

As he ran, his father's words crept into his head.

"Have faith in kindness, and it will always repay you."

He reflected on his past two weeks on the run, and the grace people had shown him. *I hope to repay them for their kindness someday. And if I can't, I hope life does, somehow.*

A few minutes later, distant clopping of horse hooves filled the air, snatching his attention. Yahshi turned, concealing himself in a gap between buildings.

Must be traders. He leaned against the wall, waiting for the carriage to pass before reentering the road. A flash of aluminum rushed by.

Aluminum.

Yahshi's eyes widened. He hadn't seen a vault in over a week. *Why would a Defense unit be in Erenford in the middle of the night?*

The vault stopped not long after passing him. He heard the box door open, followed by the plopping of boots.

A guardian cleared her throat. "Don't you think this is a bit... extreme?"

Yahshi recognized her voice.

"E-Extreme?" Galler replied. "Yes, but n-necessary. We n-need to find him."

"I don't see why it requires every guardian on the case," Evaris countered. "It makes the Force look desperate."

"Well, we are de-desperate," Galler said.

"Why?"

"B-Because..."

"See? You can't even think of a reason. What do we fix by finding him?"

Yahshi gulped. *I'm him, aren't I?*

"Evaris," a third guardian warned, "have some restraint."

Professor Famir? That can't be right. Famir was a guardian in the *Research Division*. He was Pinto's unit leader, a *professor*. An expedition with unconventional units could only mean one thing.

Yahshi's blood ran cold. *They've launched a special operation to find me.*

"What makes you b-believe he's in this area, P-Professor?" Galler asked.

"I'm not sure about Erenford specifically," Famir explained, "but he was last seen a few towns south of here. My unit's been tracing him through reported sightings, and it's clear he's been heading north."

Your unit? Has Pinto been tracing me?

Perhaps he discovered that Yahshi had stolen his key, duplicated it, and broken into the archives to steal the Bayin files. Then Pinto had paced his flat, putting the pieces together and realizing that Yahshi had been lying to him this entire time—that he'd never been his friend and was just like the Bayins.

Pinto hates me. He sighed. *He hates me...*

The guardians fell silent. Yahshi's sigh had been soft, but they were trained to pick up on the faintest of sounds.

Luckily, so was Yahshi. He closed his eyes, sensing the unit as they crept toward him. *It's only a matter of time before they find me.*

He dropped his jar of water as he bolted down the space between homes. By the time he emerged from the alleyway, his tracers' footsteps were no longer quiet.

THE BELLADONNA TRAITOR

We plunge into uncertainty, for beneath the depths of fear
lie the sunken treasures of our bravery.

♫ DON'T GIVE UP - URSINE VULPINE ♫

Yahshi darted down random alleyways, aiming to lose them in the chaos. But no matter how fast he sped up, the clattering of their boots followed him in full volume.

"Dammit," he muttered, stopping in a dead-end alleyway. He turned to find Famir at the entrance, blocking his way out. Evaris and Galler appeared at his sides with their primary tools drawn.

"Commander Yahshi," Famir said, stepping toward him.

Yahshi stepped back. *Don't call me that.*

"You were my shadow, remember?" Famir continued. "I took you under my wing. I got to know you. And this facade of yours, this *Belladonna Traitor* scheme... It's ridiculous. It's not you. It's not my shadow."

Yahshi clenched his fists. *You don't know me.*

Famir held his palms up. "We're not here to hurt you."

"Then why is she aiming at me?" Yahshi asked.

Evaris lowered her bow, but she didn't return the arrow to her quiver.

"We went through all this trouble to trace you because we have a proposition to make," Famir said.

"I don't want a deal," Yahshi spat.

Famir grinned. "If I were you, I'd at least *listen* to the deal before you rule it out. You might like it."

"I doubt that." He took another step back, flinching as he ran into the wall.

"He's right," Evaris called. "It's a good deal."

"I don't want *any* deal," Yahshi said.

Galler lowered his swords with a sigh. "Y-You'd be fo-foolish not to take this deal, Shadow."

Yahshi scanned the alleyway for an alternative exit, his eyes locking on a window to his right. He jumped toward it, his boots landing on the windowsill, allowing him to grab the roof's edge.

Famir lunged after him as Yahshi swung his legs sideways. He hooked his feet over the edge before Famir could grab them, and with a roll, brought the rest of his body onto the roof.

As he regained his footing, he saw a hand grip the edge—Famir was trying to follow him. Yahshi stomped on his knuckles until he cried out and let go.

The sound of Famir hitting the ground made Yahshi wince. *Ouch.*

He ran to the opposite end of the roof and searched for a windowsill, but the wall was flat. *I don't have time to check the other sides.* Taking a deep breath, he stared at a laundry rack in the alleyway. *I've handled worse.*

Yahshi jumped from the roof, aiming his boots at the rack to break his fall.

The structure collapsed beneath his weight, leaving him tumbling, tangling himself in clothes and broken wood. When he wrestled to a stop, he stood with nothing but a few scrapes across the back of his hands.

An arrow whipped past his face, and he turned to see Evaris entering the alleyway.

"We're not gonna hurt you!" she yelled.

Yahshi darted from the broken rack. "Then why shoot?"

As he turned the nearest corner, a sharp pain jolted through his shoulder and spread down his spine. He shrieked and curled over, gripping the wound with a shaky hand. An arrow was jammed into his flesh.

"I'm sorry!" Evaris yelled. "Please, let me explain."

Yahshi dragged himself to the end of the alleyway and encountered a cart of apples. With a solid kick, he toppled it over, and the tumbling fruits slowed Evaris down as he turned the corner.

After gaining a safe distance, he ducked behind a barrel and gripped the arrow in his shoulder. His neck tensed up as he yanked it, but the warm metal clung to him, resisting. It felt like a lifetime passed before the arrowhead released its grip on his flesh.

Blood seeped through his coat as the tool struck the ground, and he pressed a hand over his mouth to keep from screaming. He could feel his heartbeat pulsing in his shoulder, but the approaching footsteps forced him to keep moving.

A ladder on the opposite wall caught his attention. It led to the roof, atop which were a few lounging chairs. With gritted teeth, he pushed through the pain and began to climb.

Just as Yahshi reached the roof, Galler entered the alleyway. Peering over the edge, he watched the commander inch forward, his gaze fixed on the bloody arrow left behind.

Yahshi grabbed a lounging chair and pivoted, tossing it over the opposite side of the building.

The wood crashed, cueing Galler to race toward the noise.

Yahshi descended the ladder—reentering the alleyway as Galler left it— and turned the nearest corner. He stole shoes from doorsteps and snatched fruits from carts, throwing them behind as he speed-walked away.

The pounding of shoes hitting rooftops and fruits bouncing between walls woke the neighborhood in a storm, and soon enough, residents were joining his diversion, yelling their frustrations into the air.

"Who's out there?"

"Keep it down!"

"My apples!"

As the neighborhood came alive, Yahshi headed toward the silence, inevitably finding his way out of the maze and into the uninhabited outskirts of Erenford.

The pain in his shoulder intensified as he reached the woods. It felt like someone was stabbing him with every step, and when he clutched the wound, his palm came away covered in blood.

He removed his coat and tied his scarf around his shoulder.

I won't get caught this far into my journey.

Slipping his coat back on, he continued to run.

Half an hour passed before he spotted distant structures of the next town north. He concealed himself in the forest, studying the closest roads to gauge whether it'd be safe to travel through town.

His face ran cold at the sight of a parked vault, waiting for him. He had no choice but to travel around the town instead, which took three times longer than passing through it.

Yahshi was gasping for breath when he reached the other side, forced to quicken his pace to compensate for the lost time. *I still have two more towns to travel through.*

As he ran, he replotted how to locate his mother. There were definitely guardians in Atherus City, so he'd need to keep a low profile. Finding a new coat to conceal his shoulder wound would be a decent place to start. *I'll keep my eyes peeled for a laundry rack, and then I'll—*

Another vault interrupted his brainstorming session. *They're searching the outskirts?*

Yahshi stopped behind a tree and peered around it. When the box door opened, he pivoted, pressing his back to the trunk. *I'm too close. If I run, they'll hear me.* He raised his chin, eyes on the branches above.

The scattering of the guardians' footsteps urged him to start climbing. He pulled himself onto the first branch, moving sleekly to ensure the leaves didn't rustle too much. His shoulder ached as he climbed even higher, embedding himself in a web of branches.

Through the gaps between leaves, he caught glimpses of the guardians.

One of them headed his way and stopped directly beneath the tree. Yahshi couldn't make his face out from above.

Don't look up.

A branch shifted under his weight, and the guardian began to crane his head back.

Yahshi launched from the branches, landing his knees against the guardian's shoulders on his way down. The guardian collapsed beneath him, his chest striking the dirt.

While he had him disoriented, Yahshi unsheathed his swords and took a few steps away. He held the stolen blades ahead of him as the guardian groaned, pushing himself to his knees. They made eye contact and froze.

"Yahshi?" Quax asked, his voice weak. "Is it really you?"

Yahshi gripped the swords tighter as Quax stood, reaching into his overcoat. "Hey," he said, removing a dagger, "you trust me, right?"

"Don't move," Yahshi warned.

He took a step forward anyway, squinting at Yahshi's bloody shoulder. "Who did that?"

Yahshi didn't answer.

"We're not supposed to hurt you. You know that, right? We have a proposition to make."

He couldn't argue with Quax like he had with the others. The words sounded different coming from him.

"Please, trust me." Quax inched closer, raising his dagger. "Drop the tool before she sees."

"Before *who* sees?"

A dart skimmed Yahshi's cheek, hardly breaking his skin.

"Before *I* see," Cal answered, emerging from the trees. She glanced at her brother, who lowered his head with a gulp.

Yahshi pivoted to run as another dart skimmed his ear. He didn't believe Cal had thrown it until he saw her in the final position of her throwing form. It had struck him too fast. Impossibly fast.

As he took a few more steps away, his vision whirled, and he felt his grip on the sword handles loosening against his will. His sudden headache and pounding heart reminded him of the maintenance vials in his getaway bag.

I've been losing tolerance.

Cal dashed after him. He swung his swords in sloppy combinations, and she dodged every move before countering with another blade throw, each cut weakening his vision.

As Cal dodged another attack, Quax tackled Yahshi from the side. The swords slipped out of his hands as he pummeled toward the dirt.

Yahshi yelled, his wounded shoulder taking the weight of his fall.

Cal flipped him onto his back, and the sight of her silhouette against the moon made him struggle to breathe. Her black hair was pulled into a bun, and the upturned collar of her overcoat shielded her slender neck from the cold. One look into her crystal eyes made Yahshi lurch his head forward in a desperate attempt to flee.

Cal slammed her boot against his chest. "The Belladonna Traitor," she said through gritted teeth. "It's about damn time." She applied more pressure until the twigs beneath him jabbed at his skin.

When she crouched beside him, her eyes were so vivid it looked like an artist had painted them with blueberry ink.

I always had a feeling Cal would kill me someday. He choked as she traced her dagger along his neck. *But I always thought it was only a feeling.*

YOU CAN'T WIN

We foster the flame of our being, refusing to be extinguished.

♫ BITTER HEART · MEMI ♫

Yahshi grabbed Cal's wrist to redirect the dagger from his neck.

"Don't move," she warned, pressing the blade harder. It cut through a layer of skin, and he released her, his eyes welling up.

"We're not allowed to hurt him," Quax said in a quivering voice.

"We're not allowed to *kill* him," Cal corrected, "so long as he co-operates."

Their voices seemed to get farther away as Yahshi lost himself in the pain. His lungs burned, begging for air, and a droplet of blood trickled down his neck. *I can't handle any more.*

And just like that, the blade disappeared.

Am I dead?

Perhaps the relief he felt was the end of their game. He had died. Cal had won. The pain was over.

But then her boot left his chest, and he inhaled a burst of air.

No, I'm still here.

He opened his eyes to find Cal glaring down at him. "Get up."

Yahshi pushed himself to his feet as Quax retrieved his swords from the ground. When Cal tucked her dagger away, he pivoted with a burst of adrenaline. *I can still outrun them.*

Two hands met his chest, shoving him backward into Cal, who caught him by his shoulders. He froze when Vell plucked a star from her bandolier. Her hair was slicked back into a low bun, her eyes narrowed.

"Vell," Yahshi muttered. "No..."

Cal released his shoulders and stepped back. "Turn around."

He stared at Vell a moment longer before turning. His legs urged him to run, but he planted himself in front of Cal because he couldn't escape all three of them.

"I could have killed you," Cal said. "And I still can, but I don't have to, and I'd prefer not to. Killing you would be a loss to the Force."

Yahshi wiped the blood from his neck. "Why?"

"Because we couldn't trace you, even with our best units on the case. The last time that happened was with the Bayins, which means you're following their tracks. You're our key to uncovering how the Underground operates. The longer you evaded us, the more we believed it." She pulled a golden slip out of her overcoat and held it out for him. "Emperor Vakoi is offering you a pardon."

Yahshi took the slip and cautiously dropped his head to read it.

> Commander Yahshi Konya of Sitra, I offer you a complete pardon for the murder of Martu Konya and your recurring violations of Guardian Protocol.

The note included Emperor Vakoi's signature and the Imperial Stamp.

"Our priority is to support you, as fellow guardians do," Cal said. "So please, come home, tell us the truth, and we'll fix this giant misunderstanding."

"What are you implying?"

"What the article says you are is speculation. A traitor to the Vakoi Empire? A heartless murderer? A rogue guardian? We can make those titles go away. We can rewrite the story. You made a mess, yes, but we'll forgive you, and we'll fix it."

"You're lying," Yahshi said, the pardon slip wrinkling in his grip. "You're setting a trap to detain and execute me. When I return, Emperor Vakoi will deny the pardon, and no one will ever know."

"He wouldn't dare, Yahshi," another familiar voice said.

From the shadows, Pinto emerged, bow in hand. "Emperor Vakoi signed the pardon in the Complex. Dozens of us witnessed it," he continued. "Going against his word would cause an uproar. He won't do it. He wants you home. We *all* want you home."

Yahshi stared deeply into his friend's watery eye. *He's supposed to hate me.*

"This isn't a trap," Quax said, drawing Yahshi's attention next. "I grew up with you. I know there's more to the story—we all do. That's why we did everything we could to ensure Emperor Vakoi would grant you this pardon. All you need to do now is come home and talk. You can get your uniform back."

Yahshi looked at Vell, but she stared him dead in the eye and said nothing. Her silence was more painful than any shout or expression of anger because being angry would mean she cared.

A twig snapped, turning him to Keiyo.

"Hey there." He smiled at Yahshi, hands in his pockets. "You're coming home, right? It's not the same without our anxious friend to dampen the mood."

If there was anyone who understood Yahshi's hatred for the Force the most, it was Keiyo. Perhaps that's why he was the only person to ask him to come home instead of demanding him to.

"The Force just wants to understand you and learn what you know," Cal explained. "That's all there is to it."

Yahshi stared at the pardon slip in his hands. The golden page devoured his vision as he mulled over his options. He could either return to Vakoi City and betray the Underground, or die at the hands of the few loved ones he had left.

I almost made it. Yahshi remembered how close he was to reaching

Atherus City. *I was almost there.*

"Yahshi," Cal said, pressing him to choose.

If he were to reject this deal, his friends would forever see him as a traitor, a murderer, a rogue guardian. They'd see him as the monster who chose the enemy over their friendship, even after everything they'd done to protect him.

And worst of all, knowing Cal, one of them would kill him today.

Yahshi's eyes darted back to Vell. She flinched, and he waited as though the subtle movement would follow with a surge of emotions, words, or *something*. But that was all it was—a single, isolated flinch.

I could go back. I could lie to the Force about what I know. I could feed them misinformation about the Underground. I could run away again— and do it better this time.

"Accept the pardon," ordered Pinto.

"Let us fix this," offered Quax.

"Can you please come home?" asked Keiyo.

"Yahshi." Vell's eyes were watering, but the words left her mouth like blades. "Prove me wrong."

The forest died. Not a single chirp or rustle came from the branches. The air was scentless. Windless. He could feel his heart beating against his chest but couldn't hear it—he nearly believed it wasn't there.

"Look around," Cal said. "Look at the mess you've made."

Yahshi's eyes hopped from Quax to Pinto to Vell to Keiyo. "How do I fix it?"

She pointed to the vault, and he nodded.

"Pinto," Cal said, "your bow."

Pinto raised his tool with a shaky grip, aiming at Yahshi to ensure he wouldn't run.

Each step toward the vault lasted a lifetime. Yahshi's thoughts drifted to Selection Day, when Commander Roz gave him a choice to join Belladonna Guardian Academy. If he hadn't signed the contract, Sitra would have shamed him for limiting their infrastructure bonus. He would have lived with unanswered questions and personal regrets.

Next, he thought of his first shadow assignment, when Cal ordered him to slit the collector's throat. He could have chosen not to, but to oppose her would be a violation of Protocol. He would have faced scrutiny from the Academy guardians and unknown punishments.

As he raised his foot to hoist himself onto the vault floor, he thought of the choice he was making now. Emperor Vakoi was allowing him to return to Vakoi City, reclaim his job, and seek comfort among his closest friends. Not returning, however, meant his blood would forever lie on their hands.

The Force knew how to frame an impossible choice. Yahshi never had to join the Academy. He never had to kill his curiosity, or the rabbit, or that collector. But the Force ensured the alternative was always more painful. The game was set up so they would win, time and time again.

With this realization came the revival of the woods. A chilly breeze raised the hair on the back of his neck. He could hear his heartbeat again. And it was exhilarating, because for the first time, he remembered what he'd always known but never believed.

It's all my choice. It always has been.

Yahshi stopped with one foot on the platform. He chose not to return to Vakoi City and endanger the collectors who had risked their lives to help him. His friends could see him as a heartless, dishonest monster, but at least he wasn't choosing to be one.

"I reject the pardon."

He lowered his foot from the platform and turned around. His fellow graduates stared with dry eyes, wide in shock—but Cal's marble eyes became real, welling with tears.

"I murdered Chima Fernis," Cal said, her voice poisonous. "You were there, Yahshi. You remember."

He pursed his lips.

"I broke Imperial Law, just like you did when you murdered your father. But the Force saw potential in me and convinced Emperor Vakoi that I deserved a second chance. If he hadn't offered me a pardon, I never would have gone to the Academy and entered the Force. I'd be dead." She bit her trembling lip and looked away. "And here you are, rejecting the Force's mercy. They're giving you a second chance, and you're throwing it away like it means nothing."

"Because I'd rather die on *my terms* than theirs," Yahshi said.

Cal wiped her eyes. "You're ungrateful"—her upper lip curled in disgust—"and unworthy of the Force."

"You're a puppet." Yahshi's eyes watered too. "And I'm so sorry, Cal. You were vulnerable. They locked you up and pretended to save you, just so you'd dedicate your life to them."

"You can't win," Cal said. "This is how you survive. There is no other way."

There is no other way. He couldn't count how many times he'd heard that phrase. It spread like wildfire through the Force, convincing them they had no choice when they had all the choices in the world.

"No," Yahshi said. "*You* can't win, because I'd rather die than be a Nightshade." He turned to his friends. "You want the truth from me, don't you? Well, here it is—the Force *lies*. I didn't kill my father—Commander Roz did. Emperor Vakoi initiated the Eastern raids to give him an excuse to control both sides of the island. This entire time, *we've* been the bad guys. *We've* been the monsters. Maelin Vandros of Frontal saw that, and the Force killed her for it."

"No, Yahshi. No." Pinto lowered his bow, shaking his head. "The *Underground* killed Doctor Maelin. I'm from Frontal. I would know."

"Look in the archives," Yahshi said. "It's all there."

"Commander Roz would never do that," Quax countered. "He would never kill Martu and blame it on you. He would have no incentive."

"The Force killed Doctor Maelin? Emperor Vakoi initiated the raids?" Pinto scoffed. "Who's telling you these things? What kind of propaganda have you been exposed to?"

"Yahshi, stop this, please," Keiyo said, his lips downturned. "Save yourself. You deserve it."

Vell opened her mouth to speak.

"I've had enough!" Cal interrupted, turning to Pinto. "Finish him."

"Finish?" Pinto asked.

"You know what I mean."

The other guardians stepped away from Pinto as he aimed his bow again. "Don't make me do this."

"You have a choice," Yahshi said, his voice shaking. "Don't be blind."

"Hurry up," Cal said.

Yahshi stepped toward the horses leading the vault.

"Move again"—Pinto drew his bowstring tighter—"and I'll shoot."

"You're shooting regardless," Cal reminded him.

Yahshi froze, and Vell aimed her star at him.

"How could you do this to us?" Pinto asked. "You made a Vow to support your fellow guardians."

"I'm not a guardian, Pinto," Yahshi replied, his heart aching. "Don't you get it?"

"Shoot him!" Cal yelled. "Shoot him now!"

Yahshi was preparing for a final sprint of desperation when an object struck the tip of Pinto's arrow. His bow jolted aside, releasing it against his will.

A throwing star stopped in the air before falling flat by Pinto's boots.

Vell stood in the final position of her throwing form, her face red.

"Vell," Keiyo said, his voice breaking. "What did you do?"

Yahshi and Keiyo tried to catch her gaze, but she wouldn't look at them. She glared at Pinto, who stared back at her with a widened eye. She'd interfered with a direct order Cal had given him. She'd broken Protocol.

They flinched as Quax screamed in horror. The color drained from Keiyo's face when he followed his gaze, and Pinto lurched forward with a hand on his mouth.

Yahshi's breath clogged his throat when he finally looked.

Pinto's arrow had pierced through Cal's neck. She dropped to her knees, trying to speak, but only croaks came out.

The bow slipped from Pinto's grip, hitting the ground as he turned his back to the siblings.

"No, you're okay." Quax gripped Cal by the shoulders, fending off tears. "It's not that bad. You'll be fine. You're okay."

Cal ignored him, staring at Vell as she gripped her neck, blood covering her hands. Her eyes said every nasty thing she couldn't say for herself.

"Vell didn't mean to," Keiyo blurted.

Yahshi looked back at Vell, who grabbed a dagger from her overcoat.

Keiyo closed his eyes as though he knew what she was about to do.

Cal collapsed onto the dirt, and Quax began to sob. His back was turned to Vell, who ran toward them with soft footsteps. Pinto was still facing away, blind to the horrors unfolding, while Keiyo stood paralyzed, refusing to look.

Yahshi raced after her, catching up as she crouched and raised the blade, intending to end Cal's life right in front of her little brother.

Yahshi snatched her wrist.

She continued to push the blade down, fighting through his resistance. He gritted his teeth, opposing her pressure until her grip on the dagger loosened. Tears streamed down her face as she looked back at him.

"Let go," he whispered, and she did. The dagger struck the dirt as Quax continued to sob, oblivious to what could have been.

"You made me a promise, Yahshi, and you broke it." Her tears wouldn't stop streaming. "You left me alone in the capital. And the things Cal made me do..."

Quax flinched at the sound of Vell's voice. "Get away from my sister!"

"Promise?" Pinto turned around, facing them with a bloodshot eye. "What promise, Vell?"

Yahshi didn't let go of her wrist. He pulled her toward the vault because there was no other way out of what she'd done. According to Protocol, she deserved the death penalty.

Pinto swiped his bow from the ground and raced after them. "Stop!"

Yahshi and Vell mounted two of the vault's horses. She used a dart to cut through the ropes that bound them to the driver's seat, and they trotted forward just as Pinto caught up, barely escaping him.

As they galloped away, an arrow skimmed Yahshi's horse and struck a tree. Pinto wasn't trying to kill them, but he wouldn't let them escape either.

Only a few more arrows came their way before the ambush stopped. He looked over his shoulder to see Pinto on the ground.

Keiyo had tackled him, allowing Yahshi and Vell to flee.

CHAPTER 40

STILL HERE

We pledge to support each other, interlacing our roots
to form a sturdy foundation.

♫ ONLY THE YOUNG - BRANDON FLOWERS ♫

"You've been heading north," Vell said over the clopping of their horses. She rubbed her cheeks dry with her sleeve. "Destination?"

"Atherus City."

"It's about thirty minutes from here." Her horse took a slight lead. "Twenty, if you can keep up."

Yahshi sped after her, his shoulder throbbing as he tightened his grip on the reins. They weaved between trees, sometimes separating but always managing to regroup.

"Vell!" he called. "Why are you here?"

She tugged at the golden ribbon holding her bun, and her black hair fell free, flickering in the wind like a match light. A quick flash of her smile stole his breath away.

"Because you're not what they say you are," she replied.

His eyes welled up as a cold breeze stung the slashes on his cheeks—but the warmth he felt, riding away as an irredeemable traitor, was far more comforting than his guardian uniform had ever been. And the warmth took his pain away.

They galloped around two more towns before spotting a brick wall in the distance. Yahshi frowned at Vell, and they sped up in unison, stopping near the roofless structure. Surrounding the half-broken wall were endless mounds of bricks and stones.

"Atherus Palace," Vell said.

Yahshi dismounted his horse.

"What are you doing?"

"Let's walk from here."

"The main part of the City's still—"

"We have time." His watery eyes met hers, and she nodded, joining him on the ground.

He led the way into a half-enclosed room overgrown with weeds. As he ran his hand along a mossy wall, he recalled what Princess Kia had told him. Somewhere among these ruins were the ashes of two-year-old Prince Runix, a boy who had his whole life ahead of him.

Yahshi leaned his forehead against the moss. "He would have been fifteen."

Vell placed a hand on his back. "We need to go."

He closed his eyes. "Will Cal be okay?"

"I don't know. I didn't study the wound."

"And... Keiyo?"

A pause. "I don't know."

Yahshi nodded before pushing himself from the wall. They might not know for a long time.

As they reached the end of the ruins, they met a passage of trees and bushes that opened into the glowing heart of Atherus City. Yahshi gawked at the cluster of slender buildings reaching for the clouds. Laundry lines crossed like spider webs between structures, and lanterns illuminated hurried residents under the morning sun. *Despite the Palace ruins, the capital's spirit lives on.*

"You're shaking." Vell retrieved an emergency neutralizer syringe from her overcoat. "Take off your coat."

"We don't have time for this."

"Please?"

He took a deep breath and removed his coat, revealing the blood-soaked scarf wrapped tightly around his shoulder, the edge of his short sleeve barely visible beneath it. Vell's needle sank into his skin right below the fabric.

Yahshi's jaw tightened. "I would have liked a warning."

Vell smiled lightly, pressing her finger to the plunger. Too much neutralizer could overcorrect the belladonna in his bloodstream and kill him, but if he trusted anyone to administer the correct dose, it was her.

Relief came quickly, his muscles relaxing and his vision clearing, though a faint tremor remained in his fingers.

Vell removed the needle and untied his scarf to examine the wound. Her gaze sharpened as she plucked a dart from her bandolier.

"Princess Kia," he muttered. "Did she report you?"

She began to cut strips of clean cloth out of his coat. "For what?"

Yahshi concealed a grin. "Never mind."

She grabbed two alcohol vials from her overcoat and emptied them over his shoulder. He winced as she dabbed the wound with a wad of cloth.

"Who shot you?"

"Commander Evaris."

"It's not deep," Vell noted. "She's nice."

After cleaning his shoulder, she wrapped it tightly with the strips she'd cut. The bleeding had slowed, so the blood wouldn't seep through and draw attention for a while. He tucked his short sleeve inward to hide the stains from earlier.

"So," Vell said, "why Atherus City?"

"My mother's alive."

"What?"

"She lives here, and she's the only person who can bring us to safety."

"Where Dice went?"

Yahshi nodded.

"Let's hurry then." She headed for the buildings, but he grabbed her arm.

"Your uniform."

She frowned, pulling her arm free. "I can't lose the coat. My tools are in it."

"My mother won't trust you if you're wearing that."

She narrowed her eyes at him, and after a long pause, slowly unstrapped her bandolier. Her overcoat came off next, its weighted fabric falling in folds around her boots.

"Feels good, right?" Yahshi asked.

"Light," Vell said with a grin.

Lastly, she removed her tie and armored vest. The light dress shirt and pants of her guardian uniform were generic enough to pass as casual attire.

She looks so... normal.

"I can't believe I'm meeting your mother."

"I can't believe *I'm* meeting my mother." Yahshi stepped closer, adjusting her bangs to conceal her mark. "How many units are in the City?"

"Two."

He straightened his watch cap.

"I told you," she said. "You look cool in hats."

Yahshi chuckled, trailing his fingers along the dart slits on his cheeks. "Do the cuts draw too much attention?"

"They look like cat scratches."

"Perfect." He took her hand and led her toward the buildings. "Let's go."

They left the greenery behind, entering a labyrinth of bustling roads. Residents sipped hot drinks from paper cups on the way to work or school, and shopkeepers shouted sales pitches to lure them inside, occasionally succeeding. Wheeled carts parked on the roadsides sold food Yahshi had never seen before, even in other Eastern towns.

He spotted a vault at the end of the road, and they bolted down a narrow alleyway with a long string of doors on either side. Above them, zig-zagging staircases led to more floors of doors—all of which were paired with a lantern.

Checking every floor would take ages.

"Yahshi," Vell said, "what do we do?"

He slowed to a walking pace, studying a staircase as he passed it. *Collectors are most likely on the ground floor. It'd be riskier for a courier to travel upstairs to pick up smuggled goods. The Underground is cleverer than that.*

"We keep walking," Yahshi answered. They turned down a near-identical alleyway, confronting another set of doors and lanterns. "Study the lantern chains on the ground floor. I'll search the ones on the right, and you'll search the left. We're looking for one with a slightly larger top link."

Vell nodded, and they walked side by side, studying chain links. When they reached the end, they turned into another residential alleyway, where they scanned another set of chains. They repeated this process, over and over, until Vell grabbed Yahshi by the shoulders and said, "This isn't working."

"We'll find one eventually."

"The units will find us first."

And that's when Yahshi saw it. He broke free from Vell's grip and approached the door behind her, confirming that the top chain link was indeed larger.

Vell joined his side a few seconds later, and he knocked on the door.

They were greeted by a man with a red, round face and an even rounder belly. But his most defining feature was his oversized, mouse-like ears.

"You're the Nightshade on the posters," the man said. "You're *him*."

"Please, I need your help," Yahshi said. "I'm with the Underground, just like you. That's why the Force hates me—that's why I'm on the posters. You have to trust me. I need to find—"

"I know. Tonna told me to keep an eye out for you."

Yahshi's eyes widened. "She did? Where is she?"

The collector's eyes darted to Vell, who made him hesitate before leaning in. "Keep heading that way," he said in a raspy voice, waving his pointer finger. "You'll see a butcher shop a ways down. Make two immediate right turns and keep going until you reach a stand. It's some old guy. He sells— I don't know—fish pops, or something. Then make a left turn. You can handle it from there."

"Thank—"

The man slammed the door in his face.

Yahshi turned to Vell. "Do you—"

"I remember it." She headed down the alleyway. "But what are fish pops?"

He shrugged. "No clue."

When they reached the butcher shop, they made a right turn, followed by another one. A man was selling round balls of fried fish at the end of the road.

"It should be down here." Vell led Yahshi into a dark alleyway across from the stand. They stopped in front of a door.

"Is this the one?" she asked.

Yahshi studied the top chain link and nodded. "It's the one."

He wiped his palms on his pants and made a fist, but he couldn't bring himself to raise it. He'd been working for this reunion for two weeks, but he'd been so focused on surviving the journey that he hadn't put much thought into what this moment would actually be like. There were so many questions with no time to ponder them, and they filled his head like a mumbling crowd.

Vell knocked on the door for him.

"Hey!" Yahshi scolded.

She chuckled, but her humor died when the door swung open.

Facing them was not a mother but a teenage boy who looked oddly familiar. Baggy clothes hung from his body, and his facial features were as sharp as blades.

"The sky... weeps with us?" Yahshi didn't mean to say the password like a question, but his confusion had to seep out somewhere.

"Oh yeah?" the boy asked, grinning. His bold eyes darted to Vell's boots, and she took a step back.

"We're looking for Tonna," Yahshi said, his voice firmer now.

"To what? Poison her?" The boy leaned against the doorframe, guarding the entrance. "I know you're with the Force. That's why you brought *her*. What is she? Your unit member?"

"Saunti?" a woman called from another room. "Who is it?"

"No one!" the boy yelled back. "Just a—"

"Are you Tonna?" Yahshi shouted. "I'm your—"

Saunti slammed the door with a scoff, and Yahshi flinched at the click of a lock.

A few seconds passed before Saunti and the woman began to argue in hushed voices. Yahshi was about to lean his ear against the door when it swung open again.

His lips parted at the sight of a shorter woman with two thick braids. She looked harmless with her round cheeks and scattered freckles, but the stern look in her eyes made him think twice about hugging her and calling her *Mother*.

"I'm Tonna," she confirmed, summoning Yahshi and Vell inside.

The cozy room smelled faintly of fish and spices. Thick curtains covered the windows, making the fireplace their only light source.

Saunti was leaning against a bookshelf with his arms crossed. "Mother, do you really think—"

"Quiet." Tonna shut the door behind them.

He's her son? Yahshi studied Saunti, wondering if he looked anything like himself. *Are we... brothers?*

"Why are you staring?" Saunti asked.

"She's your mother?" Yahshi replied.

"No, she's my father. What the hell do you think?"

Tonna's approaching footsteps turned Yahshi back to her. He gulped, watching her scan him up and down, as though he might be an imposter. He suddenly didn't know how to stand, what to do with his arms, or whether he should smile or not.

She stopped in front of him, and the room fell silent. Her warm hands reached for his face, aggravating the cuts, but he didn't care because she was smiling now. The wrinkles around her eyes told him she'd been waiting for this reunion too.

Vell stepped toward them, but Saunti's voice stopped her. "If you touch my mother, I'll kill you. I know you're a filthy Night..."

Tonna wrapped her arms around Yahshi. "It's really you."

Yahshi closed his eyes and melted into her arms, feeling Martu's presence between them. Childhood memories of his father flashed around in the darkness. He and Tonna were reflections of Martu in each other, remnants of the joy he'd once brought into their lives.

"Okay, what the hell?" Saunti asked. "How do you know him?"

Tonna pulled away with a sniffle. "There's no time to explain." She walked to the bookshelf and shooed Saunti away.

"Who is he?" Saunti asked, and Yahshi frowned at him, seeing the resemblance clearly now. His facial structure, his eyes, his voice—they all reminded him of Martu.

All this time, Father had another son...

Tonna held a book out for Saunti. "It's time."

He looked back at Yahshi and Vell, shaking his head. "No..."

"Deliver this book to Noris. Letters are circled to form the name of the nearest courier. He's to seek him for instructions on how to reach the access point."

Saunti snatched the book. "Noris won't fit in the access point."

"I need you to be serious, Saunti."

"You're the one who can't be serious. You're about to compromise Headquarters to a pair of Nightshade *spies*."

"Go," she ordered. "Tell Noris that his first assignment as a courier begins one week from today. Take no longer than three minutes, and meet us at the access point using Route B. I'll explain everything once we're safe."

"Whatever. I had a feeling I'd die this week anyway." Saunti sent Yahshi and Vell a scowl before leaving, slamming the door behind him.

Tonna pointed at Vell. "Do you trust her?"

"I do," Yahshi replied.

"Okay. Follow me."

Tonna guided them through endless alleyways, swiftly dodging residents and food stands while Yahshi and Vell struggled to keep pace. Whenever they spotted vaults or guardians on the lookout, she'd reroute their path without hesitation.

"Is he really gone?" Tonna asked. "Martu?"

Yahshi's throat tightened. "I'm sorry."

"Was it you?"

"Of course not," he said. "It was... a guardian."

She nodded as she turned down another alleyway. Entering from the other side was Saunti. Their groups met in the middle and stopped.

"You're not thinking straight," Saunti said.

"Did you do it?" Tonna asked.

"Reluctantly."

"Good." She turned to Yahshi and Vell. "Listen, we need to enter fast. If anyone spots us, *thousands* will die."

Saunti offered them a mocking grin. "No pressure."

Tonna dropped to her knees and gripped a manhole cover at their feet. She struggled to lift it, and Saunti rubbed the frown out of his forehead before kneeling to help. They dragged the cover aside, revealing a ladder.

"You'll go first," Tonna said, peering up at Yahshi. "Then me, then"— her gaze drifted to Vell—"*you*. And Saunti?"

"Yeah?"

"You're last. Don't let her run."

Yahshi gazed down into the dark abyss.

"You heard her," Saunti said. "Down the rabbit hole you go…"

Yahshi lowered his feet onto the ladder steps and began his descent, his nose wrinkling at the stench of raw sewage.

Once everyone was on their way down, Saunti dragged the cover shut, blocking all light from reaching them. A scraping sound filled the manhole, followed by a light flickering from Saunti's fingertips. He was pinching a match as he climbed down.

Yahshi reached the platform, which was surprisingly spacious but also empty. No door, tunnel, or hideout—just a half-open sewage pipe.

Tonna joined him, followed by Vell and Saunti. Their shoulders were already touching, and when Tonna gestured for them to step away, they had to squeeze into each other to make space.

She knocked near the ladder in a three-two-one pattern. They waited in silence before hearing a *click*. Yahshi and Vell shuffled in place, searching for the sound's unknown source.

"Stop squirming," Saunti said.

They stilled as Tonna gripped the third ladder step from the floor. With a yank, a hinged block of concrete swung toward her to reveal a secret entryway.

Standing in the shadows was a teenage girl who appeared to be the same age as Saunti. Yahshi couldn't make out many of her features, but he could tell she was tall and slender with long, flat hair that reached her waist.

"Tonna!" the girl shouted. "Long time no see." Her eyes trailed over Yahshi and Vell. "Who are the kids, Cricket?"

Saunti nearly replied, but Tonna held her palm up, muting him. "Step aside, Aero. It's time."

Her eyes darted back to Yahshi with an open-mouth grin. "Holy shit. It's *him*, isn't it?"

When Tonna said nothing, Aero finally stepped aside, and they filed into a tunnel lined with torches.

Saunti entered last, closing the secret door behind them. He fumbled with a small metal block attached to it.

"Wow." Aero reached past him and twisted the block. "You don't even know how our locks work."

Saunti huffed. "How would you expect me to—"

She blew his match out with a chuckle.

"Aero," Tonna said, "as a handler, I assume you have direct access to the inventory room?"

She retrieved a ring of keys from her pocket and jingled them. "Indeed I do."

"Not many people inside, right?" Tonna asked.

"Only handlers have access."

"And you know how to get there without being seen?"

"'Course." Aero skipped to the front of the group, passing Tonna to lead the way. "Follow me."

She guided them to a ladder at the end of the tunnel, which they descended into a network of interconnected passages. The twists and turns were natural for Aero, but unlike in the alleyways of Atherus City, Tonna's steps faltered, and she gripped the walls for support. That's when it clicked.

Aero's a hider. She receives goods while Mother and Saunti deliver them.

They traveled for about ten minutes before Aero stopped to unlock a metal door. Yahshi's jaw dropped at the sight of coal, canned fish, oil, matchboxes, blankets, and other goods he'd seen Underground members collecting. He and Vell glanced at each other as they followed Tonna and Saunti into the inventory room.

This is where the smuggled goods are going. He swiped a can of beans from a shelf. *This is the one mystery the Force can't crack, no matter how long they look or how many smugglers they kill.*

"Leave us locked in here for now, and don't announce our arrival publicly," Tonna said. "I want you to deliver a message directly to the Provisional Council members."

"Got it." Aero stood in the doorway, hands in her pockets. "What's the message?"

Despite opening her mouth, no words came out. Tonna looked back at Yahshi with watery eyes.

"Tonna?" Aero prodded. "What do I tell the Council?"

Yahshi's grip on the can of beans tightened when Tonna smiled at him. Her eyes overflowed, and silent tears spilled down her cheeks.

"Prince Runix has returned."

UNDERGROUND ROYALTY

BELLADONNA, BOOK 2

While Saunti adjusts to life in the Underground with Yahshi and Vell, Pinto calls old friends into service for the Force's most dangerous operation yet.

ACKNOWLEDGMENTS

On a summer morning in 2021, my friend Angie and I woke up at 4:00, chugged a few lattes, and set off for a chilly beach near San Francisco—one of our chaotic rituals. I had just published my second novel Capsule and was grappling with what to work on next.

Angie helped me brainstorm during the drive, and we became so invested in plotting Nightshade Academy that we missed a turn and got lost. We never made it to the beach.

Thank you, Angie, for lighting a match for the Belladonna trilogy that day —and thank you, Joy, for keeping the flame going while we lived together in Thailand. You're a trooper for enduring my panicked, late-night rants throughout the editing process. Wishing you nothing but the best, Roomie.

Mom and Dad, I have no clue where I'd be if you hadn't encouraged my creative projects growing up. Thank you for being a constant pillar of support.

John, calling to nag you for plot hole solutions was one of the highlights of writing this novel. Thank you for your time, enthusiasm, and willingness to take a dose of second-hand agony.

Thank you to my aunt and uncle, Robin and Thomas Bottorff, and my grandparents, Norma and Eleuterio Torrefranca. Your encouragement when I was a teen writer has stuck with me.

Pedro Solana, thank you for an incredible week of training at Muay Thai Sangha in Chiang Mai, Thailand. Your lessons informed not only the characters in this book but also opened my eyes to so much. Being your student, just for a moment, was an honor I'll never forget.

A mega-ton confetti award of thanks to my beta readers who provided constructive criticism on early drafts of Nightshade Academy. This book would be a dumpster fire without you:

Alina Korhummel, Rara Llarenas, Saura Bhirud, Kai Kimayong, Rida Ep, Meike Liang, Hannah Wernecke, Liam Lee, Franck Picardat, Germaine Han, Brian Goss, Jesmin Maria, Ben T. Clarke, Millie Florence, Sabrey Moiraine, Fanta Sesay, Olivia Smyka, Reeha Dalin, Angeline Sieman, Rosalind Sterling, Chi Mary, Aaridhi Katiyar, Joshua Lu, Luis Rodrigues, Ananya Katiyar, Diya Mukherjee, Avelia Shindyapin, Amanda Ernar, Paurvi Bhansali, Victor Thong, Evelyn Hong, Lucy Robertson, Lara Toffanello, Emilia Hernandez, Emily Jarecke, Kayla Fachruddin, Nitya Mattey, Martine Alexandra Hassel Baardseth, Vardaa Maheshwari, Juri Al-Mutairi, Amanda Lauren, Beka Lynne, Elise Yount, Jade Gilbride, Shambhavi Kumari, Dami Jinadu, Sunshine Blair, Jimmy McCann, Chathulya B., Amethyst Pen, Laurel Glyn, Hilary-Ann Adwoa, Ruth Holst, Carol Keirn, Louise Pattison, Celeste L., Dharuni Ankani, Johan de Klerk, Astridwrites, Emilia Rodrigo

I'm extremely grateful to those I've worked with at Lost Island Press, especially Katie Flanagan for being here from the start.

Shoutout to my fellow Lost Island authors—Shira Behore, Amanda Michelle Brown, Sowon Kim, Julia Rosemary Turk. And shoutout to a few more storytellers who inspire me—Germaine Han, Sebastian Delgado, Millie Florence, Andrew Carniglia, Zoe Anastasia.

Aleksandra at MAD Book Covers, thank you for my absolute dream design. I remember sprinting around to show everyone your initial concepts for the cover art—I couldn't contain my excitement.

Gonzalo Mansilla, thank you for enhancing the interior pages with your illustrations.

Huge thanks to everyone who worked with me behind-the-scenes on the audio adaptation of Part 1. James Sinclair Stott for the Belladonna theme song, What We Are. Gita Puspita Asri for the soundtrack. Teera Music Studio for recording my narration. Juan Pablo Diaz for editing the weekly episodes.

I have massive appreciation for the audio adaptation's voice actors. Your interpretations were so compelling that I made unplanned edits to book dialogue and body language, especially in Part 2. A heartfelt thanks to the cast:

Jason Brown, Anthony Andrés Echeverry, Philip Kraaijenhof, Melissa White, Alex Bui, Patrick Vierzba, David John-Bores, Julia Ristrow, Ellie Chua, Kody Kiehl, Conner Blunck, Walter Mack, Ben Awtry, Gwyneth Evans, Jeff Rosenau, Lucas Hensley, Levi Titus, Angie Eggers, Alison Prophet, Willem Digard, Maria Palmö

Non and Ploy, your friendship has brought so much color to my life. I love the projects we work on—and our midnight instant noodle stops at 7-Eleven to procrastinate on said projects.

Mikey, I always enjoy our walks, coffee breaks, and conversations about the most random topics.

Sending my love to Grandpa Pete. I will write another, and another, and another…

Last but not least—Aunt Ginny, this book is dedicated to you. Thank you for reading my stories and being such a kind role model. I love you and will cherish our time together always.

ABOUT THE AUTHOR

MEL TORREFRANCA is a full-time author and founder of Lost Island Press. Her books feature morally gray characters, bold endings, and a pinch of awkward humor. Mel discovered her passion for writing at the age of seven and published her debut novel, *Leaving Wishville*, during high school. She also drinks way too many lattes.

MELTORREFRANCA.COM

LONE PLAYER

JULIA ROSEMARY TURK

To manage overpopulation, citizens are marked with playing card tattoos—and an annual draw from a deck determines who the Chaser Corps exterminates.

THE MEMORY JUMPER

AMANDA MICHELLE BROWN

Adelaide, an illegal Memory Jumper, lives in an underground safe house with a narcissistic mother who secretly exploits her mind-altering powers for money.

MY BROTHER'S SPARE

SHIRA BEHORE

Valeria's secret investigation to find her mother's murderer pulls her into an alliance with Alias Black, the most infamous hitman in the kingdom.

ABOUT THE PUBLISHER

LOST ISLAND PRESS publishes dystopian, sci-fi, and fantasy books. Unlike mainstream presses, we don't publish everything for everyone. We publish for *you*. Our catalog offers grounded, character-driven stories that linger long after the last page. The kind you get lost in, that keep you up at night. And because our books have the same vibe, if you enjoy one, you'll enjoy them all.

LOSTISLANDPRESS.COM

Join our newsletter to claim a free ebook